E. Daumas, James Hutton, Emir Abd El-Kader

The Horses of the Sahara and the Manners of the Desert

E. Daumas, James Hutton, Emir Abd El-Kader

The Horses of the Sahara and the Manners of the Desert

ISBN/EAN: 9783743318915

Manufactured in Europe, USA, Canada, Australia, Japa

Cover: Foto ©Andreas Hilbeck / pixelio.de

Manufactured and distributed by brebook publishing software
(www.brebook.com)

E. Daumas, James Hutton, Emir Abd El-Kader

The Horses of the Sahara and the Manners of the Desert

THE HORSES

OF THE SAHARA,

AND THE

MANNERS OF THE DESERT.

BY

E. DAUMAS,

GENERAL OF DIVISION COMMANDING AT BORDEAUX, SENATOR, ETC., ETC.,

WITH COMMENTARIES

BY THE EMIR ABD-EL-KADER.

TRANSLATED FROM THE FRENCH

BY JAMES HUTTON.

(THE ONLY AUTHORISED TRANSLATION)

LONDON:

WM. H. ALLEN & CO., 13, WATERLOO PLACE, S.W.

1863.

TABLE OF CONTENTS.

PART THE FIRST.

THE HORSES OF THE SAHARA.

PART THE SECOND.

THE MANNERS OF THE DESERT.

THE HORSES OF THE SAHARA

INTRODUCTION.

The horsemen of Numidia were famous even in the time of the Romans. The Arab horsemen are in no way inferior to their predecessors. The horse has continued down to these our days to be the chief instrument of war among those martial tribes. A dissertation on the horses of Algeria, which still retain the typical characteristics of both the Barb and the Arab stock, is not only of interest for the lovers of horse-flesh, but also for those who are responsible for the maintenance of our power in Algeria. The greatest merit of a study of this kind is its perfect accuracy as to facts. I will therefore mention the sources whence I have derived my information.

In the course of the sixteen years which I have passed in Africa, I have been intrusted with missions or have exercised functions which brought me into constant intercourse with the Arabs, a people hitherto so little known, but whom we are bound to study if we would learn how to govern them.

From 1837 to 1839 I was the French Consul at Mascara accredited to the Emir Abd-el-Kader; after that, head of the Arab Office in the province of Oran, in which at that time General Lamoricière held the chief military command; and finally Central Director of the Arab Office of Algeria under the government of Marshal the Duke of Isly. These different posts brought me into close contact with the native chiefs and the first families of the country. I acquired their language and it was through their assistance that I was enabled to publish, one after the other, my books on the Algerian Sahara, the Great Desert, Great Kabylia, and on the Manners and Customs of Algeria, works which may perchance have rendered some service to French interests by throwing light upon important questions of war, commerce and government.

The study of the Arab horse, which had long been the subject of my most careful researches, seemed to me to form the natural complement of my previous labours. Indeed, this question, full of uncertainty and contradictions, was as it still is, of the most thrilling interest. In the event of a European war must we always have recourse to foreign countries, or cannot Algeria come to our aid in supplying remounts for our light cavalry? Such was the national question I set before myself, and the reply to which I founded on patient and minute inquiries throughout my long residence in Algeria.

Besides, according to some authorities, the Arabs are the first horsemen in the world, while according others they butcher their horses. The former give them credit for whatever is good in the systems pursued by ourselves or our neighbours; while the latter insist that they know nothing whatever about riding, or about the veterinary art, or about breeding. How much of truth is there in all this? What is the real value of Arab horses? What is the nature of the service they are capable of rendering? This I was determined to find out, not by hearsay, but through the evidence of my own eyes—not from books, but from men. What I am now about to place before the reader is consequently the result both of my own personal observations, and also of conversations with Arabs of every grade of life, from the tented chief down to the simple horseman, who, as he himself would say in his picturesque idiom, has no other profession than to "live by his spurs." In other words, I made my inquiries of those who had large possessions, and of those who had very little; of those who bred horses, and of those who only knew how to ride them: in short, of every body. Thus the opinions which I am about to commit to paper do not emanate from the head of a single individual—they are gathered separately from the members of a powerful tribe. My only merit is that of having collected and arranged many documents widely scattered and difficult to obtain.

In fact, a Christian has need to employ both tact and patience to extract from Mussulmans information insignificant perhaps in itself, but which a gloomy fanaticism makes them regard as of great importance, or as perilous to their religion. Nevertheless, I have one reservation to make. I am not at all prepared to say: "This is right," or "That is wrong." I say simply: "Right or wrong, this is what the Arabs do."

REMARKS OF THE EMIR ABD-EL-KADER.

Learned Mussulmans have written upon horses a great number of books in which they discourse at considerable length upon their qualities, their colours, upon all that is esteemed beneficial or injurious, their maladies and the right mode of treatment. One of them, Abou-Obeïda, a contemporary of the son of Haroun-al-Raschid, composed no fewer than fifty volumes on the horse. This Abou-Obeïda met with a little misadventure, which shows that it is not the author of the most ponderous and numerous volumes who imparts the soundest information, and that not the worst plan is to consult men themselves.

"How many books hast thou written upon the horse?" asked one day of a celebrated Arab poet the vizir of Mamoun, son of Haroun-al-Raschid. "Only one." Then turning to Abou-Obeïda he put to him the same question. "Fifty," replied he. "Rise, then," said the vizir, "go up to that horse and repeat the name of every part of his frame, taking care to point out the position of each." I am not a veterinary surgeon," answered Abou-Obeïda. "And thou?" said the vizir to the poet.

"Upon that"—it is the poet himself who relates the anecdote—"I rose from my seat, and taking the animal by the forelock, I began to name one part after the other, placing my hand upon each to indicate its position, and at the same time recited all the poetic allusions, all the sayings and proverbs of the Arabs referring to it. When I had finished, the vizir said to me : "Take the horse." I took it, and if ever I wished to annoy Abou-Obeïda, I rode this animal on my way to visit him."

In all times the horse has been regarded by peoples and Governments as one of the most potent elements of their strength and prosperity. At the present day there is no question relating either to rural economy or to the art of war, more canvassed than that touching the amelioration of the charger. The highest authorities of the State, learned societies, agriculturists, the army, every body, in short, is taken up with it in France, and yet we are very far from being agreed upon it. For my own part, I have never wearied of studying that noble animal, from taste quite as much as from patriotism or professional necessity. I have consulted the most esteemed authors and men of great erudition, but I confess that it is among the Arabs I have met with the most just and practical appreciations of the subject. To obtain the best possible information, I have frequently applied to the Emir Abd-el-Kader, that illustrious chief who, by reason of his exalted position in Mussulman society, his science, and his skill as a horseman, was of all men the most competent to remove the misgivings which still troubled me. The following is the last letter that he wrote to me in reply to certain questions I had proposed to him as to the origin of the Arab horse. It seems to me to contain some very remarkable suggestions, even from a zoological point of view. In any case it is sufficiently curious to justify my expectation that it will prove acceptable to all who, whether at home or abroad, feel an interest in the equine race.

LETTER OF THE EMIR ABD-EL-KADER.

Praise be to the one God!

To him who remains ever the same amidst the revolutions of this world :

To our friend, General Daumas.

Peace be with you, through the mercy and blessing of Allah, on the part of the writer of this letter, on that of his mother, his children, their mother, of all the members of his family and of all his associates.

To proceed : I have read your questions, I address to you my answers.

You ask me for information as to the origin of the Arab horse. You are like unto a fissure in a land dried up by the sun, and which no amount of rain, however abundant, will ever be able to satisfy.

Nevertheless, to quench, if possible, your thirst (for knowledge) I will this time go back to the very head of the fountain. The stream is there always the freshest and most pure.

Know then that among us it is admitted that Allah created the horse out of the wind, as he created Adam out of mud.

This cannot be questioned. Several prophets—peace be with them!—have proclaimed what follows :

When Allah willed to create the horse, He said to the south wind :

"I will that a creature should proceed from thee—condense thyself!"—and the wind condensed itself. Then came the Angel Gabriel, and he took a handful of this matter and presented it to Allah, who formed of it a dark bay or a dark chestnut horse, (*koummite*—red mingled with black) saying :

"I have called thee horse *(frass)*; I have created thee Arab, and I have bestowed upon thee the colour *koummite*. I have attached good fortune to the hair that falls between thy eyes. Thou shalt be the lord *(sid)* of all other animals. Men shall follow thee wheresoever thou goest. Good for pursuit as for flight, thou shalt fly without wings. Upon thy back shall riches repose, and through thy means shall wealth come."

Then He signed him with the sign of glory and of good fortune (*ghora*, a star in the middle of the forehead).

Do you now wish to know if Allah created the horse before man, or if He created man before the horse? Listen :

Allah created the horse before man, and the proof is that man being the superior creature, Allah would naturally give unto him all that he would require before creating himself.

The wisdom of Allah points out that He made all that is upon the earth for Adam and his posterity.

Here is another testimony to that :

When Allah had created Adam, He called him by his name and said unto him :

" Choose between the horse and *Borak*." *

Adam answered : "The fairest of the two is the horse," and Allah replied :

" It is well; thou hast chosen thy glory and the eternal glory of thy children; so long as they shall exist, my blessing shall be upon them, for I have created nothing that is more dear to me than man and the horse."

Likewise Allah created the horse before the mare. My proof is that the male is more noble than the female, and he is, besides more vigourous and potent. Though they are both of the very same species, the one is more impassioned than the other, and the Divine Power is wont to create the stronger of the two the first. What the horse most yearns after is the combat and the race. He is also preferable to the mare for the purposes of war because he is more fleet and patient of fatigue, and because he shares his rider's emotions of hatred or tenderness. It is not so with the mare. Let a horse and a mare receive exactly the same sort of wound, and one that is sure to be fatal, the horse will bear up against it until he has succeeded in carrying his

---

* *Borak* is the animal upon which Mohammed was mounted when he made his journey through the heavens. It was like a mule, and was neither male nor female.

master far from the field of battle; while the mare, on the contrary, will sink at once upon the spot, without any force of resistance. There is not a doubt on the subject—it is a fact known by proof among the Arabs. I have seen frequent instances of it in our combats, and have experienced it myself.

This being granted, let us pass on to another point. Did Allah create the Arab horse before the foreign horse, or did he create the foreign horse before the Arab?

As a consequence of my former argument every thing leads us to believe that He created the Arab before all others, because he is without dispute the most noble. Besides, the foreign horse is only a species of a genus, and the Almighty has in no case created the species before the genus.

Now whence come the Arab horses of the present day?

It is related by many historians that after the time of Adam, the horse — like all other animals, such as the gazelle, the ostrich, the buffalo, and the ass—lived in a wild state. According to these writers the first man who, after Adam, mounted the horse was Ishmael, the father of the Arabs. He was the son of our lord Abraham, beloved of Allah. Allah taught him to call the horses, and when he did so, they all came galloping up to him. He then took possession of the finest and most spirited, and broke them in.

But after a while many of the animals trained and employed by Ishmael lost something of their purity. One single stock was preserved in all its nobleness by Solomon, the son of David, and it is that which is called *Zad-el-Raheb* (the gift, the support of the horseman), whence all real Arabs derive their origin in this manner.

There is a tradition that some Arabs of the Azed tribe went up to Jerusalem the Noble to congratulate Solomon on his marriage with the Queen of Saba. Having fulfilled their mission they addressed him as follows :

"O Prophet of Allah ! our country is far distant, and our provisions are exhausted : thou art a great king; bestow upon us wherewithal to take us home."

Solomon thereupon gave orders to bring from his stables a magnificent stallion descended from the Ishmael stock, and then dismissed them with these words :

"Behold the provisions which I bestow upon you for your journey. When hunger assails you, gather fuel, light a fire, place your best rider on this horse and arm him with a stout lance. Hardly will you have collected your wood and kindled a flame, when you will see him return with the produce of a successful chase. Go and may Allah cover you with his blessing."

The Azed took their departure. At their first halt they did as Solomon had prescribed, and neither zebra, nor gazelle, nor ostrich could escape them. Thus enlightened as to the value of the animal presented to them by the son of David, these Arabs on their return home devoted him to foal-getting, and carefully selecting the dams, at length obtained the breed to which out of gratitude they gave the name of *Zad-el-Rakeb*.

This is the stock whose high renown spread at a later period through the whole world.*

In fact it was propagated both in the East and the West in the train of the Arabs who subsequently penetrated to the limits of the habitable globe. Long previous to Islam, Hamir-Aben-Melouk and his descendants reigned for a hundred years over the West. It was he who founded Medina and Saklia.

Shedad-Eben-Aàd made himself master of the whole country to the borders of Moghreb, and built cities and constructed sea ports.

Afrikes, who gave his name to Africa, extended his conquests as far as Tandja (Tangiers), while his son Shamar overran the East as far as China, forced his way into the city of Sad, and destroyed it. On that account that place has ever since been called Shamar-Kenda,—because *kenda* in Persian signifies "he has destroyed",—which the Arabs have corrupted into Samar-Kand.

Since the introduction of Islamism, new Mussulman invasions extended the fame of Arab horses to Italy, Spain, and even to France, where, without doubt, they have left traces of their blood. But the event which more than any other filled Africa with Arab horses, was the invasion of Sidi-Okba, and still later the successive invasions of the fifth, and sixth centuries after the Hijra. Under Sidi-Okba the Arabs merely encamped in Africa, whereas in the fifth and sixth centuries they arrived as colonists with the intention of settling there with their wives and families, their horses

---

* It is distinguished by the size of the respiratory duct, which enables it to accomplish fabulous journeys.

and mares. It was these latter invasions which established Arab tribes on the soil of Algeria, particularly the Mehall, the Djendel, the Oulad-Mahdi, the Douaouda, etc., who spread themselves in all directions and founded the true nobility of the country. These same invasions transplanted the Arab horse into the Soudan, and justify our asserting the oneness of the Arab stock, whether in Algeria or in the East.

Thus, the history of the Arab horse may be divided into four great epochs : 1st from Adam to Ishmael; 2nd from Ishmael to Solomon; 3rd from Solomon to Mohammed; 4th from Mohammed to our own times.

It is to be clearly understood, however, that the race of the principal epoch, that of Solomon, having been forcibly divided into several branches, different varieties have been formed partly from the change of climate, and partly from the greater or less degree of care bestowed upon them, precisely as is the case with mankind. The colour of the coat has also varied under the influence of the same circumstances. Experience has satisfied the Arabs that in districts where the ground is stony, the usual colour is gray, and in those where the ground is chalky *(Ard Beda)*, white is the prevalent hue. I have myself frequently verified these observations.

There remains now only one question to settle with you. You ask by what outward signs the Arabs recognize a horse to be noble, a drinker of air. Here is my answer :

The horse of pure descent is distinguished among us by the thinness of its lips and of the interior cartilage of the nose, by the dilation of its nostrils, by the leanness of the flesh encircling the veins of the head, by the graceful manner the neck is attached, by the softness of its coat, its mane, and the hairs of its tail, by its breadth of chest, the largeness of its joints, and the leanness of the extremities. According, however, to the traditions of our ancestors the thoroughbred is still better known by its moral characteristics than its physical peculiarities. The outward signs will enable you to guess at the race, but it is by the moral qualities alone you will receive full confirmation of the extreme care displayed in coupling the sires and dams, and of the pains taken to prohibit all misalliances.

Thoroughbred horses have no vice. A horse is the most beautiful of all animals, but his moral qualities, as we think, must correspond with his physical, or he will be regarded as degenerate. The Arabs are so convinced of this that if a horse, or a mare, have given indisputable proof of extraordinary speed, of remarkable endurance of hunger and thirst, of rare intelligence, or of grateful affection for the hand that feeds them, they will make every imaginable sacrifice to get their progeny, under the persuasion that the points by which they were themselves distinguished will reappear in their offspring.

We allow, then, that a horse is really noble when in addition to a fine configuration, he unites courage with fire, and bears himself proudly in midst of battle and danger.

Such a horse will love his master, and as a rule will suffer no other person to mount him.

He will not yield to the wants of nature so long as his master is on his back.

He will refuse to touch what another horse has left.

He will take pleasure in troubling with his feet whatever limpid water he may meet with.

By the senses of hearing, of sight, and of smell, as well as by his address and intelligence, he will know how to save his master from the thousand accidents that may befall him in war or at the chase.

Finally, sharing the emotions of pain or pleasure experienced by his rider, he will aid him in the combat by combating also, and every where without hesitation will make common cause with him *(ikatel-ma-Rakebhou)*. Such are the tokens which evidence purity of race.

We possess numerous works on the characteristics of the horse, whence it appears that, after man, he is the most noble, the most patient, the most useful of created beings. He is content with little, and if considered simply with regard to strength, he is still superior to other animals. An ox of great strength will carry a hundred-weight, but if you place it on his back he will move only with an effort and be quite incapable of running. On the other hand, the horse carries a full grown man, a robust cavalier, with standard, arms, and ammunition, besides food for both, and will go at speed for a whole day and more, without eating or drinking. It is by his means that the Arab holds whatever he possesses, rushes on his enemy, tracks him down or flees from him, and defends his family and his freedom. Let him be enriched with the possession of all that sweetens life, his horse alone is his protector.

Do you now understand the boundless affection the Arabs feel for their horses! It is only equalled by the services rendered by the latter. To their horses they owe their joys, their triumphs, and therefore are they prefered to gold and precious stones. In the days of paganism they loved the animal from motives of interest and merely because it procured them glory and wealth; but when the Prophet spoke of it in terms of the highest praise, this instinctive love was transfigured into a religious duty; some of the first words he uttered on the subject of horses are those ascribed to him by tradition, on the occasion of the arrival of several tribes from Yemen with a view to accept his doctrines and to present him, in token of submission, with five magnificent mares belonging to the five different races of which Arabia then boasted. It is said that Mohammed went forth from his tent to receive the noble animals that had been sent to him, and caressing them with his hand, expressed himself in these words :

"Blessed be ye, O Daughters of the wind!"

Afterward the Messenger of Allah *(Rassoul Allah)* said in addition :

"Whosoever keeps and trains a horse for the cause of Allah is counted among those who give alms day and night, publicly or in secret. He shall have his reward. All his sins shall be remitted to him and never shall fear dishonour his heart."

Now I pray unto Allah to grant you a happiness that shall never pass away. Cherish your friendship for me. The wise men among the Arabs have said :

Riches may be lost :

Honours are but a shadow that fades away :

But true friends are a treasure that remains.

He who hath written these lines with a hand which shall one day be withered in death, is your friend, the pauper in the presence of Allah.

SID-EL-HADJ, ABD-EL-KADER, BEN-MAHHYEDDIN.

Damascus, end of Deul-Kada 1274 (end of August 1857).

P. S. For the better understanding of our correspondence, permit me to instruct you on one point. The word *ferass* is not exclusively applied to the female of the horse, as is customary in Algeria—it indicates the male as well as the female. If a mare be particulary alluded to, it is necessary to say a female *ferass;* and in like manner if the allusion be to a horse, a male *ferass* is the proper phrase. Such is the way with the true Arabs *(Arabes-es-sahh);* strictly speaking, the mare is called *hadjra* and the horse *hossan.*

The reader of this curious document will doubtless have remarked the singular admixture of legendary anecdotes with snatches of natural history sometimes true, sometimes fabulous after the manner of Pliny and Aristotle, and all of it under the dominion of a religious sentiment. It is history as written by Orientals and likewise by the Western Arabs; for both the one and the other, until now outlawed as it were from progress by their forced or voluntary exclusion from the intellectual movement going on in Europe, are still, so far as science and literature are concerned, no farther advanced than their ancestors of Bagdad or Granada.

Now, it is a remarkable fact that the more learned an Arab may be, the more are his writings imbued with that fancifulness which, for a reader accustomed to the preciseness of our European style, needs to be cleared of its poetical mysteriousness and constructed afresh, before it can be reduced to the character of a document possessed of any historical or scientific worth in the sense we usually give to those words. Thus, at first sight, the letter we have just perused is nothing more than a fragment detached from an Oriental tale. There are, nevertheless, lurking within it incontestable truths, and from beneath the exaggerations and symbols of tradition may be gathered information of a kind not wisely to be despised. Here especially is it the letter that killeth while the spirit giveth life—let us then seek for the spirit beneath the letter.

God created the horse out of the wind, symbol of fleetness, which, in the eyes of an Arab, is the first quality of a courser. The poets of Greece were inspired by the same idea. It was the wind that impregnated the mares of Thessaly, the swiftest of ancient times; and it may be that those mares were introduced into Greece from Syria, or Arabia, together with the fabulous pedigree assigned to them by the poets of both countries. If this were the case, and here history is in accord with tradition, the Arabian horses must have been, what they still are on their native soil, the fleetest and best in the world.

The Arabs, who neither understand nor practice our system of fighting in compact and serried masses, at times immovable, but who charge without any semblance of order and see nothing disgraceful in a headlong flight, are naturally disposed to love and to vaunt above all others the drinker of air. "The air-drinker," say they, "is the first in the combat to rush at the enemy; and the first after victory to fly at the booty, and in case of defeat the first to escape from danger."

A poet has said : "There are things which an intelligent King should never neglect. The first is a horse, that by its swiftness shall be able to rescue him from the enemy he has failed to overcome."

The favourite steed of the Prophet was named *Ouskoub,* "the torrent," from the word *sakab,* "quickly flowing water." The intervention of the Angel Gabriel in the creation of the horse commends that animal to the good offices of the true Believers, for the Angel Gabriel is the constant medium of communication between the Deity and the Prophets, especially Mohammed. Now it was by means and with the assistance of the horse alone that the Mussulman tribes succeeded in accomplishing that immense system of emigration, that propagand war, as far as China to the eastward, and westward to the Ocean, which was in the mind of Mohammed to impose upon them. It was indispensable, therefore, that the horse should be looked upon in the light of a sacred animal, a providential instrument of war, created by the Deity for a special purpose, and of a nobler essence than that with which He fashioned the other animals. To produce the horse in a manner beyond the common law of creation, to envelop his origin in a symbolism that wanders abroad from natural history to lose itself in mysterious legends, to place him thus beneath the safeguard of religious reverence, evinced, as the result has proved, a thorough knowledge of the spirit of the people upon whom Mohammed purposed and was about to operate.

The Koran in speaking of horses calls them *El-Kheir*, "the especial treasure," and from this simple word the commentators of the Sura, *sad,* have arrived at the conclusion that "an Arab ought to love horses as a part of his own heart, and to sacrifice for their keep the very food of his own children." A volume might be composed of phrases detached from the sacred book, or from the *hadites* of the Prophet (his conversations as handed down by tradition), and of the commentaries upon them, which under the form of maxims and precepts, prescribe to Mussulmans, as a religious duty, the love of horses. I shall quote only a few of them.

"Blessings, good fortune, and a rich booty shall be attached to the forelock of horses until the day of the resurrection." "Whoso keeps a horse for the holy war in the way of the Most High, increases the number

of his good works. The hunger and thirst of such a
steed, the water he drinks, the food he eats, every one
of his hairs, each step he takes, and every function of
nature, shall all weigh in the balance at the day of the
last judgment."

"The horse prays thrice a day. In the morning he
says : 'O Allah! make me beloved of my master.' At
noon : 'Do well by my master, that he may do well by
me.' In the evening : 'Grant that he may enter into
paradise upon my back!'"

It was doubtless under the impression of these last
words that El-Doumayry wrote in his history of animals,
Hayat-el-hayouan : "The horse is the animal that by his
intelligence approaches nearest to man." While on this
subject I cannot help remarking that the Arabs, when
they advanced this proposition, were well acquainted
with the animals which pass with us as being the most
intelligent such as the elephant, the dog, etc. How is it
then? May it not be that the Arabs, by living on such
intimate terms with the horse, have succeeded in developing faculties the very existence of which is unknown
to us, who accord to that animal only the instinct of
memory? With them, in fact, the horse is a friend of
the family. With us, on the contrary, it is no more
than an article of luxury or an instrument of labour,
which we are ever ready to change through interest or
caprice; as witness the common saying : "One does not
marry one's horse!" But the Arab does marry his horse.
Be this as it may, the maxims quoted above all tend to
the same end, to identify man with the horse. Let it
not be supposed, however, that that is all. It was necessary that the horse should be the companion of the

Believer alone, to the exclusion of all infidels,—a dogma the political bearing of which will be readily appreciated. Allah hath said : "The horse shall be cherished by all my servants, but he shall be the despair of all those who do not follow my laws, and none will I place on his back save those who know me and who worship me."

It is needless to add that the Mussulman princes have availed themselves of this dogma to prohibit in the name of Allah the sale of Arab horses to Christians, under pain of sin and damnation. These commands, though of divine origin have, I am well aware, been disobeyed in some countries. The Arab loves money, it is true; but for all that we may rest assured that for the most part the animals sold to us are of an inferior order, and that the horses or mares whose noble and precious qualities have been ascertained by proof, whether as regards speed or as breeders, are never parted with to foreigners for any price. Even if the owner were willing to let them go, the whole tribe in the name of their common interest would oppose it. This is the real truth, and probably explains the disrepute into which Arabians appear to have fallen in Europe. One seldom there meets with any except such as the Arabs have no desire to keep. But enough on that head : let us now turn to another topic.

The Emir Abd-el-Kader asserts that the horse was created *koummite,* red mixed with black, that is to stay, dark bay or dark chesnut. Desengaged from the cloudiness of fancy, this assertion will at least go far to prove that these colours have in all ages been esteemed by the Arabs as the index to superior qualities. It is a fixed idea with this observing people. It is constantly turning up. The Prophet said :

"If after having collected all the horses of the Arabs I were to make them race against one another, it is the *euchegueur meglouk,* the dark chesnut, that would outstrip the rest." Moussa, the celebrated conqueror of Africa and Spain, is reported to have said : "Of all the horses of all my armies the one that has best borne the fatigues and privations of war is the true bay, *hameur somm.*"

And the Prophet further remarked : "If thou hast a dark chesnut, conduct him to the combat, and if thou hast only a sorry chesnut, conduct him all the same to the combat."

From all this it is abundantly apparent that legendary traditions and experience are in perfect harmony in according a decided superiority to coats of deep and decided hues. Coats of a light pale colour are held in no esteem whatever. The horse's coat, therefore, must be an index to his character. The long experience of Mohammed the Prophet and of Moussa the Conqueror must have placed them in a position to speak with full knowledge of the subject, and their opinion confirmed by that of all the Arabs, the best horsemen in the world and the most interested in studying the animal, upon whom indeed depend their honour and their life, is certainly entitled to be regarded with some respect. It is beyond all question that the *koummite*—red mingled with black, chesnut or bay—is preferred by the Arabs to all others. If I might be allowed to quote my own personal experience, I should have no hesitation in saying that, if there be any prejudice in the matter, I share it with them. Besides, must it necessarily be a prejudice because it may seem to be one? No one will deny that all the individuals of the same species are, in their wild state, identical in colour and endowed with common instinctive qualities inherent in the race. These colours and these qualities undergo no alteration or admixture except in a state of servitude and under its influences, so that if any of these individuals, by a return to their natural condition more easily proved than explained, happen to recover the colour of their first ancestors, they will be equally distinguished by more broadly defined natural qualities. The canine race may be taken as an illustration. Whence it follows that a certain number of domesticated individuals being given, their coats alike and with dominant qualities, it may be fairly concluded that this coat and these qualities were those of the race in its wild state. In the case, then, of the Arab horse, if it be true that those whose coat is red shaded with black are endowed with superior speed, are we not justified in inferring that such was the uniform colour, such the natural qualities, of the sires of the race? I submit with all humility these observations to men of science.

Abd-el-Kader assures us, moreover, that it is ascertained by the Arabs that horses change colour according to the soil on which they are bred. Is it not possible, in fact, that under the influence of an atmosphere more or less light, of water more or less fresh, of a nurture more or less rich according as the soil on which it is raised is more or less impregnated with certain elements, the skin of the horse may be sensibly affected? Every one knows that with any coat, the colour changes in tone and shade according to the locality where the animal lives, the state of its health, the quality of the water it drinks, and of the food it eats, and the care that is bestowed upon it. There is perchance in all this a lesson in natural history not to be despised, for if the circumstances in which a horse lives act upon his skin, they must inevitably act also in the long run upon his form and qualities.

This point being dismissed, the last proposition in the letter of the Emir Abd-el-Kader is that which classes the history of Arab horses in four epochs : 1st, from Adam to Ishmael; 2nd, from Ishmael to Solomon; 3rd, from Solomon to Mohammed; 4th, from Mohammed to our own times.

This is the history of the Arabs themselves, so completely have they identified themselves with the horse, their necessary and indispensable companion. Between Adam and Abraham the Arabs did not exist—it was the age of a pastoral population. No wars, at least of a serious character, no pillaging. The horse appears in it only on the day of creation. He has no part to play except as a head of cattle among the flocks and herds, peacefully employed in domestic service. But on the second epoch with Ishmael, his part changes altogether. Ishmael is a bastard, disinherited, abandoned in the desert. His life is to be a struggle. He must be at open war with all mankind because he must live somehow upon the soil to which he has been banished, without taking into consideration the fact that this necessity of fighting in order to live, at the same time gratifies the resentment he entertains towards his brothers, heirs, to his prejudice, of the paternal fields. We read in the Bible, that when Hagar, in Arabic *Hadjira,* fled into the wilderness an angel appeared to her and said :

"I will multiply thy seed exceedingly that it shall not be numbered for multitude.

"Behold, thou art with child, and shalt bear a son, and shalt call his name Ishmael; and he will be a wild man; his hand will be against every man, and every man's hand against him; and he shall dwell in the presence of all his brethren."

Ishmael is the personification of the Arab people. He calls the horses to him, selects the best, and trains them for racing, for the chase, and for war. It is by their aid that he will live upon the plunder of the rich caravans that may venture upon his territory, and will make forays from the land of hunger and thirst into the land of abundance. The horse has made him King of the desert, and in return he makes a friend, a companion of his horse. Between them there is only one interest.

Nevertheless, the Arabs, hard pressed to the eastward by the powerful armies of the Kings of Abyssinia, to the northward by the people of Jehovah,—one half of them absorbed and decimated in these great struggles; and the other half shut in within their arid peninsula and divided by intestine dissensions—the Arabs degenerated, and with them their horses suffered deterioration. It was at Jerusalem the Noble, and according to the legend in the stud of Solomon, that the true type of the race was exclusively preserved. Travellers, perhaps conductors of the caravans which in those days used to arrive in Jerusalem in great numbers, receive as a gift certain horses, of whose value and fine qualities they are ignorant. But under the influence of peace commerce again discovers the long disused road from Central Asia to the seaports of Syria, and the Arabs interested in making common cause with one another reform themselves by mutual alliances between tribes. The horse, on his part, follows this new phase of their fortunes.

At a later period, a fresh degeneracy arises in consequence of the immigration into Arabia of foreigners, Jews and Christians, and from quarrels among the Arabs themselves. Some few noble and powerful tribes, such as the Koreishites, for example, the most powerful and the most noble of all, had preserved a traditional love of the horse as inseparable from their original dignity. But in order that Mohammed's task should have any chance of accomplishment, it was necessary to extend to all and to popularise this exceptional passion of a few, and equally essential was it to condense into one national unity the disunited elements of which the tribes of Arabia then consisted. We have seen with what persistance the Prophet reverts to this necessity, in the Koran, in his conversations, and in his teachings, and how he made the careful tendance of horses an obligation of Mussulman life, and an article of faith in the Believer. In this manner, from the Hidjra to our own times, the condition of the Arab horses has unavoidably gone on improving. Has he not said : "Whoso feeds and tends a horse for the triumph of religion, makes a magnificent loan to Allah"?

I have only one more word to say on the portrait of the thoroughbred horse sketched by Abd-el-Kader. The Emir takes it at one view, and as inseparable one from the other, both the physical and moral qualities. In his opinion physical qualities alone will never constitute a perfect horse. He must also by his intelligence and by his affection for the master who feeds, who tends, who rides him, unite with him as an integral part. To demand such qualities from a horse is simply placing him, in the intellectual order, immediately after man, just as, according to the legend, he has been placed in the order of creation.

The Europeans are, I am aware, far from entertaining such a high opinion of the animal, but may we not err in the opposite degree?

THE BARB.

We have often heard it said that the horse of our
African possessions, to whose rare qualities we have
endeavoured to do justice, was very inferior to the true
Arabian. Notwithstanding a conviction based on a
lengthened experience and a grave study of the subject,
we have made it our duty to take up and discuss an opinion put forth with an air of authority. We were willing
to accept as umpire in this dispute, a man whose intelligence, whose habits, whose whole life, render him a
supreme judge in all matters relating to horse-flesh—
the Emir Abd-el-Kader. We addressed to that genuine
horse-man a letter in which we frankly expressed the
objections which each of our assertions had encountered.
His reply to this letter is given below. It will be seen
from this curious document that the Emir does not confine himself to the confirmation of the proposition we
advanced, but develops by reflections or by facts the
whole of our opinions. According to his statement, the
Barbary horse, so far from degenerating from the Arab,
is, on the contrary, superior to him. The Berbers, he
says, formerly inhabited Palestine, where they reared

the animal that has become the type of a perfect war-horse. Having emigrated to Africa through the vicissitudes of their life of adventure, they paid the utmost attention to the guest of their tents, the instrument of their hunting expeditions, their comrade in the fight. Their horses thus preserved such eminent qualities, that an Asiatic sovereign engaged in a perilous war, sent for them from the Berbers. The reader will appreciate the value of this historical dissertation which, from whatever point of view it be examined, does not the less possess an interest that cannot be contested. It is quite certain that the Barbary horse is indebted to the climate in which he flourishes, to the education which he receives, to the food that is given to him, to the privations that are familiar to him, for a vigour that enables him to equal, if not to surpass the most vaunted steeds of Persia and Upper Egypt. Supported by the following letter, we hold ourselves justified in repeating that all the horses of Asia and Africa may be blended together under one common denomination. We oppose to the European horse, one identical horse—the horse of the Orient—which, thanks to our conquest of Algeria, we believe will be daily called upon to render to our country services more and more valuable and more and more valued.

This is the letter from the Emir Abd-el-Kader, which he forwarded to me from Broussa :

Praise to the one God! His reign alone is eternal!

May the profoundest peace and the most perfect divine beneficence be extended to the person of General Daumas,—of him who ardently seeks for the solution of the most obscure questions! May Allah conduct and protect him!

To proceed : You have asked us our opinion on Barbary horses, their character, and their origin. To give you satisfaction I am again turning my attention to these subjects, and can do nothing better to-day than send you some extracts taken from the poetical works of the famous Aâmrou-el-Kaïs, who lived a short time before the coming of the Prophet. They refer to the superiority of the horses of the Berbers, and I think you will there find proofs against those who maintain that those admirable animals are of an inferior stamp. The poet remarks, while addressing himself to Cæsar, Emperor of Constantinople, in a long piece of versification:

"And I answer thee, if ever I am reinstated as King, we will ride a race where you shall see the horseman lean forward over his saddle to increase the speed of his courser;

"A race across a space trampled down on all sides, where no higher marks are distinguishable to direct the traveller, than the hump of an aged Nabathæan camel loaded with years and uttering plaintive moanings.

"We shall be borne, I tell thee, on a horse accustomed to nocturnal journeys, a steed of the Barbary race; with slender flanks like a wolf of Gada; a steed that rushes along on his rapid course, and whose flanks are running with sweat.

"When, slackening the bridle, the rider urges him on still faster by striking him with the reins on either side, he quickens his rapid course, bending his head to his flanks and champing the bit.

"And when I say : 'Let us rest;' the horseman stops as by enchantment and begins to sing, remaining in the saddle on this vigorous horse, the muscles of whose thighs are long drawn out and whose tendons are lean and well apart."

Aâmrou-el-Kaïs was one of the ancient Kings of Arabia, who took infinite pains to procure Barbary horses wherewith to combat his enemies. He was doubtful of success if obliged to trust himself to the qualities of Arab horses. It is not possible, in my opinion, to give a more invincible proof of the superiority of the Barb. After testimony like this any one who should dispute it would be quite unable to adduce an allegation of the slightest value.

The Berbers, as stated by El-Massoudi, are descended from the Beni-Ghassan, while other writers affirm that they come from the Beni-Lekhm and the Djouzam. Their native country was Palestine, whence they were expelled by one of the Kings of Persia. They then emigrated to Egypt, but the souvereign of that country refusing them permission to settle here, they crossed the Nile and spread over the regions to the westward of the other side of the river.

Maleck-ben-el-Merahel says that the Berbers form a very numerous population composed of Hymiar, Modher, Copts, Amalkas, and Kanéan, who became amalgamated in the province of Sham (Syria) and took the name of Berbers. Their immigration into the Maghreb, according to this historian with whom El-Massoudi, El-Souheili, and El-Zabari also agree, was owing to their marching under Ifrikesh to the conquest of the African peninsula.

Ibn-el-Kelbi asserts that opinions are divided as to the real name of the chief under whose guidance the Berbers emigrated from Syria towards the Maghreb. Some will have it that it was under the Prophet David, others name Youssha-ben-Enoun, others again Ifrikesh, and yet others certain Kings of the Zobor.

El-Massoudi adds that they did not emigrate until after the death of Goliath and that they established themselves in the province of Barka and in the Maghreb, after having vanquished the Frendj (Franks). They then invaded Sicily, Sardinia, the Balearic Isles, and Spain. Still later it was stipulated between them and the Frendj that the latter should occupy the towns, while the former should fix themselves in the deserts which extend from Alexandria to the Ocean.

Ibn-Abd-el-Berr affirms that the establishment of the Berbers extended from the extremity of Egypt, that is, from the regions situated behind Barka to the Green Sea, and from the sea of Andalusia to the end of the deserts which border on Soudan. On this frontier line a tribe bearing the name of Berbers still exists between the Habeuch (Abyssinians) and the Zendy (Zanzibar). The author of the *Kamous* (an Arabic Dictionnary) makes mention of them, but they are a very insignificant tribe, whose trivial and obscure history records not a single important event.

The essential point here is the extract from the poet Aâmrou-el-Kaïs on the subject of Barbary horses. As for the Berbers themselves, every thing proves that they have been known from time immemorial and that they came from the East to settle in the Maghreb, where we find them at the present day.

Peace be with you, at the end as at the beginning of this letter on the part of your friend.

ABD-EL-KADER-BEN-MAHIIIDDIN.

May Allah cover him with His blessings!

Broussa, the 1st of Safer, 1269.--1854.

Since the above was written, I have received a proof confirmatory of my opinion as to the excellence of the Barbary horse and its perfect equality with other horses of oriental extraction. It is this :

Paris, — 185 —

My dear General,

I forward you a copy of the official report of the races which came off at Alexandria in Egypt on the 25th July, 1836. I give you full permission to introduce it in your work as a useful argument in support of your thesis on the excellence of the Barb. I have already related to you how these races took place in consequence of a conversation I had with Mehemet-Ali, in the course of which the Viceroy of Egypt bantered me on the arrival of a horse which my brother Jules had sent me from Tunis.

Accept, etc., etc.

Ferd. de LESSEPS.

DISTANCE RUN : 4 1/2 KILOMÈTRES (NEARLY 2.4/5 MILES) IN A STRAIGHT LINE.

1st Heat.

Nejdi horse, dappled gray, 4 1/2 yrs, the property of Suby-Bey, ridden by the owner.

Nejdi horse, bred in Cairo, bay, 9 yrs, the property of M. Jules Pastré, ridden by the owner.

Anézé horse, from Syria, iron gray, 3 1/2 yrs, the property of M. Mércinier, ridden by M. J. Dufey.

Nejdi horse, bred in Cairo, the property of H. E. Moharrem-Bey, son in law of Mehemet-Ali, and ridden by Terata-Tutemy-i-Bashi of the Pasha.

The horse ridden by M. Jules Pastré was the first in.

2nd Heat.

Barbary horse, from Tunis, bay, 4 yrs, the property of M. Ferd. de Lesseps, ridden by the owner.

Nejdi horse, white, 6 1/2 yrs, the property of M. Etienne Rolland, ridden by M. J. Dufey.

Nejdi horse, bay, 5 yrs, the property of Subi-Bey, ridden by the owner.

Nejdi horse, bred in Cairo, 7 yrs, the property of H. E. Moharrem-Bey. ridden by Cerkès-Osman-Sakallé.

The Barb ridden by M. de Lesseps was the winner.

3rd Heat.

Nejdi horse, bred in Cairo, gray, 6 yrs, the property of Hussein-Effendi, ridden by the owner.

Nejdi horse, dappled-gray, 5 1/2 yrs, the property of Dr Gaetani-Bey, ridden by M. Ferd. de Lesseps.

Nejdi horse, bred in Cairo, iron gray, 6 yrs, the property of M. W. Peel, ridden by the owner.

Samian horse, bay, 9 yrs, the property of Ibrahim-Effendi-Bimbashi, ridden by the owner.

The Egyptian horse ridden by Hussein-Effendi was the winner.

4th Heat.

Nejdi horse, bred in Cairo, bay, 8 yrs, the property of M. Henricy, ridden by M. Escalon.

Egyptian horse, from Atfeh, bay, 8 yrs, the property of M. Samuel Muir Junior, ridden by M. Sanders.

Nejdi horse, bred in Cairo, bay, 8 yrs, the property of Turki-Bashi, ridden by the owner.

Nejdi horse, gray, 4 yrs, the property of M. Roquerbe, ridden by M. Bartolomeo.

Won by the Nejdi horse ridden by M. Bartolomeo.

Recapitulation of the Winners.

1st Heat, Cairo horse, the property of M. Pastré, ridden by the owner.

2nd Heat, Barbary horse, the property of M. Ferd. de Lesseps, ridden by the owner.

3rd Heat, Cairo horse, the property of Hussein-Effendi, ridden by the owner.

4th Heat, Nejdi horse, the property of M. Roquerbe, ridden by M. Bartolomeo.

According to previous agreement the four winning horses having gone over the same ground, were to contend against one another in a fifth heat. They came in in the following order :

1st. Barbary horse, the property of M. Ferd. de Lesseps, ridden by the owner.

2nd. Cairo horse, the property of M. Jules Pastré, ridden by the owner.

3rd. Nejdi horse, the property of M. Roquerbe, ridden by M. Bartolomeo.

4th. Nejdi horse, the property of Hussein-Effendi, ridden by the owner.

Certified the accuracy of the above report.

Signed : FERD. DE LESSEPS.

To finish with the Barb and to give, over and above the other qualities he possesses, an exact idea of his strength and spirit, I cannot do better than state the weight carried in most of our expeditions by the horse of a chasseur d'Afrique.

WEIGHT CARRIED BY THE HORSE OF A CHASSEUR D'AFRIQUE SETTING OUT ON AN EXPEDITION.

	Kilogr.*	Hectogr.	Décagr.
Horseman armed and in full uniform ..	82	—	—
Equipments and pistol	24	—	—
Bread for two days	1	5	—
Biscuit for three days..................	1	6	5
Coffee for five days	—	6	—
Sugar for five days	—	6	—
Bacon for five days	1	—	—
Rice for five days.....................	—	3	—
Salt	—	—	8
Pressed hay for five days	25	—	—
Barley for five days...................	20	—	—
Three packets of cartridges	1	3	—
Four horse-shoes.....	1	6	—
TOTAL (350 lbs)............	159	6	3

159 kilogrammes, or 19 more than the horse of a carabineer, and 26 more than the horse of a cuirassier in France. This weight, of course, decreases as the column proceeds on its march.

Delivered the 31st February 1847, by Colonel Duringer, at the moment of departure of a column.

Now, a horse that, in a country often rough and difficult, marches, gallops, ascends, descends, endures unparalleled privations, and goes through a campaign with spirit, with such a weight on his back, is he, or is he not, a war horse?

* A kilogramme is equal to 2 1/5 lb., a hectogramme to rather more than 3 1/2 ozs, and a décagramme is the 100th part of a kilogramme.

To a pastoral and a nomadic people, roaming our vast grazing grounds, and whose numbers bear no proportion to the extent of their territories, the horse is a necessity of life. With his horse, the Arab trades and travels, looks after his numerous flocks, distinguishes himself in battle, at weddings, and at the festivals of his marabouts. He makes love, he makes war : space is nothing to him. Thus, the Arabs of the Sahara still give themselves up with ardour to the rearing of horses. They know full well the value of blood, they pay great attention to crossing the breed, and try every means to improve the species. The state of anarchy in which they have lived in these latter times has naturally modified some of their habits, but it has effected no change in this condition of their existence—the breeding,' perfecting and training of horses.

The love of the horse has passed into the Arab blood. That noble animal is the friend and comrade of the chief of the tent. He is one of the servants of the family. His habits, his requirements are made an object of study. He is the burden of their songs, the favourite topic of conversation. Day by day in the gatherings outside the *douar,* where age alone enjoys the privilege of speech, and which are marked by the decorous behaviour of the listeners, seated in a circle on the sand or on the turf, the young men add to their practical knowledge the counsels and traditions of their seniors. Religion, war, the chase, love, and horses, inexhaustible subjects of observation, make regular schools of these open air meetings, in which warriors are formed and develop their intelligence in collecting a mass of facts, precepts, proverbs, and sententious sayings, the application of which will only too frequently occur in the course of the perilous life they have to lead. It is thus they acquire that knowledge of horse-flesh which we are so astonished to meet with in the humblest horseman of a desert tribe. He can neither read nor write, and yet every phrase in his conversation rests upon the authority of the learned commentators of the Koran, or of the Prophet himself. "Our lord Mohammed declared" — "Sidi-Ahmed-ben-Youssef says in addition "—"Si-ben-Dyab relates "—And you may take him on trust, this learned ignoramus, for all these texts, all these anecdotes, which for the most part are only to be found in books, he for his part derives from the *tholbas* or from his chiefs, who, unconsciously come, as it were, to a mutual understanding, to develop or maintain among the people the love of the horse, useful precepts, sound doctrines, and the best rules of hygieine. The whole is sometimes tainted, no doubt, with gross prejudices and ridiculous superstitions. It is a picture with much shading. But let us not be too severe : it is not so very long since very nearly the same absurdities were proclaimed in France as indisputable truths.

I was talking one day with a marabout of the tribe of the Oulad-Sidi-Schik about the horses of his country, and pretended to question some of the opinions he had expressed. "You cannot understand that, you Christians," he exclaimed, abruptly rising to his feet, "but horses are our riches, our joys, our life, our religion. Has not the Prophet said : 'The good things of this life, even to the day of the last judgment, shall be suspended from the hairs which are between the eyes of your horses?'"

"I have read the Koran," I replied, "but have never met with those words."

"You will not find them in the Koran, which is the voice of Allah, but in the conversations of our lord Mohammed *(Hadite sidna Mohammed)*."

"And you believe in them?" I retorted.

"Before taking my leave of you, I will show you what may happen to those who have faith." And my companion gravely recited the following history :

"A poor man confiding in the words of the Prophet which I have just repeated to you, came one day upon a dead mare. So he cut off her head and buried it under the threshold of his door, saying to himself : 'I shall become rich if it please Allah' *(An-sha-Allah)*. Days, however, followed each other, but no riches came, and yet the Believer never doubted. The Sultan of the country being on his way to visit a holy spot, happened by accident to pass before the lowly abode of the poor Arab. It was situated at the end of a small plain bordered by large trees and watered by a pretty rivulet. The scene pleasing him, he halted his brilliant escort, and dismounted to rest himself in the shade. Just as he

was about to give the signal to continue the journey his
steed, which a slave was employed to look after, impatient to devour space, began to neigh and to paw the
ground, and presently broke loose. All the efforts of the
saïs (grooms) to catch him again were for a long time in
vain and every one was in dispair, when they beheld
him stop suddenly of himself at the threshold of an old
hut which he smelt at while throwing up the ground
with his forefeet. An Arab, until that moment an unmoved spectator, went up to him without frightening him,
as if he had been known to him, caressed him with hand
and voice, laid hold of him by the mane, the bridle
being in a thousand pieces, and without any difficulty
led him quietly up to the astonished Sultan.

"How have you contrived," demanded his greatness,
"thus to tame one of the most fiery steeds of Arabia?"

"You will no longer be surprised, my lord," replied
the man of faith, "when you learn that, having been
taught that all the good things of this world unto the
day of judgment shall be suspended from the hairs
which are between the eyes of our horses, I buried under
the door-way of my house the head of a mare I found
lying dead. The rest has come to pass through the
blessing of Allah."

"The Sultan instantly caused the ground to be dug up
at the spot indicated, and when he had thus verified the
statement of the Arab, he hastened to recompense one
who had not hesitated to give an entire faith to the words
of the Prophet. The poor man received the present of a
fine horse, superb garments, and riches enough to place
him beyond the reach of want for the rest of his days."

"You now know," continued the marabout, "what may

happen to those who believe," and without waiting for my reply he saluted me with the eyes after the manner of the Arabs, and withdrew.

This legend is popular in the Sahara, and the words of the Prophet on which it is founded are there an article of faith. Whether the Prophet uttered them or not, they do not the less surely answer the end proposed to himself by their imputed author. The Arab loves honours, power, riches. To tell him that all that was attached to the long hairs of his horse was to endear it to him, to bind it to him by the bond of a common interest. The genius of the Prophet doubtless went much farther. He fully understood that the mission of conquest which he had bequeathed to his people could only be accomplished by hardy horsemen, and that the love of the horse must be developed in them simultaneously with faith in Islam. These injunctions, which all tend towards the same end, are clothed in various forms. The marabout and the thaleb strung them together as sayings and legends, the noble *(djieud)* as traditions, and the common people as proverbs. Subsequently, proverbs, traditions, and legends, assumed a religious character which has for ever accredited them to the great family of Mussulmans : for it is the will of the Prophet that his own people, to the exclusion of all infidels, should reserve to themselves these powerful instruments of war, which in the hands of the Christians might become so fatal to the Mussulman religion. This inner motive, which the common people of the tent may not have seen, through the symbolical veil behind which it was concealed, has not escaped the perception of the Arab chiefs. The Emir Abd-el-Kader, when at the height of his power, inflicted death without mercy on every Believer convicted of having sold a horse to a Christian. In Morocco the exportation of these animals is hampered with such heavy duties that the permission to take them out of the kingdom is altogether illusory. At Tunis the same reluctance yields only to the imperious necessities of policy, and in like manner at Tripoli, in Egypt, at Constantinople, in short in all Mussulman States.*

If you speak of horses to a *djieud,* the noble of the tent, who still plumes himself on his ancestors having fought with ours in Palestine, he will tell you :

> The mounting of horses,
> The letting slip greyhounds from the leash,
> And the clinking of ear-rings,
> Draw the maggots out of your head.

If your interlocutor is one of those horsemen *(mekhazeni)* whose bronzed face, pepper-and-salt beard, and prominent exostosis† on the tibia announce that he has gone through many adventures, he will say to you :

> Horses for a quarrel,
> Camels for the desert,
> And oxen for poverty.

Or he will remind you that when the Prophet was engaged in expeditions, in order to induce the Arabs to tend their horses properly, he always gave two-thirds of the prize to whomsoever had accompanied him on the best horse.

---

* I know for a fact that in certain Mussulman countries in the list of obligatory presents for a Christian personage, the donor wrote down : *Kidar ala Khrater er-Roumi* — "a jade for the Christian."

† The eye of the Arab stirrup invariably produce exostoses on the front part of the leg. By them you may distinguish at once the rich man from the poor, the cavalier from the man on foot.

The voluptuous Thaleb, man of God for the world who lives in contemplative idleness, without any other occupation than that of writing talismans and making amulets for all men and women who want them, will repeat to you with his eyes on the ground :

> The paradise of earth is to be found on horseback,
> In the study of books,
>
> Or on the bosom of a woman,

he will add if no prudish ears are at hand.

Again, if you question one of those aged patriarchs who are renowned for their wisdom, their experience, and their hospitality, he will answer you :

"Sidi-Aomar, the companion of the Prophet, hath said : 'Love horses, tend them well, for they are worthy of your tenderness. Treat them like your own children, nourish them like friends of the family, clothe them with care! For the love of Allah, do not neglect to do this, or you will repent of it *in this house and in the next.*'"

Finally, if you have the good fortune to encounter in your journey one of those wandering story-tellers *(medahh, fessehh)* who pass their lives in travelling about from tribe to tribe, to amuse the abundant leisure of these warrior-shepherds, supported by a player on the flute *(kuesob),* and accompanying himself on a tabour *(bendaïr),* he will chaunt to you with a hollow but not unmusical voice :

> My horse is the lord of horses!
> He is blue as the pigeon beneath the shade,
> And his black hairs are like waves;
> He bears hunger and thirst; he outstrips the eyesight;
> And, true drinker of air,

He blackens the heart of our enemies
In the days when muzzles touch each other.
Mebrouk * is the pride of the country.

My uncle has thoroughbred mares, whose distant sires
Are counted in our tribes since the ancient times,
Gentle and timid as daughters of the Guebla †.
You would say they were gazelles
Feeding in the valleys under the eye of their dams.
To see them, is to forget the authors of our days.

Covered with *djellals* ⊘ which make our flowers look pale,
They march like Sultanas attired for a fête,
A negro of Kora ♀ tends them,
Gives them pure barley, and milk to drink.
And leads them to the bath.
Allah preserve them from the evil eye! ‡

For his much loved mares
My uncle demanded Mebrouk in marriage,
And I said to him : No;
Mebrouk is my support, I wish to keep him
Proud, full of health, dexterous and fleet.
Time turns on itself and returns;
There may be no dispute to-day, but to-morrow, perhaps, we shall see
The hour of strife approach with rapid strides.
For a skin full of blood, my uncle replied,
Thou hast made my face yellow ♂ before all my children.
The earth is vast : adieu.

Mebrouk, why this neighing night and day?
Thou betrayest my ambush and warnest my enemies,
Thy thoughts wander too much to the daughters of our coursers,

---

* *Mebrouk* is Arabic for " the fortunate one."

† *Guebla*, the south, the Sahara, the desert.

⊘ *Djellals* are woollen cloths more or less ornamented with designs according to the wealth of the chief. They are very wide and extremely warm, and cover both the chest and the croup.

♀ Slaves from Kora are in great request among the Mussulmans. They learn Arabic with great difficulty, but they are very attentive to their duties, and much attached to their masters.

‡ What the Arabs understand by the evil eye is this : Some one may say to you : " Oh! what a beautiful horse, what a beautiful mare you have there! " Fear the worst from such a one, for he has only spoken out of envy. If he had meant it in real kindliness, he would not have failed to have added : " Allah protect you, or grant you his blessing." It is not every one, however, who has the evil eye.

♂ Red and all the brilliant colours fall to the lot of good fortune, in the eyes of the Arabs; while the sombre hues, and especially yellow, indicate misfortune.

I will marry thee, o my son!
But where shall I find my friends
Whose mares are so noble, and their she camels such treasures?
Their tidings are buried in the earth;
Where are their spacious tents so pleasant to the eye?
In them were spread the carpet and the mat;
In them was offered the hospitality of Allah,
And the poor man filled his belly.
They are vanished!
The scout viewed the hillocks,
The brave marched in the front rank,
The shepherds drove the flocks after them,
And the hunters, on the track of their sharp greyhounds,
Chased the gazelle.

Have you heard speak of the tribe of my brethren?
No! Well, come with me and count their numerous horses :
There are colours which will please you.
Behold those horses white as snow that falls in its proper season;
Those black as the slave carried off from Soudan;
Those others green * as the reed that grows on the banks of rivers;
Those, again, red as blood that spirts first from a wound,
And those blue † as a pigeon when it flies beneath the sky.
Where are those rifles so straight, quicker than the winking of an eye?
That powder from Tunis, and those balls turned out in moulds, ⚬
Which pierced the bones, tore the liver,
And made the stricken perish with mouth wide open?

When I cease to sing, I am still transported thither by my heart;
For it burns for my brethren with a fire that consumes my interior.
Nowhere have I seen such warriors.
O Allah! strike with blindness those who bear them envy!
Have they not spacious tents well provided with carpets,
Mats, cushions, saddles, and rich arms?
The traveller and the orphan are they not always received there
By these words of our sires : " You are welcome! "
Their wives, bright as the corn-poppy,
Are they not borne on camels,
Those ships of the earth,
That march with the noble gait of the ostrich?

* The Arabs consider as green the colour we call a deep yellow dun, especially when
it approaches to that of a ripening olive.
† The Arabs call blue the horse of a grayish colour shot like a starling's back.
⚬ It is a matter of luxury for the Arabs and especially for those of the desert to
possess balls made in moulds.   For the most part they use rods cut into small pieces.

Are they not covered with veils
Which trailing far behind them fill even the marabouts with despair!
Are they not adorned with ornaments, gems enriched with coral,
And the blue tattoo on their arms, was it not pleasant to behold?
Every thing about them charmed the heart of the believers in Allah;
You would say they were bean-flowers created by the Eternal.

You have plunged into the southern desert,
And the days seem unto me very long!
Behold! it is well nigh a year that nailed to this wearisome * Tell,
I have seen no more of you than the traces of your encampments.
O my cherished dove
Who wearest trousers that reach to thy feet;
Who wearest a burnous that sits so well on your shoulders;
Whose wings are variegated, and who knowest the country;
O thou who cooest!
Away, fly beneath the clouds, they will serve thee for a covering;
Go, find my friends, give them this letter to read,
Tell them that it proceeds from a sincere heart,
Come back quickly and inform me if they are happy or unhappy,
They who make me sigh.

You will see *Sherifa:*† a haughty damsel;
She is haughty, she is noble, I have seen it in writing;
Her long hair falls with grace
On her white and ample shoulders;
You would say it was the sable plumes of the ostrich
That dwells in the desert and sings beside its brood.

Her eye-lids are bows brought from the negro-land;
And her eye-lashes, you would swear that it was the beard of an ear
Ripened by the eye of light◊ towards the end of summer;   [of corn
Her eyes are the eyes of the gazelle
Troubled about her little ones,
Or, rather, it is the flash that precedes the thunder
In the middle of the night.
Her mouth is admirable,
Her breath sugar and honey.
And her fine set of teeth ressemble the hailstones

* The Arabs of the desert are so fond of their independant wandering life, that
they regard as the most wearisome moment of their existence the season when they
are compelled to come to the Tell to purchase their supplies of corn.
   † Feminine of *sherif*, signifying a descendant of the Prophet.
   ◊ In their poetic effusions, the Arabs frequently call the sun *aïn ennour*, " eye of
light."

Which the winter in its fury sows over our land.
Her neck is as the standard which our warriors plant in the ground
To defy the enemy and rally the runaways,
And her faultless body outvies the marble
Which is used for building the pillars of our mosques.

Fair as the moon around which gathers the night,
She shines like a star undimmed by a cloud.
Tell her that she has wounded her lover
With two thrusts of a poniard, one in the eyes, the other in the heart.
Love is no light burden.
I ask of the Almighty to give unto us water;
We are in the spring-time
And the rain has tarried too long for the people of flocks.
I am hungry, I am fasting like a Ramadan moon.

They are at Askoura, praise be to Allah!
Bring me my horse!
And you there, strike the tents!
I go to seek my uncle;
He will forgive the son of his brother;
We shall be reconciled to one another,
And by the head of the Prophet,
I will give a feast in which the young men shall appear
With shining stirrups and saddles richly embroidered;
Powder shall be burnt* to the sound of the flute and the tabour;
I will marry Mebrouk
And his offspring shall be called the offspring of well tended mares.

O tribes of the Sahara!
You claim to possess camels; †
But camels, you are aware,
Care only for those who can defend them;
And those who can defend them are my brethren,
Because they know in the fight how to crush the bones of the rebellious.

Thus it is seen that among the Arabs every thing concurs to develop the love of horses. Religion makes a duty of it, while the agitated life, the incessant conflicts, and the distances to be traversed in a country

---

* Among the Arabs, there are no rejoicings without firing off of guns.

† When a desert tribe is at peace, the camels are sent away ten or twelve leagues to graze, and it may be easily conceived that if a sudden swoop be made upon them, it needs excellent horses and vigourous horsemen to recover them.

absolutely devoid of means of rapid communication, make it a necessity. An Arab can only live a double life, his own and his horse's.

REMARKS BY THE EMIR ABD-EL-KADER.

The best horses are chiefly to be found in the Sahara, where the number of bad horses is very small. In fact, the tribes that inhabit it and those who border on it only employ their horses to make war, or to contend in trials of swiftness. Accordingly, they never use them for agricultural purposes, or exercise them in any other way than in battle. On this account their horses are nearly all excellent.

No individual in the Sahara cares to possess ten camels until he has a horse to defend them against those who might assail them.

In the Tell most of the Arabs apply their horses to the cultivation of the land. They also make use of them to ride and for any other purpose. They have no particular preference for males because in their eyes the horse is merely an animal to be turned to any employment of which it is capable, and not kept for war alone. For this reason the horse of pure origin bred in the Sahara is preferable to the same horse in the Tell. The former, unlike that of the Tell, is subjected to fatigue, to long journeys, to hunger, and to thirst, which renders him able to achieve whatever is required of him.

The Koran calls horses "the especial good."

The servant of the Prophet used to say : "With women, what the Prophet loved best was horses."

"Aïssa-ben-Meryem (Jesus, the son of Mary),—peace be with him!—went one day to Eblis, the black demon, and said : 'Eblis, I have a question to address to thee : wilt thou tell me the truth?' 'Spirit of God,' answered Eblis, 'question me as seemeth good to thee.'"

"I demand of thee," pursued Jesus, "by the Living One who cannot lie, what is it that can reduce thy body to a liquid state and cut thy back in two?" "It is," replied the devil, "the neighing of a horse. Never have I succeeded in entering a house that contained a horse for the cause of the Most High."

Being passionately fond of horses, one of the companions of the Prophet asked him if there were any in Paradise. "If Allah causes thee to enter Paradise," replied the Prophet, "thou wilt have a horse of rubies, furnished with two wings, with which he will fly whithersoever thou willest."

A poet has said : "Who are they who will weep for me after death? My sword, my Boudaïna lance, and my long-bodied chesnut, trailing the reins to the fountain, after death has deprived him of his rider."

In all times, among the Arabs, the horse has been the object of the greatest solicitude, and this solicitude the Prophet lost no opportunity of keeping up, developing and augmenting by introducing the religious sentiment.

We find in the collection of his conversations the following precepts :

"Happiness in this world, a rich booty, and eternal rewards are attached to the forelock of horses."

"Evil spirits enter not into a tent where there is a thoroughbred horse."

"The Angels sympathise with only the three following

pastimes of men : the exercises of war—the joys of connubial love—and the running of horses."

"Whensoever any one is prevented from fulfilling his religious duties, let him keep a horse for the sake of Allah, and all his sins shall be forgiven him."

"Whoso maintaineth a horse for the triomph of religion makes a magnificent loan to Allah."

"The horse, sincerely reared in the way of Allah, for the holy war, shall save his master from the fire at the day of the resurrection."

"Whoso maketh sacrifices in order to train a horse for the holy war shall be treated in the next world as a martyr."

"Whoso traineth a horse in the way of Allah is counted in the number of those who give alms day and night, in secret or in public. He shall have his reward. Never shall fear dishonour his heart."

"Money spent upon horses passes in the eyes of Allah for alms given in a direct manner."

"Whoso keepeth and tendeth a horse for the service of Allah shall be recompensed as one who fasts during the day and passes the night in prayer."

"Horses pray to Allah to make them beloved by their masters."

"Allah comes to the aid of such as occupy themselves with horses, and lightens the expenses incurred on their account."

"Every grain of barley given to a horse is inscribed by Allah in the Register of good Works."

"Martyrs of the holy war will find in Paradise horses of rubies, furnished with wings, which shall fly whithersoever their riders desire."

BREEDS.

The tribes that inhabit the Sahara have always been better able than those of the Tell to withdraw from the caprice, oppression, and spoliation of the various conquerors of Africa. It is therefore evidently among them that the Barb has had the best chance of preserving all the qualities of grace, speed, and sobriety, that are universally regarded as its characteristics. We shall consequently confine ourselves exclusively to the horses of that region, and with a view to avoid a repetition of what every one has read in books, we shall allow the many Arabs we have interrogated, to speak for themselves. Here, then, is the outline they have drawn of the thoroughbred horse, *shareb-er-rehh,* "the air-drinker :"

The thoroughbred horse is well proportioned, his ears are small and in constant motion, his bones massive, his cheeks meagre, his nostrils wide as the throat of a lion, his eyes bright, black, and level with the head,* his neck long, his chest full, his withers prominent, his

---

* Small and restless ears as well as lively and prominent eyes are a sign, say the Arabs, of a healthy action of the heart, and that the animal is full of life.

well knit, his haunches strong, his fore-ribs long
his hinder ones short, the belly hollow, the croup
When the upper part of his legs long like an ostrich's
and furnished with muscles like a camel's, his hoofs
black and of a uniform colour, his hair fine and abundant, his flesh firm, his tail very thick at the dock but
loose at the extremity. Looked at in front he is like
unto the peak of a lofty mountain. Looked at from behind, he seems to lean forward as if he would prostrate
himself. Looked at from the side, he shows himself
robust and well set up.

To sum up : he should have four points broad, the
front, the chest, the croup, and the legs;—four points
long, the neck, the upper part of the legs, the belly,
and the haunches;—four points short, the loins, the
pasterns, the ears, and the tail. All these qualities in a
good horse, say the Arabs, prove firstly that he has real
blood in him, and secondly that he is certainly fleet of
foot, for his form combines something of the greyhound,
the pigeon, and the *mahari,* or riding camel.*

The mare ought to take from the wild boar its courage
and breadth of head; from the gazelle, its grace, its
eyes and mouth; from the antelope, liveliness and intelligence; from the ostrich, its neck and swiftness; from
the viper, the shortness of its tail.

* The *mahari* is much more slender in its proportions than the *djemel,* or common
camel. It has the exquisite ears of the gazelle, the supple neck of the ostrich, the
hollow belly of the *sloug ui* or greyhound. Its head is lean and gracefully attached to
the neck; its eyes bright, black, and prominent; its lips long and firm, covering well
the teeth; the hump is small, but the chest where it touches the earth when the
animal couches down, is strong and protuberant; the dock of its tail is short; its legs,
very lean in the upper part, are furnished with muscles from the ham and the knee
down to the hoof, and the sole of its foot is neither broad nor thick: finally, it has very
few hairs on the neck, and its coat, of a tawny colour, is as fine as that of the jerboa.
See General Daumas' work on the " Great Desert." In the desert, the *mahari* is to the
djemel what, with us, a race horse is to a draught horse.

A thoroughbred horse *(hôor)** may be known by yet
other signs. For instance, he cannot be prevailed
to eat barley out of any other nosebag than   ...
He so loves trees, verdure, shade, and runniñ 'water,
that he will neigh for joy on seeing them. Seldom does
he drink until he has troubled the water, and if the con-
formation of the ground prevents him from doing so with
his feet, he will kneel down and do it with his mouth.
He is continually shrivelling his lips; his eyes are in
constant motion; alternately he pricks up and lowers his
ears, and turns his neck to the right or left as if he
wished to speak, or to ask for something. If to all these
signs a horse adds sobriety of disposition, his owner
may deem himself the possessor of a pair of wings.

It has been remarked that a horse that is a fast galopper
has the head firmly set on, and the transverse apophysis
of the atloïd very protuberant. "He has horns," say the
Arabs.

The races most esteemed in the western part of the
Algerian Sahara are three in number : that of Hâymour,
that of Bou-Ghareb, and that of Merizigue. Their offspring are dispersed among a great many tribes, such
as the Hamyân, the Oulad-Sidi-Shikh, the Leghrouât-
Kuesal, the Oulad-Yagoub, the Makena, the Aâmour, the
Oulad-Sidi-Nasseur, and even the Harar. Every one, according to his fancy, or according to his occupation,
offers his mare to the descendants of one of these three
types. The Hâymour usually produce bay horses, the
Bou-Ghareb white ones, and the Merizigue those of a
gray colour. The Hâymour are most sought after. They

* *Hôor*, in the plural *harar*. Not unlikely, this word brought by our ancestors from the crusades is the origin of the word *haras*.

are of a beautiful shape, with a good carcass, and yet very active. They pass for the swiftest coursers of the Sahara, and preserve their strength to a very advanced age. They bring good luck, and their owners belong to the richest and noblest families.

Next come the race of Bou-Ghareb, the produce of which are taller, and are also very patient of fatigue, but less fleet than the Hàymour. Like the latter, however, they remain sound until a great age.

Lastly the Merizigue who are shorter and have less bottom than the preceding, but are solid, clean-limbed, and sober. They are chiefly sought after by common horsemen who have long journeys to make and great hardships to undergo.

The Hàymour breed is superior to all others; nor has the imagination of the Arabs failed to trace it to a marvellous source. The legend runs as follows · —A chief owned a magnificent mare, which happened to receive a serious hurt in hunting the ostrich. It was feared that she would be lame for life. Her master though he could see no improvement in her condition and was annoyed at the trouble of dragging her after him in all his removals from place to place, was still unable to bring himself to put her to death, and therefore turned her out to graze at large. On returning from a long journey he remembered his mare and inquired what had become of her. She proved to be in excellent health, and on the point of foaling. He at once brought her in, took the greatest care of her, and soon afterwards found himself possessed of a foal that was unrivalled throughout the desert. As no tribe had passed for a very long time near the place where he left the animal, the Arabs were willing to believe that she had been covered by a wild ass, *hamar el oudhhch,* and they gave to the foal the name of Hâymour, which is that of the foal of the onager.

In the central part of the Algerian Sahara, the Arbâa* affect the offspring of *Rakeby.* This breed has both height and bottom, and is found among the Aghrazelias, the Oulad Shayb, the Oulad Mokhtar, and even among the Oulad Khrelif.† For the most part they are gray or dark bay. They endure hunger and thirst with ease, and without being knocked up will cover for several consecutive days distances of twenty five to thirty leagues.◊ At the present day the finest animals are in the family of the Seuffrân. *Rakeby,* it seems, was formerly brought from Morocco by the ancestors of Sidi-Hamed-Oulad-*Tedjini,* the famous Marabout of Aain-Mady.

The Oulad-Nayl⸮ make use of the offspring of a celebrated stallion named El-Biod, "the White," formerly the property of the Oulad-Si-Mahmed, one of their divisions. This stock is renowned for its sobriety and speed.

In the Hodna and the Medjana, among the Oulad-Makrane and the Ghiras, the most highly esteemed are the descendants of a well known stallion belonging to the Oulad-Mahdi. It was named Bey-el-Hissen, and was the property of the family of El-Amri-ben-Abi-Meramer.

A good horse in the desert ought to accomplish for five or six days, one after the other, distances of twenty

---

* The nomadic tribe of the Arbâa encamps in the neighbourhood of Leghrouât. It is divided into three great sections : el Mamera, el Hedjadj, and Ouled Salah. (*Sahara Algérien,* p. 43.)

† All these tribes pitch their tents in the quadrilateral comprised between Sidi-Khaled, Tougourt, the Beni-Mzab, and Leghrouât.

◊ The French league is rather less than 2 1/2 miles English.

⸮ A very populous tribe who occupy the whole of the Djebel-Sahri and the greatest part of the basin of the Oued-Djedi.

five to thirty leagues. After a couple of day's rest, if well fed, he will be quite fresh enough to repeat the feat. "With a horse that on arriving at a resting place shakes himself, paws the ground with his foot, and neighs at the approach of the barley, then pushing his head into the nosebag begins to munch eagerly three or four mouthfuls of the grain, there is no occasion to pull up in a journey." The distances to be traversed in the Sahara are not always of such great length, but at the same time it is no very rare occurrence to hear of horses doing fifty to sixty leagues in four and twenty hours.

A tribe on receiving notice that its enemies project a razzia, at once sends out scouts *(shouâfin)* to watch them, mounted on mares, "the children of a Jew"—*benate el ihoude*—so cunning and dexterous are they. These horsemen take with them no more than a feed of barley for their horse's supper. They frequently vary their pace but are always careful to husband their steeds, and will place themselves in ambush thirty leagues from their point of departure in order to "kill the earth"—that is, to reconnoitre. If the result of their observations causes them to entertain any immediate apprehension for the safety of their brethren, they return at once at full speed to warn them to take to hasty flight. In the contrary event, they retrace their steps leisurely and will yet gain their tents before the hour of the evening prayer, after having traversed sometimes fifty to sixty leagues in the twenty four hours. Should there be a skirmish on the morrow, their horses will be in a condition to take part in it. If the horse of a *shouaf* happens to die in the course of a reconnaissance made for the good of all, it is replaced at the expence of the whole tribe.

With regard to the great distances accomplished by the horses of the desert, instances may be quoted which will appear incredible, and the heroes of which are still alive, if witnesses were wanted to confirm the truth of the story. Here is one of a thousand, which was told to me by a man of the tribe of Arbâa. I give his own words:

"I had come into the Tell with my father and the people of my tribe to buy corn. It was in the time of the Pasha Ali. The Arbâa had had some terrible quarrels with the Turks, and as it was their interest for the moment to feign a complete submission in order to obtain an amnesty for the past, they agreed to win over by presents of money the Pasha's suite, and to send to himself not merely a common animal as was customary, but a courser of the highest distinction. It was a misfortune, but it was the will of Allah, and we were forced to resign ourselves. The choice fell upon a mare "gray stone of the river," known throughout the Sahara, and the property of my father. He was informed that he must hold himself in readiness to set out with her on the morrow for Algiers. After the evening prayer my father, who had taken care not to make any remark, came to me and said: 'Ben-Zyan, art thou thyself to day? Wilt thou leave thy father in a strait, or wilt thou make red his face?'"

"I am nothing but your will, my lord," I replied. "Speak, and if your commands are not obeyed, it will be because I am vanquished by death."

"Listen. These children of sin seek to take my mare in the hope of settling their affairs with the Sultan, my gray mare, I say, which has always brought good fortune to my tent, to my children, and the camels : my gray mare, that was foaled on the day that thy youngest brother was born! Speak! Wilt thou let them do this dishonour to my hoary beard? The joy and happiness of the family are in thy hands. *Mordjana* (such was the name of the mare) has eaten her barley. If thou art of a truth my son, go and sup, take thy arms, and then at earliest nightfall flee far away into the desert with the treasure dear to us all."

"Without answering a word I kissed my father's hand, took my evening repast, and quitted Berouaguïa,* happy in being able to prove my filial affection, and laughing in my sleeve at the disappointment which awaited our sheikhs on their awaking. I pushed forward for a long time, fearing to be pursued, but Mordjana continued to pull at her bridle and I had more trouble to quiet her than to urge her on. When two-thirds of the night had passed, and a desire to sleep was growing upon me, I dismounted and seizing the reins twisted them round my wrist. I placed my gun under my head and at last fell asleep, softly couched on one of those dwarf palms so common in our country. An hour afterwards I roused myself. All the leaves of the dwarf palm had been stripped off by Mordjana. We started afresh. The peep of day found us at Souagui. My mare had thrice broken out into a sweat, and thrice dried herself. I touched her with the heel. She watered at Sidi-Bou-Zid in the Ouad-Ettouyl, and that evening I offered up the evening prayer at Leghrouât, after giving her a handful of straw to induce her to wait patiently for the enormous bag of barley that was coming to her. These are not journeys

* Berouaguïa is six leagues south of Medeah; Souagui, thirty one leagues from Berouaguïa; Sidi-Bouzid, twenty five leagues farther on; and lastly Leghrouât, twenty four leagues beyond that, or one hundred and seven leagues south of Algiers.

fit for your horses," said Si-ben-Zyan in conclusion, "—for the horses of you Christians, who go from Algiers to Blidah, thirteen leagues, as far as from my nose to my ear, and then fancy you have done a good day's work."

This Arab, for his part, had done eighty leagues in twenty four hours : his mare had eaten nothing but the leaves of the dwarf palm on which he had lain down and had only once been watered, about the middle of the journey; and yet he swore to me by the head of the Prophet that he could have slept on the following night at Gardaya, forty five leagues farther on, had his life been in any danger. Si-ben-Zyan belongs to a family of marabouts of the Oulad Salahh, a section of the great tribe of the Arbâa. He comes frequently to Algiers and will tell this story to whoever will listen to him, confirming his narrative, if required, by authentic testimony.

Another Arab, named Mohammed-ben-Mokhtar, had come to buy corn in the Tell after the harvest. His tents were already pitched on Ouad-Seghrouan, and he had opened a business communication with the Arabs of the Tell,* when the bey Bou-Mezrag, "father of the spear," fell upon him at the head of a strong body of cavalry to chastise one of those imaginary offences which the Turks were in the habit of inventing as pretexts for their rapacity. Not the slightest warning had been given; the razzia was complete; and the horsemen of Makhzen gave themselves up to all the atrocities customary in such cases. Mohammed-ben-Mokhtar thereupon threw himself on his dark-bay mare, a magnificent

---

* The Tell is the granary of the Sahara : the master of the Tell holds the people of the Sahara with the grasp of famine. They are so sensible of this that they frankly avow it in a phrase that has passed into a proverb : " We cannot be either Mussulmans, Jews, or Christians : we are forced to be the friends of our belly."

animal known and coveted throughout the Sahara, and perceiving the critical nature of the situation, at once resolved to sacrifice the whole of his property to save the lives of his three children. One of them, only four years old, he placed on the saddle before him, and another aged six or seven behind him holding on by the troussequin, and was about to place the youngest in the hood of his burnous when his wife stopped him, exclaiming : "No, no, I will not let thee have this one. They will never dare to slay an infant at its mother's breast. Away, I shall keep him with me. Allah will protect us." Mohammed-ben-Mokhtar then dashed forward, fired off his piece, and got clear of the mêlée; but, being hotly pursued, he travelled all that day and the following night until he reached Leghrouât, where he could rely upon being in safety. Shortly afterwards he received intelligence that his wife had been rescued by some friends he had in the Tell. Mohammed-ben-Mokhtar and his wife are still alive, and the two children he carried on his saddle are spoken of as two of the best horsemen of the tribe. Can there be imagined a scene more dramatic, or more worthy of a skilful artist, than this family being saved by a horse from the midst of plunder, confusion, and fighting!

And why should I look for evidence to establish these facts? All the old officers of the Oran division can state how, in 1837, a General attaching the greatest importance to the receipt of intelligence from Tlemcen, gave his own charger to an Arab to go and procure the news. The latter set out from Château Neuf * at four o'clock in

---

* A fort built by the Spaniards, and the residence of the general commanding the province.

the morning and returned at the same hour on the following day, having travelled seventy leagues over ground very different from the comparatively level desert.

One of the best and most formidable horsemen of this tribe of the Arbâa is El-Arby-ben-Ouaregla; "his ball never falls to the ground." He belongs to the section of the Hadjadj, among whom he is celebrated both by reason of his personal prowess and because of an adventure that befell him in his infancy. He was still at the breast, when his father, Mohammed-ben-Dokha, being surprised by the enemy, rolled him in his large *habaya*** and fastened him in it with his girdle. Then, whilst his family and his flocks sought safety in flight, he mounted a mare that "could wring a tear from the eye," and fighting all day in the rearguard saved his property and killed seven of his assailants.

The Arabs of the Sahara sum up the perfection of a horse in the following manner. He must carry a full grown man, his arms and a change of clothing, food for both his rider and himself, a flag, even on a windy day, and if necessary, dragging a dead body behind him, keep up at a good pace the whole day through without giving a thought to food or water. In their opinion a horse lives from twenty to twenty five years, and a mare from twenty five to thirty. As to the service to be derived from this animal, a proverb exactly expresses their idea:

> *Sebâa el Khrouya*, seven years for my brother;
> *Sebâa lya*, seven years for myself;
> *Sebâa li adouya*, seven years for my enemy.

---

* A sort of woollen shirt frequently worn by the Arabs.

It is therefore from seven to fourteen that they consider a horse as most apt for the exercises of war. I have often had the curiosity to inquire of the Arabs if they knew whence they had received the horses of which they were so proud. In reply to this question they would point with their finger to the East, and answer : "They come from the native country of the first man, where they were created a day or two before him." And as confirmation of this their belief, they would add : "Allah hath said : 'I have created for man whatsoever is upon the earth. I give it all to Adam and his descendants. Man shall be the most noble of created beings, and the horse the most noble of animals.' Now, when a chief is expected to come and rule over us we prepare a tent to receive him, carpets for him to sit upon, and various dishes to gratify his palate, and, above all, horsemen to attend upon him and execute his orders. Consequently the horse must have been created before the coming of Adam upon the earth."

THE STEED OF NOBLE RACE.

Where are those noble steeds
Whose dam never knew any but a noble sire?
The stirrup is their life; inaction is death to them.
O Father of cavaliers! the ignorant find them every where,
But they are as rare as true friends,
And when they die the very saddle sheds tears.

In the race-course of valour
May Allah bless the noble courser!
His chest is of steel, and his flanks of iron :
He loves naught but rapine, glory, and the combat;
He cherishes his master and his family,
And when he gallops, he puts the thunder to shame.
He passes, look at him : he is already out of sight;
Women, grudge him not the milk of our she-camels.

What has become of the time when I used to bestride a swimmer,
With black eye, wide nostrils,
Clean limbs, and a faithful heart!
It was a sparrow-hawk for carnage,
And life was nothing worth to me
When the briddle was out of my hands.
I was then young; I went in search of danger,
I mocked at the ill-omened ravens;
The distant always seemed to me close at hand,
And my tent overflowed with plunder.

In summer, when sleep has restored strength to my body,
When the eye of light has dispersed the shades of night,
And when the heat bites everything, even into stone,
The song of the turtle-dove fills me with soft desire.
In the boughs of the palm-tree shaken by the slightest breeze,
On the leaf that sighs and bewails itself,
She is consumed with passion.
By my head! she rekindles in my breast the fire of bygone days.

They said to me : Ah! thou art still longing for them who dye their
And I answered : No, in my eyes   [eyelids with black?
Nothing at present is equal to my horse of pure blood.
With him, I bear myself proudly; I hunt and increase my riches;
With him, I enter the strife and protect the poor and the orphan;
With him, I chastise insult and daunt my rivals;
His neigh is like the roar of a lion in the mountains;
It is an eagle hovering in the air.

Away with you, fond memories of this world!
The most potent has never carried off more than a winding-sheet.
I am known by my air-drinker, at night and in the fight;
I am known by my sabre, the shock of battle, the pen and the paper;
I am sharper than a spear, and endure hunger like a wolf.
No matter : to day I court solitude :
In solitude is happiness : age has taught me that.
Never again shall men behold me seeking a horse, or the love of
women, or the court of an Emir.

REMARKS BY THE EMIR ABD-EL-KADER.

Horses, though they are all of one and the same family, are of two different species : the first is the Arab

race, the other the race of the *Beradin*. In like manner oxen, though of only one family, are of divers species : the first that of domestic cattle, which is the best known, and the second that of buffaloes : as different from one another in agility and weight as are the Arab horses from the *Beradin*. In like manner, too, the family of camels is one, and yet includes more than one species, —the Arab race and the race *Bakhati*.*

If the foal has for its sire an Arab horse, and for its dam an Arab mare, it is indisputably noble, *hôor*.

If it has for its sire an Arab horse, and for its dam a *Beradi* mare, it is called *Hadjin*.

If it has for its dam an Arab mare and for its sire a *Beradi* horse, it is called *Meghrif*, and it is inferior to the *Hadjin*.

Hence it will be seen that the most important rôle is assigned to the sire.

It is impossible, we think, to get a pure race out of a stock the blood of which is impure. On the other hand it is a well authenticated fact that it is quite possible to restore to its primitive nobleness a breed that has become impoverished,—but without any taint in its blood,—whether through insufficient food, want of proper care, or excessive and unsuitable work : in a word, a race may be restored, the degeneracy of which has not been occasioned by any admixture of blood.

In default of public notoriety, it is by actual trial, by speed combined with bottom, that the Arabs form their judgment on horses, and recognise the nobleness and purity of their extraction. But the form likewise reveals

* The Bactrian variety, which has two humps and is much larger than the other.

the higher qualities. A thoroughbred horse is one that has three things long, three things short, three things broad, and three things clean. The three things long are the ears, the neck, and the fore-legs. The three things short are the dock, the hind-legs and the back. The three things broad are the forehead, the chest, and the croup. The three things clean are the skin, the eyes, and the hoof.

He ought to have the withers high, and the flanks hollow and without any superfluous flesh.

"Dost thou accomplish a journey at great speed with steeds high in the withers and fine in the flanks?"

The tail should be well furnished at the root, so that it may cover the space between the thighs.

"The tail is like unto the veil of a bride."

The eye of a horse should be turned as if trying to look at its nose, like the eye of a man who squints.

"Like to a beautiful coquette who leers through her veil, his glance towards the corner of the eye pierces through the hair of the forelock which covers his forehead as with a veil."

The ears resemble those of an antelope startled in the midst of her herd.

The forelock, abundant.

"In the hour of pain mount a slender mare whose forehead is covered by silky and flowing hair."

The nostrils, wide.

"Each of his nostrils resembles the den of a lion; the wind rushes out of it when he is panting."

The cavities in the interior of the nostrils ought to be entirely black. If they are partly black and partly white the horse is of only moderate value.

The fetlock, thick.

"They have fetlocks that resemble the down which is concealed beneath an eagle's wing and like him they grow black in the heat of battle."

The fetlock joints, small.

"The fetlock joints of their hind-legs are small, but the muscles on both sides stand out prominent."

The hoof, round and hard.

"The hoof should resemble the cup of a slave. They walk on hoofs hard as the moss-covered stones of a stagnant pool."

The frogs, hard and dry.

"The frogs concealed beneath the hoofs are seen when he lifts his feet, and resemble date-stones in hardness."

"When my courser rushes towards a goal he makes a noise like to that of wings in motion, and his neigh resembles the mournful note of the nightingale."

"His neck is long and graceful as a male ostrich's. His ear is split in two and his black eye full of fire."

"In the elegance of his form he resembles a picture painted in a palace. He is as majestic as the palace itself."

If by protruding his head and neck in order to drink from a stream that flows level with the ground, a horse can remain upright on all fours without bending either of his fore-legs, be assured that his form is perfect, that all parts of his body harmonise with one another, and that he is thoroughbred.

Among the horses of the tribes of the Sahara, those of the Hamyân, the Arbâa, the Oulad-Naïl, and their respective branches, are the most patient of hunger and thirst, the most capable of enduring fatigue, the fleetest gallopers, and the most able to keep up a good pace for several days together without stopping,—very different in that respect from the horses of the Tell.

There existed in ancient times several stallions whose fame has come down to us. Among others, *el Koura,* of the tribe of the Beni-Timin, and *Aouadj,* "the concave," of the tribe of the Beni-Helal. On the subject of this latter, the following anecdote is told : His master being asked, "what canst thou relate of a surprising nature in connection with thy horse?" recounted this anecdote :

"I was wandering one day in the desert mounted on *Aouadj,* when I was seized with a violent thirst. By good fortune, I fell in with a flock of ketâa* flying towards a spring. I followed them, and though holding in my horse as much as possible, I reached the water as soon as they did, without once pulling up to breath him. It is a most extraordinary example of speed, for the flight of the *ketâa,* always rapid, is greatly quickened when, driven by thirst, it makes for water... Had I not," continued the owner of *Aouadj,* "checked his speed by pulling at the bridle with all my force, I should have outstripped the *ketâa.*"

The origin of this stallion's name is this : He had not been long foaled, when his master was attacked by enemies and forced to flee. The foal being too weak to follow by itself, was put into a sack and placed upon the back of a beast of burden. Thence were derived the roundness of his back and his name *Aouadj,* which bears that signification.

---

* A species of partridge, with a " tucked up " body and very short toes.

Another celebrated stallion—here the Emir relates the origin of the race of the Haymour (see page 50) and adds : "Whoever has seen the horses of that breed will not question for a moment the truth of the tale, for their resemblance to the zebra strikes every eye."

The Arabs affirm that the best age for reproduction is from four to twelve years as regards the mare, and from six to fourteen as regards the horse. Exacting as concerns the mare, which must be of good descent, swift of foot, of good height, of sound constitution, and of a graceful form, they are still more difficult to please as concerns the horse. "Choose him" say they, "and choose him again, for the offspring always resembles the sire rather than the dam." They do not object, however, to the horse being of shorter stature than the mare, provided he be of pure race and sound in wind and limb. They attach far more importance to bottom, speed, and sobriety than to that conventional type of beauty which is so seductive in our eyes. Thus a stallion, fat, sleek, rounded in all parts, and who owes the brilliancy of his form to high feeding, indolence of disposition, or inaction, excites their distrust in the highest degree. They will say of such an animal : "Let us not be in a hurry. Let us see him at work. There may possibly be nothing there but a lion's hide upon the back of a cow." But, on the other hand they esteem as a genuine sire a horse for long journeys, whose flesh is firm, whose ribs are bare, his limbs clean and his respiration powerful. He must also be endowed with a good temper, and have given proof of being able to bear great fatigue, privations, and hardships.

As to the mare, the case has been pending for centuries. Now as formerly the custom is to picture an Arab by the side of his mare. The gold of the purchaser glitters at his feet, but whilst this gold is being counted out the descendant of Ishmael casts a melancholy look on the noble animal from whom he cannot bring himself to separate. He springs upon her back and rushes far away into the desert: "The eye knoweth not where he has passed." Such is the orthodox representation; let us now see the truth as depicted by the Emir Abd-el-Kader:

The Arabs prefer mares to horses, it is true, but only for the three following reasons. The first is because they consider the profit to be derived from a mare as something very handsome, for it is well known that as much as fifteen to twenty thousand *douros* (from £3,000 to £4,000) have been received for the offspring of a single mare. Hence they may be often heard to exclaim: "The head of riches is a mare that produces a mare." And this idea gathers strength in their eyes from it having been said by our lord Mohammed, the messenger of Allah: "Give the preference to mares; their belly is a treasure, and their back a seat of honour. The greatest of blessings is an intelligent woman, or a prolific mare." These words are thus explained by commentators: "Their belly is a treasure," because a mare by means of her offspring increases the wealth of her master; and "their back is a seat of honour," because the pace of a mare is more easy and agreeable; some even going so far as to say that the easiness of her gait will after a time render her rider effeminate.

The second motive is that the mare does not neigh in time of war like the horse, and is less sensitive as to hunger, thirst, and heat, and is therefore of greater use to a people whose riches consist principally in flocks of camels and sheep. It is known to all, that camels and sheep do not really thrive except in the Sahara, where the ground is so arid that many Arabs, being unable to procure water more than once in eight or ten days, accustom themselves to drink nothing but milk. This is one of the consequences of the great distance that frequently, on account of the pasturage, divides the encampment from a spot where there are wells. The mare is like the serpent : her strength increases in the hot season and in torrid regions. A snake that lives in a cold country or in water has very little life or venom, so that its bite is rarely mortal; whereas a snake that lives in a hot country is full of life, and the virulence of its poison is intensified. Contrary to the horse who is less capable of supporting the heat of the sun, the mare, owing doubtless to her temperament, finds her vigour doubled in the hottest season.

The third and last motive is, the little attention required by the mare. She feeds on anything. Her owner leads or sends her to graze on the same herbage as the sheep and camels. There is no occasion to place a watchman in regular attendance. The horse, however, cannot dispense with being well kept, nor can his owner send him to the pasture without a *saïs*, or groom, to look after him.

Such are the true reasons for the preference which Arabs show for mares. This preference is not caused by an idea that the foal inherits from its dam more than from its sire, or that it is better on all occasions to ride a mare than a horse. But it rests partly on substantial benefits received, and partly on the necessities of the life which the Arabs habitually lead. It may be laid down, then, as a fact that the horse is more noble than the mare, and that the sire bequeaths to the foal more than the mare does, which the Arabs express by the saying : *El mohor itebad el Fadl,* " the foal follows the stallion." I admit, however, that the best produce is that which proceeds from a sire and a dam both of pure race. In this case, it is gold allying itself with gold. I will add that the horse is stronger, of a higher courage and greater speed than the mare, and is free from the grave drawback attendant on the latter of stopping short under her rider, even in battle and at a time perhaps when everything depends on rapid movement.

There can be no doubt that the foal proceeds from the stallion and the mare. But the experience of ages demonstrates that the essential parts of the body, such as the bones, tendons, nerves, and veins follow after the sire. The mare may impart to her young the colour of her coat, a general resemblance, and something of her frame, but it is the stallion that transmits the strength of the bones, the vigour of the nerves, the solidity of the tendons, speed and all the other most important characteristics. He also communicates to his offspring his moral qualities, and if he is really noble, preserves him from all vice, for the Arabs of old have said : " The noble horse has no malice."

. . . .

No sooner has the foal seen the light than one of the bystanders takes it in his arms, and walks up and down with it for some time in the midst of almost inconceivable noise and uproar. It is supposed that a useful lesson is thus taught for the future—the animal, accustomed from its birth to horrible sounds, will never afterwards be frightened at anything. This lesson finished, the master of the tent places the right dug of the mare in the foal's mouth, and exclaims : "In the name of Allah! Allah grant that the new-born *(mezyoud)* may bring us good fortune, health, and abundance!" The friends who are present answer all together : "Amen! May Allah bless thee! He has sent thee another child."*

To teach the foal to suck, a fig or a date soaked in milk slightly salted is put into his mouth. As soon as he has taken a liking to it and begins to suck it, he is placed under his dam. After two or three attemps he soon mistakes the dug for the fig or date he has just left, and the thing is done. After that he is carefully preserved from the night-cold. But it is also necessary to accustom him to drink camel's and ewe's milk. It is done in this manner. They take a goat's skin used several years for holding milk, and fill it with air. Then squeezing it gently, they blow up his nostrils a few times. By way of complement to this operation they crush dates in milk, which impart to it a sweetish flavour

---

* Among the Arabs of Upper Asia, but chiefly in the Nedjed, when a filly is foaled, it is impossible to form an idea of the rapture that seizes the family. " Allah has sent us a blessing; our lord Mohammed has entered into our tent." Neither wives nor children would suffer themselves to substract one drop of the milk drawn from the camels, the goats, and the ewes. The whole of it is reserved for the fortunate foal, object of the love and most tender solicitude of all inhabitants of the tent. (*Voyage dans la Haute Asie*, by M. Pétiniaud.)

and then place the mixture close to the foal's mouth, forcing him every now and then to dip his lips into it. He begins by tasting and licking it and after a while drinks it, whether the dam gives him suck or not. Great importance is attached to teaching the foal to drink milk; first, because he can thus be left in the tent while the mare is again put to work; and secondly, because in after years, in default of water, he will be satisfied with milk instead, and also as food if barley runs short. Should the mare take an aversion to her young, she must be separated from him, and the latter must be brought up on camel's milk, as this is deemed preferable to the milk of the cow or the she-goat, which produces laziness and heaviness.

A few days or a few mounths after the birth of a foal, some Arabs slit one or both of the ears. This fancy is accounted for in various ways. According to one party this operation is performed on animals born in the night time, because they ought to have a better sight than those that come into the world during the day. According to others, it is done to foals born on Friday, the day of the gathering together of Mussulmans at the mosque, because it is a lucky sign. The truth is simply this : The master of a tent has a child of tender years, whom he loves very dearly. In slitting the ear of his foal he declares that he reserves him for his son so-and-so. Should the father afterwards die, no one would dispute the possession of the animal with the child thus named. Others, however, slit the ear of a foal that has the colic; the bleeding saves him.

Soon after the birth of a foal they hang round his neck amulets, and talismans (richly ornamented in the case of wealthy people) and little shells called *oudad*. They are suspended by neckbands of wool or of. camel's skin *(goulada)* which the women delight to make with their own hands, especially applying themselves to harmonise the colours tastefully. To bay or black horses they attach a white *goulada,* to those of a light colour red *gouladas.* These neckbands are useful as well as ornamental, for they serve to hold the animal by if need be, thus replacing our halters in a manner more agreeable to the eye and less irksome to the horse. As for the talismans *(heurouze-addjab)* they are simply little bags made of Morocco leather, more or less ornamented, and containing words extracted from the sacred writings, by means of which they hope to preserve the animal from wounds, from sickness, and from the evil eye.

Occasionally in war time the foal is killed immediately after its' birth, in order that the dam may be the sooner fit for service; but never do they slay a filly. Such a one is weaned and left in the tent to shelter it from the sun, and the women frequently succeed in saving its life by giving it ewe's or camel's milk. If a filly be born on the road during a journey or march undertaken for a commercial or a warlike object, in order to save it every possible fatigue it is placed upon a camel, where a soft nest is constructed for it; but it will only be allowed to approach its dam during a halt or in the night time.

During the Taguedempt expedition in 1841 I saw a cavalier of Makhzen, who had no means of transport, carry before him on his saddle for the first four days after its birth a filly which his mare had given him at the bivouac. At the end of that period it followed its dam, throughout the campaign.

When the colts are not destroyed they are usually sold in the Tell, at the season of buying grain, whereas the fillies are preserved as a source of riches through their offspring.

The greater the value attached to the mare, the earlier is the time for weaning, but it generally takes place in the sixth or seventh month. In weaning the foal they remove it from its dam, first of all for one day, then for two, and so on, gradually increasing the period of separation. To render the transition less abrupt, they give it camel's milk sweetened with date honey, and to keep it from wandering in search of its mother they tether it by its fore or hind legs with woollen cords but in either case above the knees or the hocks; whence proceed the whitish marks that are often observable. If at that age the animal were fastened by the pasterns considerable injury might be done. The foal never remaining still and puzzled by its novel situation, the processes called by the Arabs *louzze,* or almonds, would speedily be formed. Redoubled attention is paid to the foal while being weaned, for if it succeeded in getting loose and approached its dam it would be liable to fall ill through sucking a corrupt and sour milk.

In the day time while the mare is on the march or in the pasture, a sort of halter *(kuemama)* is put on the foal, the noseband of which is furnished with short porcupine's quills. The dam then refuses of herself to let the foal touch her. As soon as it is fairly weaned, it is necessary in order to prevent the accumulation of milk to draw it off from the mare from time to time, and somewhat to lower her diet. After being weaned, the foal is fed on ground barley in regularly increasing quantities, taking care, however, not to cause satiety. They use a wooden measure called *feutra*. This measure contains three double handfuls, and is common to all the tribes of the desert, because its origin dates from a religious tradition. At the *aïd-es-seghrir*, that is, at the little festival which follows the Ramadan, the Prophet recommends every Mussulman who is tolerably well off to give to the poor a *feutra* of food, wheat, barley, dates, rice, etc., according to the productions of the country in which he may be residing.

As soon as the foal is weaned, the women take possession of it, saying : "It belongs to us now; it is an orphan, but we will make its life as pleasant as possible."

REMARKS BY THE EMIR ABD-EL-KADER.

The foal follows the sire. The best stock is that which proceeds from a sire and a dam of pure extraction. The produce of a foreign mare by an Arab horse is less valued, and much less that of a blood mare by a common horse. Lastly, a colt whose sire and dam are both of foreign race has no good quality whatsoever.

The Arabs affirm that an entire horse has more vigour and speed than a mare. As a rule stallions are scarce in the Sahara. They are seldom to be met with except with the chiefs or with men of wealth, who can afford to have them properly tended and looked after, as it would be dangerous to turn them loose on to the grazing grounds. On the contrary, the mare requires very little attention, and is therefore chiefly ridden by the Saharenes.

Immediately after the foal is born it is made to swallow two or three eggs. Then, while the foal is still on the ground they rub the sole and crust of the hoof with salt dissolved in a preparation of *bouna-faâ,** which renders the horn hard and tough. After that, the foal gets up, gopes about, and seeks its dam. Twelve hours later it will follow her to the pasture. As soon as the foal is born the master of the tent hastens to arrange his ears, the forelock, the mane, and the neck, carefully collecting the hairs together from the root upwards. If the weather is cold, both the dam and the foal are kept in the tent. Seven days afterwards the mare is made to swallow a pound or a pound and a half of rancid butter not salted.

The nobler the mare, the sooner is the foal weaned, and in any case it is never permitted to suck longer than six months. In certain countries the Arabs are under the impression that a protracted suckling almost always produces a bad disposition and a hard mouth. Everywhere, where it is possible, and according to the season of the year, they give the foal camel's, or cow's, or ewe's milk, which is supposed to render the coat more soft and sleek.

"The best treasure of a man is a fruitful mare."

"Allah bade them multiply, and they have multiplied."

* An umbelliferous plant of the genus thapsia.

———

Though weaned, the foal accompanies its dam to the pasture. This exercise is found necessary to its health and to the development of its faculties. In the evening it comes home to lie down beside the tent of its owner. There, it is to every member of the family the object of the greatest care. The women and the children sport with it, and give it *Kouskoussou,** bread, flour, milk, and dates. This daily contact leads to that docility which is so much admired in Arab horses.

Sometimes tushes grow out even in one-year olds, and the animal falls away in condition until they are extracted, when it recovers its health. Should the colt at the age of fifteen to eighteen months fail to promise a fine free action of the shoulder, they do not hesitate to apply the cautery to the scapulo-humeral joint. It is generally applied in the form of a cross, the four extreme points of which are joined by a circle. Previous to the operation care is taken to trace the design with pitch if the animal be of a light colour, or with plaster if it be

---

* A kind of semolina made with wheaten flour. It is as universal with the Arabs as soup with Continental Europeans.

dark. If, again, a colt's knees are ill shaped, or indicate a predisposition to bony tumours or to thickening, fire is applied in three parallel lines. Lastly, if any apprehension is felt of the colt becoming too straight either in front or behind, they fire the fetlock-joint but only on the front part, which shows that the Arabs understand the tendons and treat them carefully. The fire is usually applied with a sickle. In performing this operation they avoid as much as possible the great heats of summer. The most favourable season is the end of autumn or the beginning of spring : there are fewer flies then, and the temperature is cooler.

The education of a colt should commence when eighteen months old, because it is the only way to make him thoroughly docile, and also because the development of the spleen is thus checked—a very important point in the opinion of the Arabs. If he is first of all mounted at a later period, he may look stronger to the eye, but in reality he will be inferior in patience and in speed.

"Every horse inured to fatigue brings good fortune."*

* During my long career, in my tribes, by my friends, or among my followers, I have seen upwards of ten thousand colts reared, and I affirm that all those whose education was not begun at a very early age and according to the principles enunciated above, have never turned out other than stubborn, troublesome horses, unfit for war. I also affirm that when I have made long and rapid marches at the head of twelve or fifteen hundred horsemen, horses however lean, if early broken in to fatigue, never fell out of the ranks, while those that were fat or mounted too late have always fallen to the rear. My conviction on this head is based on such a long experience that lately, finding myself at Masseur (Cairo), in the necessity of purchasing some horses, I refused point blank all that were presented to me that had been broken in at a comparatively advanced age.

"How has thy horse been reared? " was always my first question.

"My lord," an inhabitant of the city would reply " this gray stone of the river has been brought up by me like one of my own children, always well fed, well tended to, and spared as much as possible, for I did not begin to ride him till he was full four years old. See how fat he is, how sound in all his limbs."

" Well, keep him, my friend, He is thy pride and that of thy family. It would be a shame to my gray beard to deprive thee of him."

And Heaven knows how the Arab horse is inured to fatigue! So to speak, he is always on the march. He travels with his master who is one of the greatest travellers on horseback in the world. He travels to seek his food. He traverses long distances to find water; and this sort of life renders him abstinent, not easily tired, and ready for anything. It must be admitted that that is a method of training horses not easily surpassed.

I repeat, for I cannot too strongly insist on this capital point, the opinion of the Arabs is unanimous in favour of the education of the colt beginning at a very early age. In acting otherwise, there is a risk, they imagine, of having an unmanageable horse, or one heavy and clumsy. Exercise, on the contrary, accustoms the horse to submission, gives strength to the joints while rendering them supple, imparts firmness to the bones, develops the muscles, and brings out that power of enduring fatigue without which the animal is nothing more than source of outlay without any return for it.

At the age, then, of eighteen to twenty months the colt is mounted by a child who takes him to water, goes in search of grass, or leads him to the pasture. Not to hurt the bars he guides him with a longe, or a tolerably soft mule's bit. This exercise is good for them both. The child grows up a horseman, and the colt acquires

"And thou!" I would then ask of an Arab whom I recognised as a child of the desert, so embrowned was he with the sun, "How has thy horse been reared?"

"My lord," he would answer, "betimes I formed his back to the saddle, and his mouth to the bridle. With him I have reached a distant, very distant point. He has passed many a day without food. His ribs are bare, it is true, but if you encounter any enemies on your path he will not leave you in peril. I swear it by the day of the last judgment, when Allah shall be kadi and the angels witnesses."

"Hola, there! tether the dark chestnut before my tent," I would cry to my servants, "and satisfy this man."

(SIDI-HAMED-BEN-MOHAMMED-EL-MOKRANI, khalif of Medjana, chief of one of the most illustrious families of all Algeria.)

the habit of carrying a weight proportioned to his strength. He learns to walk, to fear nothing, and it is in this manner, say the Arabs, that "we contrive never to have restive horses." The first time the child mounts the colt, he should say, while in the act of bestriding him : "Glory to Him who has subjected the horse to us! Without Allah we should never have accomplished it."

It is at this age also they begin to shackle the colt. The clogs are at first fastened very short, as without that precaution the young animal might lose something of the steadiness of its balance and injure its chest or shoulders either in lying down or getting up again. They ought likewise to be attached loosely so as not to occasion the formation of hard knots. This mode of shackling a horse is decidedly the best. With it one never hears of a horse breaking loose, a misadventure that causes such confusion in a bivouac, drives horsemen to despair, and is the source of a thousand accidents. As the animal is forced to stoop and lean forwards to graze, one would imagine that it could not fail after a while to lose something of its uprightness. The fear is altogether unfounded. The chest expands, the limbs acquire strength. All Barbs stand well upon their legs and are admirably straight along the back and loins. The Arabs are loud in their abuse of our mode of tying up horses with a longe. They affirm that in addition to the vices and accidents it may occasion, it has the great inconvenience of not allowing the animal to lie down. Whereas with clogs a horse protrudes his head and neck and when he wants to sleep places himself exactly in the position of a greyhound basking in the sun. Besides, a great many stable vices desappear when they are used. The animal can neither entangle itself in the halter, nor slip it, nor get into the manger nor lie down beneath it, nor scratch the earth with its foot, nor rub against the manger nor contract any other bad habits of the kind: an indisputable advantage so far.

The colt being thus shackled in front of the tent, a little negro with a switch is placed near him to accustom him to remain still. It is the duty of this young slave to correct him slightly if he attempts to lash out at any-thing passing behind him, or if he bites at his neighbours. He is watched in this manner until he is brought to the most perfect gentleness. When he is sent to the pasture, the ligatures fasten together a fore and hind foot at the same side, and the cord is purposely made very short. It is observed that when the colt stoops to graze, the shortness of the cord compels the vertebral column to remain straight, and to become rather convex than concave. If, on the contrary, the cord were too long, there would be nothing to support the vertebral column, and it would easily become distorted.

When from twenty four to twenty seven months old, the colt is for the first time saddled and bridled, but with every precaution. For instance, he is not saddled until quite used to the bridle. For the first few days the bit is covered with undressed wool, partly with a view not to hurt his bars, and partly to allure him to docility by the saltish flavour of which he is so fond. When he begins to champ the bit, the task is nearly · accomplished. This preparatory exercise takes place morning and evening. Thus sagaciously handled, the young animal will be ready to be mounted in the early part of the autumn, when he will be less tormented by the flies and heat. Wealthy owners, before they allow their colt to be mounted by a grown-up man, sometimes have him led up and down gently for a fort-night, with a pack-saddle on his back supporting two baskets filled with sand. He thus gradually passes from the weight of the child that first bestrode him to that of the man who is about to mount him.

Suppose the colt now to have completed two years and a half. His vertebral column has acquired strength. The clogs, the saddle and the bridle are familiar to him. A cavalier mounts on his back. The animal is certainly very young, but he will be ridden only at a walking pace, and his bit will be a very easy one. The main point is to accustom him to obedience. The owner without spurs and holding only a light cane in his hand which he uses as little as possible, rides him to the market, or to visit his friends, his flocks and pastures, and attends to his affairs without exacting anything more than submission and docility. This he ordinarily obtains by never speaking to him except in a low voice, without passion, and carefully avoiding anything likely to elicit opposition that must result in a contest from which he might come forth conqueror, but at the expense of his horse. Particular importance is attached to keeping the young animal still and quiet for a fiew minutes before letting him start. At a later period, his owner will not fail to reap the benefit of this excellent practice.

The common people sometimes mount their colts before they are two years and a half old, and if reproached for doing so, they answer : "You are quite right; we know that, but how can it be helped? We are poor, and have no choice but to act in this manner or go on foot. We prefer the former alternative, notwithstanding its disadvantages. In the perilous life we lead, the present moment is everything."

Seeing the Arabs employ their colts so early, mounting the two-year olds and exacting from them considerable fatigue, and forced marches, and using them even as pack-horses without regard to their age or strength, many persons have concluded that this people knew nothing about the proper mode of managing horses, and have even denied that they had any love for the animal. Such persons, however, cannot have taken into account that sometimes to save their families, sometimes their property, and frequently to obey the summons of the holy war *(djehad)* these Arabs are obliged to use whatever materials come to hand. They are compelled to employ their horses through the necessities that beset them, and through circumstances quite beyond their control, but they are perfectly aware that it would be better not to do so.

It is also when he is about thirty months old that the colt is taught not to break loose from his rider when the latter sets foot to earth, and not even to stir from the spot where the bridle has been passed over his head and allowed to drag on the ground. Especial care is taken in teaching this lesson, because it is one of great importance in Arab life. The same means is adopted in this case, as in accustoming the colt to the clogs. A slave stands beside him, who puts his foot on the bridle whenever the animal is about to go off, and thus gives a disagreeable shock to the bars of his mouth. After a few days of this exercise he will stand stock still at the spot where he has been left, and will wait for his master for days together. This practice is so universal throughout the Sahara that the first thing an Arab does after killing his adversary, if he wants his horse, is to pass the bridle quickly over his head. The animal then remains perfectly still and allows the conqueror time to despoil his fallen foe : without this precaution it would have rejoined its *goum*.

Here is a scene we have all witnessed. An Arab arrives at the market, and dismounts in the midst of a score of horses or mares. You suppose that he is going to give his animal to some one to hold. Not so: he passes the bridle over his neck, lets it fall on the ground, and placing a stone upon it goes without disquietude to transact his business. Two hours afterwards he returns, finds that his horse has not moved from the spot where he left him—and to which he probably fancied himself fastened—gets on the saddle and returns to his own people.

From the age of two and a half to three years the system already indicated continues to be applied with a view to confirm the young animal in the docile habits so essential in war time. Pains too are taken to make him very quiet to mount, by using every precaution. In his life of perilous adventure the Arab has need, before all things, of a horse easy to mount. Lessons to this effect will be renewed day after day until they are no longer necessary : but not too long at a time for fear of tiring out the colt. At first the owner will be assisted by two men, one of whom will hold the bridle and the other the stirrup, and after a while he will succeed in producing a statue-like immobility. Sick and ill-shaped horses, say the Arabs, alone prove unteachable.

From three to four years old more is expected from a horse, but at the same time he is better fed. He is now ridden with spurs and, being thoroughly grounded in the foregoing lessons, he gives proof of mettle and learns to fear nothing. The cries of the animals living in the same *douar,* the roaring of the wild beasts that prowl around during the night, and the constant discharge of fire-arms, soon prepare him for war.

However, if notwithstanding all the careful management we have described, a horse takes to rearing either through laziness or vice, or to plunging, or biting, or refuses to leave the tent or the other horses, recourse is had to the potency of spurs. These are made very sharp, and their point is bent in the form of a slightly rounded hook. With these instruments the rider draws long bloody wheals along the animal's belly and flanks, which inspire him with such terror that he becomes as tame as a lamb and will track his master out like a dog. Horses that have undergone this punishment rarely relapse into their former faults. To increase the potency of the spurs, salt or gun powder is rubbed into the still bleeding wounds. The Arabs are so convinced of the efficacy of this chastisement that they do not look upon a horse as thoroughly trained for war until he has passed through this terrible experience. At the same time that the rider uses the spurs to chastise a decidedly restive horse, he strikes him a little behind the headstall of the bridle with a short thick stick, with which he is always provided when he means to break in an animal of this kind.

In certain localities to prevent a horse from rearing they attach an iron ring to his ear. If he tries to rise up a smart blow with a stick is struck upon this ring, the pain thus caused soon sickening the animal of his bad "defence." To cure a horse of plunging, he is mounted with his tail towards a thick thorny shrub *(gandoule)*. He is then urged forward, but jibs, lashes out, and pricks himself. However, after a few lessons of this kind, he breaks himself of his abominable habit.

The Arabs declare that spurs add one fourth to the rider's horsemanship, and one third to the spirit of the animal, and illustrate their assertion by the following fable :

"When beasts were first created, they had the gift of speech. The horse and the camel took an oath never to harm one another but to live, on the contrary, with a perfect mutual understanding. An Arab placed in a critical position by one of the chances of war, saw with dispair the flight of the camel on which he had hoped to save his property. There was no time to lose. 'Bring my horse!' he exclaims, and leaps on his back. He scolds him, beats him, gives him the heel. All in vain. The horse stirs not a step, remembering the promise made to his friend. The Arab then puts on his spurs, which he carried in his *djebira,** and the horse, smarting with his torn flanks, springs forward, and speedily overtakes the runaway. 'Ah! traitor!' cried the camel, 'thou hast violated our compact; thou tookest an oath never to do me any harm, and yet thou hast replaced me in the power of my tyrant.' 'Accuse not my heart,' replied the horse; 'I refused to move, but "the thorns of misery" have brought me up to thee.'"

---

* A sort of sabretache attached to the pommel of the saddle, in which the Arabs carry their ammunition, their papers, and food, etc., etc. Sometimes the *djebira* is a marvel of elaborate embroidery.

It is not an easy task to use the spurs properly. Horsemen who possess that talent are cited even among the Arabs. Some are only able to urge on their steed by constantly tickling his flanks without wounding him. Others are acquainted only with the *tekerbeda*, or the art of clashing their iron spurs against their iron stirrups in order to frighten the animal. The most skilful alone know how to raise those bloody wheals to which we have already alluded. When it is said of a horseman that he marks his horse with wheals from the navel to the vertebral column, the highest compliment has been paid to him. During my residence at Mascara, how often have I heard the Arabs assert, by way of vaunting the horsemanship of their Emir : "Abd-el-Kader! why, he crosses his spurs on his horse's loins!"

These spurs are dangerous for inexperienced horsemen, who sometimes prick the animal on the kneepan and so lame him if the wound be deep. And if a horse comes down, the spur is very apt to run into him. For this reason the Arabs generally have the leathers of their spurs tolerably loose, in order to obviate by their slackness their own awkwardness. It also enables them to disembarrass themselves more quickly in battle if their horse happens to be killed and they are compelled to flee on foot to save their lives. On the same grounds they prefer in a serious combat loose-fitting shoes to boots. Our spurs they look upon as utterly inefficient. "What benefit, in a case where your life is at stake do you expect to get from them with a horse already knocked up? They are good only for tickling a horse and to make him restive. With our spurs we draw every thing out of him. As long as there is life in him, we will get it out of him : they lose their effect only in presence of death."

Every Arab trains his own horse. In the Sahara the only riding masters are practice, tradition, and example. A reputation as a good rider is only acquired after many proofs of skilfulness. It is not sufficient to be competent to manage a horse on level ground. It is necessary, gun in hand, to make the most of him at a rapid pace over a broken, wooded, and difficult country. "Such a one," say they "is a horseman of the gun, while so-and-so is only a horseman of the heel." Perfection implies equal skill with the gun and the heel. They even go so far as to institute a difference between one who rides well over dry ground, and one who rides boldly over slippery ground. They distinguish between the horseman of summer and the horseman of winter.

What experience must not such an apprenticeship lay up! There is one point, however, which they entirely overlook—they never trouble themselves as to which leg the horse puts foremost. An Arab horse has always power and well formed shoulders which, owing to his practice as a colt of grazing on mountains, in woods, and on broken ground, have become far better developed than they would have been by means of the plate-longe and the riding school. He is also easy in his paces because the rider yields to all the movements of his body and never sets himself against them. I may add that the Arab has a perfect seat, and though he rides very short he makes up for that disadvantage by wearing very long spurs which, by the slightest movement of the leg, catch the horse on the flank, compel him to bring his hind-legs under the centre of gravity, keep him in hand, and place his head as correctly as if he had acted upon our best system of horsemanship.*

Arab horses have always a good mouth. A proverb says :

> The horseman makes the horse,
> As the husband makes the wife.

But it is not enough to have softened and tamed the horse. Although, by means of kind treatment, daily intercourse, and punishment judiciously applied, he has become docile, and a good action has been secured, his education is still incomplete. It still remains to perfect him, and to do so they train him to the following exercises :

El Feuzzda, "setting off suddenly at full gallop." To accomplish this they pursue nearly the same method as ourselves, with this difference that they avail themselves of the aid of the *tekerbeda,* which we have already described, so that a horse must be altogether impracticable if he does not act as he is required to do.

---

* "To day we went out on horseback with our host Youssouf-ben-Bender, and directed our course towards the desert. He was accompanied by his sons and grandsons, all mounted on fine horses, while his servants proceeded on dromedaries. During this excursion, we met an Arab who caused me some surprise. Without saddle or bridle, with a slight halter, the nose-band of which was a thin iron chain, and holding in his hand a wand crooked at one end with which he guided his horse, he started off at full gallop, pulled up dead halt, was off again like an arrow, turned sharp round at full speed, and while going at that pace, made his horse change his feet, off the ground, on the right line. I could scarcely believe my own eyes and I question if our most celebrated riding-masters or "sportsmen" could do better. What particularly struck me was the simplicity of the means employed by this son of Ishmael to obtain what he exacted from his courser. In Europe, we study the functions and play of the muscles, only to counteract them. In Arabia also are they studied, but in order to make use of nature, not to do her violence. Besides, it is not merely one Arab here and there who rides well; but all without exception are good horsemen, all love the horse passionately, all understand how to train him. At the bivouac an inhabitant of the Nedjed always sleeps with his head resting on the shoulder of his horse, and every horse lies down at his master's bidding. The latter thus obtains a pillow softer than the ground, and also renders it difficult for any one to steal his horse during his sleep." (*Voyage dans la Haute Asie,* by M. Pétiniaud, General Inspector of the "Haras.")

El Kyama, "going free." They rush the animal at a wall, or a tree, or a man, and pull him up short. By degrees he will learn to halt abruptly in the middle of a rapid career, on the bank of a river or on the edge of a ravine or precipice—a valuable accomplishment, oftentimes most advantageous in war. If a young horse is not a free-goer, but capers about and obstinately refuses to separate from the other horses, a fault of the last consequence to an Arab, he is cured by the following process. The owner's friends get on horseback and draw themselves up in two lines, facing each other and two or three paces apart. The horse is then ridden between these two hedges. If he stops, the horsemen beat him with sticks, while his rider plies him vigourously with the spur. A fortnight of this lesson is more than enough for the most obstinate.

El Lotema, "the wheeling round." This exercise consists in turning suddenly to the right or left, but more frequently the latter, as soon as the rider has fired off his piece. The principle is this, the trigger being pulled, the horseman strikes his horse sharply with the left hand behind the saddle, and at the same moment with his right hand on the neck. The animal understands what is meant, and in a very short time learns to obey merely the movement of his rider's body. This instruction is inculcated with the greatest care, being of great importance to the Arab, who is so often exposed to single combats.

El Djery, "the race." They first of all make the animal go at a swift pace by itself over a level plain, stimulating it with whip and spur, but only for a short distance. After a while they match the colt against an old horse of some renown. The young one becomes excited, and does his utmost to maintain the contest. These exercises being frequently repeated serve likewise to give the owner an exact knowledge of his horse's capabilities, and of what he may safely undertake with him in the future. They are not unattended with danger, but "the angels have two special missions in this world : to preside at the racing of horses and at the union of man with woman." It is their duty to preserve horsemen and horses from all accident, and to see that marriages are fruitful.

Teneguize, "the leap." Moreover, the colt must be taught to leap. This teaching is progressive and demands much patience. The lesson is not repeated more than twice or thrice in the course of one day. At first they begin with small obstacles, so as not to disgust the animal, nor is he brought face to face with any of a serious nature until he is quite docile and fully developed. Unquestionably, the Arabs regard the leap as the necessary complement of a colt's education, but they are far from attaching to it the same importance that Europeans do. Their country is for the most part difficult, full of ravines, strewed with huge stones, and covered with prickly bushes. They assert, therefore, that if they were to jump over every obstacle they encounter either in war or in hunting, they would be always jumping, which would fatigue their horses terribly and in the long run ruin them. Consequently, they go round any very rough ground, ride down almost perpendicular places, and go straight up the steepest slopes, and practice renders their horses so adroit that in a long journey they reach the end more quickly than if they had jumped over everything that came in their way.

El Nechacha, "the exciting." The horse is taught to throw himself upon that of the adversary, and bite either the rider or the animal. The rider pulls up his horse, while he pushes him with his legs, and all the time keeps on repeating the cry of *sheït,* and success is the more easy because the animal is naturally excitable. The Arabs declare that horses trained in this manner have often unseated an enemy in single combat. Sometimes, too, in razzias, they quicken the pace of the camels that have been captured. I myself have seen a Makhzen horseman thus hurry on animals that had fallen behind. His horse rushed at them and bit at them with apparent pleasure.

Horsemen of renown do not, however, confine the education of their horses to these manœuvres so necessary in battle, but they also teach them to shine at feasts and fantasias by the following accomplishments :

El Entrabe, "the caracol." The horse walks, so to speak, on his hind-legs. Scarcely does he touch the ground with his forefeet, than he again rises. One hand, in concert with the legs, soon trains to this exercise a horse of fair intelligence.

El Guetcâa, "the bucking." The horse springs up with all fours off the ground, the horseman at the same time throwing up his gun into the air and cleverly catching it. To obtain this action, the rider marks certain intervals of rest and works with his legs. He gives with the animal as he rises, in order to hold him up when he comes down again. Nothing can be more picturesque than this exercise. The horses quit the earth, the guns fly into the air, and the ample folds of the burnous float and unroll themselves in the wind, thrown back by the vigourous arms of the children of the desert. It is, in truth, the charm and crowning act of the fantasia.

Lastly, *El-Berraka,* "the kneeling." The rider remaining on his saddle causes his horse to kneel down. This is the *nec plus ultra* of the man and the animal. Not every horse is fit for this exercise. The colt is trained to it by tickling him on the coronet, pinching him on the legs, and forcing him to bend the knee. After a time the horseman will reap the benefit of these preliminary steps. He need only clear his feet of the stirrups, stretch his legs forward, turn out the points of his toes, touch with his long spurs the animal's fore-arm, and then as his piece is fired at marriage feasts and other rejoicings, his horse will kneel down amid the applause of the young maidens, piercing the air with joyful acclamations.

After the horse is completely "suppled" by all these exercises, the following feats are attempted :

Laâb el Hazame, "the girdle feat." When the horse is thoroughly trained, at a family festivals and religious solemnities, the horseman going at full gallop will pick up a girdle lying on the ground : the most skilful grasping it at three different places.

Laâb Ennichan, "firing at a mark." The target is usually a stone, or a mutton shoulder-blade. The performers start from a distance in order to get a good seat, and when fifty or sixty paces off they discharge their pieces. The Saharene will recall these lessons to mind when out hunting, and going at full speed, he brings down an ostrich or a gazelle. It is not of an inhabitant of the Tell that you must expect these prodigies of address, skilfulness, and equestrian science. Nor will you see on him the light apparel, the fine and beautiful wool of a child of the desert, whom, besides, you will always recognize by his slender, long-bodied horse, the ease with which he handles his gun, and that graceful forward movement by which he quickens his courser's pace. How many are there in the Tell who would ride a whole stage without dropping a piece of money placed between the sole of the foot and the spur?*

"And you Christians! you go at a trot. And so do we, but only when time is of no consequence and to breathe our horses. In war time we know nothing but the walk and the gallop. If we are not in a hurry, the trot is enough for us, but if there be danger it is the gallop that saves our heads."

An Arab chief would not keep a horse whose pace was not formed. The above exercises are not adopted by all Arabs. Each selects what is best suited to his position, his fortune, and his tastes. But all conform themselves to the principles we have laid down for the education of the colt. These consist in first of all reducing the young animal to the last degree of wretchedness, in order to handle him gently when between three and four years old. After these trials, his real value is konwn. These principles are, moreover, summed up in a familiar proverb that shows the amount of

---

* While with us, in France, the stirrup is not supposed to bear more than the weight of the leg; with the Arabs, on the contrary, the whole weight of the body, when going at a good pace, is thrown upon the stirrups.

interest attached to beginning by times the task of training.

> Let the one-year old colt do nothing but eat,
> And he will not strain himself:
> Mount him from two to three years old,
> Until he is quite tamed.
> Feed him well from three to four.
> Then mount him again,
> And if he does not suit you,
> Sell him without hesitation.

Let it not be supposed, however, that it is only the Arabs of our African possessions who are so mad, if I may be allowed the use of the expression, about commencing the process of breaking-in at an early age. The Arabs universally, no matter to what country they belong, profess the same principles. If proof be wanted, read what has been said on the subject by no inexperienced person, in fact by an inspector-general of the Haras, M. Pétiniaud, who was commissioned by the French Government to travel through Upper Asia to procure horses of pure Oriental blood. He shall speak for himself :—

"After three years of wanderings among the tribes encamped from Diarbekir and Aleppo to the confines of the Nedjed, I returned to Bagdad last January. Among the papers that awaited me, I found a number of the *Journal des Haras,* containing an article on the horses of the Sahara. The perusal of this only too brief memoir which denoted such a perfect knowledge of the Arab and his horse, inspired me with a desire to possess the entire work. On my arrival in France, you were obliging enough to send me a copy, for which I thank you. No one could take a greater interest than myself in a work which you might safely have entitled : "On the Arab horse of Asia and Africa;" for such is the spirit of tradition among this peculiar people that at every line I recognized in the customs of the Moghreb Arabs the customs of their ancestors of the Koreish and the Nedjed, and that after a separation of many centuries."

"In 1851 I descended the Tigris from Mosul to Bagdad, with a volume of Herodotus in my hand. All his descriptions of men and things were still strictly applicable. Thus, at a distance of two thousand three hundred years he depicted the manners of the Arabs with the same truthfulness with which you, General, have described in Africa the Arabs of Asia. Time and space are impotent in the presence of the unchangeableness of such habits : intestine feuds, the chace, *fantasias,* love of the horse, etc., etc., I have witnessed in Asia exactly what you have written of Africa."

"Your work which possesses the great merit of telling the whole truth and nothing but the truth, is calculated, as I think, to exercise a great influence on the education of the horse in France. This delightful style of reading will develop an interest in the animal in those who have never before given it a thought, while our breeders will derive some useful hints from the numerous details you relate. They will learn not to reserve their admiration for a horse that has no other merit than that of being fat, and they will at last come to understand the advantages that result from putting a colt to salutary work from his earliest age. "The horse is a labourer"—let him, then, be accustomed to it in good time."

"I observed that the Arabs used universally to fatigue

without mercy their two and three year olds, but spared them from three to four years of age. They say that sustained work at an early age strengthens the chest, muscles, and joints of the colt, at the same time imparting a docility that will remain with him until death. They also declare that as soon as these rude trials have been got over, his constitution should be developed by rest, care, and an abundant diet, because after this new stage of life he will only be able to show himself exactly what he really he is—good or bad. If good, they will keep him : if bad, they will get rid of him without hesitation, for in their eyes a bad horse is not worth the barley they give him."

I trust to be pardoned for this digression for the sake of the reflections which it suggests. Is it not wonderful to behold a people scattered over vast territories, from the Persian Gulf to the Atlantic Ocean, without means of communication, without printing machines, without telegraphs, without any one of the thousand appliances of modern civilization, but still speaking the same language, living in obedience to the same law, and preserving by simple tradition as well as we could do by books, the usages, the manners, and even the precepts of their ancestors? While seeing and interrogating the Arabs of Algeria, I saw and listened to the Arabs of the primitive stock. Is not this oneness, under such circumstances, a matter to create astonishment?

It may happen that after a horse's education is finished, vices will occasionally break out. The Arabs, however, pay little attention to these, because they consider that such faults proceed simply from too long a period of rest which renders them of lazy habits, or subject to caprice through excess of vitality. They correct them by work, the fatigues of war and the chace. The convenient disposition of their saddles enables them to keep their seat in spite of the obstinate "defences" of the animal. They are consequently never taken by surprise, nor frightened, and always end by mastering the animal completely. No one ever thinks of getting rid of his horse because he rears or plunges or is otherwise troublesome. On the contrary they take delight in these proofs of spirit, for the time will come when they will find their advantage in it. The Arabs have a saying that "The horseman who has not known how to train his horse, bestrides death every day."

The individual to whom they attribute the honour of having been the first to tame the horse is Ishmael, the common ancestor of all the Arabs. Their authority is these words of the Deity : "We placed horses under his dominion in order that he might ride them"—and the celebrated invocation of Ishmael himself : "Horses, night, and space are my witnesses, as well as my sabre, my pen, and paper." Always, always, religious tradition.

As to the really bad vices of biting, plunging, and kicking, they are almost unknown. In fact, all their efforts are directed to avert these. They make the horse live close to the tent, and receive him in some degree as an integral part of the family. In the midst of the women, the children, and the slaves, he can hardly fail to acquire habits of gentleness and docility. For the rest, this care shown to the horse is not merely the result of a sense of personal interest on the part of the owner : it takes its origin in religion. The Prophet has said : "The Believer who has trained his horse to shine in the holy war, the sweat, the hair, the very excrement of this animal shall be placed in the balance to his favour at the day of the last judgment."

However, notwithstanding all these bonds which attach man to the horse, notwithstanding the solidarity formed by habit, religion, and interest, no Mussulman will ever give to his horse the name of a man. Men's names have been borne by saints; it would therefore be a deadly sin, a sacrilege, in fact, to apply them to any animal, even though he should be the noblest of all. Besides, names of any kind are given solely to illustrious steeds, and only in the tents of the great. The following are some of their designations :—

Rakib, the Scout; *Mansour,* the Victorious; *Sabeur,* the Patient; *Salem,* the Saviour; *Kamil,* the Perfect; *Saâd,* Happiness; *Maârouf,* the Known; *Aatik,* the Noble; *Sabok,* the Rapid; *Nadjy,* the Persevering; *Moubarek,* the Blessed; *Guetrâne,* Pitch; *Messaoud,* the Happy; *Safy,* the Pure; *Ghezala,* the Gazelle; *Naâma,* the Ostrich; *Mordjana,* Coral; *El Aroussa,* the Bride; *Djerada,* the Locust; *Ouarda,* the Rose; *Guemera,* the Moon; *Hamama,* the Dove; *Yakouta,* the Ruby; *El Guetaya,* the Cutter; *Aâtifa,* the Docile; and *Leïla,* Night. Very similar names are given to slaves.

A constant practice of the Arabs, and one that must have been remarked by all who have served in Africa, is to cut the hairs of the forelock, the neck, and the tail. The rules for this seem odd to Europeans. When the colt is one year old they clip off all his hair except a tuft between the ears, on the withers, and on the dock of the tail. At two years old the operation is repeated, but this time the hair is entirely clipped off. When three years old, in the third spring, a third clipping takes place. From three to five years the hair is allowed to grow, but only that the whole may be clipped off at the termination of the fifth year. This final operation is called *el halafya,* and no instrument is ever again raised against the hair. It would be thought sinful to do so, as the only object could be to deceive one's brethren as to the age of the horse. After each clipping they never fail to rub the parts thus exposed with sheep's dung soaked in milk, or with Prussian blue diluted with melted butter. These applications soften the skin and thicken the hair. The practice of clipping is supported by several reasons. In the first place, it indicates, at sight, the age of a horse up to eight years, as it takes at least three years before the horse, having recovered his full length of hair, can be styled *djarr*—one that trails his tail along the ground. Secondly,—which is an important point in hot countries,—it compels the animal to bear patiently the stings of flies. And lastly it is supposed that the hair thus becomes thicker, longer, and more silky.

If the Arabs explain and justify this method of clipping a horse's coat until it is five years old, they do not attempt to do so for our fashion of docking a horse's tail. In their eyes it is a barbarism that has no name. It affords an inexhaustible theme for raillery. They rally us, indeed, on this subject in the most serious conjunctures. I can corroborate this assertion by an incident for the accuracy of which I personally vouch :—

In 1841 the column commanded by Marshal Bugeaud marched to Taguedempt to destroy the fort erected there at great expense by the Emir Abd-el-Kader. We were encamped on the Ouad-Krelouk one of the tributaries of the Mina. In the course of the night we were awakened by the report of a musket shot fired in the middle of the camp. Every one rushed out of his tent, hastened in the direction of the sound, and inquired what was amiss. An Arab was lying on the ground, with his thigh broken. He held in his hand a small knife with a very sharp edge and, like all professional thieves in that country, he had nothing on save a leathern girdle furnished with a pistol. The sentinel who had fired explained that having observed a bush approach, halt, and then approach still nearer, he had suspected some trickery and so fired at it at ten paces distance, just as it was close to the horses of his captain. On hearing the tale of the African veteran, his comrades in their fury were about to massacre the Arab, but the officers who were present calmed their not unnatural excitement and reported the case to the superior authorities. The Arab was carried without delay to the ambulance and had his wound dressed. On the morrow the expedition resumed its march. The fellow had received a very severe wound, and it was useless to embarrass ourselves with him. To have put him to death would only have hastened his destiny, perhaps, by a few days, without doing us any particular good, and, besides, the adventure could be turned to a better account. The Governor General decided, therefore, that he should be left upon the site of the encampment, and that a letter should be entrusted to him for the powerful tribe of the Flittas, upon whose territory we then happened to be. In this letter clear intimation was given to that hostile people that their furious dislike to us would one day be fatal to themselves; that it was useless to contend with us, that France abounded in warriors and in wealth, that Abd-el-Kader by continuing the struggle would only bring upon them unnumbered woes; and lastly that the best thing they could do, was to draw off from that man, unless they preferred to see their rich harvests destroyed and burnt before their very eyes.

At early dawn the column set out, and the rearguard was not a thousand *metres* from our bivouac when they observed some Arab horsemen arrive, dismount, and carry off the wounded man. On the following day we received the reply of the Flittas. It was addressed to "General Bugeaud, Kaïd of the Port of Algiers," and was couched to the following effect :—

"You tell us that you are a strong and powerful nation, and that we cannot contend against you. The powerful and the strong are just. And yet you seek to take possession of a country that does not belong to you. Besides, if you are so rich, what do you propose to do among a people who have nothing but powder and shot to give you? Moreover, when it pleases Him, the Master of the world humbles the strong and exalts the feeble. You threaten to burn our crops, or to devour them with your war-horses and beasts of burden. How often already have we experienced similar calamities! We have had bad seasons, we have had locusts and drought, but Allah has never forsaken us; for we are Believers, we are Arabs, and privations will not kill an Arab. We will never yield to you. You are the enemies of our religion. It is quite impossible. Nevertheless, if the Almighty, to punish us for our own sins and for those of our forefathers, should be pleased to inflict upon us some day that horrible malady, we confess we should be greatly embarrassed. With us the mark of submission is the presentation of a horse to the victors. We are aware that you care only for horses with short tails, and our mares do not produce such."

Subsequently, however, the Flittas were compelled to give us such horses as their mares did produce; but their resistance was obstinate. Since then they have always been the first to raise the cry of war and rebellion. It was they who slew the brave General Mustapha-ben-Ismaïl.* It was they who supported Bou-Maza. It was they, in short, who were the last reduced to submission.

After this episode so characteristic of our African campaigns, I cannot better conclude this chapter on the education of the colt than by giving some entirely novel details as to the manner of treating horses in Arabia, which will not be at all out of place and may be interesting to many as showing the part played by woman in the life of that noble animal.

I have often heard it asked whence come the gentle-

---

* France was indebted to the hatred of Abd-el-Kader cherished by Mustapha-ben-Ismaïl for the unfailing loyalty of the illustrious chief of the powerful tribe of the Douairs. He had been for upwards of thirty years the Aga of the Turks. Thus, when the son of Mahi-Eddin, at the age of twenty five, was proclaimed Sultan by the tribe of the province of Oran, the aged warrior refused to yield obedience to him, saying that "never with his white beard would he go to kiss the hand of a mere boy." The consequences of this enmity forced him to take refuge in the *mechouar* of Tlemcen, where for two years he held out against the *hadars*, or citizens, all of whom were devoted to the cause of him who had assumed the title of Commander of the Faithful. Only when reduced to the last extremity did he demand and obtain succour from Marshal Clauzel, whose column relieved him in 1836. From that period, notwithstanding his great age, he took part at the head of the "goums" of the Douairs and the Zmelas, in all the actions fought in the province of Oran. France recompensed this energetic attachment by a Marshal's baton and the cross of a Commander of the Legion of Honour. Mustapha-ben-Ismaïl was killed by the Flittas, on the 19th May 1843, in his eightieth year, while skirmishing in the rear, protecting the rich booty taken from the Hashem-Gharabas, at the capture of the Smala.

ness, the address, the intelligence which, every one is agreed, are to be met with in Arab horses. Are these qualities inherent in the Oriental stock? or are they the result of education? A genial climate is undoubtedly favourable to the development and improvement of the equine race. A rich and noble stock is naturally more apt than any other to yield what is demanded of it, but at the same time something must be done for it in return. The most fruitful soil will produce nothing but briars and thorns if it is not cultivated, and that in a proper manner. Starting from this standing point the Arabs apply themselves with the greatest care and the utmost tenacity to perfect, in their horses, the gifts of nature. A sustained education, daily contact with man, with the other animals, with external objects, that is their grand secret—it is that which makes the Arab horse what he is, an object worthy of our unexceptional admiration. I am aware that this feeling of admiration has not been altogether general. Imperfect knowledge has led many to accuse the Arabs of being ignorant and even of acting like butchers in the matter of horses. They rode them badly, and did not bestow upon them the sort of care so prized in Europe; they abused them from their most tender years, and were constantly drawing blood from the flanks or from the mouth, etc., etc. But truth at length began to dawn, and when it was ascertained that all their horses were intelligent, obedient to the hand and leg, quiet to mount, and inaccessible to fear, there was no choice but to acknowledge that these were great qualities which could only have been produced by a sound and logical education.

Our horses, on the other hand, are nothing more than

animals more or less tamed. They bear with man as a conqueror who disposes of them, but they have neither confidence nor affection for those who employ them. Slaves of mankind in general, they do not attach themselves to any one man in particular, because no man especially attaches himself to his horse, which is merely tended and valued like any other agricultural product that is sold as soon as possible, or like an article of commerce, or a piece of furniture that is bartered for profit or exchanged from caprice. Our dogs, it may be, are only attached to us because we do not part with them for a price.

The Arabs desire to find, in their horse, a devoted friend. With them he leads, so to speak, a domesticated life, in which, as in all domestic life, women play a conspicuous part—that, in fact, of preparing by their gentleness, vigilance, and unceasing attention, the solidarity that ought to exist between the man and the animal. On a journey or a campaign, far from the dwelling place, it is the rider who occupies himself with his horse. But at the encampment, under canvas, and in time of repose, it is the wife who directs, superintends, and feeds the noble companion in arms who so frequently augments the reputation of her husband while supplying the wants of her children. In the morning it is the wife who brings him his food, and tends him, and if possible washes his mane and tail. If the ground on which he stands happens to be uneven, broken, or covered with stones, she removes him to a spot more convenient for his repose and the just disposition of his weight. She caresses him, passes her hand gently over his neck and face, and gives him bread, or dates, or kouskoussou, or even meat cooked and dried in the sun. "Eat, O my son!" she says to him in a soft and tender tone. "One day thou shalt save us out of the hand of our enemies and fill our tent with booty."

It is in the morning also that the Arab wife goes forth to the pastures to gather for the animal she cherishes an ample supply of herbs esteemed in the desert for their tonic and nutritive properties. On her return should she see any children, as yet too young to reason, amusing themselves by teasing or ill using the horses tethered in front of the tent, she will cry to them as soon as she can make herself heard : "Children, beat not the horses. Wretches! it is they who nourish you. Do you wish that Allah should curse our tent? If you begin again, I will speak to your father."

On this subject the Arab wife is so intractable that she would not spare her own husband if he took no care of his horse. The horse is his honour, his fortune. She is proud and jealous on those points, and deems herself affected by whatever affects him. If it ever came to pass that her remarks and suggestions were passed over with neglect, she would not hesitate to carry her complaints to the chief of the tribe : "O my lord! you know that our horse is all we have, and yet my husband takes him on idle journeys, ill uses him, overrides him, and taxes him beyond his strength. It would be something if he looked after him when at home; but no, his covering is full of holes, he is never certain of being fed, and even goes in want of water. Scold my husband, I beseech you in the name of Allah. Lead him back into the ways of our forefathers. Above all, do not tell him that it was I who suggested this to you."

The Arab chief, whose interest it is in the course of his adventurous career to be followed only by well mounted horsemen, never fails to make use of the information thus given. He will summon the delinquent before him, reprove him, and warn him that if he does not change his conduct he will take his horse from him and make him walk like a common foot soldier. At last he will discharge him with these words: "Thou understandest me; go thy way; but bear in mind that in this world honour begins at the stirrup to be completed in the saddle." A lesson of this kind always produces a great effect, not only on the offender but on all who might be tempted to follow his example. And in this manner, sometimes through self-love, sometimes through the fear of punishment, the Arabs apply themselves to inculcate, voluntarily and compulsorily, on all characters and dispositions a love for the horse.

In the afternoon, a little later or a little earlier according to the season, the wife employs herself in leading the horses to water if the fountain be not too distant, and in that case she goes herself to fetch the water in goat-skin bags. When water fails entirely, she gives them ewe's or camel's milk. At this hour the tent of an Arab chief presents a truly singular spectacle. Oftentimes may be seen between the legs of the women and the horses, in presence of a crowd of picturesquely attired children, by the side of falcons beating their wings or greyhounds in a state of excitement, a gazelle, an antelope, or an ostrich, running in and out and jumping about, to beg a drop of that liquid so rare in the desert but which is nevertheless given in abundance to the favourite of the family. Now the evening is at hand. What means that dark speck on the horizon? It is the young men of the *douar** wearily regaining the encampment, mounted on horses with hollow flanks, worn out, and shoe-less. They have been out the whole day hunting, without eating or drinking. Camels loaded with gazelles, hares, bustards, etc., follow behind, but this prize, tempting though it be, will not save them from the storm that awaits them : "Young men," their mothers will exclaim with an angry voice, "it is disgraceful thus to ruin our horses for the sake of a little useless game. You would do far better to spare them for the day when the saliva will dry up in the mouth, for the day when riches will not ransom the head."

During the great heats the women bring the horses into the tent, to shelter them from the fierce rays of the sun. They wash and cleanse them, and in the evening fill the nosebags with barley to hang round the neck of their petted animals. Each one, and it is a very important point, receives a ration proportioned to his age and temperament and the work he has gone through. These every day attentions and kindnesses as we have already remarked and can not too often repeat, render the horses gentle and affectionate. They neigh with pleasure at the approach of her who tends them, and, as soon as they see her, turn their head gracefully towards her. They go up to her, and she lays hold of them whenever it pleases her, and if any one expresses surprise she will reply with perfect simplicity : "How can you suppose that our mares will not recognize the hand that caresses and feeds them? To how many gambols do they not betake themselves in

* Tents pitched in a circle, a subdivision of the tribe.

my presence? And when rising up on their hind-feet
behind my back they gently rest their legs on my
shoulders—and when they carry a young lamb in their
teeth by its wool—and when they slip into the tent to
steal our kouskoussou—these are all associations very
dear to us. Besides, is it not I who, by giving them at
proper times milk or barley, have succeeded in tighten-
ing their bellies, developping their chests, sharpening
their heads, widening their foreheads, and hardening
their limbs? Behold them pass by the side of a herd of
gazelles and you would see no difference between the
one and the other : the same grace, the same vigour in
their bounding, the same swiftness in the course. Like
the gazelles have they not eyes level with the head,
large eyeballs, bold, sharp ears, thin legs, a rounded
croup, and hoofs hard and well knit?"

REMARKS BY THE EMIR ABD-EL-KADER.

The details touching the education of the colt are true.
It is what we really do. Too great fatigue and too long
journeys do not suit the colt because they prevent the
development of his strength and stature. The *djeda,* or
less than three years old colt is like a shrub—any
impediment in his way stops his growth. But what
does suit the colt is exercise and a cautiously graduated
fatigue. He must be accustomed to the saddle and
bridle, but should only be ridden by a child or by a
man of discretion whose weight is in proportion to the
age and strength of the animal.

A very customary kind of exercise is after this manner.

The colt is mounted by a child, who, with a light stick in his hand, sets off at full gallop. When the colt is tired, he stops, and browses, and lies down as soon as he returns home. On the following morning they give him a feed of barley and take him back to the same starting point, whence he again sets off. This time he is expected to go a greater distance, and in this manner they continue until they have obtained from him a course twice as long as that of the first day.

The Arabs look for a free-going pace in a young horse, and they demand three varieties of gallop; 1st a short gallop, such as is usual in taking a ride for pleasure; 2nd a strong and regular gallop, useful in war, or in hunting wild beasts; 3rd a gallop at full speed, as in races or in fleeing for one's life. This last should not be too freely indulged in.

In fine, the education of the colt should be commenced very early. This is an excellent practice, and not to conform to it is disgraceful—it is making a horse unfit for war. An animal that is not thoroughly trained from its earliest years is intractable, difficult, and awkward : with the slightest exertion it bursts out into a sweat and is good for nothing. It is therefore incumbent in sparing the colt, as I have already said, whatever may check his growth and the full development of his proportions, to endeavour to obtain by work a horse that is supple and patient of fatigue.

The first horse possessed by the Prophet was called *Ouskoub*, by reason of his speed, for the word *sakab* denotes water that escapes.

Another horse belonging to the Prophet was named *Mortadjez*, because of the beauty of his neigh which resembled poesy and the harmonious metres of the *Aadjaz.* He was of a white colour, and was also styled "Gracious" and "Noble."

A third was known as the "Trailer," as if he trailed his tail along the ground. A fourth was *El Hezzez,* "the fixed" or "the adherent," as if he were already fixed and adherent at the goal it was proposed to reach. Others affirm that his name referred to the vigourous set of his limbs. A fifth was named the "Hill," either because of his height, or because of the power and hardness of his limbs. The Prophet's sixth horse was called the "Rose," on account of the colour of its coat, which was a cross between a chestnut and a dark bay. The seventh was named the "Swimmer," because of the beautiful movements of his shoulders, and because in gallopping he raised his forelegs as if he were swimming.

His first horse, *Ouskoub,* was his favourite. He had besides these the "Sea," the "Wolf," etc., etc.

It has been my object in recalling to mind these notices to teach the Arabs the rule they ought to follow in naming their horses, which should always be called after those of the Prophet. *Djarada,* a javelin,—*Delim,* male ostrich,—*Rakib,* vigilant [the wild ass], are likewise designations suitable to horses.

There are three kinds of horses : the first loads with crimes and belongs to Satan; the second preserves from eternal fire and belongs to man; the third brings down rewards and belongs to Allah.

Loads with crimes and belongs to Satan the horse that is trained out of pride and ostentation, and kept to support wagers to play at games of hazard, or to do injury to Mussulmans.

Preserves from the fire and belongs to man the horse reared for the purpose of reproduction, to save his owner from poverty, and to be useful to him in his personal affairs, without his wandering from the way of God.

Lastly, draws down rewards and belongs to Allah the horse destined exclusively for good works, in the interest of religion. The grass eaten by such a horse in the field or the garden, his evacuations, the water he drinks with his master on his back while crossing a river, without even any intention on the part of the latter to give him to drink, are inscribed by Allah in the register of good works.

Remonstrate with your horses, and they will avoid the faults which have brought down your anger upon them, for they understand the wrath of man. Treat them, however, habitually with great gentleness; and when you mount them, fear not to guide them into the midst of a crowd or of uproar. Let them hear the report of fire-arms, the *guellal* (the tabour), the shouts of men, and the cries of camels; let them see everything, too, which appears strange to them, and in a short time they will manifest neither surprise nor terror.

A man of a noble family of the Oued-Shelif* setting out for Mecca, started in company with a few friends who wished to do him honour. He was riding a blood mare, still in the possession of the family. Suddenly she stumbled, and to punish her he gave her a smart cut with his bridle end, which put her into such a state of agitation that for some minutes she did nothing but rear and jump about from right to left. On his return from

* A river in Algeria.

Mecca he rode the same animal, and the friends who had accompanied him on his departure went forth to meet him and give him welcome.　Scarcely had they reached the spot where the mare was beaten than she began to rear and caper about, going through absolutely the same movements as on the day she was struck.　Every one was astonished at this proof of extraordinary memory in an animal that had preserved for a whole year the recollection of a punishment, and of the place where she received it.

"Our noble coursers pass their time in vying with each other in swiftness."

"The women wipe off with their veils the sweat that runs down their faces."

"They balance their heads as if they would free themselves from the fastenings that hold them captive, and are attentive to the slightest command."

"On their backs are mounted fierce lions."

If in the Sahara ewe's or camel's milk is frequently given to horses, it must not be supposed that that is their only drink. It is more generally a substitute for barley, which is a scarce commodity, than for water, which is not usually difficult to find. The Arabs are convinced that milk maintains health and strengthens the fibre, without increasing the fat. It is needless to add that the rich who possess many she-camels are less sparing of milk than the poor, who have hardly enough to satisfy the wants of their families. The latter dilute it with water when they can. In the spring time they make use of ewe's milk, to which at other seasons they add camel's milk.

At Souf, Tougourt, Ouargla, Metlili, Gueleâa, and in the Touat, where there are more camels than horses and where grain is scarcer than in the first zone of the desert, dates oftentimes take the place of barley. When they are dry they are given in a nosebag. In eating them the horse, of himself, rejects the stones with considerable address. In certain districts the stones are taken out and crushed in a mortar, and are then mixed with the dates, which are likewise slightly bruised. Dates are also given to horses before they are perfectly ripe, and are eaten stones and all—being quite soft they do no harm. When it is desired to mix the dates with the drink, the Arabs proceed after this fashion. After the fruit is gathered they take three or four pounds of fresh dates, and manipulate them in a large vase full of water until the pulp of the date has become a sort of liquid paste. The skins and stones are removed and the mixture after being well shaken is presented to the animal. The date regimen makes fat, but does not harden the fibre.

In the first zone of the Sahara the ordinary diet of the horse is as follows for each season :— In the spring the shoes are generally removed, and the animals are turned out on the pastures, which at that period of the year abound with a succulent and fragrant herbage known under the generic name of *el àacheub*. They are clogged. Care is taken to avoid the districts where the *ledena* is met with, a velvety plant the leaves of which resemble a rat's ear. It grows close to the ground and is usually covered up and hidden in the sand. It brings on colics that for the most part terminate fatally. Persons of distinction who keep many servants, and experienced horsemen, never give green food to their war-horses. Rich or poor, no one gives barley, which is replaced by ewe's milk, which in this season is very abundant, and preserves the horse in perfect condition. The animals are watered only once a day, at two in the afternoon.

In summer the Saharenes proceed to the Tell to lay in their provision of grain. They are surrounded by unfriendly strangers, and sometimes by enemies. They do not, therefore, care to send their horses out to graze, as they would run the risk of being stolen. Nor are they sorry to have them close at hand in case of any of the numerous accidents happening which so often occur. Barley and barley straw are purchased from their hosts: it is the period of the year when the animals fare most liberally. I mention barley straw, because no Arab would ever consent to feed his horses on fresh wheaten straw. They fancy it produces jaundice if used before the winter. If, perchance, any thing should prevent them from going to buy grain in the Tell, as the plains afford no herbage but what is dried up by the sun, they make for the mountains of the Sahara, where there is a better chance of coming across rivers, or ponds, or at least marshes. If this resource fails them, they encamp in the neighbourhood of the *Kuesours** where straw can be had for money or in the way of barter. In either case the mares alone are sent out to graze, the horses being fastened in front of the tents. Whatever be the temperature, the Arabs never give their horses that mixture of bran, barley meal, and water which we call a mash, and of which we make such a mistaken use. They accuse it of relaxing the tissues and of weakening the system, while favouring the growth of fat, an evil they dread above all things. When their horses are over heated they lessen their work, and if they can procure it they give them green barley straw, and if that is not to be had they have recourse to cooling baths. As to the barley, they like it heavy, without any bad smell, and free from the dirt which gets mixed with it in the "silos,"

---

* The plural form of *Ksar*, a hamlet, village, or town of the desert.

as well as from the black, withered, and blighted grains
which have been struck by the South wind.

In autumn the horses are again turned out into the
pastures, where they find the *shiehh*, that invaluable
resource of the Sahara, so that it is said in praise of a
man who is as capable as he is modest :

> So-and-so is like the shiehh :
> He has parts, but is no prattler.

So much for the day.   At night are given handfuls of
seurr, a species of thorny shrub.   It is cut down close to
the ground, and beaten with a stick to get rid of the dry
prickles, which might injure the œsophagus, or the
membranous lining of the stomach.   It contains many
nutritive elements.   Another plant somewhat resembling
the common bramble and called *el ádem* is prepared in a
similar manner.

The horse is watered only once in the twenty four
hours, about two in the afternoon.   That time is thought
the most favourable because the water will have lost
something of its coldness,—the temperature then falling
every day.   Those who are well off give barley, but the
poor cannot always do so.

In winter the horses continue to be sent to the
pastures, which are now verdant in proportion to the rain
that has fallen.   The *shiehh,* the *ádem,* the *derine,** etc.,
are met with, and afford a very sufficient diet.   At night
bouse is thrown to them in quantities.   It is called by the
Arabs " brother of the barley," so highly do they appre-

* The *Stipa barbata* of Desfontaines.   This plant grows abundantly in the Sahara.
The inhabitants of that unproductive region wander far and wide to gather the seeds
of this grass, and often collect a large quantity.   The seed is ground down and used
for the same purposes as wheaten flour.

ciate its nutritive properties. *Bouse* is in fact, nothing else than the *alfa*, * which, at the moment of forming its ear, having been pulled by its upper part has come away and got separated from its sheath. Being gathered into small sheaves it is cut up in pieces and answers the purpose of chopped straw. The *alfa* is turned to account in yet another manner. Its roots are laid bare with a mattock and being freed from their reddish coating, are eaten with avidity by the animal. This article of food takes the name of *gueddeine* or *zemouna*, according to the locality. It is nutritious, but not a substitute for barley. Hay is unknown in the desert. The Arabs might, if they chose, lay up an abundant supply of it for the winter, but they reject it as having a tendency to make a horse heavy, to soften the fibre, and in the long run to occasion inflammatory disorders. The animals are watered only once a day as in autumn. It is a proverbial saying with the Arabs that "The food of the morning goes out into the draught, while that of the evening passes into the croup." They affirm, therefore, that if the horse has drunk sufficient over night, and eaten heartily through the night, there is not the slightest inconvenience in not giving him anything on the morrow, especially if he has to set out early in the morning. Thus in our camps, with fifteen to eighteen hundred Arab horsemen making part of the expedition, what did we witness? Every officer of the old African army can vouch for the truth of what I am about to say:

---

* This plant is very common throughout Algeria, and is much used for feeding horses. In our expeditions our chargers have often had nothing else to eat. It is the *Lygeum Spartum*. The culms of this grass do not rise above ten or twelve centimètres in height. It is the *Stipa tenacissima* used in the East for making basket work, etc.. and in some parts of Algeria the natives weave it into mats.

Contrary to our habits, to the very last moment the most perfect tranquillity continued to reign in the Arab bivouac. Not a minute was taken from the rest of the animal. They gave him nothing either to eat or to drink. The instant before starting they rubbed him down with a nose-bag. The saddle replaced the covering worn through the night. The bridle was put on, the tents struck, the morning prayer offered up, and at the hour named they were on the march. More than once I have happened to testify my surprise at such a system, but always received the same reply : "Why wouldst thou do for thy horse what thou wouldst not do for thyself? If thou leavest the table at ten or eleven at night, canst thou sit down again to it on the morrow at the dawn of day?" With this regimen the animals remain thin and slender. They are always ready to march or gallop, or do whatever hard work may be required of them. They pick up in an astonishing manner when instead, of a few handfuls of barley and what they can graze off plains parched by a burning sun, they fall in with the produce of the Tell. How would it be, then, if they were placed on the diet of European horses? Instead of their flesh being firm they would get quite fat, and so gain in our estimation, but they would lose in that of the Arabs, who little appreciate that style of beauty generally acquired at the cost of the best qualities of a war-horse.

However, if the Arab is too genuine a horseman not to attach the greatest importance to vigour, he is on the other hand too fond of pomp and distinction and the *fantasia*—to use a word already popular in Europe— not to bestow upon himself, when he can, the luxury of a horse for show and parade. It is therefore no rare thing to see Arabs of high position leave their favourite mares for three or four months fastened in front of their tents, without putting them to any work. They thus get into good condition, and are employed only at festivals and marriage feasts and on occasions when the chiefs are particularly anxious to distinguish themselves. For the chace, for razzias, and for long and arduous journeys, they keep horses of less apparent value, but of which they are sure, and do not fear to fatigue them. The mares to which we have alluded are equipped with great ostentation. The *stara,* or cloths, and the bridles are embroidered with pure gold, the stirrups are plated or gilt, and the felt saddle-cloths are as fine as cloth; the most esteemed coming from Ouareglâa.

REMARKS OF THE EMIR ABD-EL-KADER.

One of the Prophet's companions as he went out one morning found him wiping with his cloak the head of his horse. "Why, with thy cloak?" "What know'st thou?" replied the Prophet. "It may be that the Angel Gabriel has been angry with me on his account last night." "At least let me give him his food." "Ah!" cried the Prophet, "Thou would'st take for thyself all the rewards, for the Angel Gabriel has told me that every grain of barley eaten by the horse is accounted to me for a good work."

The Saharene gives his horse camel's milk to drink which has the particular property of imparting speed, so that a man—according to what is said by reliable persons who guarantee the truth of the statement—if he takes nothing else for a sufficient time, will attain to such a degree of swiftness that he may vie with the camels themselves. In fact, camel's milk strengthens the brain and the tendons, and does away with fat, which produces a relaxation of the muscles.

In some parts of the Sahara the chiefs and horsemen of renown never give green food to their war-horses. Milk, barley, and the plants known by the names of *shichh, derine, bouse,* and *seuliane* form their sole keep. This diet does not enlarge the belly or fatten like green food, which distends the intestinal canal, partly because of the enormous quantity consumed by the animal before he is satisfied, and partly because of the water it contains.

In summer the horses are not watered until three o'clock in the afternoon. In winter they are watered rather earlier—from noon to one. It is the time of day when in the open air the water has lost much of its coldness. These principles are expressed in the following proverb, known to the meanest horseman of the desert :—

> In the hot season * put back the hour of the watering-place
> And put forward that of the nose-bag;
> In the cold season put forward the hour of the watering-place,
> And put back that of the nose-bag.

Among the desert tribes, for forty days counting from the month of August, the horses are watered only every other day. The same method is pursued during the last twenty days of December and the first twenty days of

---

* The Arabs understand by the hot season from April to September inclusive, and by the cold season from October to March inclusive.

January. In cold weather the rich let their horses have as much barley as they can eat, but decrease the ration considerably in hot weather. Milk and *bouse* may be substituted for barley. It is seldom that any thing to eat is given in the morning. The horse marches upon the food of the previous evening, and not on that of the same day.

Looking at two horses, one from the Tell and the other from the Sahara, a man who has not studied the subject will always prefer the former, which he will find handsome, heavy, sleek, and fat, while he will despise the second, fool that he is, and abuse the very points which constitute his worth—that is, the fine, dry extremities, the tightened belly, and the bare ribs. And yet this horse of the desert that has never been accustomed to barley, green food, or straw, but only *shiehh, bouse,* and *seuliane,* that has never had any thing but milk to drink and from his earliest years has served at the chace and in war, will have the swiftness of the gazelle and the patience of the dog, while the other will never be any thing but an ox by his side.

The greatest enemies of the horse are repose and fat.

Grooming is unknown in the Sahara. The horses are merely wiped down with woollen rags, and covered with very good *djellale,* or rugs that envelop both the croup and the chest. In truth, labour of this sort is little wanted, the horses being habitually placed in a healthy spot, on raised ground, and sheltered from draughts. Arabs who have observed us grooming our horses morning and evening with elaborate carefulness, pretend that this continual rubbing of the epidermis, especially with the curry-comb, injures their health, and renders them delicate and impressionable, and consequently incapable of supporting the fatigues of war, or at all events more liable to disease.

When the weather is hot and facilities exist for the purpose, the horses are washed morning and evening. Frequently in winter time they are fastened up inside the tents, which are very roomy, to shelter them from the sun and rain. The great thing is to keep them clean. One day a horse was led up to the Prophet who examined it, rose up, and without saying a word, wiped his face, eyes, and nostrils with the sleeves of his under-garnment. "What! with your own garnments!" exclaimed the bystanders. "Certainly," replied he; "the Angel Gabriel has more than once rebuked me, and has commanded me to act thus."

In winter the covering is kept on day and night; and in summer until three o'clock when it is taken off, but put on again at eight for the whole night, to preserve the animal from cold and dew, which are all the more dangerous, say the Arabs, because the skin has been heated throughout the day by a burning sun. The following proverb expresses their dread of the cold of summer nights :—

> The cold of summer
> Is worse than a sabre cut.

If the Arabs do not, like ourselves, attach much importance to grooming, they are, on the other hand, very careful and particular in their choice of the food, and above all of the water, they give to their horses. Many a time during the early days of the conquest, while on an expedition, after long marches in an intolerable heat, with a south wind blowing that choked us and drove the dust and sand into our faces, when horse and foot alike panting, exhausted, without power of motion, we delivered ourselves up, worn out as we were, to a fatiguing sleep often interrupted by the alerts caused by the enemy prowling around us—at such a time I have seen the natives go a league from the bivouac in order to water their horses at some pure spring known to themselves. They preferred to risk their own lives to experiencing the pain of watering their horses at the scanty rivulets in the encampment, quickly converted into filthy drains by the trampling of men and beasts of burden.

It can hardly be necessary for me to dilate any farther on the hygiene of the horse among the Arabs.   Indeed, I could only repeat what I have already said.   It seems to me preferable to refer the reader to the various details scattered through the preceding pages, and particularly to the principles enunciated in the chapter on the education of the colt.   If I have made myself at all understood, I have shown how every owner of a horse among the Arabs is an active, vigilant, I had almost said devoted, master who watches and directs the progress, corrects the defects, and perfects the qualities of his pupil from the very first day.   This education embraces every thing, including what I may fairly call the moral faculties; and it augments, modifies, and improves the physical qualities.   Every thing is weighed and foreseen.   The drink, the diet, the exercise, the position in rest, the whole is graduated and proportioned to age, place, and season; it is all the object of incessant and sustained solicitude.   Moreover, the grand principle, and I myself think it a good one, seems to be to avoid, on one hand, excessive fatness which is opposed to all energetic work, and, on the other, any check to perspiration which is the cause of the greater number of diseases.   Once more, the question is not: is all this care well founded? are they wrong, or are we mistaken?   But after having propounded the formula, that in the life of an Arab his most absorbing and almost exclusive occupation is the rearing and training of his horse, I have shown that the Arab is not guided by mere chance, that his is not a blind, inconsiderate passion, as is supposed by those who see him from afar and bestow only a glance on him. Any one who will study him perseveringly, who will examine him, as it were, under the microscope, and analyse his daily acts and doings, will be forced to the conclusion that he is guided by traditional and logical motives. In a word, this education, this careful bringing up, of the horse is based upon fixed and constant principles having for their aim to endow the animal with spirit, bottom, and health. And what is this but hygiene?

The Arabs, says Ben-el-Ouardy, have always preferred good horses to their own children, and they love so much to show them off on occasions of rejoicing that they would deprive themselves of all nourishment rather than see them suffer from hunger and thirst. In the arduous and critical circumstances of life, especially in years of famine, they go so far as to give them the preference over their own persons and families. This is proved both by faithful narratives, and by the chaunts composed by their poets. Witness the verses addressed by the learned Ben-Sassa to the great tribe of the Beni-Aâmer.*

> Beni-Aâmer, why do I behold your horses
> Blemished and changed by misery?
> Such a condition cannot be right for them.
> Though death has an hour that no man can put back,
> Horses are your safeguard :
> Give them the good things you yourselves like best;
> With pure barley fill their nose-bags,
> And with iron furnish their hoofs.
> Love horses, and take care of them;
> In them alone lie honour and beauty.
> In taking care of them, you take care of yourselves,
> The Arab who has not a good horse can never aim at renown.
> For my part, on this earth, I know no other happiness.

* A very important tribe situated to the North-West of Oran.

And had I hundreds of gold *soulthanis.**
I should enjoy them only by sharing them with him.
I would also support my family with them,
And when they came to fail me,
I would humble my pride
Even to beg alms proudly for my friend.
All the treasures of Karoun,† without a horse,
Would not make me happy.

Does the north wind begin to blow,
Do the heavens open upon the earth,
Secure your horses from the cold rain.
Keep them warm, they deserve these attentions.
For sports, for war,
Adorn them with your richest saddles,
With bridles embroidered with gold, with superb garments,
And the Prophet will love you.

Sympathise, too, with, the mares of your poor dependents,
When in spite of all their efforts
They have not sufficed for their wants;
Bestow upon them a generous hospitality,
Share with them your ordinary food;
Associate them with your own families,
Many sins will be forgiven you.

The sabres are drawn,
The warriors are in their ranks,
The horse is about to become more precious than a wife.
The fire of battle is kindled,
I guide him into the midst of perils,
He protects me with his head, and his croup,
And makes my enemies to flee.
May Allah preserve this well-maned horse,
Whose eyes flash fire!
Love horses, take care of them,
In them alone lie honour and beauty.

In the Sahara, then, the horse is the noblest creature
after man.   The most honourable occupation is to rear

---

* Gold coins, worth from ten to twelve francs each.
† An Indian prince who flourished before the birth of the Prophet, and whose
riches were proverbial.

him, the most delightful pastime is to mount him, the best of all actions is to tend him well.

The Arabs assert that they can tell beforehand, by certain methods, what will be a colt's stature and character when he becomes a horse. These methods vary in different localities, but those most generally adopted are the following : — For the height, they take a cord, and passing it behind the ears and the nape of the neck, they bring the two ends together on the upper lip just below the nostrils. Having established this measure, they apply it to the distance from the foot to the withers. It is an article of belief that the colt will grow as high as this last measurement out-tops the withers.

When it is desired to ascertain the value of a horse by his proportions, they measure with the hand from the extremity of the dock to the middle of the withers, and take note of the number of palms. They then begin again from the middle of the withers to the extremity of the upper lip, passing between the ears. If in the two cases the number of palms is equal, the horse will be good, but of ordinary speed. If the number of palms behind is greater than in front, the horse will have no "go" in him.   But if the number of palms between the withers and the extremity of the upper lip is more considerable than in measuring from the tail to the withers, rest assured the animal will have great qualities.   The more the number differs to the advantage of the forepart, the greater will be the value of the horse. With such an animal, say the Arabs, they can "strike afar"— go a long distance —thus expressing the pace and bottom promised by such proportions. With a little practice they easily come to judge by the eye so as to have no occasion to measure. While a horse is passing they compare rapidly, starting from the withers, the hindpart with the forepart, and without going into details the animal is judged.

REMARKS BY THE EMIR ABD-EL-KADER.

Passing before a horse the Prophet began to rub his face with his sleeve, saying : "Allah has been wrathful with me because of horses." "Felicity is attached to the forelocks of horses." And it is on their account that their owners can reckon on the aid of Allah. Therefore it is your duty to wipe their forelocks with your hands. A wise man has said :—"The noble labours with his hands without a blush, in three cases; for his horse, for his father, and for his guest."

One mode of judging of a horse is to measure him from the root of the mane close to the withers and descend to the end of the upper lip between the nostrils. They then measure from the root of the mane to the end of the tail-bone, and if the forepart is longer than the hindpart there is no doubt the horse will have excellent qualities. To ascertain if a young horse will grow any more or not, the Arabs measure first from the knee to the highest point situated in the prolongation of the limb above the withers, then from the knee downwards to the beginning of the hair above the coronet (to the crust of the hoof) : if these two measures are to one another as two-thirds to one-third, the horse will grow no more. If this proportion does not exist, the animal has not done growing, for it is absolutely necessary that the height from the knee to the withers should represent in a full grown horse exactly double the length of the leg from the knee to the hoof.

In the desert the curry-comb is never used, the horses are cleaned with the nose-bag, which is made of horse hair, and are frequently washed if the weather is favourable. Milk is their ordinary drink. Should it happen to run short, the Arabs do not hesitate to go a considerable distance to find clear and pure water for them. The barley ought to be heavy, very clean, without any bad smell, and completely clear of the impurities which are unavoidably mixed with it in the " silos." The horses are covered with good *djellale,* which fully protect the loins, the belly, and the chest. They are manufactured in the tribe. Those that are made with care are water proof.

There are some coats which must be preserved with equal attention from cold and from heat. Experience has demonstrated that this is necessary for all horses of a light colour, beginning with the white, the fineness of whose skin makes him very susceptible.

> In the sun he melts like butter :
> In the rain he melts like salt.

Coats of a dark colour do not need so many precautions. When it is very hot or very cold, the horses are brought inside the tent. In the Sahara the nights are always cool; in summer, as in winter, the animals must be covered. Nothing is overlooked that may avert checked perspiration. After a long journey the saddle

is not removed until the horse is dry. Nor do they give
him any thing to eat until he has recovered the regula-
rity of his breathing, and for the most part they give
him water to drink with the bridle on. Lastly, the
encamping grounds are studiously selected.   What is
preferred is a dry ground, cleared of the stones that
might encumber it, on which the horse is placed so that
the forequarters shall be a little higher than the hind
quarters, and facing as much as possible the master of
the tent, who watches him night and day like one of his
own children.   To place a horse with his forequarters
lower than the hind quarters is to ruin his shoulders.
Particular care should always be taken of the *djellale*.
A horseman is little respected by the Arabs when it can
be said of him :

> His horse drinks troubled water,
> And his covering is full of holes.

———

The favourite coats are : —

The White : "Take the horse white as a silken flag, without spot, with the circle of his eyes black."

The Black : "He must be black as a night without moon and stars."

The Bay : He must be nearly black, or streaked with gold. "The dark red one said to the dispute, 'Stop there.'"

The Chestnut : "Desire a dark shade. When he flees beneath the sun, it is the wind. The Prophet was partial to chestnuts."

The Dark Dappled Gray, called "the grey of the wild pigeon," if resembling the stone of the river.

> He will fill the douar
> When it is empty,
> And will preserve us from the combat,
> On the day when the muzzles of the guns touch each other.

The Grays are generally esteemed when the head is of a lighter colour than the body.

The Green, or rather the yellow dun, which must be dark, with black tail and mane.

White is the colour for princes, but does not stand

heat. The black brings good fortune, but fears rocky ground. The chestnut is the most active. "If one tells you that he has seen a horse fly in the air, ask of what colour he was; and if he replies : 'Chestnut,'—believe him." "In a combat against a chestnut, you must have a chestnut." The bay is the hardiest and most sober. "If one tells you that a horse has leaped to the bottom of a precipice without hurting himself, ask of what colour he was; and if he replies : 'Bay,'—believe him."

Ben Dyab, a renowned chief of the desert, who flourished in the year of the Hijra 955, happenning one day to be pursued by Saad-el-Zenaty, sheikh of the Oulad Yagoub, turned to his son and asked : "What horses are in the front of the enemy?" "White horses," replied his son. "It is well; let us make for the sunny side, and they will melt away like butter." Some time afterwards Ben Dyab again turned to his son and said : "What horses are in the front of the enemy?" "Black horses," cried his son. "It is well; let us make for stony ground, and we shall have nothing to fear—they are the negroes of the Soudan, who cannot walk with bare feet upon the flints." He changed his course, and the black horses were speedily distanced. A third time Ben Dyab asked : "And now, what horses are in the front of the enemy?" "Dark chestnuts and dark bays." "In that case," exclaimed Ben Dyab, "strike out, my children, strike out, and give your horses the heel, for these might perchance overtake us had we not given barley to ours all the summer through."

The coats despised are :

The Piebald : "Flee him like the pestilence, for he is own brother to the cow."

> The kouskoussou arrives when he is gone,
> And he finds the dispute as soon as he arrives.

The Isabel, with white mane and tail; no chief would condescend to mount such a horse. There are some tribes even that would not consent to allow him to remain a single night with them. They call such a one *sefeur el ihoudy,* "the Jew's yellow." It is a colour that brings ill luck.

> The iron gray
> And the Jew's yellow,
> If his rider returns from the fight
> Cut off my hand.

The Roan; this is called *meghedeur-el-deum,* "a pool of blood." The rider is sure to be overtaken, but will never overtake.

The horse is to be valued that has no white spots except a star on the forehead, or a simple white stripe down the face. The latter must descend to the lips, and then the owner will never be in want of milk. It is a fortunate mark. It is the image of the dawn. If the star is truncated or has jagged edges, it is universally disliked, and if the animal adds to that a white spot in front of the saddle no man in his senses would mount it, nor would any judge of horse-flesh deign to possess it. Such a horse is as fatal as a subtile poison. If a horse has several white spots, three is the preferable number —one of the right feet should be exempt, but it matters not whether it be behind or before. It is a good sign to have stockings on both the off forefoot and the near hindfoot. It is called,

> The hand of the writer
> And the foot of the horseman.

The master of such a horse cannot fail to be fortunate, for he mounts and dismounts over white. The Arabs, it must be remembered, generally mount on the off side and alight on the near side. Two hind stockings are a sign of good fortune;

> The horse with the white hind feet,
> His master will never be ruined.

It is the same with white forefeet—his master's face will never turn yellow. Never buy a horse with a white face and four stockings, for he carries his winding-sheet with him. The prejudices of the Arabs on the subject of white spots are summed up in the following little story:

"An Arab had a blood mare. There was a dispute beforehand as to what her foal would be. So when she was on the point of foaling he invited all his friends to be present. The head first of all came in sight—it bore a star. The Arab rejoiced. His horse would one day, outstrip the dawn, for he had the mark on his forehead. Next appeared the near forefoot, when the owner in ecstasy demanded one hundred *douros* for the foal. The off forefoot then showed itself with a stocking, and the price was reduced to fifty douros. After that came the near hindfoot. It also had a stocking, and the Arab overjoyed, swore that he would not part with his foal for the whole world. But lo! the fourth foot presents itself likewise with a stocking, when the dweller in the Sahara cast the animal out, in his fury, on the refuse-heap, unable to bring himsel to keep such a brute."

A horse has forty white *Tufts*, of which twenty eight are generally considered as being of neither good nor bad omen, while to the remaining twelve a certain influence is attributed. It is agreed on all hands to regard six of these as augmenting riches and bringing good fortune, and the other six as causing ruin and adversity.

The tufts of good omen are :

The tuft that is between the two ears, *nekhlet el addar*, "the tuft of the head stall" : such a horse is swift in the race.

The tuft that grows on the lateral surface of the neck, *sebâa enneby,* "the finger of the Prophet" : the owner will die like a good Mussulman in his bed.

The tuft of the Sultan, *nekhlet essoultan*. It runs along the whole length of the neck, following the tracheal artery : love, riches, and prosperity. The horse that bear this offers up three prayers every day :

"Allah grant that my master may look upon me as the most precious possession he has in the world!"

"May Allah give unto him a happy lot, so that mine may benefit by it!"

"May Allah grant unto him the happiness of dying a martyr upon my back!"

The tuft on the chest, *zeradya,* fills the tent with plunder.

The tuft where the saddle-girths pass, *nekhlet el hazame* multiplies the flocks.

The tuft on the flank, *nekhlet eshebour,* "the tuft of the spurs." If it is turned towards the back, it preserves the rider from misadventure in war : if it is turned towards the belly, it is a sign of riches for its master.

The following white tufts bring misfortune :

Netahyat, a tuft over the eyebrows : the master will die, shot through the head.

Nekhlet el nâash, the coffin tuft, grows close to the

withers and goes down towards the shoulder. The rider will not fail to perish on the back of such a horse.

Neddabyat, the mourners; a tuft on the cheek; debts, tears, ruin.

Nekhlet el khriana, the thieves' tuft. It is close to the fetlock joint, and night and morning it prays : "O Allah! grant that I may be stolen, or that my master may die!"

The tuft by the side of the tail announces trouble, misery, and famine.

The tuft on the inner part of the thigh : women, children, flocks, all will disappear.

Such is the classification generally adopted. It is not, however, absolute, for it varies according to localities, each tribe increasing or diminishing the number of its lucky and unlucky tufts. It will be seen that I have alluded only to the principal coats without entering upon the gradation of shades, which would have carried me too far astray. Making every allowance for prejudice and superstition, it is clear that the Arabs are fond of dark and decided colours, while they look upon light and faded colours, as well as white spots upon the head, carcase, and limbs, if broad or long, as signs of weakness and degeneracy of race. Every Arab has his own favourite coat. Some like black horses and others gray, while others again affect bays or chestnuts. Their preferences and antipathies are usually based on family associations. With such a coat their ancestors achieved a brilliant success—with such another they encountered a grievous calamity. They will thus often refuse a good horse, without giving any other reason than "It is not my colour."

REMARKS BY THE EMIR ABD-EL-KADER.

The horse the most esteemed is a black one with a star on his forehead and white spots on his feet. Then comes the blood-bay, and after that the dark chestnut. Horses of other coats are placed on the same line with the exception of the piebald, with which the Arabs will have nothing to do.

The Prophet has said : "If thou wouldst go to the war, purchase a horse with a star on the forehead and stockings on all his legs with the exception of the right forefoot."

A horse with white feet, his off foreleg being alone of the colour of his coat, resembles a man who carries himself gracefully in walking, with the sleeve of his cloak floating in the air.

The Prophet has said : "If I were to gather together in one spot all the horses of the Arabs, and make them race against one another, it is the chestnut that would outstrip the rest."

According to the traditions of our Lord Mohammed the black horse is superior in the beauty of its mould and in its moral qualities, but the chestnut in fleetness. The Arabs have a saying : "If thou hast a chestnut, bring him along. If thou hast only a sorry chestnut, still bring him."

In a spacious arena constructed for races, cast thy eyes over the assemblage of noble coursers.

Thou wilt see the one who, arriving the first at the goal, has removed his master's anxieties.

Then the second who followed close at hand;—they

both reached the goal without slackening their speed.

Every horse of noble race fascinates the eyes and rivets the gaze of the enthusiastic spectator.

One of a rose colour, whose coat resembles the red tints which the setting sun leaves on the horizon.

Another of a white colour, like to a shooting star hurled against the evil genii.

A third, a blood-bay, of incomparable beauty and tall stature, in whom may be recognised traces of his paternal and maternal uncles, famous in the annals of racing.

There may also be seen a bright bay with a skin like gold.

And then a chestnut that pleases the eye with its shining mane.

Or another, black as night, adorned only with a white star on the forehead, that shines like the first light of dawn. Oh! blessed is the horse with white stars and stockings!

The Prophet abhorred a horse that has white marks on all its legs. The horse with a white mark that does not come down to the tip of the upper lip, accompanied by a stocking on the off forefoot, bears upon him the signs of the most evil omen. Thus, whosoever sees him prays to Allah to avert from himself the calamity announced by this animal. He is like the "hour poison." *

The fleetest of horses is the chestnut; the most enduring, the bay; the most spirited, the black; the most blessed, one with a white forehead.

The Arabs distinguish forty knots or tufts in a horse. Of these, twenty eight are without any significance in their eyes, and are of neither good nor bad omen. To

* Poison that is fatal within the hour.

twelve of them alone do they ascribe an influence allowed by tradition and confirmed, as they think, by personal observation.

"Horses are eagles mounted by riders tall as a lance; they arrive, cleaving the air like a falcon swooping on its quarry."

In the Sahara horses that are celebrated for their blood and speed sell easily and at a good price. There are blemishes that totally exclude a horse from serving in war. Such as *el maatcuk*, a narrow and hollow chest accompanying lean and perpendicular shoulders. It is difficult to form an idea of the importance attached by the Arabs to the development of the muscles of the chest.

Another blemish is fatness and want of prominence in the withers. You can never fix the saddle properly on such a horse, nor handle him boldly in galloping down hill. Again, the jardens "father of bleaching" (of the beard): curbs, when too far gone; ring-bone; spavin, especially when it is near the saphena; the processes known as *louzze,* or "almonds," on the ribs, and *fekroune,* or "tortoise," on the forequarters; splints, if near the back sinew; the pastern prolonged and bent; the pastern short and upright; windgalls along the tendons; and a long and concave back, are all serious objections. An animal is also rejected if he cannot see at night, or when there is snow. It is discovered by the manner he raises his feet when it begins to grow dark. The defect may be ascertained by placing a black surface before him in the day time—if he steps upon it without hesitation, there is no doubt on the subject. As the Arab passes much of his life-time in making nocturnal marches to surprise his enemy, or to escape from him, what could he do with such an animal?

Let us pass on now to the faults or blemishes which, through generally dreaded, do not prevent a horse from changing masters. These are narrow nostrils—they will leave you in trouble; long, soft, and pendant ears; and a short, stiff neck. A horse is little worth that does not lie down, nor one that switches his tail about while in quick motion; also horses that scratch their neck with their feet, that rest on the toe of their foot, that over-reach themselves in trotting or galloping, or that cut themselves by knocking their feet together. To discover if a horse cuts himself, pass the two wrists, joined together, between his two fore-arms and place them below his breast. If they are touched by the inner part of the fore-arms, be sure that the animal has too narrow a chest and cannot help cutting himself.

Distrust a horse that wets his nose-bag in eating his barley, and that seems to sip the water with the tips of his lips. An ambler is not fit for a chief: it is the horse of such as "clash the spurs," (carry messages). Beware of a horse that rears, refuses the spurs, bites, is difficult to mount, and breaks away from his rider when the latter dismounts: these are all grave faults in war time. Leave to the pack-saddle a horse that is deaf. You will know him by his hanging ears, void of expression, and thrown backwards, and also by his not answering to any sound of the voice. By sight, by smell, by hearing, a horse will warn his master of coming danger, if he do not save him from it. He saith:

> Preserve me from what is in front,
> I will preserve thee from what is behind.

"The lion and the horse disputed one day as to whose eye-sight was the best. The lion saw, during a dark night, a white hair in milk, but the horse saw a black hair in pitch. The bystanders pronounced in favour of the latter."

The highest virtue in a horse is endurance, to which, in order to constitute a perfect animal, must be joined strength. A horse is considered strong if he clears fifteen to sixteen foot-lengths in his first bound. If he covers a greater space he is deemed to be of superior strength, but if he clears no more than eight to ten feet he is set down as a heavy animal. A very fiery horse never exhibits patience of fatigue; nor one whose legs are lanky, neck too long, and buttocks too heavy to be in harmony with other parts of his body; nor one who lacks vigour in his heels. Such a horse, after a long course, will be exhausted in his legs, so that when he is pulled up by his rider he will still take several steps contrary to the latter's wishes. A horse that has neither patience nor mettle is easily recognised. The form of his body is irregular, his chest narrow, and his breathing short. Strength and wind are the two highest qualities of a horse. The absence of either is likely to affect his endurance and lower his spirit.

"Look in a horse for speed and bottom. One that has speed alone, and no bottom, must have a blemish in his descent; and one that has bottom alone and no speed, must have some defect, open or concealed.

"Reject a horse high in the middle, with a narrow chest, flat ribs, and lanky limbs and that is for ever fidgetting about and holding up his head. If you give him his head, he says : 'Hold me in!' and if you hold him in, he says : 'Let me go!'

"But if in the course of your life you alight upon a horse of noble origin, with large, lively eyes, wide apart, and black, broad nostrils, close together; whose neck, shoulders, haunches, and buttocks are long, while his forehead, loins, flank, and limbs are broad; with the back, the shin-bone, the pasterns, and the dock short; the whole accompanied by a soft skin, fine, flexible hair, powerful respiratory organs, and good feet with heels well off the ground—hasten to secure him if you can induce the owner to sell him, and return thanks to Allah, morning and night, for having sent thee a blessing."

Never burden yourself with an animal that is broken-kneed, diseased, or wounded, though they assure you that it is only a temporary accident. Recall to mind the saying of your ancestors;

> Ruined, and son of a ruined one,
> Is he who buys to cure.

It is no uncommon thing for an Arab to buy a horse in partnership with another. The usual conditions of such a compact are after this fashion. An Arab sells a mare to another for 100 *douros,* but receives only 50 *douros* in payment, the balance representing his share in the animal. The purchaser rides the mare about, and makes use of her for war, the chace, and for his private journeys. If he make a razzia, three-fourths of the plunder belong to himself, and one-fourth to his partner. Should the mare be killed in war, in an expedition mutually agreed upon, the loss falls upon them equally. But should death overtake her at a fantasia, a wedding, or any other festival, the purchaser is alone answerable—he has to make good 50 *douros* to the vendor. If the animal, however, is killed in front of the tent, suddenly, or under the horseman, while the latter is defending his wife, his children, and his flocks,—the circumstances were beyond his control, and he is not called upon for any reimbursement.

Should the mare produce a colt, it is reared until it is a year old, when it is sold, and the proceeds equally divided between the partners. On the other hand, if the mare has produced a filly, the latter is valued when a year old, and the vendor has the privilege of choosing the filly or the dam, paying or receiving the difference of value. This sort of compact is never made with respect to horses.

An Arab who wishes to sell a horse will never consent to be the first to name a price. Some one comes up and says : "Sell; thou wilt gain." The vendor replies : "Buy; thou wilt gain."

"Speak thou first."

"No, speak thou."

"Was he purchased, or reared?"

"Reared in my tent, like one of my own children."

"What hast thou been offered for him?"

"I have been offered 100 *douros*."

"Sell him to me at that price—thou wilt gain. Tell me, then, what thou askest."

"See what is written with Allah."

"Come, let us drive away the previous bidder, and do thou take 10 *douros* over and above his offer."

"I accept. Take thy horse, and Allah grant thou mayst be successful upon his back as many times as he has hairs upon it." And should he be desirous to avoid all risk of future annoyance on the subject of warranty, he adds in the presence of witnesses : "The separation between us is from this very moment. Thou dost not know me, and I have never seen thee."

It is not permitted to mount a horse for a trial until after the price has been agreed upon. Nevertheless, before the bargain is completely concluded the animal is tested against a horse that has a certain local reputation. The mode of trial is somewhat singular. The riders are barefooted, and are not allowed to touch their horse with the heel during any part of the race.

Horses whose reputation is well established in the country are never sold in the market-place. It is a positive insult to an Arab to ask him, "wilt thou sell thy horse?" before he has made known his intentions. "They must think me then in a miserable condition," he will say, "that they should dare to make such a proposal to me."

Certain tribes are particularly addicted to traffic in horse-flesh. The most noted of these Arab horse-dealers are the Beni-Addas. It is said of them :

> With others, horses are mere carrion,
> With them, they are youthful brides :
> With others, they are asleep,
> With them, they dance.

For the rest, the Arab is no horse-dealer after the European fashion. He never makes use of ginger, nor does he resort to any trickery to disguise the bad points of his horse. He simply places him before the purchaser. But for the fraud he disdains he substitutes a flow of seductive eloquence. His inexhaustible oratory pours itself forth in metaphors and hyperboles. Pointing to the animal, he will say : " Uncover his back and satisfy thy gaze."

He will then go on :

"Say not it is my horse; say it is my son. He outstrips the flash in the pan, or a glance of the eye. He is pure as gold. His eyesight is so good that he can distinguish a hair in the night time. In the day of battle he delights in the whistling of the balls. He overtakes the gazelle. He says to the eagle : 'Come down, or I will ascend to thee!' When he hears the voices of the maidens, he neighs for joy. When he gallops he plucks out the tear from the eye. When he appears before the maidens he begs with his hand. It is a steed for the dark days when the smoke of powder obscures the sun. It is a thoroughbred, the very head of horses! No one has ever possessed his equal. I depend on him as on my own heart. He has no brother in the world : it is a swallow. He listens to his flanks, and is ever watching the heels of his rider. He understands as well as any son of Adam : speech alone is wanting to him. His pace is so easy that on his back, you might carry a cup of coffee without upsetting it. A nosebag satisfies him, a sack covers him. He is so light that he could dance on the bosom of thy mistress without bruising it."

The owner of the truly beautiful offers him for sale;
The owner of the swift one makes protestations.

Ben Youssouf, having one day given in exchange for a mare of the desert twenty she-camels with their young replied to his father who had keenly rebuked him : "And why are you angry, my lord? Has not this mare brought me the agility and the softness of skin of the jerboa, the movement of the neck of the hare, the fleetness and the vision of the ostrich, the hollow belly and the limbs of the greyhound, and the courage and breadth of head of the bull? She cannot fail to turn yellow the face of our enemies. When I pursue them, she will plunder without ceasing the croups of their horses; and if they pursue after me, the eye will not know where I have passed!"

It will be seen, as I had previously indicated in tracing the outline of a thoroughbred horse as sketched by the Arabs, that they esteem it of consequence that in his form he should borrow certain details from other animals. He should unite in himself the qualities that are separately remarked in the gazelle, the greyhound, the bull, the ostrich, the camel, the hare, and the fox. It is agreed that he should have the long, clean limbs of the gazelle, the fineness and strength of its haunches, the convexity of its ribs, the shortening of its fore-legs, the blackness of its eyes, and the straitness of its armpits, He should also recall to mind the length of the lips and tongue of the dog, the abundance of its saliva, and the length of the lower part of its fore-paws. They go so far as to regard this resemblance of the horse to the greyhound as a means of guiding inexperienced purchasers : at least, such appears to be the moral of an anecdote widely circulated among them.

"Meslem-ben-Abou-Omar, having learned that one of

his relatives was travelling near the banks of the Euphrates, desired to avail himself of this opportunity to obtain one of the famous horses of that country. His relative knew nothing about horses, but was very fond of the chace, and had some very fine dogs. Despatching a servant with proper instructions, Meslem informed his relative that the form of the horse he wished for corresponded to that of the best of his greyhounds. An animal was thus procured, the like of which the Arabs have never since met with."

Merou-ben-el-Keyss replied one day to some friends who accused him of knowing nothing about either horses or women :

Yes, I have ridden horses
Sober, strong, and swift in the course,
Whose thighs were solid,
Their sinews lean and their rump rounded.
Forming as it were a channel towards the tail :
Their hoofs were hard : they could go without shoes.
By Allah ! 1 used to fancy myself on an ostrich.

To find the tall grass
Vhich grows in solitudes dangerous to traverse,
In solitudes defended by the points of lances,
And by the descent of torrents,
I have many a time galloped,
When the birds were yet asleep in their nests.

To hunt the white-skinned zebra,
Whose legs are striped like Indian stuffs,
Or to overtake the antelope that lives in wild regions,
I have ridden horses with flesh hardened by exercise,
It was Allah who created them for the happiness of Believers.

Many a time, too, have I rested my heart
On that of a maid with budding bosoms,
And legs adorned with anklets of gold !
In our incursions of horsemen,
When eye must meet eye,

> Many a time have I said :
> Forward! forward! O my beloved courser!
> Follow up the enemy routed and fleeing!

The value of a horse is in his stock.

REMARKS BY THE EMIR ABD-EL-KADER.

To a King who asked a poet for his horse named *Sakab,* the latter replied : "*Sakab* is not for sale, nor is he to be exchanged. I would ransom him at the price of my life. My family should die of hunger rather than that he should suffer."

An Arab once said : "My countrymen blame me for being in debt, and yet I contracted it for a horse of noble race and well rounded forms, who confers honour upon them and serves as a talisman to my *goum,* and to whom I have given a slave as his attendant."

An Arab one day sent his son to buy a horse in the market place, and he, before setting out, asked his father what qualities the animal should have. The father made answer : "His ears should be ever in motion turning sometimes forward, sometimes behind, as if he were listening to something. His eyes ought to be keen and restless, as if his mind were occupied with something. His limbs must be well set on and well proportioned." "Such a horse," the son rejoined, "will never be sold by his master."

Many of the Arabs of Upper Asia have genealogical trees, in which they state and confirm by evidence that would be accepted in a court of justice, the birth and parentage of the colt, so that when a proprietor wishes to sell a horse he has only to produce his genealogical tree to satisfy the purchaser that he is not deceiving him.

I have seen among the Annaza, a tribe extending from Bagdad to the confines of Syria, horses so absolutely priceless that it was impossible to buy them, or at least to pay in cash for them. These horses are usually disposed of to great personages or wealthy merchants, who pay a fabulous price for them in thirty to fifty bills, falling due at intervals of twelve months, or else they bind themselves to pay an annual sum for ever to the vendor and his descendants.

"I take them by surprise in the morning, while the bird is yet in its nest and the moisture from the dew is making its way to the river.

"I surprise them with my sleek-coated courser that by its swiftness overtakes the wild beasts and never wearies of hunting the gazelle in all seasons and far from our home.

"He has the flanks of the gazelle, the legs of the female ostrich, and the straight back of the wild ass standing as a sentinel on a hillock.

"His croup, like to a heap of sand which moisture has rendered compact, harmonizes with withers rising above the back, like the pack-saddle of the camel kept in its place by the crupper.

"The swellings behind his ears are rounded like spheres : the headstall and the headband seem as if they were fixed to the extremity of the trunk of a palm-tree, stripped of its leaves.

"Fastened by the side of other horses, he bites and demeans himself in his jealousy as if he were possessed by a demon."

Contrary to the accepted opinion, the Arabs of the Sahara are in the custom of shoeing their horses, whether on the two forefeet, or on all four feet, according to the nature of the ground they occupy. Those who shoe them on all four feet are the inhabitants of the stony districts, and these constitute the majority. Among them are the Arbâa, Mekhadema, Aghrazelia, Saâid-Mekhalif, Oulad-Yagoub, Oulad-Nayl, Oulad-Sidi-Shikh, Hamyane, etc., etc. It is the universal practice to take the shoes off in the spring, when the animals are turned out to grass; the Arabs asserting that care must be taken not to check the renewal of the blood which takes place at that season of the year.

In every desert tribe there is a *douar* set apart by the name of *douar-el-maâllemin*, "the master's douar." It is that of the farriers. A profession entirely and especially devoted to that indispensable complement of the Arab, his horse, might be expected to be made the object of particular esteem. Accordingly, numerous and invaluable privileges are accorded to them, but I am not certain if the concession of these privileges is to be regarded as an homage rendered to an art that refers exclusively to the horse, and not also, seeing that it is the only art that survives in the desert, as a remembrance of the encouragements formerly given to the able and learned men of Arabia, Egypt, Africa, and Spain, by the Arabs of the olden times, the brilliant conquerors of the Goths and contemporaries of Haroun-al-Raschid.

The Arabs of the Sahara say that their first farriers came to them from the towns on the sea-board, such as Fez, Tunis, Mascara, Tlemcen, and Constantine, since when their knowledge and their calling have been perpetuated in their families from generation to generation. A farrier must likewise be something of an armourer and iron-smith, to repair their bits, spurs, knives, guns, sabres, and pistols, besides making horse-shoes, sowing needles, sickles, small hatchets, and mattocks.

In return he enjoys the following immunities : He pays no contributions—on the contrary, when his tribe proceeds to the Tell to buy grain a collection is made for his benefit. This immunity, however, he shares with the maker of sandals. "The worker in iron and the maker of boots pay no imposts." Neither is he called upon to offer kouskoussou or shelter to any one : in other words, he is exempted from the duty of hospitality, which in certain cases is imposed upon all. The constant toil demanded by his calling, the unavoidable accidents to which he is liable through the urgent wants of his brethren night and day, the sleepless nights he has to undergo, entitle him to certain dues, called *aâdet-el-maâllem*, "the master's dues." On their return from the purchase of grain in the Tell every tent makes over to him a *feutra* of wheat and barley, and a *feutra* of butter. In the spring he receives in addition the fleece of a ewe. If a camel is killed for eating, he claims the part comprised between the withers and the tail, deducting the hump, which, being covered with fat, is esteemed a delicacy. In razzias and expeditions, whether or not he has taken part in the enterprise, he is entitled to a share of the booty. Usually, it is a sheep, or a camel, according to the value of the prize. This due is known as the horseman's ewe. The most important privilege, however, accorded to farriers, the indisputable token of the protection they formerly enjoyed and of the esteem in which they are still held, is the gift of life on the field of battle. If a farrier is on horseback, with arms in his hands, he is liable to be killed like any other horseman of the *goum*; but if he alights and kneels down and imitates with the two corners of his burnous—raising and depressing them by turns—the movement of his bellows, his life will be spared. Many a horseman has saved his life by means of this stratagem. A farrier can only enjoy the benefit of this privilege by leading an inoffensive life, absorbed in the duties of his business; but if he distinguishes himself by his warlike prowess, he forfeits the privileges of his calling, and is treated as an ordinary horseman. These advantages, on the other hand, are compensated by a serious drawback. Should he happen to grow rich, a quarrel is fastened upon him and in one way or another a portion of his wealth is taken from him to prevent him from quitting the district.

A farrier whose tribe has been plundered seeks out the victors, and on the simple proof of his trade, recovers his tent, tools, utensils, and horse-shoes. His implements consist of a pair of bellows, which are nothing more than a goat-skin bag with three openings, of which two are on the upper part in the same line, and the third at the opposite end. Through this last protrudes the barrel of a gun, or pistol, that conveys the blast to the fire. It is the wife's department to work the bellows. She kneels down before the charcoal which is placed in a hole, and takes in each hand one of the upper orifices, which she closes by clutching the skin around them. Then by alternately opening and closing her hands, she produces a movement that causes a current of air sufficient for the purpose, though not very powerful. The Arabs of the Sahara give the preference over a more perfect one to these bellows with their feeble blast, but which are easily transported in their nomadic expeditions. To the bellows the farrier joins an anvil, a hammer, files, pincers, and a vice. These instruments they obtain chiefly from the seabord, though some of them they make for themselves. Formerly they used to procure the iron in the great markets of the central desert, at Tougourt, among the Beni-Mezabe, or at Timimoun, according to the greater or less distance of those points from their own neighbourhood; but now they begin to purchase them from us. The charcoal they prepare themselves with the *arar*, the *remt*, the *senoubeur*, and the *djedary*, the last being the most esteemed.

The horse-shoes are kept ready made, and always command a sure sale, the Arabs being in the habit of laying in their supply for the whole year, consisting of four sets for the forefeet and four for the hindfeet. The nails are likewise made by the farriers. When a horseman goes to a farrier, taking his shoes with him, the latter is paid by his privileges, and when the horse is shod, its master gets on its back, merely saying : "Allah have mercy on thy fathers!" He then goes his way and the farrier returns to his work. But if the horseman does not bring his shoes with him, he gives two *boudjous* to the farrier for the complete set, and his thanks are couched in the simplest formula of Arab courtesy. "Allah give thee strength!" he says, as he takes his departure.

In the Sahara, they put the shoes on cold. In the foot of the horse, say the Arabs, there are hollow interstices, such as the frog, the heel, etc., which it is always dangerous to heat, if only by the approach of the hot iron. This aversion for the hot iron, founded on the destructive action of heat on the delicate parts of the foot, is so strong among them that in bivouacs, when they see us shoeing our horses, they exclaim : "Look at those Christians pouring oil upon fire!" In a word, they cannot understand why — especially in long marches, when the exercise draws the blood down to the foot of the horse — any one should wish to increase this natural heat by the action of heated iron.

The shoes are very light, of a soft, pliant metal. In the fore-shoes only three nails are driven in on each side. The toes are free, and never fastened. According to the Arabs, nails in the toe would interfere with the elasticity of the foot, and would cause the horse at the moment he sets his foot on the ground precisely the same sensation that a man experiences from wearing a tight shoe. Many accidents thence ensue.

The feet are neither pared nor shortened. The hoof is allowed to grow freely, the very stony ground and incessant work sufficing to wear it off naturally as it tries to get beyond the iron. The necessity of paring the feet is only felt when horses have been for a long time fastened in front of the tent without doing any work, or have remained long in the Tell. In such a case the Arabs simply make use of the sharp-pointed knives which they are never without. This method has this further advantage that if a horse casts a shoe, he can still proceed on his journey, as the sole remains firm and hard. "With you," say they, "and with your practise of paring the foot, if the horse casts a shoe you must pull up, or see him bleeding, halting and suffering."

The shoes are joined at the heel. As the horse can only suffer in the part that is quick, and not in the part that is hard, it is, of course, the frog that should be shielded from accident. The shoes should therefore follow the curvature of the frog. They give to the nail-heads the form of a grasshopper's head, the only form, as they allege, that allows the nails to be worn down to the last without breaking. They approve of our method of driving the nails into punched holes and clinching them outside, which prevents a horse from cutting himself; but their scarcity of iron obliges them to content themselves, for their part, with hammering the nails down upon the hoof, so as to render them serviceable a second time by making a new head. If a horse overreaches himself they cut away his heels and place light shoes on his forefeet, but heavier ones on his hindfeet. They are careful not to leave one foot shod and the other bare. If during an excursion a horse happens to cast one of his foreshoes, and his rider has not a fresh supply with him, he takes off both the hind shoes and puts one of them on the forefoot; and if the animal is shod only on his forefeet, the rider wil take the shoe off the other foot, rather than leave him in such a condition. Should a horse, after a long journey such as the horsemen of the desert not unfrequently make, require to be shod, it is no uncommon thing to place a morsel of felt between the shoe and the foot.

The necessity, caused partly by the nature of the ground and partly by the length of their excursions, of shoeing the horses of the Sahara, has shown the expediency of accustoming the colt to let himself be shod without resistance. They therefore give him kouskoussou, cakes, dates, etc., while he allows them to lift his foot and knock upon it. They then caress his neck and cheeks, and speak to him in a low tone; and thus after a while he lifts his feet whenever they are touched. The little difficulty experienced at a later period, thanks to this early training, has probably given rise to the Arab hyperbole: "So wonderful is the instinct of the thoroughbred horse that if he casts a shoe he draws attention to it himself by showing his foot." This exaggeration at least proves how easy these horses are to be shod, and further explains how every horseman in the desert ought to have the knowledge and the means of shoeing his own horse, while on a journey. It is a point of the highest importance. It is not enough to be very skilful in horsemanship, or to train a horse in the most perfect manner, to acquire the reputation of a thorough horseman—in addition to all this, he must likewise be able to put on a shoe if necessary. Thus on setting out for a distant expedition every horseman carries with him in his *djebira* shoes, nails, a hammer, pincers, some strips of leather to repair his harness, and a needle. Should his horse cast a shoe, he alights, unfastens his camel-rope, passes one end round the *kerbouss* of the saddle and the other round the pastern, and ties the two ends together at such a length as will make the horse present his foot. The animal stirs not an inch, and his rider shoes him without assistance. If it be a hind shoe that has been thrown, he rests the foot upon his knee, and dispenses with aid from his neighbours. To avoid making a mistake he passes his awl into the nail holes in order to assure himself beforehand of the exact direction the nails should take. If, by chance, the horse is restive, he obtains for the hindfeet the help of a comrade who pinches the nose or ears of the animal. For the forefeet, he merely turns his hindquarters towards a thick prickly shrub, or extemporises a torchenes with a nose-bag filled with earth. Such cases, however, are rare.

The Saharenes declare that our shoes are much too heavy and in long and rapid excursions must be dreadfully fatiguing to the articulations, and cause much mischief to the fetlock-joint. "Look at our horses," say they, "how they throw up the earth and sand behind them! how nimble they are! how lightly they lift their feet! how they extend or contract their muscles! They would be as awkward and as clumsy as yours did we not give them shoes light enough not to burden their feet, and the materials of which as they grow thinner commingle with the hoof and with it form one sole body." And when I have answered that we did not discover in our mode of shoeing the inconveniences pointed out by them, they would reply : "How should you do so? Cover as we do in a single day the distance you take five or six days to accomplish, and then you will see. Grand marches you make, you Christians, with your horses! As far as from my nose to my ear!"

I have stated that the Arab saddle furnishes the rider with such a firm seat that he does not trouble himself at all about certain vices in a horse that are apt to cause us uneasiness. I will therefore say a few words on the subject, though it is one now familiar to every body.

The Arab saddle consists of a wooden saddle-tree, surmounted in front by a long *kerbouss* or pommel, and by a broad troussequin behind, high enough to protect the loins. The whole is covered and held together, without nails or pegs, by a plain camel's skin which gives it great solidity. The bands rest on the animal's back, and are broad and flat, with a proper regard for the freedom of the withers and loins, and afford a roomy and commodious seat. This last is very hard, and it requires long practice to get used to it. The chiefs cover it with a woollen cushion; but the common horsemen make it a point of honour to ride on the bare wood, pretending that the use of cushions is excessive effeminacy, and by diminishing their points of contact cannot fail to invite them to sleep during a long course, and consequently expose them to injure their horses. This is all the more meritorious that for the most part, and especially in summer they ride without trousers or drawers.

The saddle-tree is concealed by a *stara,* or covering of red morocco, without ornament, in the case of individuals who are poor or not very well-to do; and by a *ghrebaria,* or covering of cloth or scarlet velvet, embroidered with gold or silver thread, 'and ornamented with fringes, in the case of rich people and chiefs. The *deïr,* or breast-piece, is very broad and is placed like that of our French saddle. Its extremities are provided with two strong buckles of iron or chased silver, and are fastened to the saddle-tree by small girth-leathers, so placed as to keep the saddle in its true position. The Arabs will have nothing to do with a crupper. They say it interferes with every forward movement by the restraint it imposes on the animal. They use it only with bat mules and donkeys, and even then they do not pass it under the tail.

The stirrups are broad and clumsy. Their lateral faces gradually diminish so as to unite with the upper bar which supports the ring for the stirrup-leathers. They are used very short, and the whole foot is thrust into them, and thus shielded from balls or falls. These stirrups are extremely painful for those who are not accustomed to them, because in raising oneself on them the eye strikes against the bone of the leg. After a time the skin hardens and an exostosis is formed that destroys all sensibility. It is by these exostoses that a horseman is distinguished from a foot-soldier, and so clearly, indeed, that in the province of Oran a certain Bey, having resolved to inflict an exemplary chastisement on a tribe that had revolted, put to death all who fell into his hands, bearing these marks. He well knew that his anger was vented only on the horsemen. The stirrups of wealthy individuals are either plated or gilt, and in former times the great Turkish officers had them made of solid silver or gold. The stirrups are suspended by leathers placed behind the girth, which are simply twisted straps of morocco or camel's skin—when doubled seven or eight times, they are of great strength. The noble make their stirrup-leathers of silken cord; but as these, let them be ever so solid, will not suffice when going at a rapid pace with the whole weight thrown upon the stirrups, they add what are called *maoune,* or stirrup-holders.

By way of horse-cloths the Arabs make use of pieces of felt fastened to the saddle, to allow of the operation of saddling being quickly performed. They are seven in number, and dyed blue, red, and yellow—the blue being uppermost. An eighth one is added, but white and unattached, so that it can be washed and dried in the sun if the horse has perspired much. When these pieces of felt are well shaped, the different colours lying one over the other and slightly projecting, form an ornament in very fair taste, while they preserves the horse from wounds and sores. Care is taken that they should partially cover the loins.

The saddle-girth is placed in front of the stirrups, and is narrower than ours. The Arabs as a rule girth their horses loosely; and they can do so without inconvenience, as their saddles never slip round.

The headstall of the bridle is very broad; blinkers are used, and occasionally, but not often, a throat band, loose and fastened to the headband. The Arab of the Sahara, however, does not approve of it, because if his horse, as may often happen, should be seized by the bridle in a fight, it deprives him of his usual resource of slipping the bridle over the head, and so escaping from the enemy, whose prize is thus reduced to the bridle alone. The blinkers have the advantage of preventing a horse from being disquieted by external objects, and are perhaps partly the cause of his not fearing anything. The head-stall and the headband of the bridle are embroidered in silk for the commonalty, and in silver or gold for the rich. The bit is attached to the bridle, and is never cleaned. The bars are broad, short, straight, and fashioned *à la Condé*. The canons are flat, and the curb is a circular ring fixed to the upper part of the mouth piece. The Arab bit allows no liberty to the tongue, and its lever-arm is much shorter than in a French bit : consequently, it is much less severe than has been hitherto imagined. The advantage it offers in wartime of being free from those curbs and hooks which are often so difficult to replace, cannot be too highly appreciated.

The reins are long. Two knots are made in them, one at the length whence a horse can be kept at a foot pace without impeding the freedom of his movements, and the other at the point where experience has shown that the horse, after shortening the muscles of the neck for a gallop, begins to bear on the hand. They are held very full, and at times used as a whip to quicken the animal. The Arabs reject the snaffle as calculated to confuse a horse. Rarely combatting with the sabre, they have never experienced the necessity of it.

As with them the horse is constantly fastened by hobbles, the Arabs do not understand the value of the halter which we employ. They replace it by a *goulada,* a thick cord of silk or camel's hair, of a more or less lively colour according to the coat of the animal. It is passed round the neck, and from it are suspended small morocco sachets, inclosing talismans that have the virtue of preserving from the evil eye, of averting sickness, and of bringing success in war. This *goulada* is, in the first place, an ornament, and, besides, it serves to hold the horse by, when required. To take him by the forelock to hold or lead him, as we do, is to dishonour him; for the Prophet has said : "The good things of this world to the day of the last judgment shall be suspended from the hairs that are between the eyes of your horses."

The Arabs of the Sahara make use of a whip to correct a horse when they are breaking him in, or to excite him in war or at the chace. It is composed of five or six twisted leather thongs, attached to a ring fixed to a bar of iron six or seven inches long, terminating in another ring. To the latter is fastened the small leather thong that is slipped over the wrist. Round the iron rod, but shorter by an inch, is a hollow cylinder, also of iron, of a diameter that allows the rod to play easily within it. The whip is used with all their might. It punishes so severely that after a time it suffices to shake it in order to make the animal dash forward at full speed—the noise made by the cylinder coming in contact either with the rings or with the bar that connects them, recalling to his memory the nearly similar sound of the *tekerbeda.*

In the desert the Arabs carry from the *kerbouss* of the saddle a club a cubit in length, and terminating in a large knob garnished with spikes. It is hung from the wrist by a leather thong. Some replace this by a longer club terminating in a hook, for the purpose of picking up booty from off the ground, without alighting from the saddle. The latter is called *el adraya,* or the despoiler. Neither the Arbâ nor the Harrars would ever mount on horseback without one of these clubs.

The spurs have only one spike, and are clumsy, solid, and long. They are kept in their place by a simple leather strap crossed, and are attached very loosely.

Every Arab carries as a complement of his equipment, suspended from the *kerbouss* of his saddle, a kind of sabretache called *djebira* or *guerab.* It contains several compartments, for the purpose of carrying bread, biscuit, a mirror, soap, cartridges, shoes, a flint, writing materials, etc., etc., according to the calling of the owner. Some *djebiras* are extraordinary rich. I am convinced that the sabretaches of our Hussars must have come to us from the East. The common people on an expedition carry also suspended from the troussequin of their saddle a kind of wallet, which they call *semmâte.* They are shorter than ours, so as not to irritate the animal's flanks.

With the exception of the great chiefs, the Arabs have no holsters to their saddles. They carry their pistols in their girdles, or in a heart-shaped case that rests on the left side, and is held in its place by a leather strap over the shoulder and another round the body. They prefer this latter mode, because they are sure of having them on their person if they chance to be separated from their horse.

Those who do not put a throat-band to their bridle generally adorn their horses with boar's tusks or lion's teeth, or with talismans which they attach to their necks by means of silk or woollen cords.

To our taste, the less covered a thoroughbred horse may be, the better are the beauty and elegance of his form displayed. The Arabs think differently. They say :

> Kohol * embellishes the bearer of babes,
> A tribe embellishes a defile,
> And the saddle embellishes horses.

During my residence in Africa, I have seen so many horses that it was impossible to dispose of when girt with an English saddle, bought up with avidity when caparisoned with an Arab one, that I am much inclined to adopt the native prejudice. Many a time also I have observed that when an Arab, who had purchased a horse from an European, had covered its back with his own saddle, the vendor was seized with regret, being struck with a beauty he had never before noticed. It is true, the only extravagance indulged in by the Arabs is in their harness; for the Prophet, while proscribing the use of gold in their garments, authorised and even enjoined it, in respect of arms and horses. He said : "Whoso fears not to spend money on the maintenance of horses for the holy war, shall be considered, after his death, as the equal of him who has always been open-handed." It is therefore no uncommon sight to see, even in these times of trouble and misery, an Arab chief treat himself to a saddle worth from £80 to £120, and on days of feasting or on solemn occasions, cover the croup of his horse with *shelil,* a silken stuff of brilliant hues.

---

* *Kohol,* sulphide of antimony, used to stain the eyelids. When a married woman has stained her eyes with *Kohol,* adorned herself with *henna,* and chewed a stick of *souak,* which sweetens the breath, whitens the teeth, and reddens the lips, she becomes more pleasant in the eyes of Allah, and more beloved of her husband.

When thou mountest a horse, first pronounce these words: *Bi es-scm Allah,* "in the name of Allah." The grave of the horseman is always open.

The cavalier of Truth should eat little, and, above all, drink little. If he cannot endure thirst, he will never make a warrior—he is nothing but a frog of the marshes.

Purchase a good horse. If thou pursuest, thou attainest : if thou art pursued, the eye presently knoweth not where thou hast passed.

Prefer a horse from the mountain to a horse from the plain, and the latter to one from the marshland, which is only fit to carry the pack-saddle.

For the combat mount a horse with a trailing tail [that is, one at least eight years old]. In the day when the horsemen shall be so crowded together that the stirrups knock against one another, he will save thee from the thick of the fight and bear thee back to thy tent, though he were pierced by a ball.

When thou hast purchased a horse, study him carefully, and give him barley more and more every day until thou hast ascertained the quantity demanded by his appetite. A good horseman ought to know the measure of barley suited to his horse, as exactly as the measure of powder suited to his gun.

Suffer neither dogs nor donkeys to lie down upon the straw or barley you intend to give to your horses.

The Prophet has said: "Every grain of barley given to your horses shall secure you an indulgence in the other world."

Give barley to your horses; deprive yourself to give them still more; for Sidi-Hamed-ben-Youssouf has remarked; "Had I not seen the mare produce the foal, I should have said it was the barley." He has also said: "Superior to spurs there is nothing but barley."

Do not water your horses more than once a day, at one or two in the afternoon; and give barley only in the evening, at sunset. It is a good practice in wartime, and, besides, it is the way to make their flesh firm and hard.

To train a horse that is too fat for the fatigues of war, reduce him by exercise, but never by lowering his keep.

So long as your horse, when at work, sweats over his whole body, you may say that he is not in good wind. But you may count upon him as soon as he sweats only on the ears and chest.

Leave not thy horse near others that are eating barley, without he has some likewise, for otherwise he will fall ill.

Never water your horse after having given him barley. It would be the death of the animal.

Never give water to a horse after a rapid gallop, for here is danger of checked perspiration.

After a rapid gallop, water him with the bridle on, and feed him with the saddle-girth on, and thou wilt not repent of it.

Be clean, and perform your ablutions before mounting your horse, and the Prophet will love you.

Whoso is guilty of an impropriety on the back of his horse is not worthy to own him. Moreover, he will suffer for it, for his horse will do himself a hurt.

Never fall asleep upon thy horse. The sleep of the rider wounds or wearies the animal.

When you put a horse to his speed, husband his strength for the time of need. He must be treated like a goat-skin water-bag, which if you open gradually, keeping the neck nearly closed, you will easily preserve the water. But if you open it hastily, the water will rush out all at once, and not a drop will remain to quench your thirst.

A horseman should never urge his horse to full speed, while going up or down hill, unless he is forced to do so. He ought, on the contrary, to hold him in.

"Which dost thou prefer?" the horse was asked one day, "The getting on, or the getting off thy back?" And he made answer : "Allah curse the point where they meet!"

When you have a long journey to accomplish, relieve your horse by changing his pace, to enable him to recover his wind. Repeat this until he has sweated and dried three times, then shift his girth, and afterwards do what you will with him. He will never fail you in a difficulty.

If, on a march, you have a strong wind right in your teeth, contrive if possible to save your horse from facing it—you will spare him various diseases.

If at the bivouac your horse is so placed that he cannot move out of the wind that is blowing violently into his nostrils, do not hesitate to leave the nose-bag suspended from his nose—you will preserve him from serious mischief.

If you have put your horse to the gallop and other mounted men are following behind, soothe him, do not urge him on, for he will be sufficiently excited of himself.

If you are chasing an enemy and he commits the error of pushing his horse on, hold in your own—you are sure to overtake the fugitive.

Never strike a thoroughbred. It humiliates him, and his pride will revolt and urge him to resistance. It is quite sufficient to correct or animate him by word or gesture.

If, after having wandered a long time in the mountains and by narrow path-ways, the horseman descends into the plain, it is good to give the animal a gallop over a short distance.

At starting the rider should not scruple to play with his horse for a few minutes, as he will thereby relax his joints, and assure himself peace for the rest of the day. In like manner, after a painful and fatiguing excursion, at the moment he reaches his tent let him perform the fantasia for a while. The women of the *douar* will applaud, saying: "Look at so-and-so, son of so-and-so!" and he will find out, besides, what his horse is really worth.

The rider who does not teach his horse a good pace is no true horseman, but an object of pity.

If, in war time or in hunting, your horse is in a lather, and you happen to come across a stream, have no fear of allowing him to swallow half a dozen mouthfuls with the bridle on. So far from doing him any harm it will enable him to continue his course.

When you dismount think of your horse before thinking of yourself. It is he who has carried you, and is to carry you again.

After a long journey, either unsaddle your horse immediately and throw cold water over his back, at the same time leading him up and down; or else leave the saddle on until he is perfectly dry and has eaten his barley. There is no middle path between these two courses.

When after a long journey in winter, through rain and cold, you at length regain your tent, cover your horse well, and give him parched barley and warmed milk, but do not let him have any water that day.

Suffer not your horse to have anything to eat or drink directly after a journey of unusual length, or you will produce inflammation.

Put not your horses to speed, unless positively compelled to do so, during the great heats of summer. The animal himself says :

> Put me not to speed in the summer,
> If thou would'st that I should one day save thee from the sabre.

In a case of life or death if you feel your horse's wind failing, take off the bridle if only for an instant, and strike him on the croup with a spur sharply enough to draw blood.

If after a rapid gallop you are able to give a little respite to your horse, you will know when to start again by the drying up of the mucus that issues from his nostrils.

If you would know, at the end of a day of excessive fatigue and hard riding, how far you can yet depend upon your horse, get off his back and pull him strongly towards you by the tail. If he remains unmoved as if rooted to the ground, you may still rely upon him.

On an expedition when, after great fatigue, you have only a moment for repose, take for your pillow some of the bridles of your brethren, and you will not be abandoned or forgotten, happen what may.

A horseman ought to study the habits of his horse and obtain a thorough knowledge of his character. He will then know whether, when he alights, he can have any confidence in him and can leave him in the midst of other animals, or whether he must keep an eye upon him and hobble him. Not one of these details is a matter of indifference in the presence of an enemy.

The proper season for calling on a horse to do great things, is the spring, before the great heats; or the autumn, before the intense cold.

The horse is what his work is.

> Yes, give the heel to your steeds,
> Learn and teach them what will be of service to you.
> In this world it is certain that, one day or another,
> Every man has to face him who demands his life.

REMARKS BY THE EMIR ABD-EL-KADER.

The Arabs have preserved the practice of racing their horses against one another, in which they indulged so far back as in the times of idolatry, prior to Mohammed.

The new law has in no way altered this usage. On the contrary it has consecrated its lawfulness, and, by impressing it with the seal of religion, has attached additional importance to it.

For racing, the Arabs subject their horses to a preparatory regimen, which is called *tadmir,* or training. Thank to this treatment, a horse acquires a wonderful speed. The *tadmir* is in this wise.

They begin by increasing the animal's allowance of food, so that he gains fat to a perceptible degree. When this result has been attained, they begin to reduce his condition by gradually diminishing his rations for forty days, until they have reached the minimum of nourishment. During these forty days, they subject him to progressive exercise. At the same time, and from the very first day from lowering his keep, they cover the animal with seven *djellale,* or horse-cloths, one of which they remove every six days. The sweating disperses all the fat, gets rid of a useless weight, gives tone to the muscles, and leaves nothing but hard flesh. By means of this treatment, a horse attains, according to the stock he comes from, the highest degree of speed. Thus prepared, the horse is brought on to the *djalba* or race ground.

Horses arriving from all districts are led on to the *djalba,* and crowds of people likewise flock thither. At no other time, except at the period of the assemblage of pilgrims, is such a concourse of men to be seen, and all the nobles and chiefs are present.

"We have taken part in the races, and, although it was yet early, the crowd was as great as at the period of pilgrimages."

Horses properly trained are never suffered to run against those that are not. They are placed in different classes, to each of which a different goal is assigned. The trained horses have much the longest course to run. The race-course in this case in called *el midmar,* and upon this the learned Bokhari has remarked:

"The Prophet caused the trained horses to run by themselves, and fixed a distance of seven miles to traverse, while for ordinary horses he fixed a distance of only three miles."*

The horses are grouped together by tens, but before allowing them to start and to prevent false starts, the following precaution is taken. A rope is stretched across touching the animals' chests, the two ends of which are held by two men. This rope is called *el mikbad,* and *el mikouas;* and in reference to it the Prophet said: "The horse runs according to his race, but placed before the *mikouas* he runs according to his chance of a rider." Or, in other words: "In ordinary cirumstances the speed of horses depends on the qualities of blood with which they are more or less endowed; but in a race success depends greatly on the skill of the rider, and not unfrequently a horse of the purest blood may be outstripped by a less noble animal." To each of the ten horses that have contended, a name is assigned indicative of his degree of swiftness. Thus the one that arrives first at the goal is called *Modjalla,* "taking away," because he takes away care from the heart of his master. The second is named *el Mousalli,* from the word *salouan,* "the extremity of the buttocks," because he follows the first so closely that the point of his nose touches the

---

* This mile is only a kilomètre.

other's hindquarters. "I must positively be the *mousalli,* [that is, the second] if I consent to thy carrying off the first prize." The third receives the surname of *el Msali,* "Consoling," because he consoles his master, who is content that there is only one horse between his own and the winner. The fourth is *el Tali,* or "the Follower;" the fifth *el Mourtah,* "the fifth finger of the hand;" the sixth *el Aâtif;* the seventh *el Hadi,* "the Lucky one," because he has his share of success with the foremost; the eighth, *el Mouhammil,* "one who gives hopes," because he caused his master to hope that he might be among the winners; the ninth, *el Lathim,* or "the Buffeted," because he has been humiliated and rejected on all sides; and the tenth, *el Sokeït,* "the Taciturn," because his master undergoes the lowest humiliation without uttering a word—shame closing his mouth. Of these ten horses seven gain a prize, but the others obtain nothing. At the further end of the course a vast tent is pitched, into which the seven winners are admitted in order to shelter them, while the three others are ignominiously driven away.

IN THE NAME OF ALLAH THE CLEMENT AND MERCIFUL.

"We took part in the horse races. Though it was early morning the crowd was as dense as at the season of pilgrimage.

"Horses were brought from every quarter, but no one knows better than ourselves how to rear and train them.

"We arrived at the peep of day with horses whose hoofs were as hollow as cups. The stars had announced good fortune to them.

"They are drawn up according to the purity of their race. The noble is placed by the side of the noble.

"Among them is a black horse with robust limbs and adorned with a white mark on his forehead. When he feels the bit in his mouth, he dashes off, clearing the lines traced to indicate the goal.

"The star that shines on his forehead equals the brilliancy of Mirzam.*

"Then a dark bay with a black mane, endowed by nature with admirable qualities, with a sleek skin, bearing also a star on his forehead, and a white mark on the upper lip.

"Next a horse completely black without a white spot any-where, but participating in the excellent qualities of the pre-ceeding.

"They have been brought to excite the admiration of the spectators, impatient to see them appear in the lists.

"Horsemen mount them, hardy as bars of iron and short of stature. Their voice is like the roaring of the lion.

"Seated on their coursers they look like starlings hovering over the table-land of a mountain.

"At last they draw up in line. In the midst of the assembly of spectators, a man, a Mussulman like the others, sits in the capacity of umpire. He has been chosen by common accord as arbiter, and surely his awards will not be tainted with par-tiality.

"The steeds let loose in the arena disperse immediately like pearls that fall from a necklace, or like a covey of *hetâa* (gray partridges) discovered by a falcon that swoops down upon them, attacking them with fury.

"The black, with a white mark on the forehead, comes in first.

"The bay with the dark mane is second, and the entirely black is without reproach, for he runs in third.

The *Tali* is the fourth, and follows the others. But how far is the inhabitant of the Tahama from the inhabitant of Nedjed!

The fifth, *el Mourtah*, is not to be blamed, for he has done as well as he could do.

The *Aâtif* is the sixth. He comes in all trembling, and his fear well nigh stopped him in mid-career.

"The seventh is the *Hadi*. The awarder of prizes will give unto him his due.

"The *Mouhammil*, who gave such hopes to his master, has

---

* A star in the constellation of Orion.

come in the eighth. He was mistaken. The unfortunate one encountered on his path the bird of ill omen. He suffered seven horses to pass before him and ran in the eighth—but the eighth horse is not one of the winners.

"The ninth arrives at last. He is the *Lathim*, the buffeted one, and receives blows from every one.

"On his traces follows, capering about, the *Sokeït*, the Silent one, with trouble in his face and humiliation on his forehead. The horseman who rides him at the tail of the others is the object of reproaches from all sides, and still more so his groom. It is of little use to ask who is his master,—no answer is to be had from those whom shame has made dumb.

"Whoso does not take to the race-course the horses that are most noble by birth ought to repent of it.

"In being present we have experienced the greatest gratification, without speaking of the glory and advantages we have carried off.

"In exchange for the seven reeds planted at the end of the course and carried off by the first seven as they arrived, we have received magnificent presents, such as it is seemly to offer.

"Striped calico from Yemen, dyed of various colours, and *haïks* of silk and of wool.

"We carried off all these stuffs spread out over our horses, with borders red as blood.

"In addition to all this they gave us silver coins by thousands, but this silver we never keep for ourselves. We distribute it among the servants who tend our horses, though we ourselves tend these with our own hands far more carefully than they do.

"These are horses that never drink any but the purest water, and never feed on any but the choicest food.

The Mussulman law distinguishes three ways of offering prizes for horse racing. The first is positively permitted, the second is so conditionally, and the third is utterly prohibited. In the first case, some one entirely without interest in the result of the race offers a prize, saying : "Whoever shall be victor in the race shall gain

the prize." Kings, chiefs, and great personages whose
rank or fortune places them in an exalted position, sometimes propose prizes in this manner, which is sanctioned
without any condition. In the second case, an individual
interested in the race, says : "I offer a prize which shall
be given to the one first in." This mode is allowed,
with the condition that if the donor himself is the first
to arrive at the goal, the prize shall be given to the
assembly. The third manner is that by which every one
interested in the race offers a prize for the benefit of him
by whom he is beaten. This style of racing is nothing
more than a wager, and consequently is absolutely forbidden. Much more is betting by persons not concerned
in the race formally prohibited.

ABD-EL-KADER ON THE ARAB HORSE.

———

Having known the Emir Abd-el-Kader during the time I held the office of French Consul at Mascara, from 1837 to 1839, and having again met him at Toulon in 1847, whither I had been ordered on special duty at the time of his first landing in France, I had full opportunity in my numerous interviews with him to appreciate his intimate acquaintance with all that related to the history of his country, as well as to all questions of horse-flesh. I did not hesitate, therefore, to ask his opinion on a subject of a purely scientific nature, which may nevertheless be of great moment, not only for the future interests of our colony, but for those of the country at large. The following is his reply, written under date of the 8th November, 1851.

Glory to the one God, whose reign alone endureth for ever!
Peace be with him who equals in good qualities all the men of his time, who aims only at what is good, whose heart is pure and his word abiding, the wise, the intelligent, the Lord General Daumas, on the part of your friend Sid-el-Hadj Abd-el-Kader, son of Mahhi-Eddin.
Behold the reply to your inquiries :—
1st. You ask me how many days an Arab horse can march

without rest and without suffering too severely.   Know, then, that a horse sound in every limb, that eats as much barley as his stomach can contain, can do whatever his rider can ask of him. For this reason the Arabs say : "Give barley and over-work him." But without tasking him overmuch, a horse can be made to do sixteen parasangs day after day.*   It is the distance from Mascara to Koudiat-Aghelizan on the Oued-Mina; it has been measured in cubits.   A horse performing this journey every day, and having as much barley as it likes to eat, can go on, without fatigue, for three or four months, without lying by a single day.

2nd. You ask me what distance a horse can accomplish in a day. I cannot tell you very precisely, but it ought to be about fifty parasangs, or the distance from Tlemcen to Mascara.   However, an animal that has performed such a journey ought to be carefully ridden on the following day, and allowed to do only a very much shorter distance.   Most of our horses used to go from Oran to Mascara in a single day, and could repeat the journey for two or three consecutive days.   On one occasion we started from Saïda about eight in the morning to fall upon the Arbâa, who were encamped at Aaïn-Toukria, among the Oulad-Aïad near Taza, and we came up with them at break of day.

3rd. You ask for examples of the temperance of the Arab horse, and for proofs of his power of enduring hunger and thirst. Know that when we were established at the mouth of the Melouïa, we used to make razzias into the Djebel-Amour, following the route of the Sahara, and on the day of attack pushing forward at the gallop for five or six hours at a stretch — the entire expedition, going and returning, being completed in twenty to twenty-five days at the outside.   During this space of time our horses had no barley except what they carried with them, about enough for eight ordinary feeds.   Nor did they find straw, or anything except the *alfa* and *shiehh*, and grass in the spring time.   And yet, on rejoining our people, we performed the fantasia on our horses, and some among us burnt powder. Many, too, who were not fresh enough for the latter exercise, were quite able to go upon an expedition.   Our horses would go a day or two without water, and once they found none for three days.   The horses of the Sahara do far more than that, for they go three months without touching a grain of barley.   Straw

---

* A parasang is equal to about 5,000 mètres. Sixteen parasangs are equal, in round numbers, to fifty English miles.

they meet with only when they go to the Tell to buy grain, and for the most part feed on the *alfa*, the *shiehh*, and sometimes the *guetof*. The *shiehh* is better than the *alfa*, but not so good as the *guetof*. The Arabs say :

> The *alfa* is good for marching,
> The *shiehh* is good for fighting,
> And the *guetof* is superior to barley.

In certain years the horses of the Sahara have gone the whole twelve months without a grain of barley to eat, especially when the tribes have not been suffered to enter the Tell. At such times the Arabs give dates to their horses, which is a fattering food, and keeps them in condition for marching or fighting.

4th. You ask why, seeing the French do not mount their horses before they are four years old, the Arabs mount theirs at a very early age. Know that the Arabs say that horses, like men, are more easily taught when quite young. They have a proverb :

> The lessons of infancy are engraved upon stone,
> The lessons of ripe age pass away like birds' nests.

They likewise say :

> The young branch is made straight without much trouble,
> But the old wood can never be straightened.

In the very first year, the Arabs teach the colt to let itself be led by the *reseum*, a species of cavesson. They call it then *djeda*, and begin to fasten and bridle it. As soon as it has become *teni*, that is, as soon as it has entered on its second year, they ride it a mile or two, or even a parasang, and after it has completed eighteen months they do not fear to fatigue it. When it has become *rebâa telata*, that is, when it has entered on its third year, they tie it up, cease to ride it, cover it with a good *djellal*, and get it into condition. They say :

> In his first year, tie him up lest he should meet with an accident;
> In his second year, ride him until his back bends;
> In his third year, again tie him up, and after that, if he does not
> suit you, sell him.

If a horse is not ridden before his third year, it is certain that he will never be good for anything but to gallop, which he does not need to learn, as it is his nature to do so : an idea thus expressed by the Arabs : "The noble horse gallops according to his race"—that is, a thoroughbred horse has no occasion to be taught to gallop.

5th. You ask me how it is, seeing that the foal derives more qualities from its sire than from its dam, that mares are always higher priced than horses. The reason is this. He who buys a mare does so with the expectation that he will not only be able to make use of her for the saddle, but will also obtain from her a numerous stock; while he who buys a horse cannot hope to get any other advantage out of him than by riding him.

6th. You ask me if the Arabs of the Sahara keep registers to establish the descent of their horses. Know that the inhabitants of the Algerian Sahara do not, any more than those of the Tell, concern themselves with these registers. The notoriety of the fact suffices them; for pedigree of their blood horses is as well known to every one as that of their masters. I have heard it said that some families possessed these written genealogies, but I cannot answer for the fact. Such books, however, are kept in the East.

7th. You ask me which are the tribes of Algeria the most renowned for the pure breed of their horses. Know that the best horses of the Sahara are unquestionably those of Hamyàn. They possess none but excellent animals, because they never employ them to till the ground, or as beasts of burden. They employ them solely on expeditions and in battle. These are superior to all others in endurance of hunger, thirst, and fatigue. Next in order come the horses of the Harar, the Arbâa, and the Oulad-Naïl. In the Tell, the horses in the first rank for nobility of race, for height and beauty of mould, are those of the Shelif, especially those of the Oulad-Sidi-Ben-Abd-Allah, near the Mina, and those of the Oulad-Sidi-Hassan, a section of the Oulad-Sidi-Dahbou, who dwell in the highlands of Mascara. The fleetest in the race-course, and at the same time of a beautiful shape, are those of the Flittas, the Oulad-Sherif, and the Oulad-Lekreud. The best for traversing stony ground, without being shod, are those of the Hassasna in the Yakoubia. The following words are ascribed to Mulay-Ishmael, the celebrated Sultan of Morocco.

May my horse have been reared in the Màz,
And watered in the Biaz.

The Màz is a district of the Hassasna, and the Biaz is the stream known by the name of Foufet, that flows through their territory, The horses of the Oulad Khaled are also famous for the same qualities. In reference to this tribe Sidi-Ahmed-Ben-Youssel has said : "The long locks and the long *djellals* will lie seen in the midst of you to the day of the resurrection," thus enlogising their women and their horses.

8th. You say that people maintain against you that the horses of Algeria are not Arabs but Barbs. It is a theory that turns against its own authors, for the Barbs were originally Arabs. A well known writer has said : "The Berbers inhabit the Mogheb. They are all sons of Kaïs-Ben-Ghilan. It is likewise stated that they spring from two great Hemiarite tribes, the Senahdja and the Kettama, who came into the country at the time of the invasion of Ifrikesh El Malik." According to both these opinions, the Berbers are decidedly Arabs. Historians, moreover, establish the descent of most of the Berber tribes from the Senahdja and the Kettama. The arrival of these tribes was anterior to Islam. Since the Mussulman invasion the number of Arabs who have emigrated into the Mogheb is beyond computation. When the Obeïdin [the Fatimites] were masters of Egypt, immense tribes passed into Africa, among others the Riahh, and spread themselves from Kaïrouan to Merrakesh [Morocco]. It is from these tribes that are descended the Algerian tribes of the Douaouda, the Aïad, the Màdid, the Oulad-Mahdi, the Oulad-Iakoub-Zerara, the Djendel, the Attaf, the Hamïs, the Braze, the Sbeha, the Flittas, the Medjahar, the Mehal, the Beni-Aâmer, the Hamian, and many more. Without doubt the Arab horses were dispersed through the Mogheb in like manner with the Arab families. At the time of lfrikesh-ben-Kaïf, the empire of the Arabs was all powerful. It extended as far west as the confines of the Mogheb, just as in the time of Shamar the Hemiarite it extended eastward to the frontiers of China, as it is related by Ben-Kouteïba in his book entitled "El Marif."

It is quite true, however, that although the Algerian horses come of Arab stock, many have degenerated from their nobleness from being employed much too often in the plough, in carrying and drawing heavy loads, and in other kinds of labour, and from other causes which did not exist among the Arabs of the olden times. It is sufficient, they say, for a horse to have walked over ploughed land to lose something of his excellence, and by way of illustration they relate the following anecdote :

"A man was riding one day, mounted on a thoroughbred, when he met his enemy also mounted on a noble courser. The one turned and fled, while the other gave chace. The latter was distanced, and despairing to overtake the former, cried out to him :

"I demand of thee in the name of Allah, has thy horse ever been in the plough?"

"He has ploughed for four days."

"Ah! mine has never been in the plough. By the head of the Prophet, I am certain to overtake thee."

" He then followed up the pursuit and towards the end of the day the pursued began to lose ground and the pursuer to gain upon him. At last the latter succeeded in coming up with and combating him whom he had at first despaired of overtaking."

"My father—Allah be merciful to him!—was in the habit of saying : 'There was no blessing for our land since we converted our coursers into beasts of burden and tillage. Did not Allah create the horse for riding, the ox for the plough, and the camel for the transport of burdens? There is nothing to be gained by changing the ways of Allah.'"

9th. You ask me further what is our practice with regard to the keep and maintenance of our horses. Know that the master of a horse gives him very little barley to begin with, and goes on increasing the quantity little by little, until he fails to consume it all, when the quantity is reduced and afterwards maintained at the exact measure of his appetite. The best time of day for giving barley is the evening. Unless on a journey, it is useless to give it in the morning. The best way is to give it to the horse saddled and girthed, just as the best way of watering him is with the bridle on. There is a saying.

Water with the bridle,
And barley with the saddle.

The Arabs greatly prefer a horse that eats little, provided he does not lose strength. Such a one, say they, is a priceless treasure. To water a horse at sunrise, makes him lose flesh. To water him in the evening, puts him into good condition. To water him in the middle of the day, keeps him as he is. During the great heats which last for forty days, the Arabs water their horses only every second day : a custom, they assert, attended with beneficial effects.   In summer, autumn, and winter they throw an armful of straw to their horses; but the substance of their keep is barley, in preference to every other kind of food. They say : "Had we not seen that horses come from horses, we should have said that it is the barley that produces them." Again :

" Of forbidden flesh, choose the lightest," that is, choose a horse that is light and nimble — horse-flesh being forbidden to Mussulmans.

" No one becomes a horseman until he has been often thrown."

" Thoroughbred horses have no vice."

" A horse in a leading-string is an honour to his master."

" Horses are birds without wings."

" No distance is far for a horse."

" Whoso forgets the beauty of horses for that of women will never prosper."

" Horses know their riders."

The pious Ben-el-Abbas— Allah be good to him! — hath said :

Love horses and take care of them,
Spare no trouble;
By them comes honour, by them comes beauty.
If horses are forsaken of men,
I will receive them into my family,
I will share with them the bread of my children;
My wives clothe them with their veils,
And cover themselves with the horse-cloths;
I ride them every day
Over the field of adventures;
Carried away in their impetuous career
I combat the most valiant.

I have finished the letter which our brother and companion, the friend of all men, the Commandant Sidi-Bou-Senna [Boissonnet], will cause to be delivered into your hands.   Peace!

THE WAR HORSE.

——

AN ARAB CHAUNT.

My steed is black as a night without moon or stars;
He was foaled in vast solitudes;
He is an air-drinker, son of an air-drinker.
His dam also was of noble race,
And our horsemen of the days of powder have surnamed him Sabok.*
The lightning flash itself cannot overtake him:
Allah save him from the evil eye!

His ears vie with those of the gazelle,
His eyes are the eyes of a woman with wiles,
His forehead resembles that of a bull,
His nostrils the cavern of a lion.
His neck, shoulders, and croup are long,
He is broad in the seat, in the limbs and flanks,
He has the tail of a viper, the thighs of an ostrich,
And his vigorous heels are lifted above the ground.
I reckon upon him as upon my own heart.
Never has mortal mounted his equal.

His flesh is firmer than that of the zebra;
He has the short gallop of the fox,
The easy and prolonged running of the wolf;
He accomplishes in one day a five days' march;
And when he stretches out at full speed, he strikes the girts with
his hocks.
You would say that it was a dart hurled by fate,

* *Sabok*, rapid, outstripping.

Or a thirsty pigeon that precipitates itself
Upon the water preserved in the hollow of a rock.

Yes, Sabok is a war horse!
He loves the chace of savage animals,
He sighs only for glory and booty,
And the cries of our virgins excite his ardour.
When I urge him into the midst of dangers,
His neighing summons the vultures
And makes my enemies tremble;
On his back, death cannot overtake me,
It fears the sound of his hoofs.

Aàtika * said to me: "Come and be without a companion!"
Docile as the sabre one draws from the sheath,
Sabok hears my spurs, and divines my thoughts;
He cleaves through space like a falcon regaining its nest,
And when I arrive near her whose eyes are languishing,
Alone, in the midst of peril, patient and immovable,
He champs his bit until my return.
By the head of the Prophet, this horse is the resource of caravans,
The ornament of a tent, and the honour of my tribe.

I am an Arab. I know how to command and to combat,
My name protects the feeble and the afflicted,
My flocks are the reserve of the poor,
And the stranger in my tent is named The Welcome One.
The Almighty hath loaded me with his gifts,
But time turns upon itself, and turns back,
And if I must drink one day of the two cups of life,
I will show that adversity cannot humiliate my soul.
My virtue shall be resignation,
My fortune, contempt of riches,
My happiness, the hope of another life;
And if poverty were to grasp me by the throat,
I would not the less glorify Allah.

* *Aàtika*, the noble lady.

PART SECOND

THE MANNERS OF THE DESERT

It is certain that the Arabs are the most experienced horsemen in the world. They know a horse thoroughly and minutely, and can rear and train one better than any other people. It is also certain that the Arab horses are better than those of all other nations. A sufficient proof of this is that they always finish by overtaking the gazelle, the ostrich, and the wild ass, which they sometimes pursue to a great distance.

"He has chased the onager, the buffalo, and the ostrich, without once pulling up, and without a single drop of sweat moistening his coat."

The nature of the horses of the Sahara is a consequence of the life led by their masters. The Saharenes are obliged to accustom their horses to support hunger through the scarcity of food, and likewise thirst through the scarcity of water, which is frequently not to be found within a couple of day's march of the encampment. Endurance of fatigue and speed are the result of the countless quarrels of these Arabs, their incessant hostile excursions, and their fondness for the chace of the swiftest animals, such as the ostrich, the gazelle, and the wild ass, which some among them hunt the whole year round without interruption.

The Most High hath said: "Put on foot all the forces you can dispose of, and hold in readiness a large number of horses, to intimidate the enemies of Allah and your own, and yet others, whom you know not but who are known to Allah. Whatever you shall have expended in the service of Allah, shall be recompensed to you. You will not be forsaken."

And the Prophet never ceased to repeat:

"Whoso possesses an Arab horse and honours him, will be honoured of Allah."

"Whoso possesses an Arab horse and contemns him, will be contemned of Allah."

THE SAHARA

BY ABD-EL-KADER.

———

Glory to God alone!

O thou who takest up the defence of the *hader* *

And condemnest the love of the *bedoui* † for his boundless horizons!

Is it for their lightness that thou findest fault with our
tents?

Hast thou no word of praise but for houses of wood
and stone?

If thou knewest the secrets of the desert, thou wouldst
think like me :

But thou art ignorant, and ignorance is the mother
of evil.

If thou hadst waked up in the middle of the Sahara,
If thy feet had trampled this carpet of sand,
Sprinkled with flowers like to pearls,
Thou wouldst have admired our plants,
The singular variety of their hues,
Their grace, their delicious perfume;

* *Hader*, inhabitant of cities.   † *Bedoui*, inhabitant of the wild parts of the Sahara.

Thou wouldst have drawn in this balmy breath which doubles life, for it has not passed over the impurity of cities.

If, going out some splendid night,
Cooled by an abundant dew,
From the summit of a *merkeb,* *
Thou hadst cast thy eyes round thee,
Thou wouldst have seen far away and on all sides troops of wild animals
Browsing the fragrant shrubs.
At that moment all care would have fled from before thee.
Overflowing joy would have filled thy soul.

What a charm, too, in our hunting!   At sunrise,
Through us every day brings terror to the savage beast.
And the day of the *rahil,*† when our red *haouadjej* ◊ are fastened on our camels,
Thou wouldst have said that a field of anemones were bedecking themselves, under the rain, with their richest colours.

Upon our *haouadjej* recline our virgins;
Their *taka* ? are closed by houri eyes.
The conductors of their animals raise their shrill chaunt;
The tone of their voice finds the door of the soul.

* In the Sahara this name is given to hillocks the outline of which resembles that of a ship.

† *Rahil,* migration, a nomadic movement.   ◊ *Haouadjej,* red camel-litters.

? *Taka,* windows: the bull's-eyes of litters.

We, swift as the air, on our generous coursers,
The *shelils* * waving over their croups,
We give chace to the *houache*.+
We overtake the *ghezal,* ◊ that fancies itself far from us.
It escapes not from our horses at full speed,
With thin flanks.
How many *delim* ⚲ with their females became our prey!
Although their running is not less rapid than the
flight of other birds.

We return to our families at the hour of halt,
On a new camping ground, free from pollution.
The earth exhales the odour of musk, ‡
But purer than it,
It has been cleansed by the rains
Of evening and morning.

We pitch our tents in circular groups;
The earth is covered with them, as is the firmament
with stars.
They of old time have said, who are no more, but our
fathers have repeated it,
And we say as they did, for truth is always truth :
Two things are beautiful in this world,
Beautiful verses and beautiful tents.

In the evening, our camels come up to us;
At night the voice of the male is heard like distant
thunder.

---

* Veils waving over the horses croups.
† *Houache,* a species of bison, or wild ox. ◊ *Ghezal,* the gazelle.
⚲ *Delim,* the male ostrich.
‡ The odour of musk remains where the *ghezal* has passed.

Light ships of the land,
Safer than ships,
For a ship is inconstant;
Our *maharis** rival in speed the *maha*.†

And our horses—is there a glory like unto theirs?
Always saddled for the fight,
When any one invokes our aid,
They are the promise of victory.
Our enemies have no place of refuge against our blows,
For our coursers, celebrated by the Prophet, swoop
upon them like the vulture.

Our coursers have the purest milk to drink,
The milk of the camel, more precious than that of the
cow.

Our first care is to divide the booty we have taken
from the enemy.
Equity presides at the distribution.   Every one receives the due reward of his valour.

We have sold our rights of citizenship.   We have no
reason to regret the bargain.
We have gained honour, of which the *hader* knows
nothing.
We are Kings. There is none to be compared with us.
Is it life to undergo humiliation?

We suffer not the insults of the unjust. We leave him
and his land.
True happiness is in wandering life.

---

* *Mahari*, a riding camel.   † *Maha*, a species of white wild doe.

If contact with our neighbour annoys us,
We withdraw from him—neither he, nor we, have anything to complain of.

What fault, then, hast thou to find with the *bedoui?*
Nothing but his love of glory, and his liberality that knows no stint.

Under the tent, the fire of hospitality is kindled for the traveller.
He finds, whoever he may be, a sure remedy against cold and hunger.

Ages have told of the salubrity of the Sahara.
All disease and sickness dwell only beneath the roof of cities.
In the Sahara, whoever is not reaped by the sword sees days without number;
Our old men are the most aged of all men.

——

The most frequent and almost daily incident of Arab life is the *razzia*. Glory is a fine thing, no doubt, and in the Sahara hearts are as open to its fascination as elsewhere. But there, the idea of glory is to injure the enemy and destroy his resources, and at the same time augment one's own. Glory is not smoke, but plunder. The thirst for revenge is also a motive; but what vengeance is sweeter than to enrich oneself with the spoils of one's enemy? This threefold craving for glory, revenge, and plunder, could not possibly be gratified more promptly or efficaciously than by the *razzia*—the invasion by force or stratagem of the ground occupied by the foe, which contains all that is dear to him, his family and his fortune.

In the desert, there are three kinds of *razzia*. First of all there is the *tehha* ["the falling," from the verb *tahh*, "it is fallen"], which takes place at the *fedjeur*, or dawn of day. In a *tehha*, the object is not pillage, but massacre: no thought is given to riches, but all to vengeance. The next is the *khrotefa*, which comes off at *el aasseur*, or two or three in the afternoon, and means nothing but rapine. And lastly, the *terbigue,* which is neither war, nor an affair of brigandage, but, at most, a thievish operation. The *terbigue* is attempted at *nous el leïl,* or midnight. When a razzia is determined upon, those who propose to take part in it say to one another *Rana akeud,* "we are a knot." The enterprise is arranged, the association formed, and a compact concluded — compact of life and death.

THE TEHHA.

When a *tehha* is contemplated, the sheikh issues orders to shoe the horses, to prepare food, and to provide a supply of barley for five or six days, more or less. These provisions are put into a *semmât,* or wallet, each taking his own. Previous to setting out, two or three mounted scouts are sent forward to reconnoitre the position of the enemy they propose to attack. The scouts are men of intelligence, well mounted, acquainted with the country, and circumspect. They take every precaution and make a great circuit, so that in the event of a surprise, they will appear from a quarter whence those whom they intend to assail are accustomed to see only friends appear. On arriving near to their destination, they place themselves in ambush, and one of them, separating from the band, penetrates on foot to the very heart of the *douar,* without exciting the slightest suspicion. As soon as they have obtained the necessary information respecting the numbers and disposition of the enemy, they retrace their steps and rejoin the *goum,* who await them at a spot previously agreed upon. Like the scouts they, too, have followed a path little calculated to inspire with apprehension those whom they propose to surprise. All necessary intelligence having been obtained, and the foe being now near at hand, it is arranged to fall upon him at the dawn of day, because at that hour they will find

> The wife without her girdle,
> And the mare without her bridle.

Before dashing into the *mêlée*, the leaders address to their followers a few impassioned words : "Listen. Let no one think of despoiling the women, driving off the horses, entering the tents, or alighting for purposes of plunder, before taking many lives. Bear in mind that we have to do with 'children of sin,' who will defend themselves vigourously. These people have butchered our brethren. No mercy! Kill! Kill! if you desire at the same time to take revenge and the goods of your enemies. I tell you again they will not give these up to you without a struggle." The *goum* then breaks up into three or four bands, with a view to strike terror into the assailed from several different quarters at the same time. As soon as they are within range they open fire, but not a cry is uttered until their fire-arms have made themselves heard.

These *razzias* are for the most part frightful scenes of carnage. The men, taken off their guard, are nearly all put to the sword, but the women are merely stripped of their clothing and jewels. If time permit, the victors carry off with them the tents, the negroes, the horses, and the flocks, leaving the women and the children, for in the desert no one ever burdens himself with prisoners. On their return the flocks are committed to the custody of a few horsemen, while the others form themselves into a strong rearguard to cover the retreat. On reaching the *douar,* the combatants divide among themselves the flocks and the booty captured without personal risk, and give to the sheikh, over and above his share, thirty or forty ewes, or three or four camels, as the case may be, besides bestowing a special gratuity on the horsemen who where sent forward as scouts.

Previous to attempting an enterprise of this kind each tribe places itself under the protection of a particular marabout to whom it is in the habit of applying in difficult circumstances. In the eyes of the Saharene, to plunder an enemy, though an incident of no uncommon occurrence, is an affair by no means devoid of solemnity. It is thus that the tribe of the Arbâa regard as their regular and accredited marabout Sidi-Hamed-ben-Salem-Ould-Tedjiny. A successful *razzia* is celebrated by great rejoicings. In each tent an *ouadâa,* or feast, is prepared in honour of the marabouts, to which are invited the poor, the *tolbas,* or men of letters, the widows, the farriers, and the free negroes.

The *tehha* is usually achieved with five or six hundred horses, and not unfrequently foot soldiers accompany the expedition, mounted on camels. Sometimes the tribe that is to be attacked has received timely warning, and been able to adopt measures for defence. The horses are saddled, the arms ready to the hand. A combat takes place, instead of a massacre, and many fall on both sides. The assailants, however, have usually the advantage, as they are not embarrassed with women and children like their adversaries; and it rarely happens that they return home without booty.

Perhaps I cannot do better than reproduce in this place

one of those popular chaunts which so well depict the
rage and the varying fortune of these bloody struggles,
that generally originate in love or jealousy.

My horse is whiter than snow,
Whiter than the winding-sheet of men;
He will bound like a gazelle,
And will bear me to the tent of thy father.

O Yamina, fools are they who foster thy pride,
Greater fools they who tell me to forget thee!
Would that I were the pin* of thy *haïk;*
A lock of thy black hair,
The *meroueud†* that blackens thy eyes,
Or, still better, the carpet thou tramplest under foot.

I watered my horse at the fountain-head,
Then lightly leaped on his back.
My *chabir* are glued to his flanks,
And I have faith in my arms as I have faith in my own heart
They betrayed me for the moon of my soul,
But time shall betray them also.

By Allah, O ye vultures!
Why hover ye in the air?
I ask of Allah to grant us one of those bloody combats,
In which every one can die in health and not of disease.
You will pass days and nights in gorging yourselves!
Our lives and those of our horses,
Do they not belong to our maidens?

Away, strangers, away!
Leave the flowers of our plains
To the bees of the country.
Away, strangers, away!

O the generous One! Behold, then, the night
In which our *goums* shall burn powder
Close to the very *douar* of Yamina,
While the women are yet without their girdles,

---

* A thick silver pin used by women to fasten their *haïk,* a long piece of woollen,
stuff with which they robe themselves. In the desert this pin is called *khelala.*

† A small piece of polished wood, with which women smear on their eyelids the
kohol, or antimony, they value so highly.

And the horses have iron fastenings on their feet,
Before the *adlatouche** has been placed on the backs of the camels,
And the horsemen have drawn on their *temag.*
Grant that I may receive seven balls in my burnous,
Seven balls in my steed,
And that I may place seven † in the body of my rival.
The best of all loves is that which causes gnashing of teeth.

Strike out, young men, strike out! ◊
The bullets do not slay;
It is fate alone that takes life.
Strike out, young men, strike out!

The horse of Kaddour is dead, the horse of Kaddour is dead!
Publish it through your tribes, for they will rejoice at it;
But, if you are not Jews,
Add that, bleeding and wounded,
He was able to save his master and bear him out of the *mêlée.*
He was not one to be false to his ancestors,
Never had he been trained to flee,
He knew only how to throw himself on the foe.
Merouau is dead for Yamina—his days were counted!

O my heart! why art thou so bent
To make the waters flow back to the mountains?
Thou art the madman who giveth chace to the sun!
Believe me; cease to love a woman
Who will never say to thee, Yes.
The seed sown in a *sebkha* ⚥
Will never produce ears of corn.

THE KHROTEFA.

The object of the *razzia* called *khrotefa* is to carry off
a flock of camels grazing at a distance of seven or eight

---

* A kind of seat, more or less ornamented according to the means of each individual, which is placed on camel's backs for the use of women who are going on a journey. *Temag* are red morocco boots.

† Many Arabs in battle load their pieces with seven balls or deer-shot; but their fire-arms are generally in such bad condition that this practice becomes the source of innumerable accidents. The number of persons maimed by guns bursting in their hands is very considerable.

◊ " Dash on at full speed." The metaphor is taken from the act of swimming.

⚥ A salt soil that yields nothing but salt.

leagues from the tribe. From a hundred and fifty to two hundred horsemen join together as "a knot" and set out on the expedition. The reconnaissance is conducted in the same manner as for the *tehha,* only the arrangements are made with a view to arrive at the appointed spot towards *el aasseur*—three or four in the afternoon—and not at the *fedjeur,* or dawn of day.

When the *razzia* has been accomplished, and four, five, or six *ybal*—or flocks of one hundred camels each—have been driven off, they divide into two parties. The one, consisting of the weakest horses, goes forward with the booty, while the other forms a sort of rearguard whose duty it is, if necessary, to make head against the enemy. After appointing a rendez-vous for the morrow, the parties separate; but, in order to throw out the pursuers, those who are to check the enemy follow a different path to that taken by the drivers of the flocks.

In these forays the shepherds are usually spared; nor do they, indeed, take much trouble to defend property that does not belong to them. But the noise and shouting soon give the alarm. Every one saddles his horse and gallops forward; then they halt and rally, and finally appear in force upon the ground. Here again the assailants have every chance in their favour. They are on the look-out, and ready to receive the enemy. Their horses have had time to rest, while those of the tribe that has been plundered are exhausted and blown. Musket-shots are nevertheless exchanged, but night supervenes; and, as soon as the darkness has thickened so that "the eye begins to grow black," the plunderers decamp and go off at full gallop to rejoin their comrades, whom they overtake at sunrise. The pursuit lasts but a

short time. The conviction that the camels cannot be recovered, and the fear of falling into an ambuscade, soon induce the plundered tribe to return to their tents.

Although the actual fighting incidental to this kind of expedition is devoid of animation and soon interrupted by nightfall, they who take part in it do not the less run considerable risk. A horseman may receive a wound sufficiently severe to disable him from continuing his march. In that case he is lost, unless he happen to be a personage of distinction, for then he is certain not to be deserted. Some strong, vigourous fellow takes charge of him, lifts him up, places him across his saddle, and carries him home dead or alive. As for slight wounds, with the Arab saddle they do not give much trouble, nor do they prevent the return to the *goum*. On rejoining the tribe, the spoils are divided among those who shared in the *khrotefa*.

THE TERBIGUE.

In a *terbigue* not more than fifteen to twenty horsemen make "a knot," and propose to drive off the flocks from the very middle of a *douar*. They send some of their party to reconnoitre the tribe, and arrive close to the tents on one of the darkest nights. An isolated *douar* is selected, to which they approach as near as two or three hundred paces. Three of them dismount and stop, while one goes round to the opposite side, and makes a noise to attract the attention of the dogs. The people of the tribe fancy it is a passing hyœna, or a jackal, and take no notice of it. In the meanwhile the two other robbers penetrate into the interior of the *douar*, loosen the fastenings of ten, fifteen, or twenty camels, according as fortune favours them, and knock their shoes together, to frighten the liberated animals and cause them to run away. They then make off as quickly as they can, rejoin their horses, and all assist in collecting the scattered camels. After that they separate into two bands, one of which conducts the captured animals, while the others, lagging a little behind, allow themselves to be pursued in a different direction. If by chance they have succeeded in letting loose the *fadle,* or stallion, their success is certain, for all the females strive to follow him.

Siner, in these operations, the secret is generally well kept, they seldom fail, nor are accidents at all common. Should the *douar* be on its guard, the attacking party at once retires. They who venture upon such enterprises are usually well mounted, and speedily escape from a pursuit that is rendered almost impossible by the obscurity which effaces all traces and inspires dread of ambush. For a *razzia* of this sort, they do not hesitate to go thirty or forty leagues.

Sometimes incidents of a grotesque nature characterise the *terbigue*. When a party of horsemen does not care to leave a reserve to fight the enemy, they conceal themselves in an ambuscade seven or eight hundred steps from the *douar;* while the most experienced robber of the band strips himself naked, and, taking only his sword with him and tying his shoes to his head to look like enormous ears, penetrates into the *douar*. He carries in his hand an old saddle-bow, which he shakes in all directions, every now and striking the earth. To this dull sound he joins cries of alarm and terror : " The *goum!* the *goum!* up! up! We are betrayed!" The clamour, the jumping about, the strange aspect of the individual, and the noise of the saddle which he keeps on shaking, strike terror into the animals. Horses, sheep, and camels rush pell-mell out of the *douar,* and are caught by the concealed horsemen. The others rush out of their tents, snatch up their guns, and spring into the saddle; but flocks and plunderers are already far away, fleeing at full speed, and protected by the night.

The *terbigue* is, in fact, a robbery, but it is at the same time almost a warlike operation — it is, at least, a *razzia*. The strength of the party that executes the enterprise, the importance of the wrong inflicted upon an entire division of a tribe, the high qualities of the perpetrators of the robbery, who, after all, are real warriors,—all these circumstances taken together, if they do not suffice as a justification in the eyes of scrupulous Europeans, are esteemed in the desert as extremely plausible motives. Since a few brave and reckless fellows have imperilled their lives to injure a hostile tribe, there cannot be otherwise than joy and triumph in that to which they belong.

In the *khriana*, however, we descend a step lower, and arrive at a mere marauding expedition, executed by professional thieves. It is no longer war, even in miniature — it is nothing more than theft. It is no longer a subject of rejoicing for a whole tribe, though still a matter for praise and congratulation among friends; always provided the robbery has not been committed on their own or on a friendly tribe—which would be a disgrace—but absolutely on an enemy. They say, "Such a one is a brave man—he robs the enemy." As may readily be imagined, all thefts are not managed in the same manner, but are adapted to the nature of the capture that is proposed to be made.

HORSE-STEALING.

This species of theft is practised towards the end of the Mussulman month. When the moon is scarcely visible, five or six men, having a proper understanding between themselves, take a supply of provisions with them in their wallets, and go forth in search of adventures. Before starting, they give alms to the poor, and intreat them to intercede with Allah for the success of their enterprise. They then swear by some well-known marabout, generally Sidi-Abd-el-Kader, that, if they succeed, they will do him homage by putting aside a portion for the unfortunate. "O Sidi Abd-el-Kader," they exclaim, "if we return with joy, loaded with spoils and free from accident, we will give thee thy lance's share, if it please Allah!"

On leaving the *douar* the robbers travel in broad daylight, but, as they approach the tribe they propose to rob, they proceed only at night, and conceal themselves, when two or three leagues from the tents, in the bed of a river, or among the herbage, or in the mountains. As soon as the darkness has become dense, they issue from their hiding-place and try the different *douars* one after the other, stopping at last at that which seems the least securely guarded, and where the dogs are the least wakeful. If the robbers are six in number, four of them remain about fifty paces from the *douar*, silent and motionless, while the two others, the most daring and adroit, make their way into the interior. Before separating, they agree upon a pass-word; and then the two thieves go to work. If they find the dogs on the watch, they return for a third companion, whom they station a little way off, in front of the tent guarded by the vigilant dogs, and they themselves enter the *douar* from another quarter. They agree upon the tent they propose to rob; and while one of them, called the *gaad,* remains as a sentinel beside it, the other, the *hammaze,* pushes on to the horses. If the latter comes upon a horse or a mare, fastened only by leather thongs ropes, he unties or cuts the knot, seizes the animal by the *goulada,* or necklace of talismans, and leads it to the side opposite to where the dogs are held engaged by the *layahh,** the third accomplice who was stationed for that purpose in front of the tent. The *gaad* stays behind ready to shoot with a pistol, or to knock down with a stone or stick, the first man who comes out of the tent, and then to mislead the rest by flying in a direction different to that taken by his comrade with the horse. He then rejoins the *layahh,* and the two quickly come up with the *hammaze,* when all three return to their expectant companions. A second robbery is committed, if the *douar,* buried in sleep, has had no suspicion of what was going on; otherwise they prepare for flight. One of them, placing his folded *haïk* on the back of the horse so as to use it for stirrups, starts forward at a gallop, after naming a rendez-vous for the morrow or the day after. The others, to escape from the pursuit which is sure to be instituted in the morning, hide themselves during the whole of the first night. The

* *Layahh*, he who amuses, or distracts the attention.

one who mounted the horse only continues his flight if the theft has been committed in the first hours of the night; otherwise, he passes the whole of the morrow concealed in a dry and stony spot, where the animal would leave no trace.

Should the fastenings of the horse, instead of being woollen, be of iron, the operation is more difficult. The preliminary arrangments are the same, but, once fairly at work, the *hammaze* cautiously raises the clog up to the knee, and binds it there with his camel's rope, which he throws round the animal's neck, and leads it out very slowly. As soon as he has rejoined his comrades and is sufficiently far from the scene of his exploits, he bethinks him of giving his prize the liberty that is still wanting. He therefore removes the clog by means of a small saw, or picklock; at the worst he turns the padlock to the outside of the animal's legs and shatters it with a pistol ball, or else fills it with powder and blows it open. The explosion, however, rouses the owners of the animal, who set out in search of it, but nearly always in vain. The night is dark, and the robbers separate; though, if things come to the worst, they abandon their prize to save their lives.

Sometime the master of a tent is troubled by the barking of the dogs, and awakens his people by calling out to them, *El hayi rah hena,* "there is somebody here." They go out, and, finding nothing, they conclude that a hyœna, or a jackal, has occasioned the uproar, and so turn in again. The thieves then come out of their hiding places, and perhaps proceed to some other *douar* that is less upon the watch.

In preparing for a *khriana,* each one provides himself

with a pistol which he secretes under his burnous, a knife, a thick cudgel with a cord at one end, and a poniard. If a robber fancies that the dogs will distinguish him because of the whiteness of his garments, he leaves them with his comrades, and enters the *douar* entirely naked, his knife in one hand and the cudgel in the other. It is a popular belief in the Sahara that a man in a complete state of nudity is invisible in a dark night. A vicious horse, or one that is thoroughbred, or entire, is safe from robbers. Their habit of neighing on seeing a man would betray the plunderers. To avoid being scented by the dogs the precaution is taken to stalk up the wind. There are likewise other details which should not be neglected — the absence of moonlight, for instance. The twenty-first of the Mussulman month is the right time for setting out, and the night of the twenty-second is usually the most favourable for the execution of the enterprise. Dust and a high wind are useful allies, but rain is treacherous, for, by moistening the soil so as to retain foot-marks, it favours the pursuit. The cold season is the best for robberies of this character. There is a common saying : "In winter, cattle-stealing, because the dog sleeps in the tent. In summer, theft in the tent, because the dog goes away to sleep."

Like all other Arabs, the robber believes that Allah does not disdain to give him warnings—whence superstitious hopes and fears. If, on leaving the *douar*, he meets a black mare, dirty, lean, and altogether in bad condition, it is an evil omen and he goes back again. Another bad sign is to hear yourself called by people who know not whither you are going. To see two partridges is an auspicious augury, but one by itself portends calamity. To find yourself, on starting, confronted by a cheerful, courageous person, well dressed, and well mounted, infaillibly betokens success. An old woman, blind or maimed, and covered with rags, will certainly prevent you from succeeding. Start, however, with perfect confidence, if you have met a beautiful woman, richly dressed, to whom you have said : "Open thy girdle, Fatma, for that will bring us good fortune." She will not refuse to open to you the door to riches. It is equally desirable to see on one's road a woman carrying milk, and to drink a mouthful of it.

On their return, the robbers divide their spoils. The vow made to the marabouts who were invoked is scrupulously fulfilled. The chief of the *douar*, and the woman who opened her girdle, each receives a present. The share that falls to the lot of the *hammaze* is the largest; for it is he who has played the most important part, and incurred the greatest risks.

CAMEL-STEALING.

Camel-stealing is practised in the same manner as horse-stealing. They choose full grown camels,—or, at least, such as no longer cry—or she-camels with foal. Having removed the clogs, the robbers prick the animal with a poniard or knife to make it go off, and get on its back as soon as they are far enough away from the tents. All that night they travel on, and if at daybreak they do not feel that they have gone sufficiently far to escape the pursuit of horsemen, they halt and conceal themselves in a spot the soil of which does not retain foot-marks. The pursuers give up the chace if they find no traces of the fugitives. In the other event they often recover what they have lost; and, unless the robbers let go their prize and hide themselves, they may pay for their daring with their life.* This is the supreme moment for invocations and vows. "O Sidi Abd-el-Kader," cries the robber, on seeing the enemy close at hand, and in dread of discovery, "if thou wilt save us yet this one time, we will make in thy honour an *ouadda* for the poor." In the Sahara, Sidi Abd-el-Kader-el-Djilaly is the patron of robbers. This very undesirable patronage is due to the charity of the holy marabout, who shrinks from leaving in trouble those who invoke his name.

SHEEP-STEALING.

Sheep are but a poor prey, and more troublesome than profitable. They walk slowly, and it is impossible to drive them far enough away by the day after the theft. The Arabs, therefore, content themselves with stealing from an enemy, in his absence, to feed themselves while lying in ambush. Nevertheless, the opportunity is sometimes tempting. A flock is seen grazing at a distance from the *douars.* The shepherd is lying down, asleep, or in some other way occupied. It is yet early morning, and there is time to cover a considerable distance before sunset, when the flocks are driven home, and the theft is likely to be discovered. Sometimes, therefore, they risk the hazard. Striking the negligent shepherd a heavy blow on the head with a stick, they throw dust

---

* In some of the desert tribes a robber taken in the act is covered from head to foot with *alfa* (mat-weed), to which they set fire, and the poor wretch rushes away, amid general hooting, to die a little way off.

into his eyes, and, tying his hands behind him, draw over his face the hood of his burnous. The robbers then share with one another the task of driving off the flock, broken up into small sections, each taking a separate course, and going slowly at first, but after a while quickening their pace. On the morrow, after traversing none but lonely paths, they meet again at an appointed spot. In an affair of this kind they take the shepherd with them, and set him free only in the middle of the night, when they have nothing more to fear from him.

A caravan has been plundered—the women of the tribe have been insulted—the right of water and pasturage has been disputed. These are wrongs which no *razzia*, not even the terrible *tehha,* can sufficiently avenge. The chiefs, therefore, assemble and decide upon war. Then they write to the chiefs of all their allied tribes, and claim their aid. The allies are loyal and faithful—are they not also enemies of the tribe to be chastised? Have they not the same sympathies, the same interests, as those who summon them? Are they not an integral part of the confederation? Not a single tribe will refuse to send a contingent in proportion to its importance. But the allies are distant. They cannot arrive within a week or ten days, and in the meantime counsels are taken, and the passion of the warriors excited by the proclamations of the chiefs :—

"You are warned, O servants of Allah! that we have to exact vengeance from such a tribe that has offered us such or such an insult. Shoe your horses. Supply yourselves with provisions for a fortnight. Forget not the wheat, the barley, the dried meat, and the butter.

You must provide not only for your own wants, but also that you may be able to afford a generous hospitality to the horsemen of such and such tribes that are coming to our assistance. Command your prettiest women to hold themselves in readiness to accompany us, and to array themselves in their finest garments, and adorn their camels and litters to the utmost of their power. Do you yourselves also put on your handsomest dresses, for with us it is a matter of *nif* [self-love]. Keep your arms in good condition. Supply yourselves with powder, and be assembled on such a day at such a spot. The horseman who owns a mare and does not come, the foot-soldier who possesses a gun and stays at home, shall be fined, the former twenty ewes and the latter ten."

Every able-bodied man, though he should have to go on foot, is bound to join in the expedition. Before setting out, the chiefs confide the flocks, tents, and baggage of the tribe to the care of experienced veterans, who are likewise charged to exercise a sort of police supervision over this assembly of women, children, invalids, and shepherds.

The enemy, on their part, likewise make their preparations. Warned by travellers, by friends, and even by relatives whom they claim in the opposite party, they hasten to write in all directions to assemble their allies. Their flocks, tents, and baggage they place in a secure spot, and then assign a rendez-vous to the horsemen with the least possible delay. To guard against a surprise, they select a position suitable for defence, and await whatever may happen. They have not long to wait. The tribe that has taken up arms to avenge itself is very soon on the march, for it has not lost a single moment. On the evening before their departure, all the auxiliary chiefs join those who have summoned them, and, in the presence of the marabouts, take the following oath on the sacred book of Sidi Abd-Allah :—

"O friends! let us swear by the truth of the sacred book of Sidi Abd-Allah that we are brothers, that all our guns shall be as one, and that, in dying, we will all die by the same sabre. If you call us by day, we will come by day, and if you summon us by night, we will hasten to you by night."

Having taken this oath, they arrange to start on the following morning. At the appointed hour a man of high birth, noble among the noblest, mounts on horse-back, orders his women, borne on camels, to follow him, and gives the signal. There is a general movement, and all set out. The eye is dazzled by the strange and picturesque confusion, the many-hued crowd of horses, warriors, and camels bearing rich palanquins in which the women are inclosed. Here are the foot-soldiers, who march by themselves—there the horsemen, who superintend the female procession. Others, again, more impetuous and thoughtless, dash on in front or spread out on the flanks, but rather as hunters than as scouts, and with their greyhounds run down the gazelle, the hare, the antelope, and the ostrich. The chiefs, however, are more serious. Upon their shoulders rests the whole reponsibility. To them will accrue the largest share of the plunder, if the expedition succeed; and upon them, also, in the event of failure, will fall imprecations, ruin, and shame. They, therefore, consult together and form their plans. Lastly, come the camels that carry the supplies. Thus the host advances, adapting itself to the irregularities of the ground, all in wild confusion, every one noisy and joyous, thinking much of the adventure, nothing of the fatigue, dreaming of glory, not of danger. The warriors relate their former exploits, while the players on the flute accompany them, inspiriting or interrupting them, and the women utter joyful cries. And above all this uproar are heard the loud reports of fire-arms. The firing ceases, and a young and handsome horseman strikes up one of those love-songs, through which the ardour of their passion scatters stranges images and striking colours, and which, in the desert, have always a fresh charm for these chivalrous nations.

> My heart burns with fire
> For a woman come forth from paradise;
> O ye who know not Meryem [Mary],
> That miracle of the one Allah,
> I will show you her portrait.
>
> Meryem, she is Osman Bey himself
> When he appears with his standards.
>   And the roll of his drums,
> And his *goums* following behind.
>
> Meryem, she is a blood mare
>   That lives in luxury
>   In a gilded palace;
>   And loves the leafy shade,
>   And drinks limpid water,
> And will have negro slaves to wait upon her.
>
> Meryem, she is the moon of stars
>   That betrays robbers;
> Or, rather she is the palm-tree
> Of the country of the Beni-Mezab,*

* The Beni-Mezab form, in the midst of the populations of the desert, a small nation by themselves, distinguished by the severity of their manners, a peculiar dialect, honesty that has passed into a proverb, and certain differences in their religious ceremonies.

The fruit of which grows so high
  That no one can gather it.

Meryem, rather is she the gazelle,
  Bounding in the desert.
The hunter covers her young;
She sees the powder flash,
Leaps forward to receive the ball,
  And dies to save its life.

She appointed to meet me
  On Monday night.
My heart beat, she came,
  All enveloped in silk,
And threw herself into my arms.
Meryem has no sister [no equal]
In the four corners of the world!

She is worth all Tunis and Algiers,
  Tlemcen and Mascara,
Their shops, their shop-keepers,
And their perfumed stuffs.

She is worth the vessels
That traverse the azure deep with their sails,
  Going in search of the riches
  Which Allah has created for us.*

She is worth five hundred mares
  The fortune of a tribe,
When they hasten to the fight
Beneath their proud riders.

She is worth five hundred she-camels
  Followed by their little ones,
Besides a hundred negroes of the Soudan,
  Stolen by the Touareug †
  To serve Mahommedans.

* The Arab pride is here revealed in its full force. The produce of our horses, our camels, and our sheep, say they, exempts us from the necessity of working, and yet we can procure without difficulty all that these miserable Christians manufacture with so much labour.

† A large tribe of Berber origin who hold the gates of the Sahara and the Soudan, and levy upon caravans a tax for entering, a tax for leaving, and a tax for passing through, their territory. They deal, also, in slaves.

She is worth all the wandering Arabs,
   Happy and independent,
And those with fixed abodes,
   Unhappy victims
Of the caprice of Sultans.

Her head is adorned with pure silk,
Whence escapes in flowing curls
Her black hair perfumed with musk,
   Or with amber from Tunis;
Her teeth, you would say they were pearls
   Set in the reddest coral,
And her eyes, charged with blood,
   Wound like the arrows
Of the savage inhabitants of Bernou.*

Her saliva, I have tasted it,
Is the sugar of dried grapes,
   Or the honey of bees
In the flower of spring time.
Her neck is the mast of a ship
That ploughs the deep seas,
   With its white sails
To float along with the wind.

Her throat resembles the peach
Which is seen ripening on the tree;
Her shoulders are like polished ivory,
   And her rounded ribs
   Are the haughty sabres
   Drawn by the Djouad†
When weary of using their fire arms.
How many valiant horsemen
Have died for her in battle!

Oh! would that I possessed
The best horse of the desert,

* A negro kingdom to the southward, in which certain small tribes still make use of poisoned arrows.

† The Arabs give the name of *Djouad* to the military nobility who derive their origin from the Mehal, the conquerors from the East, and followers of the companions of the Prophet. The common people suffer much from the injustice and oppression of the Djouad, who strive to efface the memory of their ill-treatment, and maintain their influence, by generously according hospitality and protection to all who claim them. In other words, they combine in the highest degree the two salient traits ot the national character, avidity of gain, and love of pomp and ostentation.

> To ride pensive and alone
> By the side of her white she-camel!
> That horse would fill with rage
> The young men of the Sahara.
>
> I hunt, I pray, I fast,
> And follow the laws of the Prophet:
> But, were I forced to go to Mecca,
> Never would I forget Meryem.
> Yes, Meryem, with thy black lashes
> Thou wilt always be beautiful,
> And as delightful as a gift.

At the end of a few hours the heat becomes unpleasant, and a halt is called. The tents are pitched, breakfast is prepared, and the horses are unbridled and allowed to graze—and all rest themselves. As the sun goes down, the heat diminishes—it is now between two and three in the afternoon. To your saddles and forward, ye daring cavaliers! Display in a brilliant fantasia the worth of your horses and of yourselves. The women behold you; show them what you can do with a horse and a gun. Ah! more than one of you shall be rewarded for his prowess. Do you see that negro? He is bearing to one of you the recompense of his skill in managing his arms and his steed. He is the messenger to whose care one of the lovely spectators has confided the secret of her love, in charging him to deliver to the hero of the fantasia her *khrolkhral,* or anklets, or her *mekhranga,* or necklace of cloves.

It is not enough, however, to be a brave and skilful horseman—it is incumbent on thee, also, to be discreet. Thou hast a friend; to-morrow thou wilt give him thy horse and thy garments. Urge him strongly, for thy sister* wishes it, to show himself in the midst of the

* Sister is here used in the sense of lover or mistress.

goum upon thy steed and in thy dress, so as to deceive the other horsemen. In the mean time thou wilt pass unperceived as a humble foot-soldier, and wilt walk beside the camel that bears thy mistress. Attention! watch the favourable moment, and slip into her palanquin. She is just as impatient as thyself, and stretches her hand to thee. Profit by this assistance, and let thy movements outstrip suspicion.

In love, as in war, fortune favours the bold, but they have likewise the largest share of perils. If such meetings are frequent and nearly always successful, there is nevertheless risk to life; for, if the lovers are ever surprised, both of them perish without mercy. But who is there to betray them? All who surround them are in their favour. The lover tells his good fortune to his friends, all of whom are anxious to forward his happiness, and ten or a dozen *douros* have been sent to his mistress. Nor is this all. Her confidential servant has received two or three *douros,* and money has been freely distributed among her slaves and attendants. All, therefore, keep a good watch, and give timely notice to the lover when he must glide out of the litter, in the midst of the disorder and confusion caused by the pitching of the camp at the approach of night.

Previous to sunset, the chiefs reconnoitre a spot suitable for an encampment. It must be supplied with water, grass, and shrubs for fire-wood. On arriving at the place selected, each tent is pitched, the horses are unbridled and hobbled, as are also the camels, the negroes go in search of wood and grass, the women prepare the food, and they all sup. A thousand little scenes impart to a camp of this kind an aspect full of charm and novelty. Then total darkness envelopes the scene, unless there happen to be moonlight. The fires are extinguished—there is nothing alight to diminish the darkness. In the Sahara, oil and wax are alike unknown. Immediately after supper, each tent selects a man to watch the animals and the baggage. It is his business to prevent thefts, which his most active vigilance is, nevertheless, powerless to avert.

Not robbers alone wait for the night. Protected by the same obscurity, the lover, with the privity of his mistress, cautiously approachs the tent in which she reposes, raises the canvass, and guided by a devoted slave, takes the place of the husband who, fatigued by the day's journey, is sleeping in the men's chamber,—for in the tents of the desert there are always two distinct compartments, one for men, the other for women. Besides, it is deemed disgraceful for a man to pass the whole night by the side of his wife. There is nothing therefore, to interfere with these clandestine meetings. The presence of the two or three other wives permitted by the Mussulman law would certainly not be considered an obstacle. According to an Arab proverb, only a Jewess surpasses Shitan in trickery, but next to Shitan comes the Mussulmanee. It is a thing unheard of in the desert that women should denounce one another. But if, perchance, the adventure should seem too hazardous, the woman issues from the tent when every one is asleep, and proceeds to a spot she has indicated to her lover by means of one of the usual intermediary agents, the negroes and shepherds.

At the very hour that happy lovers meet, are accomplished schemes of vengeance. A rejected lover penetrates into the tent of the woman who has treated him with scorn, goes up to her, and shoots her with a pistol. At the sound of the explosion, the other women jump up, run against one another, and utter shrieks. The murderer, however, has had time to disappear, and the crime, perpetrated unseen, nearly always remains unpunished. Love adventures are common in the Sahara. Willingly or unwillingly, an Arab woman is sure to have lovers. The jealous precautions of the husbands excite and foment to an unnatural degree the libertine propensities of the women, by the very restraints that are placed upon them. To whatever class they belong, they pass their time in inventing stratagems to deceive their husbands while they are young, and, when they are old, to facilitate the amours of others.

The night is over; the sky is covered with a golden light; it is time to depart. The chiefs now send forward scouts to reconnoitre the enemy's position, and to form an opinion, from external signs, of his moral condition, and of the reinforcements he has received. The scouts advance very cautiously, and, when they are nearing the hostile camp, travel only at night. One of them is then detached on foot, who takes advantage of every irregularity of the ground to avoid being noticed, and oftentimes, disguised in rags, penetrates boldly into the midst of the *douars*. There he makes himself acquainted with the number of foot-soldiers, horses, and tents; observes whether they are laughing and amusing themselves, or if sadness reigns in the camp; and then returns to communicate the result of his investigations. The scouts remain all night in a concealed spot, impatient to discover what will be the attitude of the enemy at sunrise.

If he executes the fantasia and discharges his fire-arms, —if shouts of joy are heard, and singing, and the sound of the flute,—it is certain that he has received reinforcements, and troubles himself very little about the approaching attack.

The tribe continues its march until it is not above nine or ten leagues from the enemy. The advance has been made by short stages. The baggage, the women, the foot-soldiers, are so many causes of delay; but what has chiefly retarded the advance are the orders of the chiefs, who are desirous to afford time for reflection to those they proposed to chastise. It was acting prudently, and they were influenced by powerful motives. Who knew but that terms of peace might be asked for, accompanied by many presents for themselves, the leading councillors? Examples were not wanting to that effect—indeed, it was the usual custom. For them would be the cotton stuffs, the garments of cloth, the guns mounted in silver, the anklets, and the *douros!* When an affair takes such turn as this, an amicable arrangement is not far distant.

The two hostile bands are at length divided from one another by no more than ten leagues, and no propositions, direct or indirect, have been exchanged. Does the tribe recognise the impossibility of resistance, or will it accept battle? If it declines the contest, it assembles the most influential marabouts, and furnishes them with money and presents, towards which each individual has contributed his share. These holy men then proceed to the opposite camp in the middle of the night, under the protection of a chief who has received timely notice of their coming, after being seduced by their gifts. By him they are conducted to another, who is in like manner induced to accept the presents offered to him.   The two now accompany the messengers of peace to a third chief, and so on to others, until they have gained the votes of all the most powerful.   Then, and not till then, do the marabouts, secure of a friendly audience, unfold the propositions they are instructed to make — expressing themselves after this fashion :— "We have come only for the love of Allah.   You know we are marabouts, and that we desire only what is right.   For our sake, you must come to terms with the Mussulmans who have sent us.   That is far better than bringing down upon us all the calamities of war, ruin and death.   If you will do what is right, Allah will bless you, yourselves, your wives, your children, your mares, and your she-camels. If you choose what is wrong, may it recoil upon your own heads.   We repeat, make peace, and may Allah curse the demon !"

Having first raised a few difficulties for form's sake, the chiefs finish by saying in reply to the marabouts :— "Well! we will make peace for the sake of Allah, and for your sake, but on the following conditions : 1st, You will restore to us the objects, goods or animals, which were taken from us when your people robbed our caravan at such a place.   2nd, You will pay the *dya*** of our people slain by yours on such a day.   3rd, You will restore to us all the flocks that were carried off from us by your people on such a day, in such a *khrotefa*. 4th, You will restore to us all the camels and horses which your thieves have stolen from us, and which are still within your bounds."

---

* Blood money. In the Sahara the *dya* is reckoned at three hundred sheep, or fifty three-year old camels.

The marabouts accept these conditions, and guarantee their fulfilment. The sacred book of Sidi Abd-Alla is then produced, and the chiefs swear to make peace. After the oath has been taken, they who have come to prevent the shedding of blood return to their tribe, to give an account of what has been decided, and compel them to execute the terms which they have just guaranteed. On the morrow the tribe that has accorded peace continues its march, and encamps within a league of the enemy. It is barely installed, when the marabouts and chiefs of the opposite party arrive with the ratification that was stipulated. The leading men of the two rival camps meet together, and again swear on the book of Sidi Abd-Allah :— "By the truth of Sidi Abd-Allah, we swear that there shall not again be between us *razzia*, or theft, or murder, or reprisals [*ousiga*], that we are brothers, and that our guns shall henceforth fire in accord."

The marabouts of both parties next read the *fatahh*, or religious invocation, and conclude with these words : "Allah bless you, our children, for having thus buried the knife of contention, and prosper you in your families and in your goods!" The marabouts are afterwards visited by the chiefs of both sides who present to them offerings called *zyara*, literally a visit.

Peace concluded, the tribe that had put itself into motion retraces its steps, and at its departure executes a fantasia of the most noisy character. The horses caracole, reports of fire-arms resound, and the women utter loud cries. All is joy, happiness, and delirium. A dozen of the chiefs of this tribe remain in the midst of their late enemies, and receive from them a splendid hospitality, and even costly presents. And at their departure they take with them some of their hosts, and requite their new-found friends with a generous welcome. These truces last a considerable time; that is, from one to two years.

Peace, however, would certainly not have been concluded if the marabouts who came to intercede for it had not presented themselves under cover of the night. Had they come in the day-time, the Arabs, discerning their intrigues, would have exclaimed out of jealousy: "By the sin of our women! we will fight. This one has received cloth-goods, that one money, another jewels, a fourth cotton-stuffs, and that other one arms. But we, whose brothers are dead, whose flocks have been carried, we have got nothing, Yes, we swear it by Sidi Abd-Allah, the powder shall speak." And, in truth, the powder very often does speak, and without the envious having had any cause to complain of the presents made to their chiefs, and without their having prevented the latter from entering into negociations, and accepting conditions from which no advantage would accrue to the commonalty. This happens when the tribe threatened has resolved to oppose force to force, and has prepared for a struggle.

In the latter event the enemy is allowed to approach within a day's march. No advances are made, no propositions offered. The march is therefore continued on the morrow, and the camp is pitched about two leagues from that of the tribe which awaits the assault. The scouts of the two parties come into collision, and, mutually exasperating each another, prelude actual hostilities by insults. A few musket shots are exchanged, and they cry out to one another :— "O Fatma, daughters of Fatma! The night has arrived; why go on to-day? To-morrow shall be called your day." Or, "Dogs, sons of dogs, wait till to-morrow! If you are men, you will meet us."

The skirmishers fall back, and the leaders on both sides organise as quickly as possible a guard of one hundred horsemen and one hundred foot-soldiers, to insure the safety of the camp. On the morrow they watch each other attentively. If one party strike their tents, the others do the same; or if they leave their tents pitched, and advance to the combat with horses and foot, and with the women mounted on camels, the example is followed on the other side. The cavaliers of the two tribes confront one another. The women are placed in the rear, ready to excite the combatants by their cries and applause, and are themselves protected by the foot-soldiers who form the reserve. The battle begins by small parties of ten or a dozen horsemen bearing down upon the flanks, and trying to turn the enemy. The chiefs, at the head of a tolerably compact mass, keep in the centre. Presently the affair grows warm and animated. The bravest and best mounted of the young men dash forward, carried away by passion and the thirst for blood. Uncovering their heads, they strike up their war-songs, and excite themselves by loud outcries :—

"Where are they who have mistresses? It is beneath their eyes that the warriors will combat this day!

"Where are they who, in the presence of the chiefs, were always boasting of their valour? It is to-day that tongues should be long, and not in peaceful gossipings.

"Where are they who run after fame?

"Forward, sons of powder! You see before you those sons of Jews! Our sabre shall drink of their blood, and their goods we will give to our women.

"Strike out, young men! Strike out! It is not the balls that kill, but fate."

These shouts madden the horsemen. They make their steeds rear up on end, and fire off their pieces. Every face asks for blood. They rush together, and at last attack each other with the sabre. One party or the other, however, soon gives way, and begins to fall back upon the camels carrying the women. Then shrieks arise from both sides. These scream with joy, to animate yet more the victors — those utter wrathful and terrible imprecations, to rally the failing courage of their husbands and brothers.

"Look at those famous warriors who show off with their bright stirrups and splendid garments at marriage-feasts and festivals! Look at them running away and abandoning even their women! O Jews, and sons of Jews! alight and let us mount your horses, and from henceforth you shall no longer be counted among men. Oh! Allah curse all cowards!"

These railings recall the spirit of the vanquished. They make a vigorous effort, and, supported by the fire of the foot-soldiers who are in reserve, they recover the lost ground, and even hurl the enemy back into the midst of his own women, who now rail as loudly as they lately applauded. The struggle is renewed on the ground that separates the women of the two tribes. During these varying phases the contest has been very desperate, and before long the side that has most men and horses wounded, that has lost the greatest number, and, above all, that has witnessed the fall of its most valiant chiefs, takes to flight, notwithstanding the exhortations and prayers of a few energetic men, who fly from right to left, trying to rally the fugitives and restore the fight. These brave fellows cry aloud:— "Are there any men here, or are there not? Hold your own souls! If you flee, they will carry off your women and leave you nothing but shame. Die! Let it not be said: 'They fled!' Die! and you will yet live!"

A beautiful and touching scene will, perhaps, then be enacted. A chief of the highest rank, in despair at being defeated, throws himself into the *mêlée* to seek death, but is held back by the young men who gather round him, and beseech him to retire. "Thou art our father!" they will exclaim; "What will become of us if thou shouldst perish? It is our duty to die for thee. We will not remain as sheep without a shepherd." A handful of warriors still endeavour to make head against the foe, but they are swept away in the general rout, and soon find themselves by the side of their women. Every one, then, seeing that all is lost, devotes himself to saving what is dearest to him. As rapidly as possible they make to the rear, only from time to time facing about to check the pursuit of the enemy.

The audacity of desperation has more than once changed the face of things. Aïssa-ben-el-Sheriff, a child of fourteen, mounted on horseback with his tribe to repel an attack directed by Sid-el-Djedid. The Arbâa were beginning to give way and take to flight, when the boy, throwing himself before them, tried to stop them: "What! he exclaimed, "You are men, and are afraid! You have been brought up in the midst of powder, and do not know how to burn it! Did you pay all that attention to your mares only to make use of them in fight?" And when the others replied, "Djedid! Djedid! Look at Djedid!" "Djedid," continued the child. "It is a single man that makes you flee! Behold, then, this terrible warrior, who puts hundreds to the rout, checked in his victorious career by a child!" With these words he dashed his spurs into his horse's flanks, and came up with the redoutable warrior. Djedid, fearing nothing from a mere boy, was off his guard, but the latter threw himself round his neck, entwined his arms round him, and, leaving his own horse, hung by one arm, while with the other he endeavoured to stab him with his knife. Astonished at such audacity, and hampered in his movements, Djedid strove in vain to shake him off, but with all his presence of mind he was unable to parry the boy's frequent thrusts. Puzzled what to do, he slipped off his horse, hoping to crush Aïssa in his fall. The latter, however, succeeded in avoiding him, and throwing himself on the courser of the dreaded chief, rejoined his tribe, to whom he exhibited a trophy that made the oldest warrior blush for the momentary panic to which they had yielded.

Were it not that the conquerors usually build a golden bridge for the conquered, the latter might be easily destroyed; but the thirst for pillage gains the day, and the victors disperse in search of plunder. One despoils a foot-soldier, another a horseman whom he has overthrown; another, again, leads away a steed, and yet another a negro. Thanks to this disorder, the bravest of the discomfited tribe succeed in saving their women, and even their tents. When the pillage is at an end, the horsemen of the victorious tribe are anxious to return home, and their chiefs encourage the desire. "We have slain numbers," say they. "We have seized their horses, captured their women, taken their guns, and refreshed our souls by making orphans of these sons of dogs. Our best plan now is to go and sleep at such a place, for the enemy, strengthened by his reinforcements, may possibly resume the offensive and attack us during the night." The baggage is sent forward in front, and, protected by a strong rearguard, during the first few days they continue their march until nightfall.

In this species of warfare, the greatest respect is shown to the captive women. Men of low birth, indeed, despoil them of their jewels, but the chiefs make it a point of honour to restore them to their husbands, with their camels, their jewels, and their ornaments. They even take pains to properly array those who have been robbed, before sending them back.

In the desert, they make no prisoners, and cut off no heads, and they have a horror of mutilating the wounded, who are left, however, to themselves to escape or perish, for no one takes any trouble about them. Rare examples of cruelty do sometimes occur, but these are acts of private revenge, when men have recognised the murderers of those who were dear to them, a friend or brother.

On reaching their own territory, the tribe is welcomed by extraordinary rejoicings. The universal exultation betrays itself by the liveliest demonstrations. The women draw up their camels in a single row, and utter cries of joy at regular intervals. The young men execute in their presence a fantasia of the wildest description. Salutations, embraces, and interrogations are exchanged on all sides. Food is prepared for the warriors and their allies, and the chiefs collect the sum that is to be divided among them. A common horseman never receives less than ten *douros,* or an article of equal value. This recompense, called *zebeun,* is obligatory, and is given over and above the plunder each may have seized for himself; and, in addition to this, three camels are bestowed upon every cavalier who has lost a horse. It is needless to add that a larger sum than ten *douros* is offered to the chiefs of the allied tribes, whose influence has been so successful. They receive their share like the others, but in secret they are presented with money, or articles of considerable value, such as carpets, tents, arms, horses, etc., etc.

A generous hospitality is offered to the allies; and on the morrow, when they set out to return to their own territories, the chiefs mount on horseback and accompany them. After riding on together for two or three hours, they renew the mutual oath never to raise but one war-shout, never to make but one and the same gun, to come in the morning if summoned in the morning, and to come at night if summoned at night. In the desert, if feuds are keen and hereditary, sympathies, on the other hand, are also numerous and profound. The following verses illustrate the extreme degree of delicacy and devotedness to which the sentiment of friendship is carried by the Arabs:

> If a friend does not walk as blindly as a child,
> If he does not voluntarily expose himself to death,
> Forgetting that suicide is a crime,

He shall have no place in the tents of our tribes.
I will obey the summons of my friend.
Though the morning light should be the reflection of swords,
Though the darkness of night should be the cloud of dust raised
by the tramp of horses,
I will go to die or to be happy.
The smallest of the sacrifices to which I have agreed is death.
Can I live far away from the place of refuge so dear to me?
Can I support the absence of neighbours to whom I have become
accustomed.

It may be naturally asked why a tribe that is menaced with an attack, but will not make the necessary sacrifices to obtain peace, does not flee, instead of awaiting the assault. To flee, is to invite pursuit while in the disorder of a retreat. It means leaving one's country, exposing oneself to scarcity of water for the flocks, or even falling into the hands of some other enemy, who would certainly take advantage of this opportunity for pillage and revenge. The wisest plan is to choose a good position, assemble the allies, and await the enemy if confident in one's own strength, or else to make concessions if conscious of weakness.

"O Allah! save us and save our horses. Every day we lie down in a new country. It may be that She remembers our vigils with the flutes and tabours."

REMARKS BY THE EMIR ABD-EL-KADER.

How can any strange people contend with us, who are brought up in the highest sense of honour, even above all the tribes collected in the great assemblies? Do we not advance against the enemy on horses of pure race, terrible as raging lions, that gallop wildly along the perilous mountain path?

I have prepared, against the time when fortune shall be unfavourable to me, a noble courser of perfect shape, and which none can rival in swiftness.

I have also a flashing sabre which severs at a stroke the body of an enemy. And yet fortune has treated me as if I had never tasted the pleasure of bestriding an air-drinker;

As if I had never rested my heart on the virgin bosom of a well-beloved maiden, with legs adorned with bracelets of gold;

As if I had never felt the anguish of separation;

As if I had never taken part in the exciting spectacle of our blood horses surprising the enemy at the break of day;

As if, in short, after a defeat, I had never brought back the runaways to the fight, by crying aloud :—

"Fatma! daughters of Fatma!

"Death is a tax levied on our heads; turn the neck of your horses, and repeat the charge.

"Time turns upon itself and returns.

"Would that I could throw the world on its face!"

On returning to their *douars* after a *razzia,* or an expedition, the Arabs of the desert proceed to divide the spoils in equal shares, a certain portion being set aside for special cases. Thus a cavalier who has slain another in battle is entitled to the horse of the deceased, to his arms, garments, harness, pouch, and *djebira*. "In fact, he has risked a life to take a life, and will have to answer before Allah for the death he has inflicted, rightly or wrongly."   A horse that is captured without its owner being killed, is comprised among the general stock to be divided.   If a horseman has been slain by several persons firing simultaneously, without it being clearly shown by whose hand he fell, his spoils are equally shared by all.   In some tribes, the plunder reverts to the chief when it cannot be proved from whose gun the fatal ball was fired.   Should a cavalier learn after the fight is over, that he has killed an enemy with his own hand, and be able to produce witnesses to the deed, he obtains restitution of the entire plunder of the slain.

When a tribe makes an expedition against another

tribe, each individual retains whatever he has taken in *haïks,* burnouses, arms, and garments; but tents, flocks, horses, mules, camels, provisions, and grain, are public property. The chief alone is entitled, over and above an ordinary share, to thirty or forty ewes, or three or four camels, as the case may be. Even should he not have accompanied the tribe in person, he would still be assigned what is called the *akeud ek-sheikh,* or the sheikh's knot. If any one, not caring to join the expedition, has lent his mare to a friend, he shares the booty acquired by the latter. If the animal be killed and any prize is made, the value of the mare is deducted and paid over to her owner, for she had gone for the service of the tribe. Should the result be unfavourable, the owner puts up with his loss—"he sought his good fortune."

Whoever offers a supply of food to a party of horsemen is entitled to a share if the party prove successful, as he was interested in the expedition.

A "lance" [one share] is given to the farrier of the tribe, for he contributes his skill and labour to the success of the enterprise. To kill a farrier is deemed infamous. It is a deed that will recoil upon the guilty tribe, who will be pursued by a curse ever after.

He who takes off his burnous and goes up to the enemy with the butt end of his rifle in the air, must also be spared.

Shepherds, likewise, have their life accorded to them.

A special share of the plunder is reserved for those who have been sent forward as scouts previous to the attack upon the enemy. It is their just recompense for offering their lives to secure the triumph of their brethren. If a scout loses his mare, he is compensated by one hundred ewes, or another mare, or by one hundred Spanish *douros*. There is no exaggeration in this estimate, for it is always the best mounted who are selected. If a band returns with booty, a "lance" is bestowed upon the woman of distinction who goes forth from her tent, and lifts up her voice in honour of the victors. In an affair of *nif* (self-love), the pretty women who accompany the expedition to animate the combatants are entitled to a share of the spoils. Whoever lends his rifle, receives one-fourth of the share that falls to the lot of the borrower.

Suppose an Arab finds a horse at pasture away from its owner, at a time when his tribe happens to be attacked, or is on the point of setting out on an expedition. Suppose he takes the animal, and places on its back a borrowed saddle. Suppose, further, that this saddle is not complete; but that he gets stirrups from one, a girth from another, a bridle and a breast-band from a third, until at last he is completly equipped. He sets out and returns with plunder; but the proprietor of the horse has no right to any portion of it. Had the animal been killed, the owner would have been reimbursed, in the event of success; but if it is brought back safe and sound, he cannot claim anything : "The animal has been nothing more than an instrument of Allah to render service to the brave horseman who exposed himself for the public good." The proprietors, however, of the different parts of the equipment are entitled to a share. The wanderers of the desert have an apologue quite in the Arab style which exactly defines the respective dues of each :

"Quoth the saddle-tree to the horseman : 'Do you

purpose to keep all the prize to yourself? Who furnished you with a seat? What would you have done had you not found me there?'

"A pretty story!" exclaims the girth. "The service you brag of, was it after all so very great? Why, you would have done more harm than good, had I not held you on the horse's back."

"Gently, gently!" cry the stirrups. "I acknowledge you may both of you have been useful in your way; but pray tell me who supported the horseman when he dashed forward? On whom did he lean when he made use of his rifle to bring down the enemy from whom he took the spoils about which you are wrangling so sharply? Who was it that enabled him to look far ahead, to stoop down, or turn round, according as he wished to strike a blow, or to avoid one with which he was threatened?"

"It was you," replied the bridle. "There is no deny-ing the truth. And yet, O my sons, by Allah, master of the world! our horseman would not have much riches to boast of to-day had he employed only your services. You did not take the road to the plunder, and assuredly you would be far enough from it now had I not guided you. Cease, then, these disputes. The palm is mine, for it was I alone who enabled you to reach the goal."

"Ah! that is rather too much of a good thing!" the horse ironically observes, after listening thus far without uttering a word. "Somehow I fancied that the greatest praise was due to myself. I thought I had seen you lying forgotten in a corner, and that you were picked up only because I had been found. I was dreaming, no doubt, and it is you who have carried me. I own that I was mistaken. Take me back, then, as quickly as possible to my pasture, or at least let me hear no more of your squabbles."

"To put an end to all this jangling, the horseman divided his booty into six equal parts, one of which he gave to the saddle-tree, one to the girth, and one to the bridle, and kept the three others for himself. Leading the horse back to the pasture he said to him : 'I do not give thee anything, for thou hast the honour of having been useful to thy tribe.'"

If any one lends a saddle complete, he is entitled to one-half share. This distribution is called *âadet esserdj*, or the custom of the saddle.

When on the point of starting on an expedition, the *goum* offers up the following invocations : " O Sidi Abd-el-Kader - el-Djilaly! O Sidi -Sheik-ben-el-Dine! O Sidi-el-Hadj-bou-Hafeus! If we succeed and return safe and sound, we promise a camel to each of you. Protect us!" Before any division takes place these three camels are always put aside for the marabouts.

The division of the plunder, as may be imagined, is never carried out without many remonstrances, for the prevention or repression of which the *mekadim* were instituted. Sometimes the chiefs make choice of five or six individuals of approved discretion. At other times, after a *razzia* or capture of property, the booty is divided into four equal parts. They who execute the enterprise form themselves into four sections, and each section names a *mekadem* whose business it is to manage the subdivision. The *mekadim* search out and demand the restitution of all articles concealed by dishonourable persons, such as jewelry, money, coral, etc. When an

Arab is suspected of having purloined things in this manner, and nothing is found upon him, the *mekadim* make him swear by Sidi-Ben-Abd-Allah, and that oath clears him. In the Sahara, Sidi-Ben-Abd-Allah is held in great veneration. No one would dare to invoke his name falsely, through fear of dying, or of seeing his flocks waste away. The *mekadim* are acknowledged to be honest among pilferers. They are well treated and receive a handsome remuneration, consisting for the most parts of articles not included in the division of the spoils.

REMARKS BY THE EMIR ABD-EL-KADER.

I have surprised them with horses of pure race, with sleek coats, foreheads adorned with stars announcing good fortune, flanks lean through exercise, and flesh firm and hard. I have fallen upon them like a cloud charged with lightning that hangs over a defile.

It is a horse that, without ever being fatigued, always finishes by asking pardon of his rider. His head is lean, his ears and lips fine, his nostrils well open, his neck slender, his skin black and soft, his coat sleek, and his joints large. By the head of the Prophet! he is of noble race, and you would never ask how much he cost if you had seen him marching against the enemy.

When you see the horses of the *goum* marching proudly, their heads up, and making the air re-echo with their neighings, rest assured that victory accompanies them. But, on the other hand, when you see the horses of the *goum* marching sadly, with their heads down, without neighing, but lashing themselves with their tails, be sure that fortune has abandoned them.

Nevertheless, Allah is wiser than man.

Oh! would that I could see my blood flowing over my *haïk,* white as ivory from Soudan! It would be the more beautiful for it.

In the desert there are two principal modes of hunting the ostrich—on horseback, and in ambush. There is, indeed, a third method which is only a modification of the second, and consists in killing the bird while drinking at a stream of water.

The true sport is on horseback. Watching for the bird is no better than taking a sitting shot with us. The former is a noble and royal pastime, the latter is only fit for a common fellow, or a poacher. It is not enough to kill, the thing is to run the bird down. For this purpose the general sort of education given to a horse will not suffice. A special preparation is required, just as a race-horse needs a particular training for some days previous to the contest.

Seven or eight days before a hunting expedition, both grass and straw are entirely stopped, and nothing but barley given. The horse is watered only once a day, at sunset, when the water begins to get cool, and he is then washed all over. He is taken out for a long ride every day, now walking, now galloping, during which the rider carefully ascertains that nothing is wanting to the equipment proper for the purpose. At the end of these seven or eight days, say the Arabs, the belly disappears, while the neck, chest, and croup show firm flesh. The animal is then ready to endure the fatigue. This special training is called *teshaha*.

The equipment also is modified with a view to lighten the weight. The stirrups should be much less heavy than usual, the saddle-bow very light, the two *kerbouss,* or pommels, of less than the ordinary height and without the *stara*. The breast-band is likewise omitted, and instead of the seven pieces of felt only two are used. The bridle, in like manner undergoes several metamorphoses. The blinkers and headstall are omitted as too heavy, the bit being simply fastened to a tolerably stout camel-rope, without any throat-band, and kept in its place by a make-shift headstall of cord. The reins are also very light, but strong. All four feet are shod.

The most favourable season for this sport is during the great heats of summer. The higher the temperature, the less energy does the ostrich possess to defend itself. The Arabs describe the exact period by saying that it is when a man, standing upright, casts a shadow no longer than the sole of his foot. Ostrich hunting implies a regular expedition lasting over seven or eight days. It requires preparatory arrangments which are concerted by ten or a dozen horsemen bound in "a knot," as for a *razzia*. Each hunter is accompanied by a servant, called a *zemmal,* who is mounted on a camel that carries, besides, four goat-skin bags filled with water, barley for the horse, wheaten flour, another kind of flour parched, dates, a pot to boil the food in, leather thongs, a needle, and a set of horse-shoes and nails.

Each hunter should take only one woollen or cotton shirt, and one pair of woollen trousers. He winds round his neck and ears a kind of thin stuff called in the desert *haouli,* and fastens it with his camel-rope. His feet are protected by sandals attached by cords, but he also puts on light gaiters [*trabag*]. He takes neither rifle, nor pistol, nor powder. His only weapon is a club of wild olive or tamarisk, four or five feet long and terminating in a very heavy knob. The party do not start until they have ascertained from travellers, or caravans, or from messengers sent forward for that purpose, where a large number of ostriches are collected at one point. These birds are generally met with in places where there is a good deal of grass, and where rain has recently fallen. According to the Arabs, whenever the ostrich sees the lightnings flash and a thunder storm coming on, it immediately hastens in that direction, however distant it may be, for it thinks nothing of going ten days on the stretch. In the desert it is proverbially said of a man who is particularly careful in tending his flocks and supplying them with what is necessary, that "he is like the ostrich—where he sees the lightning flash, he is there."

The start is made in the morning. At the end of one or two days' march, when the hunters have arrived near to the spot where they were told to look for ostriches, and where tracks are observable, they halt and bivouac. On the morrow two intelligent servants, stripped to the skin, and wearing nothing but a handkerchief round their loins, are sent forward to reconnoitre. They take with them a goat's-skin bag suspended from the side, and a small quantity of bread, and walk on until they come upon the ostriches, which usually keep to the high ground. As soon as they have sighted them, they lie down and observe their movements; and then, while one remains, the other returns to the camp, and says that he has seen thirty, forty, sixty ostriches—it is alleged that *djeliba* or troops to that number are really to be met with. At certain times, and especially when mating, the ostriches are seldom found more than three or four couples together.

Guided by the man who has brought the information, the hunters advance cautiously in the direction of the ostriches, and on nearing the hillock on which the birds were sighted, they use every precaution to avoid being seen. Having at length reached the last inequality of ground that affords them any sort of cover, they dismount, and two scouts crawl forward to make sure that the birds are still in the same place. If these bring confirmation of the former tidings, each rider gives his horse a small draught of the water brought on a camel's back, for it is rare to find a place where water is to be had. The baggage is piled up where the halt takes place, without any one being left to watch it, so certain are they of being able to retrace their steps to the identical spot. Every hunter is provided with a *chibouta,* or goat's-skin bag of water. The attendants follow the tracks of the horses—the camel carrying only the horses' evening feed of barley and his own, and water for both men and animals.

Carefully reconnoitring the ground occupied by the ostriches, the hunters concert their mode of attack. Spreading out, they gradually form a circle, in which they inclose the quarry at a sufficient distance not to be seen, for the ostrich is very far-sighted. The attendants fill up the gaps between the horsemen. Then, when all are at their respective posts, the latter advance straight upon the ostriches, who flee panic-stricken, but are met by the horsemen, who at first content themselves by driving them back within the circle. The ostrich thus exhausts its strength by the rapidity of its movements; for, when surprised, it does not "husband its wind." Again and again it repeats the same manœuvre, always trying to break through the circle and always driven back in affright. At the first symptoms of fatigue, the hunters dash at them, and presently the troop scatters in all directions. Those that are losing strength open out their wings, which is a sure sign of weariness. The hunters, now secure of their prey, hold in their horses. Each one picks out a bird, rides after it, overtakes it, and, either from behind or from the side, fetches it a terrible blow on the head with the cudgel already mentioned. The head is bald and very sensitive, whereas others parts of the body would offer greater resistance. Stunned with the blow, the ostrich falls to the ground, and the hunter, springing out of his saddle, cuts its throat, taking care, however, to hold it away from the body, so that the wings may not be stained with the blood.

The *delim,* or male bird, when its throat is cut, especially if near its young ones, moans in a lamentable manner, but the *reumda,* or female, utters not a sound. When the ostrich is on the point of being overtaken, it is so exhausted that, if the hunter is willing to spare its life, it is easy for him to lead it away captive, guiding it with his cudgel; for by that time it can scarcely walk.

Immediately after being bled, the bird is carefully skinned, so as not to spoil the feathers, and the skin is stretched on a tree or on a horse.   When the camels arrive, salt is plentifully rubbed in.

The servants now light fires and prepare the pots, in which they boil for a long time over a fierce fire all the fat of the bird.   As soon as it is reduced to a very liquid state, it is poured into a sort of leather bottle formed of the skin stripped off from the thigh to the foot, and strongly tied at the lower end; it would spoil if put into skin taken from any other part of the body.   The fat of an ostrich in good condition ought to fill both its legs.   When the bird is brooding, it is very lean, and at that time its fat would certainly not fill both legs; and it is, at that time, hunted only for the sake of its feathers. The rest of the flesh is served up for the hunters' supper, seasoned with flour and pepper.

The attendants having watered the horses and given them a feed of barley, and the hunters having refreshed themselves, they hasten, no matter how fatiguing the chace may have been, to return to the spot where they left their baggage.   There they remain forty eight hours to rest their horses, on whom they bestow the greatest care.   After that, they regain their tents.   Sometimes they send the produce of the chace to the *douar,* whence the servants bring back a fresh supply of provisions, and, on receiving favourable intelligence, they start on a new expedition.

In the desert, the male bird is called *delim;* the female, *reumda;* a one-year old, *ral;* over one year, *oulid gleub;* a two-year old, *oulid bou gleubtin;* a three-year old, *garah,* at which age the bird attains its full growth.

The fat of the ostrich is used in the preparation of food — of kouskoussou, for instance — and it is likewise eaten with bread. The Arabs also apply it as a remedy in many diseases. It is sold in the market-place, and in the tents of the rich a store of it is often kept to give away to the poor, as a medicine. It is not, however, by any means expensive — one pot of ostrich grease being exchanged for only three pots of butter.

The plumes are sold in the *kuesours,* at Tougourt and at Leghrouât, and among the Beni-Mzab, who, at the time of the purchase of grain, bring ostrich skins down to the seaboard. Among the Oulad-Sidi-Shikh the skin of the male was formerly sold at from four to five *douros,* and that of the female at from ten to fifteen francs; but of late the price has risen considerably. In the Sahara, before our time, the beautiful ostrich plumes were only used to ornament the top of a tent or a straw hat. The Shamba strengthen their shoes with the skin of the under part of an ostrich's foot. They place a strip under the toes, and another under the heel, and the sole will thus wear a long time. With the sinews they make laces to sow the saddles, and to mend various articles made of leather.

In the eyes of the Arab ostrich hunting possesses the double charm of profit and pleasure. It is a favourite exercise of the horsemen of the Sahara, and it is also a remunerative enterprise, the value of the skin and fat much more than covering the expense. Notwithstanding the numerous train indispensable for this species of sport, it is not by any means the exclusive privilege of the rich. Any poor man who feels that he can acquit himself well can generally contrive to join a party of horsemen who propose to hunt the ostrich. He goes to a wealthy Arab, who lends him a camel, a horse and harness, and two-thirds of the barley required, two-thirds of the goat-skins, and two-thirds of the supply of food. The other third of all things is provided by the borrower, and the produce of the chace is divided between the two in the same proportions. The servant who, during the expedition, rides the camel lent to the poor man, receives from the latter two *boudjous* for every male killed, and one *boudjou* for every female. He is, besides, fed from the provisions taken with him by the horseman.

The ostrich is also hunted by lying in ambush, after it has laid its eggs, or towards the middle of November. Five or six horsemen, taking with them a couple of camels loaded with supplies for at least a month, go in search of places where rain has recently fallen, or where ponds are to be found. In such localities there is certain to be abundance of herbage, which never fails to attract the ostriches in considerable numbers. To avoid idle wanderings to and fro, they question every individual, every caravan, they happen to meet: besides, they know beforehand the most likely stations. On these occasions they provide themselves, not with a cudgel, but with a rifle and an ample supply of powder and ball.

As soon as they come upon ostrich tracks, the hunters examine them closely. If they appear only in the form of patches here and there eaten down to the ground, it shows that the ostrich has come here merely to graze. But if the tracks cross each other in all directions, if the grass has been trampled under foot, but not eaten, it is a sure sign that the ostrich has made her nest in the

neighbourhood. The hunters thereupon search attentively for the spot where she has deposited her eggs, and
approach it with the greatest precautions. While the
ostrich is digging out her nest, all day long her plaintive
moanings may be heard, but after her eggs are laid she
never utters her usual cry until about three in the
afternoon.

The female sits on her eggs from morning till mid-day,
while the male goes to the pasture. At noon he returns,
and the female goes to feed in her turn. When she
comes back, she places herself four or five paces from
the nest, in front of the male, who incubates all night.
The male himself keeps watch over the eggs to defend
them from all enemies. Jackals, among others, often
times place themselves in ambush near at hand ready to
play them an evil turn, and their bodies have frequently
been found by the hunters lying not far from the nests,
stricken to death by the male—the female being too
timid to inspire any fear.

It is in the morning, during the time the female is
sitting, that the hunters dig on each side of the nest,
and not above twenty paces distant, a hole deep enough
to contain a man. They then cover it over with the
long grass so common in the desert, so that only his rifle
is seen. The best marksmen are, of course, placed in
these holes.

Seeing all these preparations, the female takes fright,
and runs off to join the male, who beats her and compels
her to return to the nest. If these preparations were to
be made while the male is brooding, he would go off to
join the female, and neither of them would ever come
back again.

When the female returns to the nest, they take care not to molest her, it being the rule to kill the male in the first instance.   It is, therefore, customary to await his return from the pasture, which happens about noon, when the hunter holds himself ready.   The ostrich, while engaged in incubation, spreads out its wings so as to cover all the eggs.   In this position, with its legs bent under the body, the thighs are very conspicuous. This circumstance is favourable to the marksman who aims to break the leg of the bird.   All chance of escape is thus cut away, which would not be the case were it is wounded in any other part.   As soon as the ostrich is down the hunters run up and cut its throat.   The two marksmen come out of their holes, and their companions, attracted by the report, lend their assistance.   All traces of blood are quickly covered with sand, and the body of the bird carefully concealed.   At sunset the female returns as usual to pass the night close to the nest. The absence of the male causes her no anxiety, for she fancies he has merely gone away to feed, and she quietly sits upon the eggs.   She is then killed in the same manner as her mate, by the hunter who has not previously fired.   The one who shot the male receives a *douro* in addition to his proper share; but if, what rarely happens, he should miss his aim, he pays to his companions the value of the bird : "We chose thee," they say, "as the best shot : we placed thee in the good position to do us a benefit, and lo! thou workest us such a wrong as this.   Thou shalt pay for it."   The hunter who killed the female receives only an egg over and above his share.   If he miss, he forfeits what would have come to him from the price of the male and the eggs.

The one who is to fire at the male is appointed before-hand.

The nest of an ordinary couple contains from twenty five to thirty eggs, but it frequently happens that several couples combine to lay in common. In that case, they form a large enclosure, and the oldest couple are placed in the centre, with the others around them in regular order—so that, if they are four in number, they will occupy the four angles of a square. When the eggs are all laid they are pushed towards the centre, but not min-gled together; and when the oldest male comes to sit the others take their places around, where their eggs were laid—and the same with the females. These companies are composed of the young of the same family—in fact, of the young of the oldest couple. They do not all lay the same number of eggs. The one-year olds, for instance, do not lay more than four or five, and those of a small size. At times as many as a hundred eggs are found in the same nest. These family gather-ings are most common where the herbage is most abundant. The Arabs have observed a very singular circumstance. The eggs of each couple in these monster nests are carefully piled up together, with one egg conspicuously at the top. It is the one first laid, and it serves for a special purpose. As soon as the male perceives that the moment has arrived for hatching, he breaks with his beak the egg he judges to be the most forward, and at the same time very carefully makes a small hole in the one which surmounts the others. The latter furnishes their first meal to all the young ones as they are hatched, and, though open, will remain sweet for a considerable time. This quality is peculiarly useful; for the male does not break all the eggs on the same day, but only three or four at a time, when he hears the young ones moving inside. The egg which sup-- plies them with nourishment is always liquid, whether through the prevision of nature, or that the old birds have instinctively avoided sitting on it.

The fledglings, after having partaken of their first meal, and being speedily dried in the sun, begin at once to run about, and at the end of a few days follow the parent birds to the pasture : in the nest, they always nestle under their wings. The nest is generally of a circular form, and is formed in a sandy soil. The ostrich constructs it with its feet, by simply throwing out the sand from the centre to the circumference. The dust raised by this operation may be seen at some distance. The period of incubation lasts ninety nights.

The hunters eat the eggs if they are fresh, and not near ready to be hatched. The shells they either throw away, or take with them, to give as presents to friends, or to deposit them in the *koubba*.* However, for some time past, the Arabs have become aware that eggs are an article of traffic on the seaboard, and they now reserve them for that object.

The ambush hunt is very lucrative. It is quite possible to kill several birds and carry off their eggs. At that season, the ostrich itself is very lean; but, on the other hand, the feathers are better and hold more firmly together. Where several couples are assembled together in one nest, it is only the oldest male and female that are killed. Were the hunters to make as many holes as

* A small square chapel surmounted by a dome, in which a marabout has usually been interred. Solitary travellers find in them a resting place.

there are birds, they would very soon be discovered, and the whole company would take to flight.

According to the Arabs, ostriches kill vipers with a stroke of their beak, and swallow them. They eat, also, serpents, locusts, scorpions, lizards, and a very large fruit called *hadj,* abundant in the desert, and produced by a creeping plant, bitter as turpentine, having leaves like those of a water-melon : in short, they digest anything, even stones. Such is the voracity of this bird that where it is kept in a domesticated state, it bolts everything it comes across, knives, jewelry, bits of iron. The Arab who gave me these details declared that a woman one day had a coral necklace snatched from her neck and swallowed by an ostrich, and I have heard an officer of the African army relate how one tore off and bolted a button from his tunic. It is at the same time very adroit, and will snatch a date from a man's lips without hurting him. When lightnings flash and announce a coming storm, they cannot contain themselves for joy. They jump about, and hasten towards the water of which they are so fond, though capable of long endurance of thirst.

Paternal love is a strong passion in the male ostrich. He never deserts his young, and fears no danger, be it what it may, whether from dogs, hyœnas, or man himself. The female, on the contrary, is easily frightened, and forsakes all in her terror. Thus, in speaking of a man who defends his tent with courage, they compare him to the *delim;* while a feeble, timid man is likened to the *reumda.* Ostriches are generally met travelling together in couples, or in family parties of four or five couples. But, where rain has fallen, one is certain to find two or three hundreds of these birds together. From a distance, they resemble a flock of camels. They never approach a spot that is inhabited except to drink, after which they flee away in haste.

The Arabs hunt the young of the ostrich by a very simple method. Once upon the track, and at a short distance from the birds, they begin to shout aloud. The young ones, being frightened, run for protection to the parent birds; and the hunters, coming up with them, seize upon their prey in spite of the male, and under his very eyes. The *delim* becomes terribly excited, and exhibits the most poignant grief. Sometimes greyhounds are employed in this sport. While the old birds are defending themselves against the dogs, the hunters carry off the little ones without any difficulty, and bring them up in their tents, where they are easily tamed. They play with the children and sleep under the canvass. In the wanderings of the tribe they follow the camels. There is no instance of any bird brought up in this way taking to flight. They are full of spirits, and frolic with the horsemen, dogs, etc., etc. Does a hare happen to start up, away go the men in full chace, and the ostrich, becoming excited, rushes after them and takes part in the hunt. If it meets in the *douar* a child with something in its hand of an eatable nature, it lays him gently on the ground, and endeavours to take it from him. The ostrich is a great thief; or rather, as I have already said, it desires to swallow everything it sees. The Arabs, therefore, distrust it when they are counting out money, for two or three *douros* would soon disappear.

It is no uncommon thing to see a wearied child placed

on the back of an ostrich. The bird proceeds with its burden straight to the tent, the little fellow holding on by its pinions. But it would not submit to carry a heavier load—a man, for example, but would hurl him to the ground by a blow from its wing. On the march, in order to keep it from running about to the right or left, they pass a cord round one of its hocks, to which they fasten another cord by which to hold it. In the desert, the ostrich has no other enemy to fear than man. It can repel the dog, the jackal, the hyœna, and the eagle, but yields, perforce, to man.

I mentioned that there was a third mode of hunting the ostrich, when on its way to water. The Arabs simply make a hole near the water, conceal themselves in it, and fire upon the creature as it approaches to drink.

Ostrich hunting, in the Sahara, makes numerous and excellent marksmen, who practice at hitting nothing but the head, in order that the blood may not stain the feathers. A marksman of note always carries a chaplet of talismans behind the lock of his rifle, and his name is quoted in the tribes. Among the defenders of Zaatcha there was more than one crack hunter of ostriches.

The ostrich drinks every fifth day if water is to be had : if not, it can endure thirst for a long time. Ostrich hunting is a very profitable sport. The Arabs say of a successful speculation : "It is an excellent transaction —as good as an ostrich hunt."

The Arab to whom I am indebted for these particulars is an Oulad-Sidi-Shikh, named Abd-el-Kader-Mohammed-ben-Kaddour, a professional hunter. According to him, the country for ostriches is comprised in a triangle contained by lines drawn from Insalah to Figuig, from South to North—from Figuig to Sidi-Okba, from West to East—and from Sidi-Okba to Ouargla, from North to South.

The chace of the gazelle is not, like that of the ostrich, at the same time a lucrative and a toilsome enterprise—it is merely an exercise, a pastime, a party of pleasure. The gazelle is barely worth a franc or a franc and a half, and it is not for such a valueless prey that an Arab will prepare, train, fatigue, and even risk the loss of a horse, —as frequently happens in ostrich hunting. Besides, in this species of sport, the chief credit belongs neither to the man nor to the horse,—for whom it is, properly speaking, nothing more than a promenade—but to the greyhound, that other companion of the noble of the desert, of whom I shall have occasion to speak hereafter.

If the gazelle be of little value, it is because it is by no means rare. Everywhere, but above all in Sersou, is found the *sine,* or diminutive gazelle; in the Tell and in mountainous districts, the *ademi,* the largest kind; and in the Sahara, the *rime,* or intermediate species, distinguished by the whiteness of its belly and thighs, and the length of its horns. All these varieties alike travel in herds of four, five, ten, twenty, thirty, a hundred; and not unfrequently as many as two or three hundred are found herding together. At a distance they may be taken for the flocks of an emigrating tribe. A herd of gazelles is called a *djeliba*.

Gazelle hunting is not a sport exclusively reserved for horsemen. In the incessant and daily wanderings of the Sahara tribes, as soon as the camp is fixed near a fountain or river, the hunters set off in great numbers, taking care to go up the wind. The gazelles possessing a very fine sense of smell, the scent of the men wafted on the wind would soon put them to flight. The hunter advances under shelter of bush after bush, and from time to time imitates the cry of the gazelle. The latter stops, looks about on all sides, and seeks the companion it supposes to have gone astray. The hunter approaches close to it, and may even be seen without scaring it away. At a proper distance he pulls the trigger, and rarely misses his aim, "unless a spell cast upon his rifle causes it to hang fire, and prevents it from going off during the whole day." At the sound of the report the entire herd dashes off at top speed, but at the end of a league or a league and a half, their fright has passed off with the recollection of the cause of their alarm, and they again halt and go on browsing as before.

The genuine hunter is a hardy, indefatigable walker. Experience teaches him in what direction the herd is likely to stop, and to that he bends his steps. Again he conceals himself and repeats the former manœuvre. In this manner, in the course of the day, he can bring down three or four gazelles, which his friends or servants will lift up and carry to the camp in triumph. In the spring time, when the *djedi,* or fawns, sleep amidst the *alfa,* having taken their fill of the milk of their mother, it is easy to catch a dozen or fifteen of them in a single morning. It is the old hind that generally betrays them.

But not such is the sport of persons of distinction, of the real horsemen. What the great chiefs affect is to hunt them on horseback. A dozen or fifteen cavaliers take the field, accompanied by their servants, and seven or eight greyhounds, and carrying with them tents and provisions. Directing their course towards a place where gazelles are usually found, they ride forward at a venture. When a herd of gazelles appears in the distance, they proceed towards it, covering their advance as much as possible by means of shrubs and the inequalities of the ground. When they get within a quarter of a league, the attendants who hold the hounds in leash, squeezing their throats to prevent them from giving tongue, dismount and let them slip. No sooner do they find themselves free than they go off like an arrow, the Arabs stimulating them to still greater speed by shouts and passionate invocations: "My brother! my lord! my friend! there they are!" The horsemen follow leisurely at a gentle gallop, so as not to be quite thrown out; and behind them comes the baggage. The best greyhounds will not fairly overtake the herd until after a course of two or three leagues. Then, at last, the spectacle becomes full of incident and interest. A thoroughbred greyhound picks out the finest animal of the herd, and springs forward. A contest of agility and swiftness ensues. The gazelle doubles, now to the right, now to the left, bounds forwards and backwards, leaps even over the greyhound, and strives sometimes to throw him out, sometimes to strike him with its horns. Its windings and doublings are all to no purpose. Ardent and indefatigable, its enemy hangs close upon its track. When on the point of being pulled down it utters plaintive cries, and chants, as it were, its death song—song of death to it, but of victory to the greyhound who seizes it by the back of the neck, and snaps the vertebral column with its teeth. The gazelle falls to the ground, and lies motionless at the feet of the victor, until the hunters come up and cut the throat of the still living animal.

Now, as every true Believer should conform to the Law, and as it is possible that he may not reach the spot for a quarter of an hour after the gazelle has been pulled down, the hunters, before letting the hounds loose, do not omit to exclaim : *Bi es-sem Allah! Allah akbar!* "In the name of Allah! Allah is great!" For the Prophet hath said : "When thou hast let loose thy dog and hast invoked the name of Allah, if thy dog has not killed the game that he has overtaken, and thou hast found it yet alive, cut its throat to purify* it; and if it was already dead when thou hast found it, and thy dog has not eaten of it, thou mayest eat of it." If the previous invocation was omitted through accident, the game may still be eaten; but not if the omission has been voluntary.

The horsemen who are well mounted, and own the best greyhounds, renew the chace, and not until the evening do men and animals take rest. Sometimes the hunters cook the gazelle on the spot where they have pitched their camp. At other times, on their return home on the morrow, they send the product of the chace to their friends and relatives, and these presents give rise to

---

* In order to make the purification complete, it is necessary to cut through the œsophagus, the tracheal artery, and the two jugular veins.

family feastings at which the chief dish consists of the flesh of this animal, so highly esteemed by the Arabs. Gazelles are brought up in the tents, and are driven with the sheep at every change of encampment; but in the end they always contrive to escape. The winter is the proper season for hunting the gazelle and the antelope. The earth, softened by the heavy rains, retards and embarrasses their flight, while the dogs and horses find water everywhere. When the snow is on the ground, if a party of Arabs come upon a herd of gazelles, a regular massacre ensues. They are then unable to run, and being famished are easily overtaken. Ten or a dozen may be killed by each Arab. In hunting this animal the Arabs take with them three burnouses, boots, and shoes, and carry the horse-cloth upon the top of the saddle.

The proverbial beauty of the gazelle's eyes, and the whiteness of its teeth, have given rise to a curious practice. Women with child have one brought to them that they may lick its eyes with their tongue, in the belief that the eyes of their infant will have the same lustrous melancholy. Under a similar idea they touch its teeth with a finger, which they afterwards put into their own mouth. The horns, shaved thin and mounted in silver, are used by women as instruments to put *kohol* on their eyes; and the skin, after being carefully tanned, is made into *mezoueud,* or cushions, in which they enclose their most valuable articles.

If it were necessary to prove how aristocratic are the habits of the people of the Sahara, how lordly their tastes, I could give yet another very simple proof, which some persons may regard as puerile—I mean the love they have for the *slougui,* or greyhound.

In the Sahara, as in all Arab countries, the dog is looked upon as a servant in disgrace, troublesome, and cast off, no matter how useful he may be in guarding the *douar,* or in looking after the flocks. The greyhound alone enjoys the esteem, the consideration, the tender attention of his master. The rich as well as the poor regard him as a companion of their chivalrous pastimes; while for the latter he is also the purveyor that supplies them with food. They do not grudge him, therefore, the most assiduous care. The couplings are as scrupulously superintended as those of their horses. A Saharene will go twenty or thirty leagues to couple a handsome greyhound bitch with a dog of established reputation; for one that is really famous will run down a gazelle. "When he perceives a gazelle cropping a blade of grass, he overtakes her before she has time to swallow what she already holds in her mouth." This is an hyperbolical expression, no doubt, but still it is based on a certain degree of truth.

When the *slouguïa*, or bitch, has pupped, the litter is never lost sight of for an instant. The women will sometimes give their own milk to them. Visitors arrive in troops, the more numerous and eager according to the reputation of the mother. They surround the owner, offering him dates, kouskoussou, etc. There is no sort of flattery they will not lavish upon him in the hope of obtaining a pup: "I am thy friend. Prithee, give me what I ask of thee. I will attend thee in thy hunts," etc. To all these solicitations, the owner usually replies that he will not decide upon what pups he means to keep for himself until after seven days. This reservation has its motive in a very singular observation, or fancy, of the Arabs: in every litter, one of the pups gets upon the back of the others. Is it a sign of greater vigour? or is it mere chance? To ascertain this point they remove it from its habitual position, and if it returns to it for seven consecutive days, the owner builds upon it such extravagant expectations, that he would not accept a negress in exchange. A prejudice causes them to attach the greatest value to the first, third, and fifth pups, in fact, to all the odd numbers.

The pups are weaned at the end of forty days, but are still fed with goat's, or camel's milk, thickened with dates, or kouskoussou. In the Sahara, the flocks are so numerous and milk so abundant, that it is not at all surprising that wealthy Arabs, after having weaned their greyhound pups, should set aside so many she-goats for their nourishment. When the pups are three or four months old, their education commences. The boys drive out of their holes the jerboa, or the rat called *boualal,* and set the pups at them. The latter by degrees get excited, dash after them at full speed, bark furiously at their holes, and only give up the pursuit to begin another. At the age of five or six months, they are assigned a prey more difficult to catch—the hare. Men on foot lead the greyhound close to the form where the animal is couched. Then, by a slight exclamation, they set the young dog, who rushes at the hare, and soon acquires the habit of coursing with speed and intelligence. From the hare, they pass to the young of the gazelle. The Arabs approach the spot where these are lying near their mother, and direct the attention of the greyhound to them. As soon as he is thoroughly excited and rears up with impatience, they let him go. After a few lessons of this kind, the greyhound understands perfectly what to do, and begins to press forward resolutely in chace of the old hinds themselves.

When a year old the greyhound has very nearly reached its full strength. His scent is developed, and he follows the gazelle by its slot. Nevertheless, he is kept under some restraint, and not until the age of fifteen to eighteen months is he regularly allowed to hunt. From that period, however, he is held in leash, and often with great difficulty; for the Arabs say that when the greyhound scents the game, his muscular power becomes so great that, if he stiffens himself upon his paws, a man can hardly make him lift a leg. As soon as he sights a herd of thirty or forty gazelles, he trembles with joy, and looks up at his master, who cries to him : "Ah son of a Jew! thou canst not say this time

that thou didst not see them." The hunter then takes
off his goat's-skin bag, and pours a little water on the
back and belly of the hound, who, in his impatience,
casts a suppliant eye on his master. At last, he is free
and bounds forward. Presently, he tries to hide himself,
stoops down, and follows a circuitous course until he is
within an easy distance, when he springs forward with
all his might, and picks out for his victim the finest male
in the herd. When the hunter cuts up the gazelle, he
throws to the *slougui* the flesh around the kidneys. If
he were to offer him the intestines, he would reject them
with disdain.

The greyhound that cannot hunt at two years old, will
never be able do so. There is a saying to this effect,

> A greyhound after two years
> And a man after two fasts [fifteen years];

meaning thereby that that is the proper age to judge
what either will ever be worth.

The greyhound is an intelligent animal and full of self-
love. If, in slipping him, a fine gazelle is pointed out to
him, and he kills only a common looking one, he is very
sensible of the reproaches addressed to him, and slinks
off, ashamed of himself, without claiming his portion.
He has no lack of vanity, and indulges much in fantasia.
A thoroughbred *slougui* will neither eat nor drink from
a dirty vessel, and refuses milk in which the hand has
been dipped. Has he not been taught this disdainful
daintiness? And yet the utmost that is done for the
common dog, their faithful and vigilant guardian, is to
let him find his food among the offal and bones that are
lying about. And while the latter is driven with hoot-

ings from tent and table, the greyhound sleeps in the
compartment reserved for men, on carpets by his
master's side, or on his very bed.   He is clothed and
sheltered from the cold, like the horse, and is even
preferred for being chilly, as that is an additional proof
of the purity of his race.   The women take pleasure in
bedecking him with ornaments, in tying collars of shells
round his neck, and in securing him from the evil eye
by fastening talismans on him.   He is fed with care,
nicety, and caution, kouskoussou being lavished upon
him.   In summer-time, to give him strength, they make
a paste of milk and dates, of which the stones have been
extracted.   There are some who never feed their greyhounds during the day.   Nor is this all.   The *slougui*
accompanies his master when on a visit, and receives
the same hospitality with him, having a portion of every
dish.

A thoroughbred greyhound will hunt with no one but
his master.   By his cleanliness, his respect for decency
and the graciousness of his manner, he shows that he
recognizes the attention paid to him.   On his master's
return after a somewhat prolonged absence, the *slougui*
leaps with a bound on to his saddle, and caresses him.
The Arabs talk to him: "O friend, listen to me!   You
must bring me some meat.   I am tired of eating dates,"
and flatter him in many ways.   The petted animal leaps
about in a frolicsome manner, and seems not only to
understand but to wish to reply.   The death of a *slougui*
fills the whole tent with mourning, the women and
children bewailing him as if he were one of the family.
Sometimes it falls to the greyhound to find food for all,
and one that nourishes a family can never be for sale.

Now and then, however, he may be given away in compliance with the supplications of women and relatives, or of the most respected marabouts.

A greyhound that catches with ease the *sine* and the *ademi,* is worth a she-camel; but one that can overtake the *rime* is priced as a valuable horse. They are very generally named *ghezal* or *ghezala,* "a gazelle." Frequently wagers are laid on such or such a *slougui,* the stakes being sheep, or a feast of *taam,* dates, etc.

The greyhound of the Sahara is far superior to that of the Tell. He is of a tawny colour, and tall, with a sharp snout, broad forehead, short ears, and muscular neck; the muscles of the hindquarters being, also, very prominent. He has no belly, clean limbs, well detached sinews, the hock near the ground, the under part of the paw small and dry, the palate and the tongue black, and the hair very soft. Between the two ilia, there should be the breadth of four fingers, and the tip of the tail should be able to pass under the thigh and reach the hip-bone. Both the fore-arms are generally fired in five lines to harden the muscles.

The most renowned greyhounds of the Sahara are those of the Hamiân, the Oulad-Sidi-Shikh, the Harar, the Arbâa, and the Oulad-Naïl.

———

The sporting equipments of a noble of the Sahara are complete when he has a *thair el horr,* or a bird of race; for there men of distinction are still addicted to falconry. The *thair el horr* is of a dark yellow plumage, with a short, powerful bill, thick, muscular thighs, and very sharp talons. It is very rare, and is caught in the following manner. When a *thair el horr* has been sighted, they put a tame pigeon into a small net, and throw it up into the air in front of the bird of prey, who swoops down upon it. Her talons, however, get entangled in the net, so that she can neither draw them out, nor fly away, and is thus easily secured. When the falcon finds herself a prisoner, she shows no signs of fear or anger. There is a saying in the desert which is often quoted in seasons of calamity :

A bird of race, when she is caught, never frets.

Rings are passed round her legs and she is fastened to a small perch prepared for her in the tent. To accustom her to the presence of men, they cover her head with a hood, which allows only the beak to appear.

Her master unhoods her, gives her fresh meat, holds her on his fist, and caresses and speaks to her as much as possible before a numerous company, to accustom her to noise. At the end of a month the bird knows her master, and is thoroughly tamed. They then take a leveret and tie it by one leg, the hawk also being held fast by a very long "creance." They unhood her, and let the leveret go before her eyes. As soon as the bird sees it, she rises into the air, uttering cries. The leveret stops and squats down, when the falcon swoops and kills it with a blow of her talons. The owner runs up, draws the leveret, and gives a portion to the bird. This manœuvre is repeated until the falcon shows no desire to fly away, which is known by her remaining beside the animal she has killed. The falcon, naturally disposed to seize her prey, is further looked upon as trained, when she answers to the call before she has pounced upon her quarry.

Having arrived at this point, the bird may |be taken out to hunt. The owner mounts his horse and takes her with him, hooded, and perched upon his head or his shoulders. As soon as he sees a hare, he unhoods her and excites her with his voice. The falcon soars into the air, and swoops down suddenly with a sharp cry, and kills the animal with a single blow; after which the hood is immediately put on again. Sometimes the hare is killed so far off that the hunter cannot bleed it in time, according to the religious injunction; but this inconvenience is obviated by his exclaiming, when he throws off the bird, *Bi es-sem Allah! Allah akbar*—"in the name of Allah! Allah is great!" If the falcon has devoured a part of the game, the rest may be eaten by the hunter, because the bird of prey has been trained to return to her master when he calls her, and not to eat the game. A bird of race will no more eat carrion ¡than will an eagle. She will kill hares, rabbits, the young of the gazelle, the *habara*—a bird, they say, as big as a bustard—pigeons, and turtle-doves.

The principal tribes of the Sahara that practice hawking are : in the province of Constantine, the Douaouda, the Selmya, the Oulad-Moulat, the Oulad-ben-Aly, the Sahari, the Oulad-Mahdi, the Oulad-Bou-Azid, the Rahman, and the Oulad-Zid; in the province of Algiers, the Bou-Aysh, the Oulad-Mokhtar, the Oulad-Yagoub, the Oulad-Shayb, the Oulad-Ayad, the Mouidat, the Zenakha, the Abadlya, the Oulad-Naïl; and in the province of Oran, the Hassasna, the Rezayna, the Oulad-Mhalla, the Beni-Mathar, the Derraga, the Harar, the Angades, the Hamyân, the Oulad-Sidi-Shikh, and the Oulad-Khelif; and the inhabitants of all the regions where *alfa* grows in abundance. Hawking is also pursued in the higher table-lands, on the borders of the Sahara.

REMARKS BY THE EMIR ABD-EL-KADER.

The Arabs recognize four species of birds of noble race, which they employ in the chace. These are the *berana,* the *terakel,* the *nebala,* and the *bahara.* The *berana* and the *terakel* are the most esteemed; especially the *terakel,* which is the largest—the female sometimes attaining the size of an ordinary eagle. This species has black wings, gray on the under side. The belly is black and white, the tail black, as is also the head when young, but gradually turning gray and then white as the bird grows older. Its beak is very hard and sharp, and its talons solid and vigorous. The *berana* is less strong and somewhat smaller than the *terakel*. Its wings are of a whitish gray, its breast white, its tail gray and white, the latter predominating. The head is of many hues, but there also white is the dominant colour. The *bahara* is almost entirely black, with the exception of a few whitish spots on the breast. "It is a negro, and not worth much." In the *nebala*, gray predominates; there are some white spots, however, on the wings, and the feet are yellow. All these birds mew at the end of summer.

In certain districts, the following species are likewise valued; the *shashin,* the *aogab,* the *meguernes,* and the *baz*. The *baz* is the most courageous. Its plumage is of a dark red, its eyes deep set, with arched eyelids, its shoulders wide apart, its feathers soft, its breast broad, its rump thick, its tail short, its thighs wide apart, its legs white, and its feet broad. The heavier it feels on the hand, the swifter it is on the wing. It is said that its wind is bad.

The bird of noble race is given away rather than sold; whoever catches one takes it to the master of a large tent, who makes him a present in return. It is in the summer-time that they endeavour to procure these noble birds, in order to have time to train them for the hawking season, which is towards the end of autumn. They go to work in the following manner.

They envelope a pigeon in a sort of shirt made of horse-hair and a quantity of wool. A horseman rides about a desert place carrying this lure with him, and when he sees a bird of race, throws it up into the air and then hides himself. The falcon stoops and strikes it, but her legs and talons become entangled in the wool and hair, and her struggles only make her position worse. At last, stupefied and exhausted, she finishes by alighting, or rather by falling on the ground, when the horseman issues from his hiding place and secures her. A perch is prepared for her in the chief's own tent, to which the bird is fastened by an elegant thong of *filali*.* It is needless to add that the greatest care is taken to attach the jesses, so as not to hurt the bird, or cause her unnecessary inconvenience. The master of the tent feeds her with his own hands once a day, about two in the afternoon. Her ordinary food is raw mutton, very clean, and carefully cut up. She is not stinted as to quantity, may eat to satiety, and is even expected to improve in condition.

By way of commencing her education, they proceed in this manner. They show her a large piece of flesh, and at the same time call to her three times, with a cry that may be represented by the sound long drawn out of "Ouye! ouye! ouye!" The bird throws herself upon the meat, which is not given up to her, but which she fights hard to get hold of. They draw it away slowly, still showing it to her and teasing her, until she is quite exhausted, when they give her several small morsels on her perch. Up to that time, the falcon is kept scrupulously within the tent, remaining hood-winked all day, and also during the first few nights, until she is accustomed to live with the women and children, the dogs

* A kind of leather dressed at Tafilalet.

and other animals. This last point is difficult to manage, and is never completely achieved.

When the "gentle" bird has got thus far, when she is used to accept her food upon the perch, in the manner above described, the circle of her prison is extended. She is fastened by the foot to a cord, or creance, of camel's hair, soft and pliable, from fifty to sixty cubits in length, which allows her to go abroad. Outside of the tent, they repeat the lesson of calls to come and be fed, cautiously feeling their way. The falcon is in this manner tended a long time within the tent, going out only to receive her food. When her master is quite sure of having accustomed her to himself, he takes her with him on his fist to a considerable distance, putting on and off her hood several times, at different intervals. It is not without difficulty, without many struggles, that the bird accommodates herself to the scene abroad, but by degrees she becomes used to that also.

At this period, the last touch is given to her education, by means of the same calls, the same alternations of teasing and gratifying; but far from the tent and the *douar,* without hood and without leash, her food is given to her. As soon as she is gorged, the hood and leash are replaced. After that, her master never moves a step without her perched upon his fist. But this is not enough. The bird is only tamed—she has yet to be trained for the sport. Accordingly, they take a hare and cut its throat, disclosing the gash by drawing back the skin, so as to let the flesh appear. Then, inside the tent, they take off the hood of the falcon, who springs at the throat of the animal, and is allowed to worry it for a time in order to get a taste for it; and a little later they give her some of the flesh. This manœuvre is repeated seven or eight days following, with a live hare, whose ears the master keeps pulling to make it squeal, while he himself utters the call "Ouye! Ouye!" The falcon precipitates herself on the head of the animal and fights for it, pecking out the eyes, and sometimes the tongue. The hare is then opened, and some of the flesh given to the bird. This exercise is repeated more or less frequently, according to the bird's aptitude for learning.

The hawking season is now at hand. The bird must be put to the proof, to ascertain if she has profited by these lessons so skilfully graduated, by this education so laboriously inculcated, and so appropriate to her nature and to the style of sport for which she is intended. They go out, therefore, on horseback, taking the "gentle" bird hood-winked, and proceed to an open plain, or a vast plateau, having first provided themselves with five or six live hares. Having reached the appointed spot they take a hare and, having broken its four feet, let it go within the scope of the bird's ken. Squeaking and moaning it hobbles on as well as it can, when they unhood the falcon, and throw her off—exclaiming *Bi essem Allah! Allah akbar!* The *terakel,* impatient, soars straight up toward the sky, and from a great height swoops down upon the hare, which she kills, or stuns, with a single blow with her tightly closed talons, as with a fist. The hunters come up, bleed and open the animal, and give the entrails, the liver, and the heart to the bird, who devours them on the spot. After repeating this lesson several days in succession, the training of the bird is considered complete.

This course of instruction has extended from summer

to near the end of autumn, which is the favourable season, for the falcon only hunts well in cloudy and cold weather. She cannot endure the glare of the sun, nor yet thirst or heat. She would leave her master to go in search of water, which she sees from afar, and would never return. At that period, then, a party sets out after a light breakfast, at about eleven in the morning, with the falcon on the shoulder or on the fist. The only provisions they take with them are camel's milk, dates, bread, and dried grapes.

But the sport does not begin until after a tolerably long ride, towards three in the afternoon. The cavalcade is usually a numerous one. Having reached a suitable spot, they scatter about, beating the brush-wood and tufts of *alfa* in the hope of starting a hare, which they drive towards the man who holds the falcon. As soon as the quarry is sighted, the latter unhoods the bird, and throws her off; pointing with his finger to the hare, and exclaiming *Ha hou!* "there it is!" While her master is pronouncing the sacramental *Bi es-sem Allah! Allah akbar!* the bird is off, soars out of sight, keeping the hare in view all the time with her piercing eye, and then precipitates herself upon it, and strikes it, either on the head or on the shoulder, one blow with her closed talons, violent enough to stun, if not to kill it. The horsemen, seeing the falcon stoop, gallop up from all quarters, surround her, and generally find her engaged in picking out the eyes of the hare. To make her let go, some one draw out from below his burnous the skin of another hare, and throw it down a little way off, when she immediately pounces upon it. Her *curée,* or reward, is not given to her until after their return to the *douar.*

It will be readily understood that, though the bird was fed abundantly, and even to excess, during the time she was being tamed, and taught to obey the call, she is kept somewhat sparingly during the hawking season, to avoid making her dull and depriving her of her full power, and in order to make her a good hunter, that is, ardent and alert.

It is no uncommon thing with two or three falcons to kill from ten to fifteen hares in a day. A lage bird called the *habara** is also hunted with the *thair el horr*, and in this wise. The hunters ride on until they meet with *habaras*, who generally go in couples, or in companies of half a dozen and more. The falcon is on the fist. Her hood is removed, and the birds are pointed out to her. When thoroughly roused, she is thrown off with the invocation, *Bi es-sem Allah!* She soars aloft, stoops upon her quarry, strikes it on the head, and holds it in the pitiless grasp of her talons in spite of the desperate struggles of the victim, until the horsemen come up and snatch it from her. One of them then bleeds it to death, and gives the falcon her reward. The flesh of this bird intoxicates the falcon, according to the Arabs, either because of the perfumed vapour emanating from it, or because she is proud of the capture of a *habara*, a dainty fit to set before a Sultan. Thus, when she is replaced on the shoulder, she struts and balances herself, and executes her fantasia. If the *habara* attempts to fly, the falcon soars, and both mount together, the latter rising higher and higher till she is well above the other, when she precipitates herself upon it like a thunder-bolt, and breaks, first a wing, and then the sternum. They

* Probably the Guinea-fowl.

fall together, tumbling over and over, but the falcon always managing to keep uppermost and to hold her victim beneath her, so that it alone may feel the shock of this frightful fall.

The "gentle" bird hunts, also, the *scroun,* the *hamma,* and the *agad.* Some falcons will not hunt the *habara.* They are never trained to hunt partridges, as it is feared that, if they became accustomed to it, they would prefer a feathered quarry to one with a skin. If a bird delays to return to her master, a horseman, holding in his hand the skin of a hare furnished with ears and feet, gallops up towards her and throws this lure to her, at the same time hooping "Ouye!" : she generally answers to the call. This interjection, if I may so express myself, is the vocative of the bird of race. The falcon, when properly trained, seldom betrays, that is, escapes from her master. They are sometimes lost, however, by their passion for a desert bird called *hamma,* which they pursue with fury.

The *biaz*—such is the name of the falconer, the individual whose special duty it is to tend and feed the falcon—sometimes entertains a blind and fatal attachment for his pupil. He will pet and pamper her to excess; and although it is proverbially said that "vanity is her only counsellor and sole motive of her actions," yet, if she be not hungry, instead of hunting, she resumes her liberty. A bird, however, must be exceedingly well trained and even renowned, to be kept for more than one year. As a rule, unless she has displayed an exceptional prowess, she is turned loose at the end of the season, as another is sure to be obtained before the time comes round again. Birds that have been kept for three years are quoted as something quite out of the common run.

When the *djouad*, or nobles, go out hawking, it is in parties of five-and-twenty to thirty, without reckoning their attendants, and wagers are often laid. For a trained falcon, a camel is given, or a hundred *boudjous*, and at times even a horse. The falcon is regarded as a member of the family. She lives in the tent, and is the object of the most constant attention. Some chiefs are never to be seen without their falcon, which they carry about with them everywhere. It is a sign of distinction and of gentle birth to have marks of a falcon's muting on one's burnous. In the Sahara, little or great, rich or poor, all alike love and caress the "gentle" bird.

"And how should it be otherwise?" said to me one day a noble Arab; "we love pomp, splendour, and magnificence, and one must be more or less than an Arab not to feel joy and excitement at the sight of our warriors returning from hawking. The chief rides on in front, followed by many horsemen, and carrying two falcons, one on his shoulder, the other on his fist, guarded by a leather gauntlet. The hoods of these birds are enriched with silk, morocco leather, gold, and small ostrich plumes, while their jesses are embroidered and ornamented with silver bells. The steeds neigh, the camels are loaded with game, and their drivers murmur, in a melancholy tone, one of those chaunts of love, or war, which never fail to find the way to our hearts. Yes; I swear by the head of the Prophet, next to a goum taking the field, there is nothing so striking as the departure or return of a hawking party. Thus, however weary, exhausted, and out of breath one may be, sleep is less refreshing than the hope and expectation of re-commencing on the morrow."

THE CHACE

BY ABD-EL-KADER.

It is related that an Arab Sheikh was seated in the centre of a numerous group, when a man who had lost his ass presented himself before him, and asked if any one had seen the animal that had gone astray. The Sheikh immediately turned to those around him, and adressed them in these words :— "Is there any one here to whom the pleasures of the chace are unknown? Who has never pursued the game at the risk of life and limb, if he fell from his horse? Who, without fear of tearing his clothes or his skin, has not thrown himself into the midst of brushwood bristling with thorns, in order to overtake the wolf? Is there any one here who has never experienced the happiness of again meeting, the despair of leaving a woman who was dearly loved?"

One of his hearers answered : "For my part, I have never done, or experienced any of those things you mention."

Looking to the owner of the ass, the sheikh thus spoke : "Behold the beast you were looking for! Lead him away."

The Arabs, indeed, have a saying that "he who has never hunted, nor loved, nor felt emotion at the sound of music, nor prized the perfume of flowers, is not a man, but an ass." With us, war is especially a contest of agility and craft. Consequently the chace is the highest of all pastimes, as the pursuit of savage animals teaches how to pursue men. A poet has written the following enlogy of that art :

"The chace disengages the mind from the cares by which it is harassed. It adds to the vigour of the intelligence, brings joyfulness, dissipates chagrin, and renders useless the science of the physicians by maintaining perpetual health in the human body.

"It forms good horsemen, for it teaches them to spring quickly into their saddles, to alight promptly on the ground, to rush a horse across rocks and precipices, to clear stones and bushes at full gallop, to push on without stopping, even though some part of the harness has been lost or broken.

"Every one who gives himself up to the chace, makes progress day by day in courage, and learns to despise accidents.

"To fully enjoy his favourite diversion, he withdraws from perverse people. He puts falsehood and calumny to the rout, escapes from the corruption of vice, and emancipates himself from those fatal influences which tinge our beards with gray, and burden us, before our time, with the weight of years.

"Days spent in the chace are not counted among the days of one's life."

In the Sahara, the chace is the sole occupation of the chiefs and rich people. When the rainy season sets in,

the inhabitants of that region transport themselves to
the shores of the small lakes formed by the rain; and, if
game get scarce at one spot, they open up a new scene
in their wandering life. A legend familiar to every Arab
shows with what force the passion for the chace may
seize upon the heart of an African.

A man of distinction fired at a gazelle and missed it.
In a hasty moment, he took an oath that no food should
come near his mouth until he had eaten the animal's
liver. Twice again, he fired at the gazelle, and with no
better success, but not the less did he continue the pursuit for the whole of that day. At nightfall his strength
gave way; but true to his oath, he refused to take any
nourishment. His servants, therefore, resumed the
chace, which lasted for three days more. At last the
gazelle was killed, and its liver brought to the dying
Arab, who touched it with its lips and yielded up his
last breath.

The Arabs hunt both on foot, and on horseback. A
horseman who would chace the hare must take with him
a greyhound, which is called *slougui,* from Slouguïa, a
spot where they were originally produced from the coupling of she-wolves with dogs. The male *slougui* lives
twenty years, the female twelve. Greyhounds that are
able to run a gazelle down are rare. Few of them will
give chace either to the hare or to the gazelle, even if
those animals pass close to them. Their customary
object of pursuit is the *bekeur-el-ouhash,* which they
generally catch by the ham and pull to the ground. It
is said that this animal, in trying to recover itself, falls
forward on its head and is killed. Sometimes, the *slougui*
seizes the *bekeur-el-ouash* by the throat, and holds it until

the hunter comes up. Many Arabs hunt this beast on horseback, and strike it from behind with a spear. It is also on horseback that they generally hunt the gazelle, which goes in herds. They select from among its companions the animal they intend to bring down, and shoot it without for a moment pulling up their horse, on which they started at full speed. There is an Arab proverb : "More forgetful than a gazelle." This pretty creature, in fact, appears to have the giddy brains as well as the soft, mysterious glance of woman. The gazelle, if missed, runs a little way further on, and again stops, without heeding the ball which, in another minute, will again seek its life. Some Arabs hunt this animal with the falcon, which is trained to strike at the eyes.

It is especially among the Arabs of the Eshoul country that this variety of sport chiefly prevails. I have there met with a small tribe, called the Es-Lib, who lived entirely on the products of the chace. Their tents were made of the skins of gazelles and of *bekeur-el-ouhash;* and their clothing, for the most part, was nothing but the skins of wolves. A member of this little tribe of hunters told me that when he went out to hunt he generally took with him an ass laden with salt. Each time he knocked over a gazelle, he cut its throat, opened the belly, and rubbed the entrails with salt, and then left it to dry on a bush. After a while he retraced his steps, and carried to his family all the animals that he had thus prepared, for in that district there are no beasts of prey to dispute with a hunter for his game. The Es-Lib are so accustomed to feed upon flesh, that the children threw away the biscuits I gave to them, never supposing that they were good to eat.

The hunt in ambush is often practised against both the male and female of the *bekeur-el-ouhash*. When the great heats have dried up the ponds in the desert, a hole is dug close to the springs whither they resort to drink, and they meet with their death while in the act of quenching their thirst. The chace that demands the greatest intrepidity is that of the *lerouy,* an animal resembling the gazelle, but larger, though without attaining the size of the *bekeur-el-ouhash.* The *lerouy,* which is likewise called the *tis-el-djebel,* or mountain goat, frequents rocks and precipices, among which it must be pursued on foot, amid a thousand perils. As these animals have very little speed, any ordinary dog can catch them easily if they descend into the plains. But they have a singular peculiarity, as I am assured. A *lerouy* closely pressed by hunters throws itself down a precipice a hundred cubits deep, and falls on its head without receiving any hurt. The age of the animal is known by the knobs on its horns—each knob indicating a year. Both the *lerouy* and the gazelle have two incisor teeth, but they have not those situated between the incisors and the canine teeth.

If *lerouy* hunting be the glory of the pedestrian, ostrich hunting is the glory of the horseman. In the season of the sirocco, when a sort of burning sleep seems to weigh down all nature, when it might be thought that all animated beings must be condemned to repose, the dauntless hunters mount on horseback. Of all animals, the ostrich is known to be the least provided with craft. It never takes a circuitous course, but, confiding in its swiftness alone, endeavours to escape in a line straight as that of an arrow. Five horsemen station

themselves at intervals of a league in the direction it is
certain to take.   Each one acts as a relay.   When one
pulls up, the next dashes off at a gallop in pursuit of
the bird, which is thus deprived of a moment's rest, and
has to contend against horses that are fresh.   The
horseman who is the last to start is necessarily the
victor, but his victory is not achieved without danger.
In falling, the ostrich, by the movement of its wings,
inspires the horse with a panic that is often fatal to the
rider.

On horses that have to accomplish this terrific running
they place only a saddle-cloth, and a saddle of extreme
lightness.   Some hunters use only wooden stirrups, and
an extremely light bit attached to a simple pack-thread.
Each one takes with him a small leathern bottle filled
with water, and from time to time moistens the bit, in
order to keep the animal's mouth tolerably cool.   This
racing of five horsemen is not, however, the only mode
of hunting the ostrich.   Sometimes, an Arab who is
thoroughly acquainted with the habits of the bird, takes
his post by himself close to a spot where it is in the
habit of passing—near a mountain defile, for instance
—and as soon as the ostrich comes in sight he gives
chace at full gallop.   But it is rare for a hunter to
succeed by himself, as very few horses can overtake the
ostrich.   However, I once possessed a mare that excelled
in this sport.

Although the horse is usually employed in this as in
other kinds of hunting, he is not indispensable to man.
Craft may sometimes of itself overcome the ostrich.   In
the laying season the hunters dig holes near the nests,
in which they squat down, and kill the parent bird as it

comes to visit its eggs. The Arabs have recourse, likewise, to disguises. Some of them will clothe themselves in the skin of the bird, and thus approach close to those they wish to kill; but hunters, disguised in this fashion, have sometimes, they say, been shot by their own companions. If an ostrich has had a leg broken by a ball, she cannot, like other bipeds, run along, hopping on the other leg. This is because there is no marrow in its bones, and, without marrow, bones will not mend when they have been fractured. The Arabs affirm that the ostrich is deaf, and that the sense of smell replaces that of hearing.

The hyœna is a powerful animal, with formidable jaws, but a coward and afraid of daylight. For the most part it dwells in caves which it finds in ravines and among rocks. It seldom goes abroad but at night, and searches for carrion and dead bodies, and commits such ravages in graveyards, that the Arabs, by way of prevention, bury their dead at a great depth. In some districts they even construct two chambers for a single corpse, which is then interred in the lower one. As a rule, it does not attack the flocks; but sometimes at night, prowling round an encampment, it carries off a dog. The Arabs take little notice of it, though they amuse themselves by hunting it on horseback, 'and let it be pulled down by their greyhounds, but never pay it the compliment of firing at it. After they have carefully reconnoitred the cave in which it makes its lair, it is no uncommon thing to find Arabs who despise the beast sufficiently to penetrate boldly into its den, after having carefully closed the entrance with their burnouses, so as not to allow any light to enter. Having got thus far, they go up to it, talking with great energy, seize hold of it, gag it, without the slightest resistance on its part —so terrified is it—and then drive it out with heavy blows with a stick. The skin of such a cowardly brute is little esteemed. In many tents they would not permit it to enter, for it can bring nothing but misfortune. The common people eat the flesh, which is not at all good, but they carefully abstain from touching the head or brains—contact with which, they believe, would make them go mad.

Let us leave this ignoble animal, and pass on to one much more to be feared, and the chace of which presents some striking scenes, though its reputation is far from being in the eyes of the Arabs what it is in the imagination of Europeans—I allude to the panther.

The panther is found over the whole surface of Algeria, though it inhabits only wooded coverts, and broken, difficult ground. There are several species. Some never quit the neighbourhood of their lair, and are called *dolly,* that is, keeping to the house. Others, again, which are called *berani,* or strangers, frequently wander away from the place where they usually dwell, and prowl about the surrounding districts to a considerable distance.

The *dolly* panther is larger, stronger, and more dangerous than the other species. Its coat is speckled with spots more elegantly disposed, of a very dark shade, and close to one another. The colours are black, white, and yellow. On the jowl, limbs, and back-bone, there are no spots, but stripes. Those on the jowl are arranged diagonally. The upper points start from the lower eyelids, the nostrils, and the corners of the mouth, and descend towards the neck, gradually melting away into yellow, and finally lost in the white.

Panthers lap like dogs. They generally roam in couples. In districts that are well peopled, they are never seen in the daytime. In uninhabited regions, although they do go abroad in the day, they hunt only at night. They have not more than two or three cubs. The Arabs are far from regarding the panther with the esteem they accord to the lion. The lion, say they, if attacked, harassed, wounded, and surrounded by enemies, feels his courage heighten in the midst of the uproar and in the thick of the danger. He fearlessly encounters his assailants and fights to the death, while the panther only accepts the combat when it finds no way to retreat. In a word, the lion, as soon as the combat has fairly commenced, never retires, while the panther escapes whenever an opportunity presents itself. Another difference is this—the lion will devour a man, the panther never. The latter generally strikes at his head, lacerates him with its claws, and inflicts terrible bites, and then, preferring the flesh of other animals to that of a son of Adam, it leaves him there and goes in search of other prey. In a country where it is able to supply itself with the flesh of wild boar, sheep, cattle, and game of all kinds, and where it can satiate itself with the carcases of animals, it kills man, not because it is hungry, but in self-defence, as the only way of shaking off an enemy. In the case of the lion, man is often the game in guest of which he stalks abroad; while in that of the panther he is an adversary to be avoided, and never to be provoked. You may pass boldly and confidently close to the thick brushwood that conceals it, and, if you do not begin the attack, it will remain couched as close as a partridge, even holding in its breath.   But if you fire and miss, it will spring upon, bite, and lacerate you, and then, still distrustful of itself, will take itself off.

The Arabs have remarked, from the numbers of persons who have come in collision with panthers, and been wounded without being killed, that it uses only its teeth; its bite being like that of the dog, and injuring only the flesh. The lion, on the other hand, by his violent shaking, breaks the bones of the victim he holds in his powerful jaws. When the panther has inflicted its bite, it does not trouble itself as to its being fatal or otherwise, but makes off with fear and caution. The lion grows more and more furious, and returns to the attack again and again. It is not enough that the enemy be disabled—he must feel the whole weight of a lion's wrath. The lion bounds into a *douar,* and plunders boldly, at his leisure. He seizes his share without any concealment; he has no fear; he is exercising his right, the right of the strongest. The panther covers its advance, glides, creeps, crawls along like a thief, accompanied by shame and fear. The panther's spring, when enraged, is like a flash of lightning; but after that tremendous effort, its pace is less swift than that of an ordinary horse. If a panther be surrounded, tracked down, and hard pressed—maddened by terror rather than by rage—it will spring on the tree in which the hunters are stationed, and close with them. But at another time, if only one or two men are lying in ambush, and it be not shut in on all sides and a path is left for escape, it forgets its power and runs away. Everywhere and at all times, the lion is a dangerous enemy, to encounter whom is a terrible undertaking; whereas no one need dread the panther unless he has first attacked it. The cry of the latter animal resembles the clear, shrill, impotent neigh of the mule, and is in no way calculated to inspire terror like the roar of the lion, which is as the growling of thunder. But it is quick and agile, and its movements baffle the eye. If the natural disposition of the panther leads it to spare, or at least to avoid, man, and to choose for its prey animals wild or tame, such as sheep, cows, gazelles, and antelopes, that cannot defend themselves, it is equally instructed by instinct to modify its mode of attack upon animals whose habits or courage render them difficult or dangerous to assail—against such, it has usually recourse to surprise. It will not attack a horse in the centre of a *douar*. Its habitual circumspection and cowardice will restrain it from seeking to seize upon a prey that might be rescued in time, or promptly avenged. Even when out grazing, a horse by itself might escape by galloping off; but if it has not been seen, or suspected, if with a single bound it can fall upon the horse, he is lost.

Nor is the wild boar an easy victim. If it be full grown, and have had warning, and there be room enough, it will defend itself successfully. At times, indeed, it comes off absolutely victorious—the Arabs having found panthers in desert places, ripped up by a boar's tusks. A frequent struggle, perhaps the only one which the panther openly engages in, is with the porcupine; but the latter, though it grows to a considerable size in Africa, is more formidable in appearance than in reality. It has indeed, the property of bristling up its long, hard, sharp-pointed quills, which it can even throw to some distance; but these arms cannot save it. The slightest wound completely paralyses the muscular contractions by means of which it places itself in a state of defence : besides, it cannot do anything without something to fall back upon, such as a tree or a stone.

However timorous and apt to run away the panther may be under ordinary circumstances, it becomes really dangerous if its cubs have been carried off in its absence —or under its very eyes by force, which only happens when the hunters are in considerable numbers. At such times it will sometimes perish in the attempt to save them—at least, the *dolly*, or larger species will do so; but the *berrani,* or small panther, makes off, uttering the while lamentable cries. The cubs, thus torn from their mother, are given to chiefs residing in towns, to Sultans, Pashas, and Beys; but they are never kept in a tribe, for when still quite young they are dangerous even in their play, and no sort of attention will ever tame them or guarantee the master of the tent, or his wives and children, from a momentary outburst of fury on the part of the perfidious and capricious brute. We may mention, however, that in certain *zaouïas* lions are tamed by marabouts and led up and down the tribes. Thus summoning curiosity to the aid of charity, they augment the amount of the alms which they beg for their congregation. The most celebrated *zaouïa* in which tame lions are kept is that of Sidi-Mohammed-ben-Aouda, a tribe of the Flittas in the province of Oran.

With this special exception the Arabs—and it is a characteristic trait worthy of note—never rear any but inoffensive animals. There is not a tent without a gazelle, an antelope, a jackal, an ostrich, or a falcon:

but in no *douar* is a savage beast ever to be seen, such as a hyœna, a panther, or a lion. Some tribes take pleasure in rearing a young wild boar, under the idea that it amuses the horses, which like its smell. The little pig is faithful and always in motion. When the tribe is changing ground, it trots about, grunting joyously in the midst of the other animals, and accompanies the sheep and the calves to the pasture. It is called "the father of good fortune," and strangely enough, it is a lucky omen to meet a wild boar on issuing from one's tent. Prior to Mohammed the Arabs used to eat swine's flesh, but the Prophet forbade it to them, as well as the blood of animals and the flesh of every creature that has not been bled.

The panther, as I have already remarked, seldom goes abroad during the day; but if, by chance, shepherds or travellers happen to alight upon one near an inhabited neighbourhood, they utter in shrill tones *ha houa!* "there it is!" These cries are repeated with incredible rapidity. The entire population swarms forth—horse and foot, armed with whatever first comes to hand, guns, sticks, swords, spears, or pistols, and followed by their dogs and greyhounds. Surrounding on every side the spot whither the beast has retired, generally difficult ground, covered with thick high brushwood, they attack it fearlessly and usually end by killing it. It rarely happens that it escapes while it is light.

But when, instead of this sudden outbreak of an entire population against an unexpected enemy, a genuine hunt is projected, certain preparations are made before starting. It is true, the panther will run away if it has the chance, but it is always possible that it may show fight; and although, in the long run, it is sure to be mastered without a single casualty on the side of the hunters, it is as well to guard against the wounds it may inflict, however insignificant in themselves. It usually flies at the head. Against the lacerations of its teeth and claws a sufficient defence is the thick woollen cap, the *shashia,* the numerous folds of the haïk, the hood of the burnous, and the long, coarse camel's rope. But the enemy may with a single bound spring on to a horse's croup, and with one blow on the head with its paw knock over, stun, and even kill the rider. On this account they not unfrequently don a helmet—a helmet of modest pretentions, which at other times serves as a kettle.

The panther is also killed, like the lion, from an ambush. A hole is dug in the earth and covered over with branches, through which an opening is made for the rifle of the concealed hunter, who fires at the distance of about fifteen paces, as the animal approaches to devour the carcase of a sheep or goat placed there for that purpose. But lest the brute, if only wounded, should spring upon the *melebda,* as the hunter's hiding place is called, the latter is always provided with two or three guns, and perhaps with pistols likewise. At other times a gun is fastened to a tree, and at the muzzle of the barrel is fixed a bait, to which a string is tied, that passes round the tree and is attached to the trigger—so that if the bait be pulled at all forcibly the gun is sure to go off. And if the panther is not shot dead, it is certain to be wounded, and the hunters set off in pursuit, guided by the tracks of blood it leaves on its path. There is yet another mode of killing the panther, which is by surprising it while sleeping. Should it happen to be awake, it is merely a disappointment, not a danger, for it runs away at sight of a man.

But whatever be the nature of the sport in which the Arabs indulge, the least timorous are liable to superstitious fears. As it is not always possible to relinquish an enterprise when they have once entered upon it, they endeavour by all means to avoid chances of sinister omen. On the other hand they become emboldened, and take courage if, on setting out, they are greeted by one of those encounters which are reputed fortunate—with a jackal in the morning for instance, or with a wild boar in the evening.

> Let thy morning be with a jackal,
> And thy evening with a wild boar.

A hare or a fox is of ill omen; as is, also, a single crow, or a white mare. A still worse and more detestable omen is the sight af an old woman. But it is a good chance for whoever sees two crows or a mare of any colour; and, above all, success, glory, and plunder, await the *goum* that, when starting on an expedition, is met by a beautiful young and noble maiden, who will uncover her bosom and show one of her breasts. It is the custom; and if the damsel were to refuse this blessing to the warriors of her tribe, they would dismount to compel her, were she the daughter of the chief and though he were himself at the head of the *goum*—all the better, indeed, if her birth were so exalted, for the nobler the damsel, the happier the augury. In the west, young girls loosen their girdle. If, in the morning, you hear affectionate and courteous words, you will have a pleasant day; but it will be the reverse if on first awaking you are greeted with an imprecation or an insult. Do not go out to hunt on a Tuesday, a Thursday, or a Friday.

We now come to the sport that is really worthy to sharpen the intelligence and inflame the souls of warriors. The Arab hunter acts upon the aggressive with the lion. In this daring enterprise there is all the more merit, because in Africa the lion is a formidable monster, regarding whom there exist many mysterious and terrible legends, with which an awe-struck superstition surrounds his dread Majesty. With that keenness of insight which characterises them, the Arabs have made a series of observations on the subject of the lion that are worthy of being collected and preserved.

In the daytime the lion rarely seeks to attack man. Very commonly, indeed, if a traveller happens to pass near him, he turns aside his head and affects not to see him. At the same time, if any one, walking close to the bush in which he is couched, be rash enough to cry aloud *ra hena*—"he is there!"—the lion will at once spring upon his denouncer and the disturber of his repose. As night comes on, his humour completely changes. When the sun has set, it is perilous to venture into a wild, woody, and broken country. It is there the lion lies in ambush —it is there he is met on the pathways, which he intercepts by barring all further advance with his body. The Arabs thus describe some of the nocturnal scenes which are continually happening. If a solitary individual, a courier, traveller, or letter-carrier, chancing to meet a lion, possess a courage of the highest temper, he will walk straight towards the animal, brandishing his sword or gun, but carefully abstaining from using the one or the other. He simply cries out : "Oh, the robber! the highway-man! the son of a mother who never said No! Dost thou think to frighten me? Thou canst not know, then, that I am so-and-so, the son of so-and-so? Get up, and let me proceed on my journey." The lion waits till the man has come close up to him, and then goes off to lie down again a thousand paces farther on. The traveller has to endure a long series of terrific trials. Each time that he quits the path, the lion disappears, but only for an instant. Directly afterwards he again presents himself, and all his movements are accompanied by horrible noises. He breaks off innumerable branches with his tail. He roars, howls, growls, and emits gusts of poisonous breath. He plays with the subject of his fantastic and manifold attacks, and keeps him constantly suspended between fear and hope, like a cat playing with a mouse. If a man involved in such a difficulty does not allow his courage to fail him, if—to use an Arab phrase—he succeeds in firmly holding his soul, the lion will finally leave him, and seek his fortune else-where. But if, on the contrary, the latter perceives that he has to deal with a man whose countenance betrays his fear, whose voice trembles, and who dares not articulate a word, he repeats over and over again, in order to terrify him still more, the manœuvre above des-cribed. He will approach him, push him out of the way with his shoulder, cross his path every other minute, and amuse himself with him in various ways, until at last he devours his victim already half dead with terror.

There is really nothing incredible in the facts thus

stated by the Arabs. The ascendancy of courage over animals is indisputable. The professional robbers who roam abroad at night, armed to the teeth, instead of shunning the lion, cry out to him if they meet with him: "I am not what thou seekest. I am a robber like thyself; pass on, or, if it please thee, let us rob in company." It is said that the lion sometimes follows them, and attempts an assault on the *douar* towards which they are bending their steps. It is even affirmed that this good understanding between the robbers and the lions frequently displays itself in a striking manner. Robbers have been seen, when taking their meals, to treat the lions as other people treat their dogs, and throw to them at a certain distance the feet and entrails of the animals they themselves are eating.

Women likewise have been known successfully to have recourse to intrepidity in opposing a lion. They have run after him when engaged in carrying off a ewe, and have forced him to let go his prey by giving him a shower of blows with a cudgel, crying aloud all the time: "Ah, robber! son of a robber!" The Arabs say that the lion is seized with shame, and makes off as quickly as possible. This trait shows that in the eyes of the Arabs the lion is a peculiar sort of creature midway between men and beasts, which, by reason of its strength, appears to them to be endowed with a special order of intelligence. The following legend, intended to explain how it is that the lion allows a sheep to escape him more easily than any other prey, is a confirmation of this belief. Enumerating one day the various feats his strength enabled him to accomplish, the lion remarked: "*An sha Allah*—if it be the will of

Allah—I can carry off a horse without distressing myself. *An sha Allah*, I can carry off a heifer, without being prevented from running by its weight." But when he came to the ewe, he deemed it so much beneath him that he omitted the pious formula, "if it be the will of Allah;" and, to punish him, Allah condemned him to be never able to do more than drag it along.

There are several modes of hunting the lion. When one makes his appearance in the midst of a tribe, his presence is indicated by a multitude of signs of all kinds. The earth shakes, as it were, with roarings. Then a series of losses and accidents take place. A heifer, or a colt is carried off, or a man is missing. The alarm spreads through all the tents. The women tremble for their property and for their children. Lamentations arise on all sides, and the hunters decree the death of their troublesome neighbour. It is published in the market-places that on such a day and at such an hour, all who are capable of joining in the chace, whether on horseback or on foot, must assemble in arms at an appointed spot. Prior to this, the thicket has been discovered to which the lion retires during the day. Everything being ready, the hunters set out, the men on foot leading the way. When they have arrived within fifty paces of the bush in which they expect to find the enemy, they halt and await him. Closing up, they form three deep, the second rank ready to fill up the gaps in the first if succour be necessary, while the third, firm and compact, and composed of capital marks-men, forms an invincible reserve. Then commences a strange spectacle. The front rank begin to insult the lion, and even send a few balls into his hiding place to make him come out : "Look at him who boasts of being the bravest of all, and yet dares not show himself before men!   It is not he—it is not the lion—it is a cowardly thief, and may Allah curse him!"   The animal sometimes comes while they are abusing him in this manner, and, looking round serenely on all sides, yawns and stretches himself, and appears perfectly insensible to what is passing around him.

One or two balls now hit him, upon which, magnificent in his audacity, he stalks forth and stands in front of the bush which sheltered him.   Not a word is spoken. The lion roars, rolls his glaring eyes, draws back, couches down, again rises up, and by the movements of his tail and body snaps off all the branches that surround him.   The front rank discharge their pieces, whereupon the monster bounds forward, and generally falls dead beneath the fire of the second rank, who step forward and fill up the intervals left in the first.   This is the critical moment, for the lion resigns the contest only when a ball has struck him in the head, or in the heart. It is no rare thing to see him continue the fight with ten or a dozen balls through his body.   In other words, he is seldom overpowered until he has killed or wounded some of his foot assailants.   The horsemen who accompany the expedition have nothing to do, so long as their foe does not quit the broken ground.   Their part commences when, as occasionally happens, the men on foot have succeeded in driving out the lion upon a plateau, or into the plain.   The combat then assumes a new aspect, full of interest and originality.   Each horseman, according to his hardihood and agility, spurs on his horse at full speed, fires at the lion as at an ordinary mark, at a short distance, and, wheeling his horse round the moment he has fired, gallops off to re-load his piece before making a second assault. The lion, attacked on all sides and wounded at every moment, faces about in every direction, rushes forward, flees, returns, and falls, but only after a glorious struggle. His defeat, indeed, must inevitably terminate in his death, for against horsemen mounted on Arab horses success is impossible. He makes but three terrific bounds, after which his pace is by no means swift, and an ordinary horse will distance him without trouble. To form a just idea of such a combat, it is absolutely neces-sary to have witnessed one. Every horseman hurls an imprecation; there is a wild confusion of sounds, the burnouses fly out, the powder thunders, the hunters crowd together or scatter widely apart. The lion roars, the balls whistle, and the whole forms a scene of movement and animation. . But notwithstanding all this tumult, accidents are very unusual. The hunters' have little to fear, unless a fall from their horse throws them under the paw of their enemy, or—which is more frequent misadventure—they are hit by a friendly but ill-directed ball.

Such is the most picturesque, the most warlike aspect that lion-hunting assumes. Other measures, however, are sometimes adopted, both more sure and more speedily efficacious. The Arabs have observed that on the morrow after he has carried off and devoured sheep or oxen, the lion, suffering from a weak digestion, remains in his lair, fatigued, oppressed with sleep, and incapable of moving. When a place that is usually disquieted with roaring is undisturbed for a whole night, it may be inferred that the formidable inhabitant who dwells therein is plunged in this state of lethargy. Upon this, a man of devoted courage, following the tracks that lead to the covert in which the monster is concealed, will go up to him, take a steady aim, and shoot him dead upon the spot with a ball between the two eyes. Kaddour-ben-Mohammed, of the Oulad-Messelem, a section of the Ounougha, is reputed to have killed several lions in this manner.

Recourse is likewise had to various forms of ambush. The Arabs sometimes excavate a hole in the path the lion usually takes, and cover it with thin woodwork, which the animal breaks by its weight and is caught in the trap. At other times they dig close to a dead body a hole covered by thick boards, between which a small opening is left to allow the barrel of a gun to pass through. In this hole, or *melebda,* the hunter squats down, and when the lion approaches the body, he takes a careful aim and fires. Not unfrequently the lion, if he has not been struck down, throws himself on the *melebda,* shatters the barrier, and devours the hunter behind his demolished rampart. On other occasions, again, a single man will undertake an adventurous and heroic enterprise, recalling the feats of chivalry. Si-Mohammed-Esnoussi, a man of approved veracity, who inhabited the Djebel-Guerzoul, near Tiaret, thus describes his own mode of going to work :

"I used to mount a good horse and proceed to the forest on a bright moonlight night. In those days I was a capital shot, and my ball never fell to the ground. Then I began to cry aloud several times, *Ould el ataïah!* —'Daughter of a mother who yields herself up!'— The lion would come forth, and direct his steps towards the spot whence issued the cry; and at that moment I fired at him. Occasionally the same thicket would contain several lions, who would issue forth all together. If one of these brutes approached me from behind, I would turn my head and fire at him over the back of my saddle, and then go off at full gallop in the fear that I might have missed him. If I was attacked in front, I wheeled my horse round and repeated the manœuvre."

The people of that district affirm that the number of lions killed by Mohammed-ben-Esnoussi amounted to nearly a hundred. This intrepid hunter was still alive in the year 1253 [A. D. 1836]. When I saw him, he had lost his eyesight. May he participate in the mercy of Allah!

A yet more dangerous sport than hunting the lion himself, is hunting a lion's cubs. There are individuals, however, adventurous enough to undertake even this hazardous enterprise. Every day, about three or four in the afternoon, the lion and lioness quit their lair to make a distant reconnaissance, with the object, no doubt, of procuring food for their litter. They may be seen upon the summit of an eminence, examining the *douars*, and taking note of the smoke that issues from them, and of the position of the flocks. After uttering some horrible roars, an invaluable warning to the surrounding population, they again disappear. It is during this absence that the hunters cautiously make their way to the cubs and carry them off, taking care to gag them closely, for their cries would not fail to bring back the old ones, who would never forgive the outrage. After an exploit of this nature the entire neighbourhood is obliged to be doubly vigilant. For seven or eight days the lions rush about in all directions, roaring fearfully. The lion under such circumstances is a truly terrible monster. At such a time the eye must not encounter the eye.

The flesh of the lion, though sometimes eaten, is not good, but his skin is a valued gift, and presented only to Sultans and illustrious chiefs, and occasionally, to marabonts and *zaouias*. The Arabs fancy that it is good to sleep upon one, as it drives away the demons, conjures up good fortune, and averts certain diseases. Lion's claws, mounted in silver, are used as ornaments by women; while the skin of his forehead is a talisman worn by some persons on their head to preserve the energy and audacity of their brain. In short, lion-hunting is held in high repute among the Arabs. Every combat with that animal may take the device : *Kill or Die!* He who kills him, eats him—says the proverb— and he who kills him not is eaten by him. In this spirit they bestow on any one who has killed a lion, this laconic and virile eulogy : *Hadak houa*—"that one is he!" A popular belief illustrates the grandeur of the part played by the lion in the life and imagination of the Arabs. When a lion roars, they pretend that they can readily distinguish the following words : *Ahna ou ben el mera*— "I and the son of woman." Now, as he twice repeats *ben el mera,* and only once says *ahna,* they conclude that he recognizes no superior save the son of woman.

THE CAMEL.*

It was said by the Prophet : "The good things of this world, to the day of the last judgment, are attached to the forelocks of your horses;

"Sheep are a blessing;

" And the Almighty has created nothing, as an animal, preferable to the camel."

The camel is the ship of the desert. Allah hath said: "You may load your merchandize in barks and on camels." As in the desert there is very little water, and there are long distances to be traversed, the Almighty has endowed them with the faculty of easily enduring thirst. In winter they never drink. The Prophet more than once gave the following advice : "Never utter coarse remarks on the subject of the camel or of the wind : the former is a boon to men, the latter an emanation from the soul of Allah." Camels are the most extraordinary animals in the world, and yet there are none more docile, owing to their being so much with

* I am aware that this is not the denomination bestowed by science upon this animal, which is actually the dromadary. However, I have adhered to the appellation of " Camel," because it is the only one used in Algeria. Besides, the Arabic word *djemel* applies to the camel as well as to the dromadary.

20

men. So great, indeed, is their docility, that they have
been known to follow a rat, that, in the act of gnawing,
pulled a rope smeared with butter, by which they were
fastened. Such is the will of Allah. These apoph-
thegms suffice to show that the camel is, of all created
animals, the most useful in respect of the wants of the
Arabs.

The Arabs of the Sahara can tell the age of a camel
by its teeth. They say it is long-lived, though they
cannot give any very precise information on the subject.
They put the case, however, in this manner. If a camel
be born on the same day with a child, it has reached old
age by the time the latter has distinguished himself in
combats, which implies the age of eighteen to twenty-
five years. Camels require much care and experience
in managing them. Whenever it is possible, the male
camels are led to a different pasture from the females.
After the 15th of April, they are not sent out to feed until
the afternoon, because it has been remarked that the
grass is covered with a sort of dew that lays the founda-
tion of fatal diseases. Care is also taken to prevent the
camels from eating within the *douar* what remains in
the morning of the small quantity of grass given to the
horses overnight. These precautions are necessary
during the six weeks or two months in which the dew
is observed. Throughout the whole winter, the end of
autumn, and the beginning of spring, the camels may
be permitted, with advantage, to browse on shrubs with
a salt flavour; but in the beginning of April, and at the
end of May, they must not be allowed to do so for more
than five or six days.

The shearing of the camels takes place in the latter

part of April. They are made to lie down, and are operated upon by the shepherds and female slaves, a woman standing behind them to gather the fleece which she thrusts into bags. It is a somewhat slow operation. *El oubeur*, or camel's fleece, is used in making canvas for tents, camel-ropes, sacks called *gherara,* and *djellale,* or horse-cloths. It is mixed almost invariably with common wool.

The ordinary burden of a camel is two *tellis* of wheat, or about 250 kilogrammes. If not over-driven, it can go from dawn to sunset, at least if it be allowed, as it journeys along, to elongate its neck and pluck the herbage that grows on either side of its path. In this manner it will cover from ten to twelve leagues in the twenty four hours, and every fifth day it must be permitted to rest. In the desert, camels are let out to hire, not by the day, but by the journey, going and returning, according to the distance. For instance, from El-Biod, among the Oulad-Sidi-Shikh, to the Beni-Mzab, or about fifty leagues, costs from two to three *douros,* and from the same point to Timimoun six or seven *douros.*

The flesh of the camel is eaten as food. The animal, however, is seldom killed unless it has a broken leg, or is sick. The flesh is sometimes salted, and, after being dried in the sun, is kept as a provision on a journey. The love and veneration felt by the Arabs of the Sahara for their camels are quite intelligible. "How should we not love them?" they exclaim. "Alive, they transport ourselves, our wives, our children, our baggage and provisions, from the land of oppression to that of liberty. The weight they can carry is enormous, and the distance they traverse very considerable. In other words, they further the relations of commerce and render aid in war. Thanks to them, we are able, whenever we please, to shift our encampment, whether in search of new pasturages, or to escape from an enemy. Moreover, we drink their milk, which is also useful in the preparations of food, and neutralises the injurious qualities of the date. Dead, their flesh is everywhere eaten with relish, and their hump is sought after as a savoury dish. Their skin serves as shoe-leather. If soaked, and then sewed to the saddle-tree, it imparts, without the aid of a single nail or peg, a solidity that nothing can affect. Then, their sobriety and endurance of heat and thirst permit them to be kept alike by rich and poor. They are truly a boon from Allah, who hath said :—

> Horses for a dispute,
> Oxen for poverty.
> Camels for the desert.

No cattle are reared in the Sahara, owing to the scarcity of water, the scantiness of the herbage, the stony nature of the ground, and the frequent removals from one place to another. But, if the desert be unfavourable for the rearing of cattle, it is, assuredly, the veritable country of the sheep. This animal finds there the salt shrubs eaten by the camel, as well as many fragrant and nutritious plants known by the generic name of *el adsheub.* Water it obtains from the ponds supplied by the rains, or from the basins formed by the side of wells, and kept up with great care. The wells themselves are, for the most part, surrounded with masonry, and sheltered from the driftings sands. Sheep, besides, are patient of thirst. In spring, they are given to drink once in five or six days; in summer, every other day; in autumn, every third day; and in winter every fourth day. During the great heats of summer, they are not allowed to touch the pools of water lying on the surface of the ground,—experience having shown that at that period of the year stagnant water, rendered tepid by the sun's rays, is very unwholesome. If a drought happens to have prevailed during the first two months of spring, and if rain falls plentifully in the third, the herbage grows luxuriantly, and is called *khelfa,* or compensation. As if to make amends for their long abstinence, the sheep eat it greedily, but it is apt to give them a sickness named *el ghoche,* or treason. This disease does not manifest itself until after the summer heats. The head and lower jaw become much swollen, the animal coughs continually, and death usually supervenes. According to the Arabs, a rainy autumn, by causing fresh grass to spring up early, greatly tends to mitigate the pernicious effects of the *ghoche.*

Sheep are very prolific. They generally lamb twice in the year—in the early part of spring and autumn. The large tribes possess from two to three hundred thousand sheep, which are divided into flocks of four hundred, called *ghelem* or *aâssa* [a stick]. Wealthy individuals have from fifteen to twenty *ghelem,* and the poorest a half, or even a quarter *ghelem.*

In the Sahara there is a species of sheep that yields a magnificent wool, very soft but not very long. This is the wool employed in the manufacture of articles of luxury. These animals are nearly red in the head, and the ewes give a great deal of milk.

It is said of the finest ewes of this breed :

> They see like an owl,
> And walk like a tortoise.

Their wool descends to their hoofs and so completely covers their head that, literally, nothing but their eyes is visible. In the Sahara and in the *kuesours,* a *zedja,* or fleece, is worth only one *boudjou,* but the price is greatly enhanced by the time it reaches the Tell, and especially the sea-coast. Some sheep have no horns, and are called *fertass* [bald]. Others, again, have four, and are known as *el kuerbourb;* while others have horns that are bent back, and are named *el kheroubi.*

The Arabs take no care whatever of their sheep. They have no sheds in which to shelter them from the severity of the weather, nor supplies of forage to save them from starvation. Consequently, in bad seasons they frequently lose one-half of their flocks, and if blamed for this carelessness, or offered advice, they answer quite simply : "To what purpose is all that? They are the property of Allah [*Kher Eurby*]. He does with them as it pleases Him. Our ewes give us two lambs every year. Next year our losses will be repaired."

The following sentiments are ascribed to sheep : —

"I love the close hand, that is, to belong to a miser who would neither sell us, nor slaughter us for the entertainment of his guests.

"I love distant market-places; for when they are near to my master, for one reason or another we are sold, or slaughtered.

"And every day a new house; that is, fresh and more abundant pasturage."

Sheep are the fortune of the child of the desert. He says of them : "Their wool serves to make our tents, our carpets, our garments, our horse-cloths, our sacks, our nose-bags, our camel's-packs, our ropes, our cushions. And what remains in excess of our own necessities we sell in the *kuesours* or in the Tell, when we go there, after harvest, to buy grain. Their flesh we eat, or give it to be eaten by the guests of Allah. Dried in the sun, it will keep, and be of use to us in our journeys.   Their milk is very serviceable to our families, whether as drink or food.   We make of it *leben* or *sheneen* [sour milk], and what is over we give to our horses.   We also get butter from it, which enters into the preparation of our food, or which we exchange in the *kuesours* for dates.   Of their skin we make cushions, and buckets to draw water from the well.   With it we ornament the *adtatouches* * of our women, or we dress it for shoe-leather.   We have no need to plough, or sow, or reap, or thresh out the corn, or to fatigue ourselves like vile slaves, or like the wretched inhabitants of the Tell.   No; we are independent, we pray, we trade, we hunt, we travel, and if we have occasion to procure that which others can only obtain by sweat and toil, we sell our sheep, and forthwith provide ourselves with arms, horses, women, jewels, clothes, or whatever else affords us gratification, or embellishes our existence.   The owner of sheep has no need to labour, nor is he ever in want of anything. So Allah has willed it!"

* A sort of arm-chair placed upon the backs of camels.

LIFE IN THE DESERT.

In studying life in the desert, I have been greatly struck by its analogy to that of the Middle Ages, and by the resemblance which exists between the horseman of the Sahara and the knight of our legends, romances, and chronicles. This analogy will appear yet more real, this resemblance yet more striking, on a close observation of the accessory characteristics which I now propose to sketch with a rapid hand.

By the Arab of the Sahara, I do not mean a dweller in the *kuesours*. The latter is rallied by the wandering tribes as much as the inhabitants of the Tell, and receives at their hands all sorts of derisive epithets. Grown fat through his habits of indoor and commercial life, he is called "the father of the belly," the grocer, the pepper-dealer. This rearer of fowls—the Arab of the tent possesses no fowls—this shopkeeper resembles the simple citizen of all countries and of all times. He is, at bottom, the villain, the churl of the Middle Ages. He is the Moorish citizen of Algiers — he has the same placid, apathetic, crafty physiognomy.

It is of the master of the tent that I propose to speak :

of him who is never more than fifteen to twenty days without changing his abode; of the genuine Nomad, of him who never enters "the tiresome Tell" but once a year, and then only to purchase grain. My horseman, my hunter, my warrior is the man with a hardy iron-nerved constitution, a complexion embrowned by the sun, limbs well proportioned, in stature rather tall than short, but making light of the advantage of height, " of that lion's skin on a cow's back," unless adroitness, activity, health, vigour and, above all, courage be combined with it. But if he values courage, he also pities rather than despises, and never insults those who "want liver." It is not their fault, he good-humouredly remarks, but the will of Allah. His abstinence cannot be exceeded, but, accommodating himself to circumstances, he never neglects an opportunity of making a good and hearty meal. His ordinary diet is simple and without much variety; but, for all that, when the necessity arises, he understands how to entertain his guests in a becoming manner. When the *ouadâa,* or peculiar festival of a tribe, or *douar,* comes round, at which his friends will be present, he would not offer them the slight implied by his absence, and though it may be at a distance of thirty or forty leagues, he will not fail to go there and fill himself with food. Besides, they know well that he is quite ready to return their hospitality, and that they have not to do with one of those stingy town traders who never offer more than a space of four square feet to sit down in, a pipe of tobacco, and a cup of coffee either without any sugar at all, or sugared only after many preliminary phrases, carefully enunciated in recommendation of coffee without sugar.

Among the Arabs, everything concurs to give power to the development of the natural man. Nervous, hardy, sober, though occasionally displaying a vigorous appetite, their eye-sight is keen and piercing. They boast that they can distinguish a man from a woman when two to three leagues distant, and a flock of camels from a flock of sheep at double that distance. Nor is this mere bragging. The extent and clearness of their vision arise, as in the case of our sailors, from the incessant habit of looking far ahead over an immense and objectless space. And, accustomed as they are to scenes and objects always the same and which encircle them within narrow limits, it would be strange if they did not recognize them under almost any circumstances. Nevertheless, diseases of the eye are very common. The refraction of the sun's rays, the dust and perspiration cause numerous misadventures, such as ophthalmia and leucoma, and blind and one-eyed men are numerous in many parts of the desert—for instance, among the Beni-Mzab, at El Ghrassoul, Ouargla, and Gourara.

The dweller in the desert, in infancy and youth, has beautiful white, even teeth; but the use of dates as his habitual and almost exclusive diet spoils them as he advances in years. When a tooth is entirely decayed, he is compelled to have recourse to the armourer or farrier, who is privileged to torture his patient, to break his jaw with his pincers, and tear away the gums together with the tooth that was troubling him.

The genuine chief, the real great lord, rarely leaves the saddle, and very seldom goes on foot, though he wears both boots and shoes. The common Arab, however, is an indefatigable walker, and in the course of a days will get over an incredible distance. His ordinary pace is what the French call the *pas gymnastique* [which is quicker than the English "double"], and what he himself calls a dog-trot. On flat ground, he generally takes off his shoes, if he happens to have any, partly that he may walk faster and more comfortably, and partly that he may not wear them out. Consequently, his foot is like that of antique statues, broad and flat, and with the toes wide apart. He is never troubled with corns, and more than once Christians, who have insinuated themselves into caravans, have been detected by this infallible sign and expelled. The sole of the foot acquires such hardness, that neither sand nor stones affect it, and a thorn sometimes penetrates to the depth of several lines without being felt. In the desert, properly so called, however, the sand during the great heat of summer is so burning hot that it is impossible to walk upon it with naked feet. Even the horses are obliged to be shod, or their feet would become painful and diseased. The dread of being bitten by the *lefâ*, a viper whose venom is fatal, also compels the Arabs themselves to wear buskins rising above the ankle.

The most common disease of the foot is the *cheggag*, or chaps, which are healed by having grease rubbed in, and by being afterwards cauterised with a hot iron. Sometimes these chaps are so long and deep that they are obliged to be sewed up. The thread used for the purpose is made of camel's sinews dried in the sun, and split into parts as fine as silk; spun camel's hair is, likewise, employed. All the inhabitants of the desert make use of this thread to mend their saddles, and bridles, and wooden platters. Every one carries about with him a housewife, a knife, and a needle.

Not a few turn their powers of pedestrianism to a good account, and make it their profession. Hence come the runners and messengers, who gird themselves tightly with a belt. These who are called *rekass* undertake affairs of great urgency. They will do in four days what the ordinary runners take ten to accomplish. They scarcely ever stop, but if they find it necessary to rest they count sixty inhalations of the breath and start again immediately. _ A *rekass* who receives four francs for going sixty leagues thinks himself well paid. This modest reward, however, is the more highly appreciated because it is paid in actual money. Specie is rare, and is the smallest portion of an Arab's fortune. The restricted circulation, and the facility of providing for the principal necessities of life without buying or selling, by simply having occasional recourse to barter are far from lowering the value of coined money.

In the desert a special messenger travels night and day, and sleeps only two hours in the twenty four. When he lies down he fastens to his foot a piece of cord of a certain length, to which he sets fire; and, just as it is nearly burned out, the heat awakens him. In 1846, an Arab, named El-Thouamy, a native of Leghrouât, was sent by the Kalifa Sid-Hamed-ben-Salem to Berryân, a town situated in the country of the Beni-Mzab. Starting at five in the morning from Kuesyr-el-Heyrân, he reached his destination about seven in the evening of the same day. In fourteen hours he had covered 168 kilomètres, travelling at the rate of twelve kilomètres an hour. This same Thouamy set out one day from

Negoussa to go to Berryân, a distance of 180 kilomètres, charged with an important message, and accomplished the journey in sixteen hours. During both of these courses this man eat only a few dates and drank about two *litres* of water.

In 1850, El-Ghiry, of the tribe of the Mokhalif, was hunting the ostrich, and, while wholly absorbed in chasing a *delim,* his horse broke down just as his last drop of water was exhausted. All trace of his companions was lost. For thrice twenty-four hours he wandered about at random, in the desert, without food or water. During the day he slept under a *bethoum,* and walked all night. His family had given him up entirely, when at length they saw him approaching. At first they could hardly recognize him, so utterly exhausted was he, so blackened by the sun, and reduced to such a skeleton. He afterwards related that he believed he owed his life to his dreams, in which he beheld his mother tending him, and giving him something to eat and drink. These visions, he said, had comforted and sustained him in his sore distress.

Let us now pass on from these examples of vigour and abstinence, which might be multiplied to infinity, and give a tolerably correct estimate of the goods and chattels of a Saharene nomade. This inventory will afford a far better idea of life in the desert than can be obtained from a long description. I take a man of influential family, and assume that his household is constituted after the following fashion. Himself, four wives, four sons, the wives of two of his sons, each of whom has a child, four negroes, four negresses, two white men servants, two white women servants : in all, twenty five souls. He may also, of course, have daughters, but they are sure to be married, and are no further trouble to him.   Such a household as this will possess:

A spacious tent in thoroughly good condition, to make which will require sixteen pieces of woollen cloth, forty cubits long by two in width, each worth from 7 to 8 *douros*, making a total of about..................	112 *douros.*
Two Arab beds, or rather carpets of shaggy wool, thirty cubits in length by five broad; dyed with madder. 20 *douros* each; if dyed with kermes, 25 *douros*........	50
A carpet, twelve cubits long by four wide, hung up as a curtain to separate the men's apartment from that of the women. It is dyed with kermes and costs.....	16
Six cushions, to contain wearing apparel and used as pillows : the price of each is 2 *douros*................	12
Six cushions of tanned antelope's skin, also used to contain dresses and spun wool, and to lean against in the tent..	6
Six pieces of woollen stuff, made into a sort of palanquin carried on camels' backs, and in which the women travel......................................	12
Five red *haïks* to cover the palanquins.................	50
Twenty woollen sacks for the carriage of corn..........	40
Six *hamal,* or loads of wheat..........................	48
Twelve loads of barley.................................	60
Ten woollen sacks in which are kept jewels, wearing apparel, cotton stuffs, gunpowder, *filali,** money, etc., at 2 *douros* each..................................	20
Fifteen goat-skin bags to hold water...................	25
Twelve sheep- or goat-skin bags to contain butter, valued each at 4 *douros*..............................	48
Four sheep- or goat-skin bags to hold honey, which is an expensive article, as it comes from the Tell; at 8 *douros* each....................................	32
Eight *hamal* of dates. These *hamal* are sacks lined with wool..	64
Six *tarahh,* each *tarahh* comprising six skins of morocco leather; in all, thirty six skins, at one *douro* a piece..	36
Gunpowder...	30
Lead..	5

* Goat-skins, generally dyed red, and prepared at Tafilalet in Morocco : it is what we call morocco leather.

Flints..	4 *douros.*
Ten *mektaa,* or pieces of cotton stuffs....................	20
Two *meradjen,* or vases of copper lined with tin, with handles, to drink out of.................................	2
Two *tassa,* or vases, also for drinking purposes..........	2
Two *guessaa,* or large wooden bowls for making or eating kouskoussou.......................................	4
Six *bakia,* or drinking vessels of wood...................	2
A copper pot for cooking the food........................	2
Three *metreud,* or wooden platters for strangers to eat from..	3
Two *fass,* or mattocks, for preparing the site of the tent, fixing it, etc., and for clearing wood....................	2
A *kadouma,* or small hatchet for shaping wood..........	1
Ten *meudjesa,* a kind of sickle for sheep-shearing.......	1
Two *rekiza,* or uprights of the tent........	2
A *âeushut-el-zemel,* or tent with carpets, cushions, etc., for travelling, or for receiving strangers...............	30
Total......	741 *douros.*

The wearing apparel of five men will consist of:

Eleven white burnouses, three for the father, and two for each of his sons: a burnous costs 4 *douros....... .*	44 *douros.*
Five *haïks,* at 4 *douros* each............................	20
Five *habaya,* or woollen shirts...........................	10
Five *mahazema,* or belts of morocco leather embroidered in silk...	10
Five pair of *belghra,* or morocco shoes....................	2
Five *shashia,* or morocco *fessy*...........................	2
Five *kate,* or complete suits, for grand occasions, consisting of an *oughrlila* or outer garment, a *cedria* or waistcoat, a *seroual* or pair of trousers; a *haïk* of silk, a silken cord replacing the camel's rope; and a cloth burnous : each suit at 60 *douros* will make	300
Total......	388 *douros.*

The wearing apparel of six women will consist of:

Six women's *haïks,* dyed with kermes....................	60 *douros.*
Six pair of morocco leather boots, embroidered.........	6
Six woollen girdles.......................................	12
Six white *haïks* worn over the head......................	6

Six *benica*, or silken hoods........................... 6 *douros*.

Six *aâsaba*, or thread cord by which the women fasten the *haouly*, or white *haïk*, over their heads................ 2

Six pair of *kholkhale*, or silver anklets, 20 *douros* the pair. 120

Six pair of *souar*, or bracelets, 7 *douros* the pair........ 42

Twelve *bezima*, or silver buckles, used by women to fasten the *haïk*, 6 *douros* the pair.......................... 36

Six *bezimat el gueursi*, or throat buckles, used to fasten the *haouly* under the chin after it has encircled the head.. 12

Twelve *ounaiss*, or silver ear-rings set in coral.   Every woman wears two pair.................................... 24

Six *mekhranga*, or necklaces of coral and pieces of money. 48

Six necklaces of cloves interspersed with coral......... 5

Six *zenzela*, or silver chains with a small circular plate in the middle, called "the scorpion:" the chain stretches from ear to ear.................................... 13

Six *kuerrabar*, or silver boxes which the women hang from their necks, and in which they put musk and benjamin... 18

Eighteen *khatem*, or silver rings....................... 6

Six *melyaca*, or bracelets of djamous horn............. 6

Women in the desert do not wear any ornaments of gold; the whole of their jewelry is in silver.

Total...... 815 douros.

The arms for seven men are:

Five guns for the masters, procured from Algiers, and mounted in silver...................................... 100 *douros*.

Two guns for the servants............................... 20

Five sabres, two of them mounted in silver............. 40

Five pistols, two of them mounted in silver............ 85

Four pistols for the negroes........................... 12

Four sabres for the negroes............................ 12

Total...... 219 douros.

Harness and horsemen's equipment consist of:

One saddle for the master............................. 100 *douros*.

Four ordinary saddles................................. 160

Two common saddles for the servants.................. 20

One master's *djebira* of tiger-skin.................. 17

Four ordinary *djebira*............................... 28

One pair of master's *temag*, or boots of morocco leather. 12

Four pair of ordinary *temag*..................................... 24 *douros.*
One pair of master's spurs, mounted in silver and orna-
   mented with coral.. 6
Four pair of ordinary *shabirs,* or spurs..................... 4
Five *medol,* or straw hats adorned with ostrich feathers. 5

                              Total...... 3̅.6 *douros.*

Horses, cattle, negroes, etc., consist of:

A stallion for the chief of the tent.................... 100 *douros.*
Four blood mares for his sons........................... 320
Two servants' mares..................................... 60
Six asses... 18
Two *slougui,* or greyhounds [not purchasable]........... »
Four negroes.. 240
Four negresses.. 200
Twenty *ghelem,* each *ghelem* a flock of 400 sheep........ 8.000
Four *ibeul,* or droves of 100 camels each : of these 400 ani-
   mals, 130 are she-camels which command a higher
   price than the males, but I value them all round at
   30 *douros* a head.................................... 12,000
Ten he- or she-goats, the only use of which is to make
   the sheep keep moving on a march..................... 50
Two tame gazelles, a young antelope, and an ostrich
   [these are never for sale]........ .... »

                            Total...... 20,988 *douros.*

The chief of a tent of this importance ought besides to possess, in depôt, in three or four *kucsours,* or small towns :

Twelve hundred *zedja,* or fleeces, worth each half a *boud-*
   jou .... 200 *douros.*
Thirty white burnouses, at 3 *douros* each............... 90
Thirty *haïks* at 2 *douros*................................. 60
Forty *habaya,* or woollen shirts at 2 *douros*............. 80
Forty loads of dates at 7 *douros*........................ 280
Thirty camel loads of wheat............................. 240
Thirty loads of barley.................................. 150
Four *khrabya,* or enormous earthen vessels filled with
   butter.. »

                            Total...... 1,100 *douros.*

I estimate at 600 *douros* the amount of what he may
have lent or sold, to the people of the *kuesours* with
whom he has business transactions.................. 600 *douros.*
In his tent he has.. 600
Buried in a house belonging to him in one of the
*kuesours**... 1,000

Total...... 2,200 *douros.*

He has likewise a house in a *kuesour* in the charge of
a *khremass,* containing his most valuable property... 60 *douros.*

RECAPITULATION.

Tents and furniture, etc............................... 741 *douros.*
Wearing apparel of both sexes........................ 815
Arms 219
Harness and Accoutrements............................ 376
Horses, cattle, etc.................................. 20,988
Deposits... 1,100
Loans, etc... 2,200
House.. 60

Total...... 26,499 *douros.*†

An Arab who possesses such a fortune does no work.
He attends the meetings and assemblies of the *djemâa,*
hunts, rides about, looks at his flocks, and prays.   His
only occupations are political, warlike, and religious.   A
poor Arab equally disdains manual labour.   He is not
forced to it, for there is no other kind of cultivation than
that of date-trees, which is left to the inhabitants of the
kuesours.   Negroes are numerous and cost very little,
and, with the assistance of a few white servants, suffice
for the services which the free men refuse to perform for
themselves.   Some of the latter, however, mend their
sacks and harness, but they form the exception.   There

---

* Money is never buried in the desert as it is in the Tell, lest the floods of winter
should betray the hiding places.

† About £5,721.   The *douro* worth about 4 shillings and 6 pence.

are likewise farriers, but these, in fact, are artists—the privileges that are accorded to them, of which I have already had occasion to speak, constituting them a sort of special corporation. The armourers are, in truth, mere workmen who repair, but cannot manufacture, arms. The Arabs of the desert are for the most part worse armed than those of the Tell, though their chiefs yield to none in pomp and luxury. This is easily accounted for. As they obtain their arms from Tunis by way of Tougourt, or from Morocco through the Gourara country, the great distance to be traversed prevents them from getting their arms repaired as soon as they need repairs, and the unskilfulness of those who undertake this business will not permit them to do their work very efficiently. Many of the Saharenes are still armed with lances, which they seldom use except when pursuing runaways. Their spears consist of a shaft of wood six feet long, with a flat double-edged head of iron, and are usually carried in a bandolier.

The Arab of the Sahara is very proud of his mode of life, which is not only exempt from the monotonous toil to which the inhabitant of the Tell is subject, but is full of action and excitement, of variety and incident. If beards grow white at an early age in the desert, it is not only because of heat, fatigue, journeys, and combats, but much more from care, anxiety, and grief. He alone does not turn gray who "has a large heart, is resigned, and can say : It is the will of Allah!" This pride in their country and in their peculiar mode of existence amounts to positive contempt for the Tell and its inhabitants. What the dweller in the desert chiefly plumes himself upon is his independence; for in his country the lands are wide and there is no Sultan. The chief of the tribe administers and renders justice, a task of no great difficulty where every delinquency has been provided for and its appropriate penalty fixed beforehand. Whoever steals a sheep, pays a fine of ten boudjous. Whoever enters a tent to see his neighbour's wife, forfeits ten ewes. Whoever takes life, must lose his own; or, if he makes his escape, all that belongs to him is confiscated, save only his tent, which is given up to his wife and children. The fines are set apart by the *djemâa* for defraying the expences of travellers and marabouts, and of presents to strangers. Thefts within the tribe are severely punished. If committed on another tribe, they are looked over, and, if a hostile tribe be the sufferers, are even encouraged.

The women attend to the cooking, and weave various kinds of carpets, sacks, stuff for tents, horse-cloths, camel-packs, and nose-bags, while the negresses fetch wood and water. Burnouses, *haïks,* and *kabaya* are made in the *kuesours.* If rich, an Arab is always generous; and rich or poor, he is sure to be hospitable and charitable. He seldom lends his horse, but would regard it as an insult if the animal were sent back to him. For every present he receives he makes a return of greater value. Some men are quoted as never having refused anything. It is a common saying : "He who applies to a noble never comes back empty-handed." It is needless to speak of alms. Every one knows that next to a holy war, and on the same line with going on a pilgrimage, alms-giving is the act of all others the most pleasing to Allah. If an Arab is sitting down to a meal, and a mendicant, who happens to be passing, exclaims : *Mtâ rcbi ia el moumenin*—" of what belongs to Allah, O Believer!"—he shares his repast with him if there be enough for two, or else abandons it to him entirely.

A stranger presenting himself before a *douar,* stands some little way off, and pronounces these words : *Dif rebi*—"a guest sent by Allah." The effect is magical. Whatever may be his condition of life, they throw themselves on him, tear him from one another, and hold his stirrup while he alights. The servants lead away his horse, about whom, if he be a man of good breeding, he will not give himself any further trouble. He himself is almost dragged into a tent, and whatever is ready to hand is set before him, until a banquet can be prepared. Nor is less attention shown to a traveller on foot. The master of the tent keeps his guest company throughout the whole of the day, and only leaves him to make way for sleep. No indiscreet questions are ever asked, such as : Whence comest thou? Who art thou? Whither goest thou? There is no instance of any evil having ever befallen a stranger thus received as a guest, even though he were a mortal enemy. At his departure, the master of the tent will say to him : "Follow thy good fortune;" and after the guest has fairly taken his departure, his entertainer is no longer answerable for anything. In retiring from the hospitable repast, if the stranger pass before a *douar* and be seen, he is obliged again to accept the invitations that are pressed upon him.

A certain class of men live entirely on alms and hospitality. These are the dervishes. Absorbed in prayer, these pious individuals are the object of universal veneration. "Beware of offering them an insult, for Allah will punish you." A request made by them is never refused. By the side of these mendicant monks, who so exactly reproduce a particular feature of the Middle Ages, it seems appropriate to place the *tolbas,* or learned men, and the "wise women," who fill in the Sahara the part that belonged in the olden times to the magicians, alchemists, and sorcerers, and those other impostors celebrated by Tasso and Ariosto, and ridiculed by Cervantes. It is to these *tolbas* and aged dames that both men and women apply for a philter, composed of various herbs prepared with solemn invocations and awesome or grotesque ceremonies, which is mixed with the food of the swain or damsel whose love is longed for. It is they, again, who write magic words and the name of the hated one on a piece of paper and a dead man's bone taken from a cemetery, and then bury together the paper and the bone, which will soon be joined by the enemy, "with his belly full of worms." They will teach you, too, the formula you must pronounce while closing your knife, in order to sever the life of an odious rival; and that which you must throw into the furnace over which is being cooked the food of the family you would poison; and that which you must write on a copper plate, or flattened ball, to be flung into the stream whither repairs to drink the woman on whom you would avenge yourself — seized with a dysentery as rapid as the river, she will die, if she do not yield herself up to you. To effect her cure, the first sorcery must be counteracted by a second.

After these come the long train of spectres, the phantoms of those who have died a violent death. If one of them pursue you, lose no time in exclaiming : "Return to thy hole. Thou canst not frighten me. I feared thee not when thou didst carry arms." It will follow you yet a little, but will soon desist. If you are seized with terror and attempt to flee, you will hear in the air the clashing of arms, and a horse in full pursuit behind, with yells and horrible uproar, until you drop exhausted by fatigue.

In Morocco, on the banks of the Ouad Noun, about twenty days march westward of Souss, the most famous sorcerers are found. There is there a whole school of alchemists and necromancers, and of occult sciences, besides a talking mountain, and many others marvels of the magical world. The common people alone are debased to these superstitions. The wealthy, the marabouts, the *tolbas* of the *zaouïa;* and the *sheurfaa,* scrupulously follow the precepts of religion and read the sacred books; but the vulgar herd are plunged in ignorance, and barely know two or three prayers and the confession of faith. They likewise pray very rarely, and only perform their ablutions when they find water. The chiefs do their utmost to dispel this ignorance. Even on a journey they take care that the *moudden* never fail to proclaim the hour of prayer, and they establish schools in their tents. But a life of fatigue, wandering, and migration, soon causes the Arabs to forget the lessons of their childhood. Men of all ranks, however, take pleasure in having them recalled to mind in the garb of poesy by the *meddah,* or religious bards, who go about at festivals singing the praises of Allah, and the saints, and the holy war, accompanying themselves the while with flute and tambourine. These bards are rewarded with numerous presents.

"Take a thorny shrub," said the Emir Abd-el-Kader to me one day, "and water it for a whole year with rose-water, and it will still yield nothing but thorns. But take a date-tree, and leave it without water, without cultivation, and it still will produce dates." From the Arab point of view the nobles are this date-tree, and the common people that thorny shrub. In the East, great faith is placed in the power of blood and in the virtue of race. The aristocracy is regarded not only as a social necessity, but as an absolute law of nature. No one ever dreams of revolting against this truism, which is accepted by all with a placid resignation. The head is the head and the tail the tail, is what the lowest of the Arab shepherds would say.

In addition to this long descended and sacred nobility composed of the *sherifs,* or descendants of the Prophet, there are two distinct classes of aristocracy—the one the aristocracy of religion, the other the aristocracy of the sword. The marabouts and the *djouad*—for such are their designations—the former deriving their position from their piety, the latter from their courage, the former from prayer, the latter from battle, regard each other with an implacable hatred. The *djouad* reproach the marabouts with the offences which in all countries are eagerly attributed to religious orders that aim at the direction of human affairs. They accuse them of ambition, of intriguing, of underhand proceedings, and of an insatiable covetousness for the good things of the earth masked by a pretended love of Allah and of Heaven. One of their proverbs declares "From the *zaouïa* * a serpent is ever issuing." From this it appears that the Arabs, while chaunting the praises of the aristocracy, do not hesitate, sound Believers as they are, to speak the truth with regard to their priesthood. The marabouts, on the other hand, charge the *djouad* with violence, rapine, and impïety. This last accusation furnishes them with a terrible weapon of offence. They stand in the same relation towards their rivals as did the clergy of the Middle Ages towards the lay nobles who, notwithstanding the imposing appearance of their warlike power, could yet be reached by an anathema. In like manner, if the *djouad* exercise an influence over the people through the memory of perils encountered and blood shed, and all the prestige of military achievements, the marabouts on their part are armed with the omnipotence of religious faith acting on popular imagination. More than once has a marabout, feared or loved by the people, imperilled the power and even the life of a *djieud*.† Nevertheless it is the *djieud* whom I now propose to portray, because the life of the

---

* Religious establishments, generally comprising a mosque and a school, and the tumbs of their founders.

† Singular of *djouad*.

desert is especially the life of the warrior. To exhibit at one glance a noble of the Sahara in all the pomp, noise, and animation of his existence, it is necessary to depict the interior of a great tent at the moment when the day begins, from eight o'clock to noon.

The poets of antiquity have many a time described the crowd of clients who were wont to inundate the porticoes of a patrician palace in ancient Rome. A great tent in the desert in these days resembles in its way the luxurious mansions painted by Horace and Juvenal. Gravely seated on a carpet, with that dignified demeanour which is the peculiar privilege of Orientals, the chief of the tribe receives in their turn all who come to invoke his authority. This one complains of a neighbour who has endeavoured to seduce his wife, that one accuses a wealthy man of refusing to pay a debt, another is anxious to recover some cattle that have been stolen from him, while a fourth demands protection for his daughter whom a brutal husband maltreats in the most shameful manner. The first quality in a chief is patience. Assailed on all sides by violent recriminations, he lends an attentive ear to each, and strives to heal the wounds of every description which are disclosed to him. "A man in authority," says an eastern apophthegm, "ought to imitate the physicians who never apply the same remedies to all diseases." In these "beds of justice" that recall the primitive manner in which our ancient kings disposed of the private interests of their subjects, the Arab chief employs the utmost sagacity, the greatest force of character, with which he may have been endowed. To some he gives orders, to others advice: to no one does he refuse the aid of his wisdom and influence.. Nor has he need only of the quality that Solomon demanded of the Lord. Wisdom must be combined with generosity and valour. The highest praise that can be awarded is to say of him that "his sabre is always drawn, his hand always open." He must never weary of practising the somewhat ostentatious, and yet at the same time noble and touching, charity, enjoined by the Mussulman law as an obligation on all Believers. His tent must be a refuge for the unfortunate, nor may any one die of hunger in his neighbourhood; for the Prophet hath said: "Allah will never accord his mercy but to the merciful. Believers, give alms, if it be only the half of a date. Whoso gives alms to-day shall be amply recompensed to-morrow."

If a warrior loses the horse that was his sole strength, if a family is robbed of the flocks that furnished its subsistance, it is to the chief, and to the chief alone, the sufferers address themselves. However strong may be the love of pelf, it never goes so far as to make him risk the loss of his influence; and the Arab noble, while in so many respects resembling the Baron of the Middle Ages, differs from him in one essential point—he abhors gambling. Neither cards nor dice ever wile away the leisure hours in a tent. An Arab chief may neither indulge in play, nor lend money at usurious rates of interest. The only way in which he may turn his money to account, is by indirect participation in some commercial enterprise. He hands over a certain sum to a merchant, who trades with it, and, at the end of so many years, divides with the lender the profits he has gathered. It must not, however, be supposed that riches are therefore despised by Orientals. With them, as in every other part of the world, wealth is one of the indispensable conditions of power. Whoever falls into poverty, falls also very quickly into obscurity, while he who makes a fortune enters upon the path of honours. But, in order to follow out an ambitious career, it is by the right arm rather than by industry that wealth must be acquired. When a warrior has made a number of razzias that have brought him at the same time glory and gold, he is surnamed Ben-Deraou, "the son of his arm," and may aspire to the highest dignities of the tribe. This brings us back to the quality which should be the groundwork of every noble Arab's soul—valour.

"Nothing," said Abd-el-Kader, "throws out so well as blood the dazzling whiteness of a burnous." An Arab chief, like our captains in the olden times, should be more valiant than all his men at arms. He must distinguish himself by warlike feats as much as by his bearing at fantasias. His influence would be for ever lost if he were suspected of faintness of heart. But it is the reality, not the appearance, which the Arabs appreciate. What they admire is a spirit nobly tempered, and not the frame of a mere giant, or athlete. This is the place to combat the widely spread prejudice that a lofty stature and bodily strength make a deep impression upon them. Such is far from being the case. They take pleasure in man's being robust, patient of thirst and hunger, and capable of enduring severe fatigue; but they care very little for tallness of stature, or for muscular force like that of our porters, or showman's Hercules. They reserve their esteem for activity, address, and courage. It little matters to them whether a man be tall or short; and not unfrequently, while looking at some

Colossus whose huge proportions are being vaunted in their presence, they may be heard to murmur sententiously : "What to us is the stature or strength! Let us see the heart. After all, it may be only the skin of a lion on the back of a cow."

But notwithstanding this admiration of valour, there is no point of honour among the Arabs such as prevails among ourselves. In their eyes there is no cowardice in retreating before superior numbers, or even in fleeing before an enemy of inferior strength, if there is nothing to be gained by fighting. They often laugh among themselves at our chivalrous scruples. Fond as they are of riding at furious speed, and of the noisy discourse of fire-arms, they nevertheless desire to have some object of public utility as their motive for battle. Full of ardour so long as Fortune leads them on, they disperse and disappear as soon as she betrays them. In forming, therefore, their judgment of acts of bravery, there are many essential points of difference between them and ourselves. Their respect for courage never urges them to excessive severity towards those who are deficient in that quality. A coward will never rise to any post of dignity in his tribe, but neither will he be an object of contempt. They will merely say of him, with that absence of anger which usually accompanies fatalism : "It was not the will of Allah that he should be brave. He is to be pitied rather than blamed." A man of faint heart is expected, however, to redeem his shortcomings by the prudence of his counsels, and above all by an unfailing generosity.

Braggadocio is treated with greater contempt than cowardice. "If thou sayest that the lion is an ass, go and put a halter on him," is an oriental proverb in very general use. In spite of the heat of their blood and the hyperbolical character of their speech, the Arabs demand from true courage that dignified silence which they regard so highly. In this respect they have nothing in common with the nations with whom they fought in the time of the Cid; nor yet under the head of single combats, which are entirely unknown among them. A tradition, which probably dates from the crusades, asserts that in the olden time illustrious chiefs met each other in single combat, but the oldest members of the tribes of the present day have no personal recollection of anything of the kind. If a man deems himself seriously affronted, he avenges himself by assassination. There are individuals with easy consciences and complacent dispositions who, for a very moderate sum, will rid you of an enemy. But if the aggrieved happens to be more sparing of his gold than of his life—his hand being more ready to strike than his purse to open—he watches his opportunity to fall upon the man who has wronged him. He kills him, or is killed by him. In the former case it is a common thing to bequeath to another the debt of blood; for, in the absence of duelling, private revenge is in a very flourishing condition among the Arabs, and descends from generation to generation. Among them still prevail those family feuds which formerly dyed red the pavements of Italian cities, and which even in the present day stain the soil of an island of France.

The ordinary causes of the Arab *vendetta* are disputes as to wells, pasturage and landmarks, the rape of a young wife or daughter, the murder of a jealous husband, of a successful rival, or of a woman who has refused compliance,—or rivalries of chiefs, whose quarrel is espoused, first of all, by their relations, friends, and clients, then by the whole tribe, and at last by the tribes in alliance with them. As a natural consequence of the absence of the duello, private disputes are settled by assassination, and the feud, being transmitted from kin to kin and constantly provided with new fuel, goes on to eternity. The *vendetta* is either of a private or public nature, according as the injury to be avenged affects an individual or a tribe. If from any cause a man happen to lose his life through the act of a chief, or even of a humble member of a neighbouring tribe, the homicide can arrange the affair legally by paying the *dya*, or blood-money, to the heirs of the deceased. The *dya* is the same as the *Wehrgeld* of the Germans, with this difference—that not only is it legal, but from its first institution it assumed a religious character. According to the *tolbas*, it may be traced back to Abd-el-Mettaleb, the grandfather of Mohammed, and was indirectly the cause of the birth of the Prophet. Abd-el-Mettaleb, chief of the tribe of the Koreishites, had no children, and in his despair he offered up the following prayer to Allah: "Lord, if thou wilt bestow upon me ten sons, I swear to sacrifice one of them unto thee as a thanksgiving offering." Allah heard his prayer and made him ten times a father. Faithful to his vow, Abd-el-Mettaleb left it to the drawing of lots to decide who should be the victim. The lot fell upon Abd-Allah; but, the tribe opposing this sacrifice, it was resolved by the chiefs that, instead of Abd-Allah, ten camels should be set aside as a stake and recourse again had to lots until they turned up in favour of the lad, ten camels being added to the first for every time the lots had been unfavourable. It was not until the eleventh trial that Abd-Allah was redeemed, and one hundred camels were sacrificed in his place. Some time afterwards Allah manifested His satisfaction with this exchange, for He caused Mohammed his Prophet to be born to Abd-Allah; and ever since then the price of an Arab's life has been fixed at one hundred camels. Circumstances, however, sometimes occur to reduce this high standard.

There is scarcely an instance on record of a homicide who has paid the *dya* being otherwise proceeded against, or of the parents or the children of the deceased hesitating to accept this satisfaction. But if he be too poor to pay it, or if the Government has thought fit to interfere in the matter, he is condemned to suffer like for like, an eye for an eye, a tooth for a tooth, a life for a life. When I was consul for France at Mascara, in 1837, accredited to Abd-el-Kader, I had an opportunity of witnessing the application of the *lex talionis* in its utmost rigour. Two children having quarrelled in the street, their father interposed, and from insults proceeded to threats, until one of them, gradually becoming infuriated, drew his knife and stabbed his adversary, who fell down dead upon the spot. The latter received five wounds; one on his right, a second on his left, breast, two in the stomach, and the fifth in the back. A mob collected, and the *shaoushs,* or police agents seized the murderer and led him before the *hakem,* or mayor of the town. The *aoulemas,* or doctors of the law, immediately assembled, and constituted themselves a tribunal. In less than half an hour the witnesses were heard, and the culprit was sentenced to undergo the full penalty of the

lex talionis at the hands of his victim's brother.   At a
signal given by the Cadi, two *shaoushs* bound his wrists
together with a rope, and, placing themselves on either
side of him, conducted him, preceded by the executioner,
to the market-place, thronged at the time by two or
three thousand Arabs.   However horrible might be the
singular drama about to be acted, it furnished me with
an opportunity for a rare experience, and I succeeded in
overcoming the instinctive repugnance, which I at first
felt, to being present.   By the time I reached the spot,
the *shaoushs,* by dint of freely plying their sticks, had
forced back the crowd to the circumference of a spacious
circle, the centre of which was occupied by the executioner and his victim, the one with his knife in his hand,
the other calm and indifferent to what was about to
happen.   According to the sentence, the murderer was
to receive as many stabs as he had inflicted, and in the
same order and in the same parts of the body as the man
he had murdered.   When all was ready,—and the preparations were merely what I have described,—a *shaoush*
raised his staff, by way of signal.   The Arab with the
knife immediately rushed on his victim, and stabbed him
first on the right and then on the left breast, but evidently
without touching the heart, for the poor wretch cried
aloud: "Strike! Strike!   But think not that it is thou
who takest my life.   Allah alone takes away life."   The
punishment, however, was continued with horrible fury,
and the criminal, whose entrails protruded from two fresh
wounds he received in the belly, never ceased to revile
his executioner.   There still remained one other blow to
give.   The wounded man turned round of himself, and
the blade of the knife disappeared entirely in his loins.

He staggered, but did not fall. "Enough! Enough!" cried the mob. "He gave only five blows, and he ought not to receive more." The execution was over, and the unfortunate man who underwent all this torture had still sufficient strength to return to his own house on foot. M. Warnier, physician to the consulate, arrived there almost at the same instant as himself, and while he was endeavouring to sew together the gaping mouths of the two wounds in the belly, the patient kept crying aloud: "Oh! I pray you, heal me! They say thou art a great physician; prove it, heal me, so that I may kill that dog!" It was all in vain, for that night he died.

But if the murderer be the master of a great tent, and sufficiently influential to induce the tribe to exercise forbearance towards him, and therefore refuses to pay any blood money, he will sooner or later expiate that refusal with his life, which the *vendetta* will overtake though justice lag behind. From his death, however, will arise a deadly feud, as I have already shown. I could give many instances of the *vendetta;* and the one that follows, being equally illustrative of the customs of a powerful Saharene tribe, the Shamba, and of those of a people of the Great Desert, the Touareg, separated from one another by at least two hundred leagues, will afford a just notion of those obstinate hatreds, of that thirst for vengeance which always embody themselves in the same acts of violence. A band of the Shamba, commanded by Ben Mansour, chief of Ouargla, surprised, near the Djebel-Baten, some Touaregs who were watering their camels in the Oued-Mia, under the leadership of Kheddash, chief of the Djebel-Hoggar. An implacable hatred, the origin of which is unknown, divides the Shamba from the Touaregs—the latter, besides, being in a state of perpetual vendetta against the Saharenes, either because they are Berbers and not Arabs, or because they levy a tax on the caravans to and from Soudan. A bloody conflict ensued, and the Touaregs were put to the rout, leaving ten of their party dead upon the ground, and among them their chief, whose headless body they found some days afterwards. Ben-Mansour had carried off his head, which he exposed, as a trophy of his victory, over one of the gates of Ouargla. The tidings spread mourning throughout the Djebel-Hoggar, and an oath was taken: "May my tent be destroyed if Kheddash be not avenged!" Kheddash left behind him a widow of great beauty named Fetoum, and one young child. According to usage, Fetoum was entitled to rule, assisted by the Council of Nobles, until such time as her son should be of age to assume the leadership. One day, therefore, when the leading men were assembled in her tent, she said to them: "My brethren, whichever of you will bring me Ben-Mansour's head shall have me for wife." That same evening all the young men of the mountain armed themselves for war, and went to her, saying: "To-morrow we will set out with our servants to seek thy wedding present." And at the dawn of day three hundred Touaregs, commanded by Ould-Biska, a cousin of Kheddash, set out on their march to the northward. Hardly had they taken up their position at their first halt, when they beheld coming up behind them half a score of camels with riders, and among them one fleeter of foot and more richly accoutred than the others. They at once recognized the camel of Fetoum, for Fetoum had come in person to join their little army.

She was greeted with loud acclamations, for it seemed to them, and perhaps with reason, that she had come expressly to be able more promptly to fulfil her promise. It was the month of May, when water is to be found in every ravine, and the sands are clothed with herbage. During the halt on the eighth day, the scouts came in with the news that a strong body of the Shamba, commanded by Ben-Mansour, were driving their flocks towards the grazing grounds of the Oued-Nessa. The Shamba, however, having received intelligence of the approach of the Touaregs, had turned suddenly towards the north and had already gained the Oued-Mzab. But their retreat was speedily discovered, and by a forced march of a day and a night, the Touaregs placed themselves in ambush in ravines and brushwood at a distance of only a few leagues from the enemy, who had now no suspicion of their presence. All that day they rested, and when night came they again took to the plain, putting their camels to a long swinging trot. At length about midnight the barking of the dogs betrayed the *douar* of which they were in search. The next moment, on a signal given by Ould-Biska, they dashed forward uttering their war-cry. Of the Shamba, at the most not more than five or six escaped, and one even of these was wounded by Ould-Biska who, with a thrust of his long spear, struck him in the loin. Run away with by his mare, the ill-fated horseman, rolling from side to side but still keeping his seat, went on a few steps, but presently he sank forward and fell over on to the sand, dragging down with him in his fall a child seven or eight years of age whom he had till then kept concealed in his burnous. "Ben-Mansour! Ben-Mansour! knowest

thou Ben-Mansour?" demanded Ould-Biska. "He wa
my father—behold him!" replied the boy, calm and erec
beside the dead body. At that moment, Fetoum came up
followed, surrounded, and closely hemmed in by a group
of the Touaregs. "It is I who have slain him!" cried
Ould-Biska. "And it shall be done as I said," answered
Fetoum; "but take thy poniard, open the body of the
accursed, tear out his heart, and throw it to the dogs."

While Ould-Biska, kneeling on the ground and stoop-
ing over the corpse, proceeded to execute this order,
Fetoum, her lips compressed and her whole frame trembling with nervous excitement, gloated over the shocking
spectacle. And when at last the *slougui* had finished
their horrible repast, her revenge being now complete,
Fetoum remounted her *mahari* and gave the signal for
retreat, without taking any heed of the booty her followers were piling up, or of the flocks they were driving
together. As to the son of Ben-Mansour, his life was
spared, but they abandoned him to his fate. For two
days he remained there, weeping, thirsting, hungering,
and exposed to the sun, but on the third day he was
found by some shepherds who conveyed him to Ouargla,
where he was living in 1845. Thus the dogs of the
Touaregs have eaten the heart of the chief of the Shamba,
and it may be easily imagined that this will be the
subject of an undying feud, that will know neither
respite nor mercy.

I will not dwell any further upon customs impressed
which such savage energy. By way of contrast, I will
now trace some family sketches, commencing with the
reverence attached to the paternal authority. So long
as the child is in his infancy, the tent belongs to him,

and his father is in some respects the first of his slaves. His sports are the delight of the family, his whims the life and soul of the domestic circle. But as soon as he attains to puberty, he is taught the utmost deference. He is not even allowed to speak in the presence of his father, or to attend the same meetings. This absolute respect which he is bound to exhibit towards the head of the family, he is also obliged to pay to his eldest brother. However, notwithstanding their aristocratic severity, the customs of the Arabs do not come up to the gloomy rigour of the Roman Patricians. A father, for instance, would never condemn his son to death unless he has dishonoured his couch—for any other offence he would merely banish him from his presence.

Thus far I have sketched with a coarse and rapid pencil the character of the Arab aristocracy; I will now endeavour to represent the actual life of a noble in some of its most solemn moments.

The day on which a child is born in a great tent is one of much rejoicing. Every one visits the father of the new-born, and says to him : "May thy son be happy!" And while the men press round the father, the mother is not neglected, for the women of the tribe flock to see her. Both men and women have their hands full of presents, proportioned to their means. From camels, sheep, and costly apparel, down to grain and dates, all the treasures of the desert abound in the tent which Allah has just visited with his blessing. The recipient of all these tokens of affection and respect is obliged to exercise a large hospitality. Sometimes for twenty consecutive days, he feeds and entertains his guests. These festivals in the desert have that air of grandeur which belongs to all the scenes that are enacted in this solemn theatre of primitive life.

As soon as the child is old enough, he learns to read and write, which is an innovation among the *djouad,* for until recently the marabouts alone cultivated letters. The man of the sword, like our mediæval barons, held learning in contempt. It seemed to him that, in cultivating his mind, some sort of injury was done to his energy of character. But since they have beheld the humblest of our soldiers possessed of knowledge without their courage being impaired, the Arabs have changed their opinion on the subject. Besides, those who took service with us soon dicovered that education conferred a title to favours. Many of them too, murmur to one another with a tone of sad resignation : "Formerly we were able to live in ignorance, for peace and happiness were with us; but in this time of trouble through which we are compelled to pass, science must come to our aid." Our influence thus gradually accomplishes, in the very heart of the desert, the work of civilisation, of which some among us speak so despondingly, and others so lightly.

The culture of letters, however, does not lead, in the education of the Arab, to any neglect of the art of managing a horse or of handling fire-arms. As soon as a child can sit on a horse, he is placed, first of all, on the back of a colt, and then on the full grown animal. When his frame begins to take form, he is taken out hunting, and taught to fire at a mark, and to bury his spear in the flanks of a wild boar. By the time he has attained his sixteenth or seventeenth year, has learned the Koran, and has been accustomed to fast, he is married. The Prophet has said : "Marry when young.

Marriage subdues the glance of the man's eye, and regulates the conduct of the woman." Up to that epoch, paternal tenderness watches over the purity of his manners with unceasing vigilance. The lad is never left to himself. A tutor or an attendant accompanies him wherever he goes. Men of dissolute habits and women of a loose course of life are carefully kept away from him. He is expected to bring to the companion of his life a body in robust health, and a soul untainted by pollution. They select for him a youthful maiden of birth equal to his own, of unspotted reputation, and, if possible, of great beauty. It is the women of the family who ascertain these points, being permitted to examine the tents in which dwell young girls of marriageable years. A betrothal takes place, followed in due time by the wedding.

The first of these days of festival, which like those at the birth of a child, last for some time, is called *nahr refoude,* or the day of the rape. Four or five hundred horsemen, magnificently attired, riding their finest horses, carrying their most valuable arms, and conducted by the kinsmen of the bride, proceed to the tent of the latter. They are accompanied by women closely veiled and mounted on camels and mules. The youngest and most beautiful damsels of the tribe are chosen for this joyful mission. The journey, which sometimes lasts three days, is one continual fantasia. The horsemen gallop to and fro, there is a constant discharge of fire-arms, and the women utter that long-drawn cry of love and joy which fills the heart of the children of the desert with ineffable emotion. At the arrival of this triumphal procession, the father of the bride comes forth and exclaims · "You are welcome, O guests of Allah!" Then follow banquetings and rejoicings until the morrow when they again set out. This time the bride forms on of the cavalcade, mounted on a camel, or mule, richly caparisoned. She has taken no leave of her father. An almost false sense of delicacy forbids her to appear in his presence at a moment when her fate is about to undergo an entire change. She is equally prohibited from seeing her elder brothers. Her girlhood's life is finished. Henceforth she belongs to another family.

When she is on the point of starting, her mother tenderly embraces her and says: "You are going away from those from whose loins you sprang. You are going far away from the nest that has so long sheltered you, and whence you issued forth to learn to walk, and that in order to go to a man whom you know not, and to whose society you have never been accustomed. I advise you to be to him as a slave, if you wish that he should be to you as a servant. Be satisfied with little. Keep a constant watch over all that is likely to come under his eyes, and let not his eyes ever behold an evil action. See to his food and his sleep. Hunger causes anger, the want of sleep produces ill humour. Take care of his property. Treat his kinsfolk and slaves with kindness. Be dumb as to his secrets. When he rejoices, show no signs of sorrow. When he is sorrowful, show no signs of joy. Allah will bless you!"

While this nuptial journey is being accomplished, the bridegroom prepares a tent richly ornamented, which he places under the safeguard of some of his friends. Into this the bride enters with her mother and female relatives. A choice banquet is presented to her, and outside a festival is celebrated, which, with gunpowder and music, combines all that enters into the desert notion of rejoicing. At ten at night the husband glides into the tent, now silent and deserted.

A wedding feast is often prolonged over three days and nights, and is repeated each time the husband takes a fresh wife. An Arab chief is permitted by the law to have four wives at the same time, but even these do no suffice for the gratification of these fickle and voluptuous temperaments. It is in vain that, by a custom which recalls to mind Biblical manners, a Mussulman husband is allowed to associate concubines with his legitimate wives. Even this tolerance is insufficient, and recourse is had to divorce to appease these insatiable and ever craving appetites. Instances have been known of an Arab chief having had a dozen to fifteen lawful wives. As may easily be imagined, peace is far from reigning in households where the law recognizes the existence of such elements of discord. Sometimes the tent is divided into two parts, one chamber being exclusively reserved for the women, the other belonging to the husband, who selects from among his wives the one he fancies for that night. Terrible jealousies secretly spring into being, and, gradually gaining strength, finish by an explosion. Frequently a wife who is preferred to her fellows is seized with a mysterious illness, under which she languishes, fades away, and dies—a poison prepared by a rival's hand has passed into her veins. This is the gloomy side of eastern manners—crime allying itself to lust.

The immense part played by wives in the life of the Mussulmans is shown by the following fact. Tell an Arab that he is a coward, he will submit to the insult— if he is a coward, it is the will of Allah that it should be so. Call him a thief, he will smile; for in his eyes theft is sometimes a meritorious act. But address hi as *tahan*—a word which the language of Molière cou alone translate with concise forcibleness—and you w. kindle in his breast a fury that blood only can extinguish. The only man whom an Arab will never forgive is one who can with truth cast in his teeth that ill-omened epithet.

After marriage the noble of the desert enters upon a new life, and upon a sphere of individual action. ' 'He is now emancipated, though not in an absolute fashion unless he is the head of the tent, and master of his own goods and chattels, or if his father is still alive. However, even under these circumstances, he henceforth counts among his tribe as a man of action and of counsel, and by accumulated experience he will put the finishing touch to his training as a great lord, thus far sketched out by the habit of seeing good examples and hearing good advice. Already he has his own clients, his own horses, his own greyhounds, his own falcons, and all the equipments for war and the chace. His clients are young men of his own age, the courtiers of his future eminence. His horses have been chosen from among those that bring good fortune, and of the best authenticated descent. His greyhounds have been fed on dates crushed in milk, and on the kouskoussou of his own meals. They have been broken in by himself; and, while the vulgar dogs of the tribe bark all night at the hyœnas and jackals, they lie couched at his feet, beneath the tent, and even upon his very bed. His falcons have been reared under his own eyes by his own falconer, and he himself has taken care to accustom them to his cry on throwing them off and on calling them back. Among his hunting and warlike equipments there are guns from Tunis, or Algiers, damascened and mounted in silver, the stocks incrusted with coral or with mother of pearl—sabres from Fez with scabbards of chased silver—and saddles embroidered in gold and silk on a groundwork of velvet or morocco leather. To complete his accoutrements, I may mention the sabre-tache ornamented with panther's skin, plated spurs incrusted with coral, the *medol,* or high-crowned broad-brimmed straw hat, with a plume of ostrich feathers, and the *mahazema,* or cartridge-box of morocco leather pinked with silk, gold, and silver.

At some future days when his father has paid "the contribution levied by Allah on every head," that spacious tent will be his, with all its luxurious furniture, carpets, pillows, jewel-bags, silver cups, and supplies of arms, ammunition, and food for the whole family, consisting of from twenty five to thirty individuals, including master and servants. His, also will be that stallion and those mares picketed in front of the tent, those eight or ten negroes and negresses, those stores of wheat, barley, dates, and honey prudently placed beyond all danger of a *coup de main* in a town or village of the desert, those eight or ten thousand sheep, and those five or six hundred camels scattered over the grazing ground, in the care of shepherds who follow their wanderings. His fortune may then be estimated at from twenty-five to twenty-six thousand *douros* [nearly £6,000].

At the age, however, at which we parted from him, that is, at eighteen or nineteen, he will have no need as yet to trouble himself about the management of this fortune. At present, he is merely a man of pleasure.

In time of peace, he goes forth on horseback, accompan
by his friends and followed by his attendants moun
on camels, who hold his greyhounds in leash or ev
carry them on their saddle-bow, and proceeds to i
distant pasturages to inspect his flocks, taking advantage of the opportunity to hunt the ostrich, or the gazelle,
or the *bekeur el ouhash,* according to the nature of the
ground and the season of the year. His leisure hours
will be especially devoted to the peculiarly aristocratic
and lordly pastime of hawking. These violent sports,
which I have already described, mould the nobility for
the toils of war and the razzia, to which these children
of the desert consecrate all the adventurous ardour and
energy that enter into their character.

But as he advances in years, the Arab becomes more
sedate. Every white hair in his beard leads him to
thoughts of a religious nature. He more and more
frequent the society of the men of Allah, and loads them
with gifts; and more and more rarely he is seen at the
chace, at wedding feasts, and the fantasia. His occupations as a chief leave him, besides, much less idle time.
He has to administer justice, increase his means, bring
up his children, and contract alliances. Nevertheless,
the chivalrous spirit of his youth is only slumbering
within him. Let the powder speak to redress an insult
offered to his tribe, he will not be the one to remain in
his tent. Too happy, he will say, to die like a man in
battle, and not like an old woman. Some great families
loudly boast that there is no tradition of any one of their
ancestors having died in his bed. If, however, he
escapes that coveted end, as soon as he feels the hand of
death upon him, he summons his friends to his bed-side,

for the presence of friends is desired at all the great acts of human existence. "My brethren," he will say to them if he be able to speak, "I shall never see you again in this world; but I was only a pilgrim upon the earth, and I die in the fear of Allah." He will then recite the *shehada,* or symbolical act of the Mussulman faith: "There is only one God, and Mohammed is the messenger of God." If his lips refuse to pronounce these sacred words, one of those present takes his right hand and lifts up the forefinger. This sign, to which the dying man adheres with all the energy still remaining in his earthly tenement, is a testimony offered to the unity of the Deity. After he has accomplished the *shehada,* he can die in peace.

Funeral ceremonies are not wanting to the Arab chief, especially to a warrior who has fallen in combating for his tribe. He is wrapped in a white shroud, and exposed to view on a carpet, the borders of which have been turned back. The *neddabat,* that is to say, the women who in the East replace the hired mourners of antiquity, stand round the corpse, their cheeks blackened with smoke, and their shoulders covered with tent-canvass, or with camel-hair sacks. A few paces off, a slave holds by the bridle the favourite mare of the deceased, and from the *kerbouss* of the saddle hang a long gun, a yatagan, pistols, and spurs. A little further off, the horsemen of the tribe, old and young, in silent sorrow, sit in a circle upon the sand, their *haiks* held up close to their eyes and the hood of their burnous brought down over their brow. The *neddabat* chaunt to a melancholy rhythm the following lamentations :

Where is he?
His horse has come, but he has not come;

> His sabre has come, but he has not come;
> His spurs are there, but he is not there;
> Where is he?
>
> They say that he died on his day, pierced to the heart.
> He was a sea of kouskoussou [generosity];
> He was a sea of powder;
> The lord of men,
> The lord of horsemen,
> The defender of camels,
> The protector of strangers.
> They say that he died on his day.

THE WIFE OF THE DECEASED.

> My tent is empty,
> I am a-cold;
> Where is my lion?
> Where shall I find his equal?
> He never struck but with the sabre;
> He was a man for the dark days:
> Fear is in the *goum*.

THE NEDDABAT.

> He is not dead! He is not dead!
> He has left thee his brethren.
> He has left thee his children;
> They shall be the bulwarks of thy shoulders.
> He is not dead! His soul is with Allah.
> We shall see him again some day.

After these funereal lamentations, the *adjaïze*, or old women, take possession of the body, wash it carefully, place camphor and cotton in all the natural orifices, and wrap it in a white shroud sprinkled with water from the well of Zem-Zem*, and perfumed with benzoin. Four relatives of the deceased then lift by the four corners the carpet on which it is laid, and take the road to the

---

* A well at Mecca, the water of which is carried away by pilgrims. It is said to be supplied from Paradise.

cemetery, preceded by the Iman, the marabouts, and the *tolbas,* and followed by the others. The former chaunt in a grave manner : "There is only one God!" to which the latter respond in chorus : "And our lord Mohammed is the messenger of God!"

For a brief space resignation soothes their despair. Not a cry, not a sob, troubles these prayers offered in common, these professions of the faith of the deceased, which the pious assemblage repeats on his behalf. On arriving at the cemetery, the bearers depose their sacred burden on the edge of the grave, and the Iman, placing himself by its side and surrounded by the marabouts, recites with a strong sonorous voice the *salat el djena-zat,* or the burial prayer :

"Praise to Allah who gives death and who gives life!

"Praise to Him who raises up the dead!

"To Him reverts all honour, all greatness. To Him alone belong the commandment and the power. He is above all!

"Let praise be also to the Prophet Mohammed, his kindred, and his friends! O Allah! watch over them and grant them Thy mercy as Thou didst to Ibrahim, and his, for to Thee belong glory and praise!

"O Allah! N*** was Thy worshipper, the son of Thy slave. Thou didst create him, and didst bestow upon him the good things which he enjoyed. Thou, too, didst take his life away, and Thou wilt raise him up again from the dead!

"Thou knowest his secrets and his innermost thoughts!

"We come here to intercede for him, O Allah! Deliver him from the horrors of the grave and from the fire of Hell. Forgive him. Grant him Thy mercy. Grant